BABANANGO

IN THE RANKS OF DEATH

DJG PALMER

CRANTHORPE
—MILLNER—
PUBLISHERS

Copyright © DJG Palmer (2024)

The right of DJG Palmer to be identified as author of this work has been asserted by them in accordance with section 77 and 78 of the Copyright, Designs and Patents Act 1988.

All rights reserved. No part of this publication may be reproduced, stored in a retrieval system, or transmitted in any form or by any means, electronic, mechanical, photocopying, recording, or otherwise, without the prior permission of the publishers.

Any person who commits any unauthorised act in relation to this publication may be liable to criminal prosecution and civil claims for damages.

This book is a work of fiction. Names, characters, places and incidents are either products of the author's imagination or are used fictitiously. Any resemblance to actual events or locales or persons, living or dead, is entirely coincidental.

First published by Cranthorpe Millner Publishers (2024)

ISBN 978-1-80378-245-4 (Paperback)

www.cranthorpemillner.com

Cranthorpe Millner Publishers

Printed and bound by CPI Group (UK) Ltd
Croydon, CR0 4YY

Dedicated to the memory of Captain A.P. Florence BA Man.

My dear friend Alan, in memory of you, of our friendship and of all that you did for me.

I hope this fulfils my pledge.

Prologue
Zululand, January 1879

A few short weeks ago, the British Colonial Government of Natal presented the Zulu king with a provocative ultimatum designed to elicit the king's refusal and ignite war. That ultimatum expired, and a British Army invading column of the 110th Foot, The West Rutlands Regiment, crossed into Zulu territory. In support of the infantry were guns and rockets of Royal Artillery, volunteers and irregular cavalry comprising both black and white Africans, and sappers of the Royal Engineers, sent far from their home in Chatham, Kent. Bridging rivers, digging roads and erecting fortifications, the sappers drew blood with the mythical, fearsome Zulu Impi during the initial river crossing and on the firing line during pitched battle... their first major contact as soldiers.

From their longest serving to their rawest recruit, these men now understood what it was to kill in service to their country. Among them were a junior officer and his young batman, who had become closer than many of their respective ranks could even imagine...

Lieutenant Albert Hugo Bond sat up suddenly, his camp bed jolting sharply as he did so, the penetrating rays of first light illuminating the opaque, parchment canvas of his tent canopy.

He was drenched in sweat, from the thick, collar length strands of his bronze hair to the beard on his chin. Moisture trickled from his broad, freckled shoulders and rounded triceps to the matted, coppery hair which tapered from his pectorals to his abdomen. Wiping his face with yesterday's shirt, which, devoid of collar and studs, would probably also serve as todays, he hastily drank down last night's water, lukewarm in its tin beaker, and glanced at the drum that served as his nightstand.

His revolver lay where he had left it, the holster still bound up in its long leather shoulder strap.

His boots and topi stood as before, the boots now clean and denuded of yesterday's grime, the helmet quite the opposite, still glistening with a fresh coat of mimosa oil lately applied, like a newly shelled conker. With an emerging smile, he knew that Coleman had been in the night, seen to his kit, and gone again, without a word, yet doubtless not without a stolen look.

The habit of his adult life still prevailing, Bond swung his underclad legs from beneath the clammy blanket and reached unthinkingly into the pocket of his black braided, blue patrol jacket for his watch. A pang brought recollection of the gold timepiece, now impawned forever to the seedy London broker, for the meagre price of a few cab rides, an iota of a mess bill, and some priceless anonymity. With a mirthless grimace, he raked back the damp, tumbling curtains from off his forehead with both hands and prepared himself for his morning toilet.

Sapper John Jacob Coleman, habitually known as Jack, ended the night by seeing in the day as it crept over the horizon. As the early morning mist lifted, he watched the dark indigo sky pale to lilac, thence to mauve and mars violet, until the stars faded and the silhouettes, sounds and sensations of the African veldt were once again revealed to the awaking morn. A gentle red glow began to bleed into the hazy skyline, flooding the planes with morning light.

Jack removed his topi and exchanged a mute, fraternal nod with the oncoming sentry, who blinked back, bleary eyed, broke wind, then scratched his crotch in response.

Jack had managed to pull a dog's watch on account of his nocturnal duties for his officer, Lieutenant Bond. Fatigues completed, he smiled as his mind's eye envisioned his handsome officer, and the freedom and privilege that access to his quarters bestowed upon an officer's batman. Upon *him*. Jack felt a smug sense of fulfilment as he began his stand-easy, knowing full well how he intended to spend it, propping his rifle against the box and sack rampart as he shrugged off his valise and his red serge jacket. Now down to his shirtsleeves, through which his muscles bulged substantially for an eighteen-year-old, he rolled back the flannel from his broad forearms, then wriggled back into the harness of his discarded webbing.

The adjusted valise straps and weighty expense pouches pressed against the coarse grey cloth of his shirt in definition of his chest as he shifted and tightened. Going jacketless after stag was one thing, but casually lugging his ammo about was quite another, especially if Sarn't Friday caught sight of him!

Re-shouldering his rifle, Jack paused to glance out across the swaying grasses of the veldt.

The sapphire of his eyes, though cornflower, was not so deep a blue as the collar and cuffs of his red serge, nor was the flax blond of his hair, his thick fringe shifting slightly and bouncing as he walked, quite of the yellow-gold worsted that trimmed and bordered the carmine cloth.

The long lashes that framed his eyes rose and fell as he blinked away the fatigue, pursed his soft lips and blew upwards, momentarily lifting and fanning his hair.

His second wind gained after his broken yet wakeful nightshift, Jack turned his gaze towards the stalagmite forest of bell tents, and the one in which he knew his officer to be stirring...

Chapter One

At roughly the same time as the sappers, infantrymen, and a few irregulars were waking up to their third day within the sandbag-walled and damp earthworks of Fort Penfold, the men of Commandant Gillespie Flambard's irregular army were welcoming the morning under entirely different circumstances.

Since their astonishingly easy victory, Colonel Roystone's column had enjoyed a slow, steady, unmolested progress across country in the direction of the Blackwater River. In the last three days, the only forms of Zulu life that they had come across had either been in the form of a few elderly men and women populating largely deserted homesteads, or a few solitary herd boys driving cattle. The cattle were seized and, although under normal circumstances the homesteads would have been flattened, the colonel showed remarkable restraint and desisted. This tactical magnanimity owed more, in fact, to the general's orders to cultivate and secure the surrender or defection of any rank of chieftain, the location of any of whom continued frustratingly to elude them. This worried Roystone to no small extent. After all, having defeated what seemed to have amounted to the entire local impi in the short space of a morning, he fully anticipated that every household for miles around would be hurling itself into the path of his column and begging for the acceptance of their surrender.

'I told you it would never be as simple as shocking or starving the Zulus into submission,' Flambard informed the three colonels irritably. 'The Zulu impi, as with any African war machine, are intelligent and tactical as a whole, and a lone warrior is capricious and wilful! But kraaling their people, burning their crops, and rustling their beef makes spies and insurgents of every wife, child, and grandsire among them!' Flambard's oration continued.

'For goodness's sake,' Colonel Henderson interrupted, turning to Roystone, 'Harry, when are you going to stop listening to this ridiculous language and start facing facts? If we had simply burned down the kraals and seized cattle, they would soon have told us where the old chief was hiding out. He may even be dead, for all we know.'

'Yes, and if you and Harry had allowed Gillespie to search the field when he wanted to, we might at least know one way or the other,' McEnry interjected.

'Arthur is right, Francis. One warrior might look the same as an induna to you, but the commandant has at least met the man before. You might at least have listened...' Roystone chided.

'Sometimes, Colonel, I wonder whose side you're on!' Henderson snapped back in disgust. 'Whether he's dead or alive, we have broken his force and have only to worry about flushing out the stragglers and driving them towards the central columns.'

'Thank God you weren't in New Zealand,' Flambard muttered indignantly.

'Gentlemen, please!' Roystone grumbled impatiently, only too aware of the proximity of his Boer interpreter and the other ranks of the mounted infantry who made up their escort. 'We mustn't squabble. Gillespie,' he added, turning to Flambard, 'we ought by now to be practically on top of the Aloe Valley. Would you take your irregulars, the Lyndhurst fellows and whomsoever else you can muster, and see about scouting a safe route across it?'

'Pleasure, Colonel,' Flambard replied brightly, but inside his oils were well and truly boiling.

'That bloody man, Faunce!' Flambard was cursing and complaining to the large lieutenant some half an hour later and nearly five miles ahead.

'Which bloody man?' Faunce enquired airily. 'Was that Henderson, Colonel Roystone, or are we back on McGonagle?'

'Oh, leave off, Faunce, do!' Flambard continued to gripe as they surmounted the crest of the hill and gazed into the valley beyond. 'Although, now you mention it, all of 'em!'

'Look, Commandant, there's a homestead on the opposite side.'

'Hmm, that means we shall have to expect bother,' Flambard remarked to those on either side of him. 'Inspector West!' he called back to the officer in charge of Oscaarsberg's police. 'Can you and your constabulary make your way into the bed of the valley and ascertain whether it is safe to proceed?'

'Yes, Commandant,' replied the inspector obligingly. 'Sergeant,' he went on, turning to his NCO, 'can you bring up the African Special Constables as well, please? I want them in a screen on either flank!'

'Bother, Colonel?' Faunce enquired with puckered brow. 'I thought that the Zulus had all been pacified in this area?'

'Don't you believe it, Faunce!' Flambard replied. 'Just because we did so well before – whether or not we did do as well as some among our number are given to presume, to which I say nothing – there are no guarantees that we may not run into a smaller impi on its way to the king.'

'Another?' Faunce-Whittington gasped in alarm.

'We may even run across a larger impi, sent from Ulundi with orders to attack the column,' Flambard persisted.

Faunce went quiet in response.

As it turned out, the commandant didn't need to wait for the answer. Almost as soon as the main body of his detachment successfully began to pick their way down the boulder-strewn hillside and into the valley, they were treated to several bursts of discordant and sporadic rifle fire from the crags and caves beyond.

'Enfields, or I'm no solider,' observed the commandant, as a lead ball ricocheted off a large rock to the left of him. 'I used one for long enough myself!'

'They're not very good, are they?' Faunce remarked.

'You tell that to the first battalion!' growled back Flambard. 'Volume surpasses accuracy, which is how the woolly shots in our infantry get by half the time!'

Puff after puff of thick white smoke billowed from the gaps in the rock face, and Inspector West's police contingent had little work in identifying the sources of musketry. As they advanced firing however, several more organised volleys began to echo alarmingly back.

Within a few minutes, the inspector and his detachment lay helpless at the foot of the hillside, all either dead or mortally wounded.

'Not such fools, it seems,' Flambard reflected ruefully. 'We walked into that.'

'Colonel, couldn't I take an assault party? Shoot the snipers in their foxholes?' Faunce enquired of Flambard.

'You might well say that, Faunce,' Flambard replied coolly. 'And I might well be inclined to let you, were it not precisely what I intend to do myself. Take the local men, together with your own troop, and move down there to the cover of those rocks. We have support from the Lyndhurst men if required.'

'Behind you all the way, sir!' replied the captain of the Lyndhurst Mounted Rifles, and set about advancing his men, in their distinctive dove grey uniforms, down the slopes on either side of Lieutenant Faunce-Whittington's flanks.

'Fire at the source, men!' cried Flambard. 'And remember: take advantage of cover where you can. Shoot not at where you fancy the smoke to be coming from, but where your eyes confirm it to be true. Follow the flash, not the report!'

The shooting intensified, and Flambard himself was very soon down amid the very thick of it, exhorting the men on either side of him and at the same time firing his own Swinburne-Henry carbine at the snipers' places of concealment among the rocks above.

The Africans, sent out in front as always, had suffered badly, and had retired, enticing several concealed Zulu warriors to break cover, hurling insults and further badly aimed shots.

The Lyndhurst men, who had concealed themselves in readiness. burst in upon these exposed positions and were soon engaged in bitter, hand-to-hand combat amid the rocks and brambles.

As discipline amid the Zulu defenders momentarily broke down, Flambard seized his chance. With a cry of, 'Forward, men!' the indomitable magistrate drew his revolver and advanced at the head of his troops. The smoke was thick all around from the firing.

Even as Lieutenant Faunce-Whittington staggered breathlessly up the slope with his men, the sound of shooting close at hand cracked upon his ear.

To the left of him, one of the Lyndhurst men fired his carbine with a deafening clap and a blinding cloud of thick smoke. He struggled on a bit further; his throat swollen and a stinging sensation beginning to throttle even the dehydrated gasps. His ears sang from the reverberating sounds and noises going up all around him, and he felt as if he was ready to drop. *Just a few yards more*, he told himself.

At that moment, in the far corner of his periphery, a warrior of about twenty summers sprang up from behind a place of concealment, armed with some antiquated old blunderbuss, and pointed the muzzle straight at him. Hardly able to fathom how he found the strength, the officer raised his revolver and fired. It took two or three shots to fell the young warrior, but just so long as he was down, Faunce wasn't about to get picky over conserving ammunition. *Volume surpassing accuracy*, he reflected ironically. The commandant, as ever, had been right about that.

Through the acrid white smoke and discordant noise ran an African soldier. This fellow paused, brought his rifle up to his shoulder, and fired at a Zulu who was crouched amid the thickets, waiting to fire on him. They both missed, but the trooper ran forward and clubbed down the warrior with the butt of his carbine. He sank beneath a hail of blows, and Faunce caught a brief glimpse of the bloodied mess as he and the others rushed swiftly on. A second later there was a rip, followed by the sound of metal on flesh and a loud scream.

Another warrior had caught the trooper from behind, and the blade of the assegai had cut a across the dark blue cloth of his tunic, before the point had plunged between his shoulders. Hunched and mortally wounded, the trooper gave a low moan and sank to his knees in the scrub. Pausing, the warrior began the cutting from chest to abdomen in a figure of disembowelment, which Faunce clearly recognised for the ritual enacted on the dead by the Zulu. Before the blade of the assegai could come even close to the intestines of the now dying policeman, Faunce had sprung forward, revolver in hand. He fired twice; both shots hitting the grey-headed induna in a grizzly shower of blood, bone, and matter. The glossy black sakabuli feathers, worn as rank, flew up in the air and came fluttering gradually back down amid a fog of smoke and a spray of debris.

Appalled and yet hopelessly exhilarated, Faunce-Whittington soldiered on up the slope. As soon as the next head appeared from behind a rock, Faunce raised his revolver and blew a hole in it.

With a guttural growl, as another fell before him, Commandant Flambard led his troops in an advance up the red earth and yellow grass of the bitterly contested hillside. Another musket ball flew past his ear, and Flambard suddenly realised that two of the enemy had left their positions and were charging towards him with a spear and a knobkerri between them. Unable to reload his carbine, the magistrate whipped out his big revolver and pumped four or five shots at the oncoming pair. As the smoke cleared and the ferocity of the attack began to tell on his furiously depleted energy, Flambard realised that he had killed neither one, but that both were seriously wounded. The one thing the commandant had learned in fighting the Maori was respect for one's enemy, whether fallen or alive. Knowing that their wounds would claim them before the orderlies could be brought up, Flambard cocked his revolver, pausing a moment, their screams reverberating through his skull, before mercifully shooting them dead.

They advanced in stages, scrambling frantically up the grassy slopes and firing madly into the cracks and crevices around and about them.

Faunce-Whittington, who was almost at the top now, crouched behind a large boulder and proceeded to fire the fresh contents of his revolver into the small depression on the other side, from whence a Zulu warrior had been mercilessly strafing the ascent of the irregular troops. His efforts were greeted with a long moan, and to his grave satisfaction, Faunce was able to peer into the natural depression and observe the leering, lifeless features of yet another dead warrior.

Further down the slope however, all was not going so well. Several men had taken hits, and more than one officer had fallen during the fight.

'Colonel, we need help!' Faunce called down to where his commandant was unsuccessfully trying to conceal his immense bulk behind a decidedly inadequate clump of bushes. 'We've got as far as we can, but every time one of the irregulars puts his head around a rock, some Zulu shoots it off!'

'Fire into the cave mouths, Faunce!' bellowed back the commandant irritably.

He did not like being pinned down in the undergrowth while his men emaciated themselves on enemy fire. The whole thing smacked of New Zealand where he, as a new lieutenant, had learned of the Maori method of hiding themselves away in earthworks known as pahs and waiting for the British "pahekas" to simply present themselves for massacre in the form of hopeless charges.

'Let them waste their ammunition on the ones lower down, then simply pull the fellows out and put them to the butts of your carbines!' he called above the din of the fighting.

This in fact proved to be easier in theory than in practice. Nonetheless, Faunce and his men obediently applied the principles of their gallant commander, and succeeded in hauling several truculent, diehard Zulus from their positions and battering them unmercifully with whatever came to hand. Flambard was back on the offensive now, and he and his men scrambled from hole to hole, firing their pistols into the darkness and listening for the rewarding moans and groans of their wounded opponents. The result was quite remarkable indeed. Half the valley bed was strewn with the bodies of Zulu snipers. A great many more hung lifelessly about the rocks and protruding branches of the cliff face, and several prisoners had been ignominiously dumped by the side of the cart track, all of whom were suffering from blunt trauma to various parts of their anatomy.

'Not so bad for you, is it?' Flambard demanded of his detractor, as Henderson grudgingly congratulated the magistrate on his morning's work, before dispatching several of the more aggressive white irregulars to "get what they might" from the captured Zulus.

'I must say it represents a none too welcome change in circumstances,' Roystone reflected gloomily, as the field officers took their lunch later that morning.

'I fear you may be right, Harry,' Colonel McEnry replied, thoughtfully playing with the food on his plate yet exhibiting no desire whatsoever to consume it.

'I don't mind telling you, Arthur, I'm worried stiff by this,' Roystone continued, his concerns making no difference at all to his own insatiable appetite.

'All I know,' volunteered McEnry, 'is that this time three days ago, we three fellows sat around our table on the other side of that damn drift congratulating ourselves on the annihilation of his entire local force. Either we have made a grave error in ignoring Commandant Flambard's warnings about the old chief's reserves, or we have another local force to deal with, which may mean that old Manama had absolutely no intention to surrender at all.'

Roystone nodded gravely, and thoughtfully twitched the streaks of grey in his bushy black beard. 'I think I have it,' he announced at last. 'Flambard may have been right about the reserves after all, but for all that and everything, Arthur, you saw the mess we made of that impi. Do you imagine therefore, that there can be as many more of them as he fancies? Or did these boys represent a few stragglers from a local force?'

'Not really, Harry,' McEnry replied, his face betraying more doubt than speculation.

For a tense few moments, the two men looked speculatively out across the now quiet valley, now silent of the report of rifles and the clash of human conflict.

'If that is all we have to say on the matter,' the colonel announced, 'then we have only one course open to us. The execution of our orders, as presented to me by the general himself, and everything that stands before it we shall just have to face up to as best we may.'

He looked again at McEnry. His ashen face had turned to the grey of his hair.

A rumble to the far south of their position distracted their attention from their luncheon.

'Looks as if a storm is gathering somewhere on the other side of the mountains,' a rather sullen Colonel Henderson remarked by way of a greeting to his comrades. 'I imagine we'll catch it in a couple of hours' time.'

'Where's Commandant Flambard?' Roystone enquired,

with a note of melancholy evident in his normally commanding tones.

'He's gone,' Henderson replied simply. 'Rode off about twenty minutes ago with around half his men. Says he's running low on everything, and that he wants to see what's happening about the supply convoy.'

Roystone merely shuddered. There was a sudden chill in the air, and the concept of an open row with Flambard did not appeal. He was already aware that his initial misgivings about the Zulu reserve must have filtered through to the men, because there were whisperings about an even bigger Zulu army lain in wait for them beyond the plains. Even if he could have caught up with the commandant, Roystone reflected, what was the advantage?

Chapter Two

By contrast to the bloody and arduous morning passed by their brethren, the occupants of Fort Penfold awoke to a bright and rather beautiful sunrise. The hitherto thick, cold, and unfriendly grey mists of early dawn had just begun to lift, and all the way down the river valley the grass lay thick, green, and lush, still teaming with the silvery dew. A pale sun burned through the hazy canopy of white, which clung still with a great tenacity to the tops of the mountains, shrouding them in a veil of mystery. Here and there, a vague suggestion of a pale blue began to make itself apparent to the men of the Royal Engineers, as gradually the crickets started up and the rays of sunlight began to burn through the mist. As it did so, the welcome glow of morning began slowly to penetrate even the damp canvas of the tent canopies, warming stiff and idle bones and preparing the men for their morning rituals by releasing the camp from the dense, grey fog. Across the valley a secretary bird began squawking its outrage to the world. Like a bugle blowing reveille, the call was soon taken up by other fauna and carried by all around, hidden as they were for miles by the still dispersing canopy of mist, and the dense foliage of the soaking wet bush.

Blinking but happy, glad to see the bright sunshine after a night of darkness and warmed to the marrow by the sun's gentle rays, Lieutenant Bond took a deep breath and plunged his face into a bowl of icy cold water. Refreshed, utterly awake and chillingly invigorated by the shock of such extreme temperature, he pushed his lengthening bronze curls back off his smooth forehead and gasped as the droplets trickled down his bare back. Half laughing, half spluttering, he then stood back and smiled in anticipation as Coleman, watching the proceedings and beaming encouragement, repeated the ritual upon himself. With a broad grin across his handsome face, Coleman let out a gasp as he lifted the vessel above his own head and slowly emptied the freezing contents, flattening his sleek blond hair on either side of his face with a torrent of water and spluttering for breath. Spitting, shaking the water from his hair, and rubbing the drops out of his screwed up blue eyes, the young sapper smiled reverently at his officer for approval. Bond freely granted the same and suggested in a murmur that the two of them should take a walk up the hillside and see what lay beyond.

They had often taken early morning walks together. Jack loved that time of day, too, and sometimes if they rose even earlier than usual, it might just be possible to snatch a bite to eat off a friendly cook and then be gone and back again before anyone had time to notice. As they walked, a fly buzzed past them in restless haste. The sun was really beginning to beam down on them now, and a gentle breeze had begun to pick up, blowing and caressing their glossy wet hair, gradually drying it out to a smooth, silky sheen. They paused for a moment on a grassy knoll and gazed dreamily across the landscape. Kloofs and spruits lined the bottom of the river valley, and their sandy beds were choked and cluttered with rocks, brambles and aloes. Deep green pastures and lush, dripping cacti verged their route up the hillside to the top, and the morning air was fresh and gentle, not yet over-warmed by the heat of the penetrating sun.

Once safely on the other side of the hill, away from the prying eyeglasses of the garrison below, Bond and Coleman gently subsided in the long grass and took in the sight of each other's faces as they gazed longingly into each other's eyes.

'You're beautiful,' Bond sighed in wonderment.

The steam was still rising from the valley floor beyond the crest of the hill, and the gentle breeze was now beginning to ripple on the surface of the knee-high yellow grasses with a faint and suggestive rustle.

'It's just like the summer corn in the fields at home,' Bond remarked dreamily.

'Like the tide on the Medway when a ship makes steam,' Coleman responded, equally dreamily but a little less romantically.

The sun was really becoming hot in the sky now, and where a vague hint of lilac had been a few moments earlier there now shone a canopy of most vivid blue.

Bond, his bronze locks falling back off his head as he lay on his back, lazily stretched out his arm to Jack, as if somehow incapacitated by the beauty of their surroundings. Coleman responded with equal drowsiness, reaching out with an effort, and gently feeling for the officer's hand in the grass.

A second later there was a loud rustle, followed by yet another exclamation. This time it was not the cry of fun, but the genuine horror mixed with shock and incredulity of one genuinely frightened. The two of them sat bolt upright and, in a moment of panic, realised that they had been sharing their bed with a very large centipede. Jumping up in sheer disgust at the size of the appalling insect, the two men could only stand and watch in grim fascination as the coiled monster gradually wriggled out from the flattened grass they had so lately vacated and scuttled off into the undisturbed pasture. Positively aghast at what they had just seen, frozen to the spot by fear and revulsion, Bond and Coleman exchanged significant glances and looked in shifting disquiet at the spot whereon they had previously been so comfortable. Neither, however, showed any inclination to sit back down there.

'They never told us about them during training,' Coleman murmured at last.

'Nor at the Shop,' Bond replied monotonically.

The truth was of course that the atmosphere of magical tranquillity and early morning solitude that the two of them had sneaked up there specifically to induce had suddenly been swept away. The horror of their chance encounter had left both parties with a peculiar urge to remain standing and, since the tops of their heads were now just above the crest of the hill, Bond suggested that they move further down on their side.

Coleman readily agreed and, after a short scramble down the grassy slopes, they found themselves among a strange displacement of rocks, piled up almost after the fashion of a landslide, and standing about twelve feet high out of the undergrowth. It was on one of these precipitous protrusions, a flat piece of stone about five-foot square and well concealed by those that rose higher on the other three side of it, that the two of them made their second impromptu resting place. The rock was veined and staggered in pattern like the huge black crags that stick out below the cliffs at low tide, and was sloped inwards in a sort of displaced camber, set almost as a stone basin within the others. Ever the subaltern, Bond began quietly to reflect on what a good point of cover such a rock would make during one of the creeping advances that he and his troop had practiced so often at home. He was brought back down to earth from Heaven, or rather the reverse, by the gentle touch of something against his arm. Panic being the downside of a cautious nature, he promptly jumped about three feet in the air and clapped hands on his revolver.

'Please don't shoot me, Mr Albert,' Jack pleaded, subsiding forlornly on his knees in a pose of mock supplication, which seemed so genuine that Bond found it very difficult not to find it dangerously attractive.

For a second only, a flash of bitter pain darted across the officer's countenance. It reminded him all too much of the pathetic way in which Coleman had so humbly sought his forgiveness after falling in the docks at Durban, despite his own humiliation. As he looked searchingly at the face of the young sapper, and their eyes met once again, he searched his mind for any possible reason why anyone would want to harm him. Coleman seemed to sense this and smiled, as if in appreciation. Then Bond's open mouth fell into a relived smile, and all the stress, tension and trauma of their stolen assignations and brushes with horrific insects suddenly evaporated as he fell into the welcoming arms of his young batman. Passionately, yet with a certain submissive inferiority, like a shell with his head boy at school, Bond buried his head in Jack's shoulder.

'It's unjust!' he moaned. 'Why must we have to conduct ourselves in this way, skulking about like cowards? We're soldiers. Have we not earned the right to feel, live and love as we will? I care for you so deeply, and we harm no one! Can there really be anything so terrible in that?'

He looked up, and Jack looked back at him. For a moment, the unspeakable burden of a thousand things unsaid and unseen flickered across his face. Then he broke into another endearing grin, and a glow danced in his twinkling blue eyes, creasing the corners in a flash of white teeth. For once, he looked roguish, a cocksure estuary boy-chap. Bond could not help but smile back.

'You're a clever lad, Jack,' he grinned. 'You're far smarter than I am, in many ways.'

'You ain't daft, Mr Albert,' Coleman whispered gently. 'There are just times when you think too much. It's the way you are,' he could not help adding.

'Oh, *it's the way I am* now, is it?' Bond persisted with mock indignation. Now it was his turn to play the part. 'Do tell me more, you wise, worldly man, you!'

With that, he reached out, and his fingers deftly unfastened the five brass general service buttons down the front of the young sapper's tunic, his thick bronze hair flopping over his forehead as he did so. Coleman reached up and stroked the hair back off the officer's face. Bond lifted his eyes, looked up and smiled.

'You're right handsome, sir,' Coleman sighed in wonder.

'Am I?' Bond replied incredulously.

'An' well you know it, 'n' all, I reckon,' Coleman smirked. 'Strong, but not rough.'

'Neither are you,' Bond replied. 'You're the most handsome boy I've ever seen,' he added self-consciously. 'Truly, I never saw a man as I see you now.'

Coleman simply blushed at the compliment and fell to scrabbling frantically with the hooks and eyes down the inside of the mohair braid on the officer's blue patrol jacket.

'I don't understand why these things are so tough to undo,' he grumbled, as Bond's own fingers now set about the buttons on the front of his grey army issue shirt, delicately lifting back the material and gazing in wonder at the smooth skin beneath.

'They bind. It's probably because they don't get your lustrous polishing,' Bond explained.

He had both his jacket and the now slightly tatty satin-striped shirt below it off his own back in a trice, and Coleman

21

was able to touch and stroke the officer's bronzed, freckled chest and arm muscles as Bond had done with his.

Now entwined in each other's arms, closer than they had been all day, they kissed each other tenderly as their bodies lowered on to the smooth surface of the rock.

Bond, who was underneath, with the young sapper's arms around his neck and golden locks tumbling softly onto his shoulder, suddenly let out a gasp as the bare skin of his exposed back impacted the scalding hot stone. He laughed, exhaled, then breathed a sigh, which metamorphosed from agony to ecstasy in the length of a heartbeat. Coleman grinned and proceeded to further spread-eagle him to the baking stone, until Bond could only groan in submission, his arms stretched out on either side of him and his fingers scraping the surface of the rock.

'Is it really that hot, sir?'

'Hot?' Bond repeated with a dry smile. 'You try it, if you like!'

Coleman giggled at this. He writhed to get comfortable on top of Bond, his smooth cheek silkily caressing the young lieutenant's firm torso as he buried his face in the light brown chest hair with affection. Bond, blissful and utterly lost in the man let his chin rest on the blond hair and pressed a kiss on the top of his head. Jack, his face now pressed against Bond's as he moved upwards a little, closed his eyes and smiled as he breathed in the smell of the damp grass and the scent of his companion's body, and basked in the glorious heat of the sun's rays.

The sudden crack and deafening boom of what sounded like an artillery shell woke them from their state of semi-consciousness after what seemed like hours of peace and contentment.

'What in heaven's name was that?' Bond gasped, as the two of them sat bolt upright a second time, and poor Coleman nearly toppled off the rock all together.

Bond caught hold of him just in the nick of time and for a moment, the two of them just held onto one another in a prolonged and increasingly tightening embrace.

'Oh, I see what it is,' Bond observed gloomily, as he looked properly upwards for the first time.

The entire panorama of vivid blue, unbroken by a single white cloud when they had first subsided among the rocks, was now so black that it was impossible to tell it from the night sky. The grass had a putrid green glow about it, and all they could feel was a strange oppressive stillness; the sweet and sour pastures, the green and gold of the hillside, and the dusty red of the earth sharply contrasted by the gathering density of the darkening sky. A sudden rumble heralded the second barrage of the gathering thunderstorm, as all around insects flew for cover and birds tore across the black thunderclouds in the direction of the trees and bushes.

'Come on, then,' Bond muttered reluctantly. 'I suppose we'd better move, before we both get drenched again.'

Coleman smiled again; Bond was able to discern that roguish twinkle in his sparkling blue eyes.

'That *was* fun though, wasn't it, sir?'

Bond smiled and nodded. There was something so marvellously innocent and yet terribly dark about the preservation of formality between the two of them, which he felt sure that only Coleman could engender.

He gave a candid wink. 'You really are sweet, boy, Now, let's see how we get out of this one.'

'It's all right,' Coleman added quickly. 'I left one spade just inside the camp, and another over by the way we came. I did it first thing this morning,' he added, smirking victoriously.

'Clever. I'll have to keep an eye on you on duty,' Bond chuckled, placing a warm, freckled arm around Jack's shoulder as they ascended the hill. 'What's the matter?' he asked, as the smile on the young sapper's face suddenly fell into an alarming frown.

Coleman pointed at the front of the officer's jacket, which he was now struggling to don as well as his dishevelled shirt. 'You've lost one of them... things, Mr Albert.'

Bond looked pained for a moment. 'What things? Oh, you mean the olivettes.' He brushed the matter aside with a wave of his hand as he examined the black braid across the front of his navy patrol jacket and saw that one of the small decorative fastenings was indeed missing from its place. 'I don't care. I'm not fond of those,' he added childishly.

'Soft, silky, like your hair,' Jack interrupted dreamily, as he caressed the velvet on the cuff of the officer's jacket between thumb and forefinger.

'Silk velvet,' Bond replied, winking. 'Come on, we'd better move.'

Yet even as they ambled back in the direction of the camp, a white fork of lightening ripped across the dark and thunderous sky, momentarily lighting up the blue-cuffed right hand as it carefully picked up the lost olivette from its place in the long yellow grass. They did not see the red-sleeved arm reach up to scratch the sunburned bald head, nor the pursed lips between the curly moustache, and the long straggly beard.

Sergeant Friday had followed the first set of young Coleman's footprints as they led him from the camp to the place where the first spade was hidden, expecting it to lead to the latrine. Now he stood on top of the rock at the bottom of the hill and stared in bewilderment at the single black netted button, exclusive to modern patrol jackets, and wondered what exactly an officer could have been doing to lose such a thing in hills.

Never at any point during their separate excursions from the camp had either party given a thought to the presence of Zulu scouts, or to the potential risks posed by sneaking off unarmed and unsupported into the countryside.

The wind was really beginning to whip up a storm by the time the two young sappers came within sight of Fort Penfold. Black clouds had begun to roar and rumble overhead, and the crack of thunder echoed across the valley with a threatening report of heavy weather to come. More lightening ripped across the purple sky as Bond and Coleman dashed towards the open embrasure at one end of the wagon laager, laughing uproariously as they tried to beat the incoming rain.

A fierce gale had caught up with them now and began to toss and maul where before it had touched and caressed, rippling through the carpet of long grass like some wild animal and shaking a nearby tree until it trembled to its very roots. The skies opened at last, just as they had succeeded the mealie bag barricade, virtually blown in by a strong gust at their back. Yet another terrible prong of brilliant white cut across the tumultuous curtain of cloud, ripping through the oncoming torrent of rain and ghoulishly illuminating the entire African landscape for miles around, before returning them to the gloomy state of almost total darkness. Gideon Knight was not amused.

'What on earth do you mean by running around like schoolboys in these conditions?' he demanded sternly. 'More to the point, what on earth have you been doing all this time, Albert?'

Coleman, who had almost frozen stiff at the first syllables

uttered by the irate officer, snapped swiftly to attention and braced himself for a roasting.

'Oh, for goodness's sake, let the poor lad get under cover, Gideon!' Bond retorted, as he pushed the strands of wet hair back off his face with his hands.

Knight looked at Bond, then he looked at Coleman, frozen to attention and standing just a few feet away from the shelter of the canvas awning, like some bedraggled urchin outside the workhouse gates and softened... slightly.

'Stand easy, Sapper. Back to your own tent.' He sighed in capitulation adding, 'Sergeant Friday will have words with you later I'm quite certain...' He paused, his handsome brow puckering under a new and unwelcome misapprehension as he turned to Lieutenant Bond. 'Albert, where exactly *is* Sergeant Friday?'

Bond's eyes widened in amazement. The bald sergeant was never other than exactly where he should be, and right at that moment, that would have been his elbow. 'Corporal Denham!' Bond yelled across the open space of the now deserted wagon laager, to a hastily erected canopy under which his corporal, several sappers and now young Coleman were huddled together for shelter.

'Sir?'

'Where is Sergeant Friday, Corporal?'

'Beggin' your pardon, sir?' called back the corporal.

'Friday!' Bond repeated, bawling across the void to make his voice distinguishable above the rain. 'Where is he, man?'

'Latrine, sir,' put in one sapper at last.

Raising both eyes to Heaven, Bond abandoned all hope of a protracted conversation and made a dash across the open arena, now reduced to the consistency of a quagmire by the heavy torrent of rain. Slipping and slithering under the awning on the other side, Bond staggered to his feet, scraped the mud off his boots, and tried his best to look officious, while also trying not to look at Coleman whom, he was sure, would be helplessly fighting with the giggles.

'Latrine, sir,' one of the sappers repeated quietly.

'How long ago, son?' Corporal Denham enquired on the officer's behalf.

The sapper shrugged. Then, checking himself in the presence of the officer, stood to attention and affirmed that he had not noted the time that the sergeant had left the camp.

'Where did he... go, exactly?' Bond persisted. He was himself becoming ever so slightly alarmed at this point. For Friday to be out of place was one thing, but to be physically absent from camp portended of the direst calamities.

'Over yonder, sir, across them hills,' another sapper put in respectfully.

Bond did not look at Jack. Up until then it had been a conscious effort, now it would be a necessity. To look at him and see the same expression on that beautiful face that the officer was, at that moment, so certain that he bore himself, would mean immediate exposure. Could Friday have been there? *Then?*

'What could have happened to him, sir?' asked one of the Irish sappers in alarm.

Bond thought for a moment. There were no known Zulu units or homesteads left in the area, and it was unlikely that they would have simply settled on one middle-aged NCO and not bothered to attack the camp. Zulus did not take prisoners, nor did they kill quietly or covertly, rather out in the open and with candid, almost ceremonious movement.

Numbly, as the cold and damp began to seep into his bones, Bond reflected on the ghastly creature that he and Coleman had come across earlier that day and wondered whether Friday had fallen foul of some other horror, peculiar to the African veldt.

'What if something's... got him?'

Bond snapped back from his musings. It was Coleman, and his suggestion was one of alarming veracity. Since leaving Chatham before Christmas, indeed since arriving on the Cape, they had all been subjected to the hideous and sensational horror stories of old sweats of long service and the men of the native contingent. Everything in Africa, it seemed, was bigger, more wildly exaggerated and far more poisonous than anything at home. The colonial volunteers had long been simply lyrical on the dangers of scorpions, snakes, and stampeding buffalo and, although none of these tales seemed to them to have been delivered without the ghost of a twinkle in the eye of the teller, their threat had been taken at face value. In fact, it was almost true to say that the men of the Royal Engineers' Field Company, whilst cooped up in the tiny earthwork fort, had quite probably ended up more afraid of the fauna and wildlife than of the enemy they had already engaged. Not one of them had yet seen the results of a snakebite.

'S'pose he's caught a scorpion down his—'

'That's enough, men,' Bond told them with impatience.

His own mind was racing. All the possibilities were dashing through his mind like a heard of wildebeests as the potentially disastrous visions flashed before his tired eyes. What could have happened to cause the sergeant to remain out there in such terrible conditions? Two ponderous possibilities hung like a bad smell in the confines of the officer's consciousness: what if Friday had been ambushed, perhaps in the act of disturbing a Zulu scout? Worse still the possibility that Friday had been somewhere near their trysting place and... seen something?

Morality aside, the second felt worse than the first.

Suddenly, the distant report of a firearm distracted his attention, and shook Lieutenant Bond from his grim projections. 'Was that thunder?' he barked.

'Sounded like a rifle, sir,' Coleman responded truthfully, far from convinced that his statement was something either of them cared to confront.

'Sounded like it, sir,' Corporal Denham confirmed, not liking to be left out of the analysis.

Bond hummed in disquietude.

The rain was really hammering down around them by this time, beating the canvas above their heads, and the droplets were gathering like stalactites in the places where the awning sagged under the weight of the water. Much more of this torrent and they would have it in on them, Coleman reflected, as another great swelling drip finally parted company with the canvas and dropped disconcertingly on the top of his head.

Gideon Knight was by no means as analytical when the crack of the rifle sounded upon his hearing. This was a situation he had feared since the battle, and there was no way in which fate was going to find him unprepared.

'Bugler!' he called across the sandbag redoubt, now literally shining from the volume of rain that had fallen. 'Sound stand-to, immediately.'

The lieutenant's orders were greeted by a multitoned blast from the lips of a bugler. If the men were reluctant to relinquish the protection of their shelters and stagger out into the elements, it did not show on their faces. Soaking wet, bedraggled, and bogged down by the mud and rainfall, the company of sappers filed obediently into position and took up their stations all around the sandbag perimeter. Many had not had time to put on their greatcoats when the alarm had been sounded, and these poor individuals could be seen here and there as dark patches of sodden serge cloth amid an otherwise austere line-up of knee-length grey. Rifles were held protectively close, with the stocks almost hidden beneath the folds of the men's overcoats, expense pouches strapped around the waist, awaiting the order to load.

In the centre of the laager, it was Earnest Penfold who finally broke the silence of his two brother officers. 'What now, Gideon?' he called above the downpour, which was arguably louder and more incessant than the sniffs, grunts, spits and snorts of the sappers on the barricade.

'We wait,' Knight replied passively but firmly, studiously examining the rounds in his revolver for the hundredth time.

Bond's face was a mask as he quietly dragged his feet across the muddy camp and quietly instructed Sapper Whelan and Doyle to haul one of the flatbed wagons across the embrasure, and to take up positions behind it.

'Do we tell them to load yet?' Penfold enquired nervously, clearly under the impression that silence was not the greatest aid to morale on such an occasion.

Knight merely nodded, but refused to break his own silence.

All around, the officers, standing alone in the middle of the laager, could be heard: the rustle and rattle of fingers fumbling around in pouches; brass-cased rounds being pushed home by thumbs; the snapping shut of the well- oiled breech blocks on the soldiers' rifles.

'I would have preferred to have bayonets as well,' Knight broke forth at last.

Bond looked at Penfold, but the little officer merely shook his head. If the senior lieutenant and officer commanding didn't feel the need to speak again, then there was no need for anyone else to.

Chapter Three

The rain was falling even harder now; so much so that the dark brown mud and mimosa dye used by the men to camouflage their helmets was beginning to run quite freely, dripping from peaks. It dripped disconcertingly onto the toes of boots, leaving the former a dirty brown colour and the exposed headgear an altered shade of yellow.

Bond turned up the collar on his coat, glanced across at his brother officers, and shivered. The blood was starting to run cold in his veins, not just because of the freezing temperatures and damp state of his clothes, but more in consequence of the doubt that now surrounded their impending activity. What exactly *were* they supposed to do next? If indeed it was yet another Zulu impi, fresh from Ulundi and raring to destroy them, then why on earth did they not just come on? he wondered.

'It is madness!' Penfold broke forth at last, from somewhere beneath his beard.

Looking at his companion, Bond could see that he was trembling.

'Don't worry about your arm, old chap,' Knight reassured him warmly. 'Just as long as you can fire your revolver all right and shout at the men if they need it, we'll all see that no harm comes to you. Right, Albert?'

Bond nodded. 'Absolutely,' he assented. 'They won't come

within a mile of you, Earnest. Not if my boys have any say in the matter.'

Penfold remained silent. Whether in humility at his companions' words, an acute awareness of the futility in talking through the downpour, or in fear, they really couldn't say.

A few hundred yards further down the line, his flat stomach resting on a mealie bag and his elbow balanced on top of a rampart of biscuit boxes, Sapper Coleman sighted his rifle and tried hard to ignore the rain as it hammered down on and around him.

'Please, God,' he murmured as his left hand tightened around the leather-covered stock of his carbine, and the smooth wooden butt stroked against his cheek, 'let Mr Knight and Mr Penfold have the medals. I just want to see Mr Albert safe from them spears.'

'Whatever happened to Sarn't Friday, I sure hope it were quick,' one sapper muttered.

'Sarn't's lucky,' opined the corporal. 'It's us poor sods what's got it to come, right?'

'No' Coleman exclaimed, anger flashing across his face, already flushed by the elements. 'The sarn't has been good to me, and I ain't having no one say he's gone! No one! He wouldn't go down without a fight, he wouldn't.'

'You watch your mouth, blue eyes!' Corporal Denham warned the boy ominously. 'Ain't so good to be the sergeant's pet if he ain't here, is it?'

'Leave it out, Corp,' Coleman protested vehemently.

Denham thought for a moment, then he patted Coleman's shoulder. 'You'll be all right, boy,' he confided with a wink. 'You just stick with us, and see as you do what we tell you, and you'll be all right.'

Coleman smiled tightly and nodded his head. *I know more than all of you bastards put together*, he wanted to scream. He still had the gold sovereign given to him by the colonel, tucked away in the heel of his boot. *I had better make sure I don't lose it*, he thought reflectively. He was looking forward to giving that to his mother when he got home, and showing her his backpay, just to see the look on her face. She'd rest a few weeks on that lot. No theatres, no pubs... No need for anything else, either.

'How was your ole ma before we left?' an old sweat enquired fondly, seeming to read his thoughts.

'She was fine,' Coleman responded tartly. He did not like talking with the others about her, since many of them had been at Brompton for years before he joined, and there was no telling which, or indeed how many, of his mates she had entertained during her time at the King's Head.

'She gave a smashing show at the Palace Theatre,' the sapper continued unthinkingly. 'At least, no offence, lad, but—.'

Coleman bristled. The rain was virtually horizontal now. It seemed to be blowing straight into his face, blinding him, and running down his raw fingers so that soon he would not be able to feel anything at all. His clothes were soaking.

'That song what she sung that last night? You know, *pom pom pom, bobom bom pom*' the sapper resumed incautiously.

Coleman shook his head. 'Dunno, mate,' he replied peevishly.

'You remember that song what the reg'ment played when we marched,' he persisted. '*De de de didit de de*!' he continued.

Coleman braced himself; he could feel it coming any second now.

'That time what you fell in the 'arbour!' the sapper exclaimed triumphantly. He chuckled for several moments, clearly delighted at his own revelation and the colourful picture provided by the episode he recalled.

'Steady now, lads,' put in the corporal. 'Officer's a comin'!'

Coleman looked up quickly then smiled for the first time since the rain. Lieutenant Bond had grown utterly impatient standing in a puddle in the middle of the perimeter, alternately checking his revolver and watching the toes of his boots sink deeper and deeper, as the mud became wetter and wetter. Armed with a spare Martini-Henry acquired of one of the wounded men, who was doubtless tucked away, dry, and happy in the redoubt, the officer now made a slow and steady progress around the inside edge of the barricade. As he passed the men from his own troop, he addressed each of them individually, speaking to those whose names he did not know with confirmed courtesy and warm encouragement.

Coleman's pride radiated from under his helmet.

'He's a gent, is Mr Albert,' the sapper next to him muttered. '"andsome and smart and a proper gent. Don't you agree, lad?'

Coleman broke into an involuntary grin and nodded.

'A good officer, if ever there was one,' he continued. 'I've known seasoned officers, but he's a good sort, is Mr Albert. A good, virtuous Christian man, and a proper man, engaged to a proper lass from an army family 'n' all.'

Coleman felt a look of malice betray itself. *If that man just goes on...* he thought.

'For all that,' the sapper continued, oblivious of the danger from angering the young man at his elbow, 'Oh, man, what I wouldn't give to have old Friday back here now.'

The officer's remarks, when he arrived, only echoed the sentiments expressed by the sappers. 'Well done, Corporal,' he said, taking care not to address Coleman before he spoke to the NCO. 'I see you have everything here in order.'

'Yes, sir. Thank you, sir!' Denham replied briskly. 'Eyes front, that's what I told them lads, sir,' he added.

Smug bastard's after his third white stripe, Coleman brooded. Where, oh where, was Friday?

'I expect you miss your sergeant, as I do,' Bond opined to the three of them. During the whole time he had carefully addressed his remarks to all three of his men, but it was his eye contact with Jack that seemed to be doing all the talking. 'You fear him dead, Corporal?' he added shortly.

'Ah, not him, sir,' Denham replied after a moment's pause. 'He'll turn up sooner or later.'

You're a dirty rotten liar, Coleman screamed internally. *Why, you'd have him dead in the ground and them gold stripes off his arm, you would.* Even so, he held his tongue and kept his wits about him.

'This is madness,' Penfold repeated for the hundredth time, as the hands on his watch began to wander from the numeral of eleven to that of midday.

He, Knight, and Bond had been taking it in turns to mount up and sit in the centre of the laager at different times during the day. This way, should action suddenly occur, at least one officer would always be well placed to see what was happening, and issue according to instructions to the men on the walls.

'You ought not to worry so, Earnest, old chap,' Knight remarked lightly. His own stomach was rolling over as he spoke but seeing Penfold shaking his head and looking about him like a worried old man had the effect of reminding Gideon that he was, after all, in charge, and must not be seen to let the side down. 'We have enough ammunition to see off a dozen more chieftains, and you've made such a first-class job of this position that I doubt whether a Zulu would get within a hundred yards of the ditches, let alone the walls themselves.'

'A good job then, seeing as we don't have any bayonets,' Penfold retorted with customary gloom. 'I tell you, Gideon, if I am to stand here or sit on my horse in this downpour much longer, I expect that I shall catch a chill and die before we see so much as a matchstick on the hillside.'

'Just so long as they don't have the wit to put us to the siege,' Bond interjected suddenly. 'We can do all right for bullets, but three more days in this and the latrines will be flooded out.'

Knight wanted desperately to dismiss the theory at once but didn't have the heart. *Perhaps it is poor Penfold's pessimism rubbing off on me,* he thought.

They remained in a state of flux for the rest of that long and decidedly uncomfortable day. The rain continued to fall, the ground became waterlogged, tents became more porous, and traversing the boggy grass within the confines of Fort Penfold began to present even more of a challenge. Each one of the three officers took it in turns to place themselves on alert, both in and around the perimeter of the camp, for the rest of that afternoon, while his two colleagues retreated within the sandbag redoubt and made considerable efforts at drying both themselves and their clothes.

As for the sappers, Gideon Knight considered the little garrison too few for any two of his men to return to their duties, and consequently every single one of them were stood to at the defences.

At around 3:00 in the afternoon, Bond took Sapper

Coleman and three of the walking wounded from the column on a draining enterprise: hammering stakes into the slippery slime into which the sea of mud had begun to degenerate, in the hope of reducing the level of the flooding.

'It's a shame we cannot get out there and extend the drainage ditches,' Penfold complained bitterly on one of the rare occasions when he and Lieutenant Bond both found themselves together in the redoubt.

'You speak for yourself, Earnest. Unless of course you are volunteering,' Bond retorted huffily, pouring the water out of his boots, and wringing the wet out of his hopelessly crumpled patrol jacket. 'I've had quite enough of digging around in the mud and slops for one lifetime, so if the Zulus should jump out and attack us today, I for one shall be quite pleased to see them.'

Penfold gave his friend an unconvinced look and tapped the lid of an ammunition box with his fingers. 'Don't push your luck, Albert,' he told him. 'You seem to have more of it than many of us and, if it came to it, I don't doubt for a moment that it would be you who came off well.'

'Oh, come on, old fellow!' Bond objected haughtily. 'I know exactly what it is that you're fretting about. Some great military heroes have fought one-armed, you know.'

'You try,' Penfold replied quickly. 'It hurts as well.'

Bond nodded sympathetically and apologised. 'I'm sorry, old chap. But we do still have a good defensive position with a considerable concentration of firepower, a couple of sound NCOs and some marvellous recruits.'

Penfold smiled uneasily. 'Coleman again,' he observed. 'You really do hold that boy in high regard, don't you?'

Bond smiled, adding, 'At least we are unlikely to run out of bullets, whatever else happens today!'

Penfold managed to laugh a little. 'I had better go,' he said at last. 'It sounds as if that's Gideon now.'

The hour of 4:00 p.m. came and went, but the rain remained constant. All three officers had once again turned out and were just concluding that their reaction had been precipitated, when the sound of yet another single shot pierced the air, and everyone there jumped once more to the alert.

Bond, who did not have any field glasses, simply scanned the blustery murk with a hand across his brow to keep the rain off.

Coleman, who was a matter of feet away from his officer, hugged his rifle to his shoulder, took a deep breath, and listened hard.

Corporal Denham spat out the tobacco he had been chewing, raised his rifle to his elbow, and shifted into a better position on the mealie bag wall.

Well back behind the secondary line of defence, Penfold did his best to wipe the rain from the lenses of his field glasses with the saturated velvet on his cuff, while Gideon Knight cocked his revolver, and took a few paces nearer towards the perimeter as slowly, sedately and with as much ease and deliberation as a funeral cortège as the distant images began to take shape in the mist.

'This is it, sir,' Coleman whispered.

'Lord 'elp us,' Corporal Denham muttered.

'All of us,' Bond concluded.

'Amen,' echoed both his men sincerely, as the first of the approaching stream of shadows crested the top of the ford.

'Hello, this doesn't look—' Knight began, but he was staring so hard that his speech fell off completely as, gradually, the figure of a rider began to emerge properly into their blurred view.

Dressed from head to foot in what appeared to be black, and mounted on a black horse, he might just as easily have passed for a Zulu chief, were it not for the long steel-cased sword which he wore suspended from his left side. The fact that Zulus did not ride horses seemed entirely beside the point.

The second figure to emerge was most definitely an African, carrying as he did the spear and shield by now so familiar to the men of the garrison, together with some article of antiquated firearm, but dressed around the head with the clearly visible red rag of the native contingent. More traditionally armed African irregulars followed, and just as the defenders were beginning to think that some half-crazed officer had bought a small impi of tribesmen over the border, the first of the wagons came ambling slowly into their view.

'It's a wagon. It's wagons, Sarn't!' Coleman exclaimed, glancing round in wonder. His face soon fell however, as he remembered that the man to whom he had involuntarily addressed the remark was no longer with them. 'Corp,' he corrected, mournfully.

'Could it be that our days of eating through more Boxer rounds than meals are over?' Penfold sighed, thinly veiling relief with sarcasm. 'I feared we might have to ration the rations!'

'It certainly looks that way, Earnest,' Knight replied. 'Although I should just wait until we've seen some red among that lot before getting hopes up.'

Even so, the first coloured coat of their desire suddenly popped into view, seated beside the driver of one of the lumbering supply wagons. It was a rotund, well-built man and, although small in stature, appeared to the defenders to be all boots and beard. Yet, as the column began gradually to amble further and further within hearing distance, the officer on the wagon could clearly be seen and heard to be barking orders and cupping his hand around his ear to ascertain the responses. It was unmistakably Captain McGonagle.

Then as the first, second, and third wagons of the small convoy came staggering and tottering out of the thick fog of rain that had shrouded their progress, two whole lines of redcoats came filing out of the darkness, flanking them in their laborious progress. A loud and spontaneous cheer went up from all behind the bulwark, officers included. As the advancing convoy approached the drift itself, the sappers manning the southerly barricade began to hear shouts and the discordant notes of music from somewhere amid the train of wagons. The sound of orders being barked and spat by the bearded old man on the principal vanguard began gradually to filter across to them, and soon all within the walls of the fort could at last see the lines of Africans in buff uniforms, trailing arms and marching in file as they approached the camp. Rows of oxen pulled their burdens through the mud in teams, snorting and groaning, but above all, the sound they could all hear by now was the comfortingly steady tramp of the Ninety-First Regiment of Foot and the sound of their company piper.

'Looks as if you were wrong about Albert's uncle, Gideon,' Penfold remarked delightedly, scarcely able to conceal his mirth at the miraculous apparition.

Gideon said nothing. He was reserving judgement for their meeting, and the first formal introduction to the infamous captain. 'Albert, can you mount up and come with me to greet the advance party?' he called across to Bond, as the tension began to evaporate, and everyone began to relax a little at the arrival of a friendly force.

'It will have to wait a moment, Gideon,' Bond replied hastily. 'I'll just tell Earnest to stand the men down, then I'll ride across and join you.'

Knight looked suspicious but nodded in acceptance of the terms.

As it transpired, Lieutenant Penfold was taken up with rather more than merely issuing an order to the bugler. They were engaged in small talk for some time, before the necessity to break off, which Bond had been dreading, was suddenly underlined by a sharp rebuke and an unmistakably concise gesture from the mounted Lieutenant Knight.

'I suppose I had better go and pass a word or two,' he sighed at last.

'Why?' Penfold asked. 'Gideon *is* the senior, after all.'

'I know, I know,' Bond repeated. 'But the old boy has turned up trumps with the supplies at long last, and I ought to try and keep him happy. At least,' he added as an afterthought, 'I shall try to keep him from being even *less* happy than he otherwise might be.'

Penfold laughed, wished him luck, and waved him off. As soon as he had gone, the officer retreated gloomily into the redoubt, took out his journal and began furiously scribbling away with his pencil.

Chapter Four

As many had already discovered, Captain AW McGonagle was not one to suffer those whom he regarded as fools, nor inconvenience, gladly. As a result, when the men of his Highland company had risen at sunrise on the morning following their encampment by the river, now some two days earlier, the officer had not been pleased to be greeted by another day of boiling tumult. The sun beat down unmercifully, as usual; a swarm of demented midges seemed to have descended from the heavens, and the mosquitoes appeared to have been making liberal use of his exposed skin while he slept. Consequently, McGonagle was in none too brilliant form, and was not pleased to be informed by his subordinate that it was time to strike tents and move towards the drift at a time when he had barely opened his eyes.

'I'll give the orders, laddie!' he barked irritably at Simonides. 'Sergeant Andrews, strike tents and prepare to move out! Now,' he resumed, 'where's ma porridge?'

The men groaned almost as rhythmically as they trudged, the heavy red clay stuck to their boots, clinging thickly about their gaiters and to the bottoms of their trews. Walking of any kind under such harsh conditions was no mean business, but in the heat of the march it became utterly unbearable, and the men had been at it for three days.

'McGonagle!' Simonides broke forth at last, just as the

party came clattering within sight of a rocky escarpment on the opposite bank.

'Speak to me,' McGonagle replied, with an almost unprecedented joviality evident in his tones. This affability was soon to alter however, when the message in Simonides's words suddenly became apparent.

'This is not right, I tell you!' the mean little officer exploded at last. 'If we don't stop soon, we'll never make it at all.'

'The heifers are fine,' snapped back McGonagle.

'But the men are not!' Simonides protested. 'The *Africans* can hardly stand it, half dressed, and half equipped than our own men!'

The captain, who was mounted and a little way further up the line than his subaltern, merely breathed a deep sigh and removed his straw hat to mop his brow with a cotton handkerchief.

Enraged at being so undermined in front of the men, Simonides spurred his horse on up the grassy camber, catching up with the elderly officer as his own horse lumbered up to the crest of the hill. 'McGonagle!' he repeated. 'We must stop, at least for the horses!'

'I've told you before, laddie,' McGonagle drawled laconically, still refusing to acknowledge Simonides by turning to look at him. 'I am Captain to the likes of you. You do what I command, not the other way around.'

'We have to stop!' Simonides persisted, all the time remembering his father's autocratic, obnoxious belligerence, even in the face of the most earnest entreaty. 'I refuse to defer to your rank while you dismiss what I consider to be pertinent!'

'*You* consider?' he repeated and snorted.

Simonides's eyes narrowed to slits.

McGonagle paused, removed his spectacles, and mopped

their gold rims with his now saturated handkerchief. For a moment, he looked at Simonides, with the result that the young officer thought he was in for yet more verbal abuse and adjusted himself accordingly. Finally, just as the men at the end of the column had caught up with the two officers mounted by the side of the road and engaged in their verbal stalemate, McGonagle was able to look in silence at the wearied, muddy, and bedraggled troops.

Then his face softened, and he raised his hand to indicate that a halt was being commanded, all the time staring at his fuming subordinate with crushing contempt.

'Thank you,' Simonides managed to murmur.

There followed another momentary pause, during which it seemed as if the old captain was to do or say something quite extraordinary – conciliatory, even. Then, he stiffened. 'What for?' he snapped, and turned away.

The men fell almost instantaneously on the ground about the wagons, many plumping down exactly where they were and not even bothering to cast around for a dry place to sit or lay as they started to build their cooking fires.

Gunshots had been heard by some of them at around 9:00 that morning, and now, just to the northeast, a light cloud of smoke could just be seen above the distant mountains on the other side of the river.

'The first cries of engagement,' McGonagle sighed wistfully. 'And if those reports we hear are anything to reckon by, I should say that the column has its first sight of the enemy ba now.'

'Not the first,' Simonides contradicted. 'Look, there is fresh earth been turned over just down here, and those rocky cairns on the other bank look to me like burial mounds.'

If McGonagle was a man who did not like to be questioned,

he was also one who did not enjoy being proven wrong. It had happened too often before. 'Sergeant Andrews!' he called out, summoning the presence of the large, red-bearded soldier whose name had borne the full force of the officer's tongue in virtually every sector between India and Natal.

'Aye, sir?'

'Mr Simonides here believes those piles of rock o'er the other side of the river to be burial cairns. Fetch two or three of ma boys, and pick your way across and find out for me.'

'Aye, sir!' the sergeant repeated briskly.

'Oh, Sergeant?' McGonagle called after him mischievously.

'Aye, sir?'

'You will be sure to tell me if Mr Simonides is wrong, won't you, Sergeant?'

'Aye, sir!' came the stock retort, this time with the breath of a sigh.

'Well, go on with you then, laddie!' he cried, rounding on Simonides with all the venom of a disturbed cobra. 'You'd surely not have me send them boys off on your foolish errand while you skulk about here, would you? Be off with you!'

Lieutenant Simonides scowled, remounted his horse, and left with the soldiers, leaving McGonagle alone with his hip flask.

Simonides's horse was very soon across the water and was waiting on a gravelly spit for Sergeant Andrews and his men to follow up.

When at length they had struggled across the river to join their officer, they found him stooping over a handmade cross of roughly-sawn plank, inscribed with the name of an officer and the regiment in which he served.

'I knew the West Rutlands had been here,' Simonides announced triumphantly. 'Now we see who was right, don't we McGonagle?' he added aloud, incautiously.

'There's more about here, sir,' put in the sergeant.

'Which further proves my point. I can see at least five mounds, which probably equate to the same number of men per mound, and the grass about here is littered with spent cartridges,' the officer snapped back. 'Sergeant, go back and take a roll of the African men. I do not want any of them wandering off and vanishing in the scrub on either side of the river. Do I make myself clear?'

'But Captain McGonagle said—' began the NCO.

'Captain McGonagle outranks me,' the officer bit back nastily, 'yet I outrank you. So, obey my orders, Sergeant, if you value your stripes, and leave *me* to worry about *him*.'

Andrews grumbled mutinously, but in the end he could only do as he was bidden.

'Major Theodore Hector Turnpenny? Never heard of 'im!' was McGonagle's response upon being informed of the identity of the dead officer, and the confirmation of a recent engagement. 'Probably some fool of a staff officer who'd no business being out here!'

Simonides fumed, so much so that he failed to remark upon the irony, either inwardly or otherwise. He was fed up with being dismissed; rebuked, told off, and shouted down and treated like an enlisted man. He was supposed to be second-in-command after all, he reasoned. Yet how was he supposed to be expected to retain ascendancy when even the NCOs had been taught to regard him as some sort of adolescent apprentice?

Thus had their route proceeded, and for the seemingly endless period spent by the sappers in awaiting the arrival of their supply wagons, the Highlanders had been picking their way across the site of the last major battle. Pausing only for McGonagle to venture off with a couple of men and an African guide to shoot up the local wildlife with his treasured twelve-bore, they had finally arrived and crossed the drift, before pressing on to Fort Penfold, arriving late in the evening though a curtain call of African rain.

Chapter Five

'Albert,' Knight began as they rode out towards Simonides, 'I didn't want to say anything back there, not in front of poor old Earnest, but I'm terribly worried about him.'

'Is that why you didn't ask him to ride out with us?' Bond enquired, as the pair of them struggled out across the muddy and, for the most part, trackless open ground between Fort Penfold and the drift.

'Not entirely,' Knight replied. 'Although I am quite sure that more of this rain would have done the poor fellow no favours at all.'

'Well, I shouldn't fret too much about the arm, if I was you,' Bond continued. 'Only I am quite sure he could manage the reigns with a little help in mounting.'

'No, no, you don't seem to understand my meaning,' Knight rejoined, a little too hotly for his companion's liking.

'Well, supposing he is a little bit under the weather just now,' Bond dismissed peevishly and glancing upwards for effect. 'It's the same for us all, you know. When it comes to being cooped up here for days, it's not just us who suffer. The men don't enjoy it, either.'

'I do miss Warren's advice,' Knight lamented, seeming to have missed the point of his companion's words. 'There have been times, I must confess, when I have been very hard pressed to know what to do next. I sometimes wonder whether I am cut out for this,' he added, as the vanguard of McGonagle's column came paddling up to greet them.

The African troops were the first up, grinning and squinting at them through the pouring rain with a remarkable lack of chagrin, considering they had been marching for days on end with poorer rations and provisions than the redcoats, and perfunctory motivations. Effusive and fraternal towards their new comrades, the Africans smiled and nodded up at them, though most scowled back mirthlessly and in a manner decidedly unbecoming a resupplied, reinforced garrison.

'Don't these chaps look familiar, Gideon?' Bond enquired of Lieutenant Knight.

'Absolutely,' he replied, but demonstrated very little in the way of interest as he watched the remaining wagons advance.

The first white soldier with whom they made contact was, predictably, Simonides. He rode up, came to a halt, and leered at them from beneath his sun helmet. All Bond could manage at this point was a forced and very tight smile. From the moment they met he knew he would be unable to bring himself to like Simonides, although he could not clearly define why. It was just that there appeared to be something in that officer's manner that made him feel uncomfortable and, from the faces that the fellow was pulling in the effort of smiling, Bond could see that the feeling was not entirely one-sided. Perhaps it was Simonides's associations with his uncle that he found so immediately off-putting.

Equally, as the shouts, coughs and irritably barked instructions from the elderly officer became louder and louder still, he began to wonder whether his own association with McGonagle might be equally distasteful to Simonides.

'Good day, Simonides!' he found himself able to squeeze out at last, above and amid the clanking of bits, the rattle of harnesses, and the sloppy tramp of both boots and oxen hooves in the squelching mud.

'Good day,' Simonides retorted tartly. 'Shall I affect an introduction myself or might I impose upon you to do so on my behalf?' he added, casting an acidic glance in the direction of Lieutenant Knight. 'I find the weather a little inclement for ceremony.'

Bond began to colour. He knew he had not been wrong to judge this officer so harshly. Now he remembered exactly why he had. 'Gideon Knight, Royal Engineers,' he informed Simonides. 'Gideon,' he added pointedly, 'is the senior officer here.'

'Lieutenant Simonides. And not for much longer he isn't,' Simonides retorted, pre-empting further discourse as a creaky old, covered wagon came lumbering up through the sloppy wagon ruts left by the previous vehicles. 'This,' he added sharply, 'is Captain AW McGonagle, of India'

'Ninety-First Highlanders!' McGonagle barked in correction.

'I believe we've met,' Bond rejoined, equally sharply.

He did not care for the way in which Simonides had previously spoken to him, nor in fact did he like the way that this mean-spirited little man had so curtly presented his own flesh and blood to Gideon Knight.

In the event, neither did McGonagle. 'God damn it, boy! Can I not call out my own name without your usurping?' he demanded sourly, Celtic bile ringing out above the continuous din of the rain on the canvas as he examined the two ambassadors through misted up spectacles.

'I see you're in fine spirits this evening, sir,' Knight replied incautiously.

Fortunately for all involved in the interview, the rain

overwhelmed the remark.

'Captain Alec McGonagle,' Bond resumed, by this time a weary of shallow introductions. 'May I present—'

'I heard,' McGonagle interrupted. 'Now can we please get on, lieutenants? I'm fair fed up with tattling in this miserly weather, and I want ma' dinner!'

Bond, Knight, and Simonides looked at each other, then looked at McGonagle.

He was peering enquiringly over the rims of his spectacles, the rain was pouring in torrents over the brim of his hat, and the expression above and between his soaking wet beard hinted at anything but conviviality.

'Right, well then,' Knight smiled weakly after a long and embarrassed silence. 'Albert, could you ride ahead and ask the men to prepare some dinner? Then perhaps we can all see to our own arrangements and have something to eat.'

Bond simply nodded and rode away. He was done with talking and, as the rain lashed across his face, and the smell of the mud and the steam from the horses' nostrils flew up all about him, he began to think he was done with the army too.

The Highlanders did not take long to settle once the packs were off their backs and the majority had fallen under the relative shelter of their communal bell tents. The wagons were run inside the perimeter of the camp, and a small kraal formed for the teams of oxen. Simonides's horse, together with McGonagle's – which he rarely rode, but insisted upon always having prepared for use – were tethered with the other officers' mounts, given water and nosebags, while their owners joined the sapper officers at table. Indeed, although the heavy rain precluded much in the way of the proper formalities of conventional dining, the ever-resourceful Sapper Coleman had managed to drag together a few of his mates, and together they had succeeded in rigging up an improvised mess tent. This awning was slung between two wagons, held fast on either side with long ropes and anchors from the pont building equipment, and drawn down at either end to afford the officers some privacy at their meal table. This action drew praise from everyone universally, although it had to be said that most of it undoubtedly came from the ever-benevolent Lieutenants Bond and Penfold. McGonagle, for once, was also impressed, and proceeded to give loud vent to his high opinion of sappers, which was totally at odds with his previous pronouncements.

Simonides was characteristically less charitable, and very deeply resented the fact that yet another good-looking member of a service corps inferior to a prestigious infantry regiment appeared to be receiving superfluous commendation from someone who was not normally in the business of liking anyone. As ever, this owed far more to the fact that McGonagle had ruthlessly ignored Simonides throughout the day, and suddenly seemed to be all over this wretched example of a nephew who plainly regarded the old man with almost as much hostility as he did.

For Lieutenant Knight, no mess tent, however well intentioned, could in any way temper his ill humour to the lingering implications of Simonides's remark about him not being in command "for much longer". That McGonagle was a captain was incontrovertible. Equally, did the old fool intend to take over the fort, the sappers or both? Or had he received orders to drag them all back across the border to sit out the war – that Knight was supposed to be winning – in the anonymity of some depot? Was he simply to lose his first independent command to yet another officer, who this time wasn't even Warren Westgate?

Chapter Six

The meal was, despite the lingering note of negativity harboured by one or two members of the mess, a surprisingly convivial affair. McGonagle, who if nothing else had an excellent eye with a twelve-bore and an equally excellent palate for wine, had kindly presented the sapper officers with several guinea fowl and several additional articles of bagged game, which he had shot that morning.

Further to the surprise and delight of his hosts at such unexpected cordiality, the elderly captain also managed to unearth a particularly good drink from amid the chaos of his personal belongings in two of the wagons, and consequently the evening passed off with considerably altered spirits. Two brass oil lamps lit the tent itself, as well as several candles stationed in the necks of bottles up and down the table. The light played and flickered merrily on the yellowing canvas above and around them, while the clink of plate and the buzz of conversation helped them almost to forget the miserable conditions they had so lately left outside. Coleman, handsome as ever in dry serge borrowed for the occasion, poured the wine, and served as steward.

When the meal was complete, the five gentlemen lit their cigars, while McGonagle proceeded to further disarm them by magically producing yet another bottle, this time a sweet wine, which was passed around in liberal quantities. Despite the constraints imposed upon them by their duties in the field, each officer had taken some measure in improving his own personal appearance for the occasion of the reception.

'I know it's a liberty,' Penfold had said to his incredulous batman amiably, 'but would you be so kind as to let me have your serge for this evening?'

It was a request with which the boy had naturally complied, and consequently Earnest was looking decidedly below himself in rank, if a little dryer and less crumpled.

Bond, although still dressed in his one and only patrol jacket, which was still missing an olivette and looked as if it had just been exhumed, had made concessions to decency by having Coleman trim up his beard a little. He had also swapped his utterly ruined cord riding trousers for a pair of dark blue army ones, emblazoned with the broad red stripe of the Royal Engineers.

'He does a wonderful job servicing all of my needs,' Bond had spoken in praise of Jack, who was now blushing furiously in the corner and looking at his boots. 'The only downside is that my coat looks older and even filthier than it did before.'

'Tish, laddie, you'll do!' McGonagle remonstrated loudly with him. 'I've seen a lot worse than you, believe me,' he added, casting a little more than a brief glance at Simonides, who had done nothing about his own dress at all.

Simonides himself, who appeared to be scowling less and less as the wine went down in the bottle, had taken the rather unfortunate step of removing his own beard all together. This ill-advised measure of cosmetic alteration had, far from improving things, made the poor hideously-favoured officer look even more toothy and gaunt than he had been to begin with. In fact, it was a stiff fight not to end up staring at him in distaste as the wine flowed ever further, and propriety was gradually drowned in a glass.

Gideon Knight, on the other hand, had abandoned completely any notion that he might have had about his hopelessly degraded uniform, opting instead for a pair of cord riding breeches and a civilian Norfolk jacket in a brown tweed.

'Aren't we bonnie tonight?' McGonagle asked for the hundredth time.

'Best to agree with him,' muttered Simonides, drink getting the better of his usual introspection as he addressed Earnest Penfold, next to whom he had been seated.

Penfold nodded and smiled awkwardly. It was just like Gideon and Albert to land him with this odd fish who, worse still, now appeared bent on engaging with him alone.

'How long have you served?' McGonagle was asking of Gideon Knight.

'Twelve years next month,' Knight replied politely. 'And yourself, sir?'

Bond tried to stop him, frantically shaking his head, and trying to nudge the officer under the table. It was too late however: McGonagle's metaphoric cork was out of its bottle.

Rising, the full splendour of his Highland regalia of kilt, plaid, sporran, and his short bolero mess jacket, the captain addressed the officers. 'More than thirty years I have served in this captaincy,' he began.

'Self-indulgent old basket,' Penfold muttered to Gideon below his breath. 'I thought it was you who was supposed to be hosting tonight?'

'Oh, I know,' Knight replied. 'But it does well to be diplomatic, especially since the old boy's brought out his cellar as well as these jolly decent birds. Just humour him, and I'm sure he'll pack it in sooner or later.'

Penfold's observations, in fact, were not entirely devoid of truth. Ever since they had sat down together, and McGonagle had planted himself royally at the end of the improvised table of boxes and planks, he had taken over proceedings. When McGonagle finished, Coleman cleared away. When he took out his cigar and lit it, so did everyone else. Now he got up, stood at the head of the table, and toasted the Queen until he almost fell over.

Bond, having also been imbibing a good deal more than usual, rose to his feet and lifted his glass above his head in salute. 'To the Ninety-First McGonagleshires!' he proclaimed, to rounds of applause and shrieks of drunken laughter from his well-oiled companions.

McGonagle was doubled up in fits as the decanter was set down upon the tablecloth. He had just been busily engaged in one of his more long-winded anecdotes, equating the war with the Zulus to a drive for pheasant, when young Jack Coleman attempted to attract the old captain's attention by stepping up to refill his glass.

'It's all very well the colonels chasing individual chieftains for their support,' he was saying, 'but if they all begin breaking away from the royal household, there's really no controlling them. Better to keep them together, and then defeat them all with one mighty swipe. Draw 'em down, then knock 'em flat, eh, gentlemen?'

Bond coughed pointedly. Coleman took another pace forward. He was ignored.

'It's the same with the dogs,' the captain continued. 'If one of them gets the scent of a rabbit, they're off in another direction entirely. It all rests with how dominant the top dog is, you see. Hello, what have we here by damn?'

The officer's decidedly blurred vision had suddenly incorporated the image of Coleman, who was still waiting patiently for McGonagle to stop waving his glass around like a conductor's baton and allow him to top it up. Having noticed the boy for the first time that night, McGonagle promptly proceeded to emulate the dogs of his metaphor by veering off on the subject of "this fine wee laddie"; Coleman's blond hair flopping down over his deeply colouring face as he stooped to pour the liquor.

'My, but you're a handsome fellow,' he told the cringing sapper merrily. 'I remember a drummer boy like you we had in India. Just sixteen, he was, when—'

'Uncle, leave the poor fellow alone!' Bond exclaimed above the din of his colleagues' laughter and Simonides's muted growling.

The truth was that he did not entirely care for anyone, especially his uncle, expressing so lightly sentiments so alarmingly close to home for him. It was as though his uncle were speaking his own thoughts, and he was too aware of how Jack was being humiliated, and sought to bring the ugly scene to an end.

'Tish, laddie, I'm only having a joke!' McGonagle cried with intoxicated indignation, staggering once again to his feet as he spoke. 'I was a boy soldier myself, you know!' he continued, to the sound of a collective groan. 'Ensign of just fifteen, I was, in the Queen's *other* army... that of India!'

The mess erupted in spontaneous applause; Coleman smiled weakly and blushed even harder, and Bond felt his head fall into his hands.

'Aye,' continued the captain, aware at last that he had secured his audience. '"The minstrel boy to the war is gone",' he began, to drunken shouts and catcalls of derision, '"in the ranks of death you'll find him".'

'Uncle, that is enough!' Bond stormed indignantly.

Poor Coleman looked searchingly to his own officers, particularly Bond, for help. He remembered the old defunct town stocks, rotting away in Rochester's high street near the guildhall. Only now did he fully understand their purpose in use.

'"His father's sword he hath girded on",' McGonagle persisted, proving that he clearly did not give a hoot, '"and his 'ain true harp slung behind him".'

'Sir, I must protest! This is most undignified!' Simonides interjected, apparently utterly fed up with Bond and his wretched friends stealing all the attention. Besides, such tributes were not to be conferred on a pretty boy with the rank of nothing at all.

Coleman was really looking poorly now.

'Uncle!' Bond repeated, louder.

'Nephew!' McGonagle exclaimed and threw open his arms in demonstrative affection.

'Gentlemen!' Gideon Knight intoned, seeking to end the embarrassing spectacle.

Simonides snarled, and a flash of pure malice flickered through his eyes for a second. Hurling his napkin on the tablecloth, he rose and left the mess tent.

'Bad form!' McGonagle cried delightedly. 'Add a port fine to his mess account!'

'Er, gentlemen!' Knight repeated, rising to his feet, and joined in amid the growing bedlam. 'Our thanks to Captain McGonagle for his most generous provider, wonderful anecdotes and his, er, recital. However, we all have a long day ahead of us tomorrow, so if I could ask for your appreciations for the steward—'

He needn't have bothered. McGonagle had passed out, together with Earnest Penfold; Simonides had stormed off in the darkness; Bond and Coleman were nowhere to be seen. With a sigh of resignation, Gideon Knight lifted his brandy glass and swallowed its contents. He would pay Coleman tomorrow. Tonight, everything else could go hang.

Coleman, who had just been glad to get out of that terrible mess tent and was now busy scraping the mud off his boots, felt a wave of tiredness overcome him as a further gust of wind-driven rain thrashed across his shirt-covered back. He scrubbed away, and soon the layers of thick red clay began gradually to dissolve in the water, parting from the leather like butter from a hot knife. He was just going to tip the contents away, and start washing Mr Albert's riding trousers, when a thin cough made him spin round instantly and drop what he was doing.

'Sir, what are you doing round here this late?' he asked in surprise, standing to attention with his bare feet sinking into the mud.

Lieutenant Simonides, who had quit the mess tent ahead of everyone else in a stage of some inebriation, had been maliciously watching Coleman in his labours for some minutes before stepping out of the shadows and making the young sapper aware of his presence. Now, as the refracted light from a nearby tent filtered across the glistening wet grass, a tenuous glow just lighting up the gleaming blond hair and the opaque blue shirt on the firm, youthful body, the bitterness of rage began to well up inside the miserable officer.

'You... dislike me too, I suppose?' he demanded, staggering from the edge of an empty wagon to the steadying aid of a mooring rope from one of the nearby tents.

Coleman, frozen to the spot and fixed by the piercing gaze of the mesmerizing grey eyes, could only remain at attention and stare straight out in front of him.

'I said, *do you dislike me*, soldier?' Simonides demanded, his thin little voice rising almost to screeching proportions in the darkness.

'Sir?'

It was a stock response, often employed by other ranks when they had nothing better to say in reply to a question from a superior. Or something far worse.

'Dumb insolence!' Simonides snarled, and stumbled forward a pace or two.

Coleman flinched, but remained at attention, the rivulets of rainwater surging down off his hair and streaming into his eyes. Before he knew where he was, the bony little officer had seized hold of him, and was forcing him down by his own body weight over the pail in which he had been washing his things. Simonides was drunk, but Coleman was frozen stiff with horror and that physical paralysis which the system had beaten into him, from his days in the back streets of Chatham to the rigid drills of the parade ground. You just clenched your teeth and held on to your nerve. Now though, as the disgusting smell of meat and intoxicant reflux came hissing forth from between the yellowing teeth, and the saturated fringe of thin hair hung like some malignant black spider in front of this horrible officer's face, dripping water into his eyes, Jack could no longer suppress revulsion. With a cry of terror mixed with pitiful supplication, Coleman slid under Simonides's arm. The officer was small and slight, and he had been drinking, but the animal rage with which he grabbed hold of young Jack's arms, the bony little fingers digging the sharp nails into his muscles, seemed to render the poor sapper completely and utterly helpless.

'Please, sir!' he begged, gritting his teeth. 'This ain't proper. You're an... officer!'

'Oh, *you're* too good for *me*, are you?' Simonides murmured, so low it was almost inaudible. 'The body of a man, face of a woman! You must be used to this. Pretty mudlark! Urchin! How else did you turn a penny? Go with sailors, did you? Or soldiers? Do you still? Well, I'm wise to your dirty tricks!'

Coleman sobbed again and screwed up his eyes as he felt the fingers fumbling about with the buttons on his shirt. He forced back a wretch and felt his fists begin to close. You didn't get to eighteen summers and look like he did among the pubs and brothels without knowing how to keep unwanted advances at bay. This bastard was an officer, but this wasn't a parade ground, and this certainly wasn't usual.

As the quick-fisted street lad began to overmaster soldierly deference, the snide voice in his ear was suddenly quieted, and replaced by an abrupt crack, like the breaking of an egg.

Simonides, consumed by a frenzy of vindictive arousal, felt a sudden overwhelming impact. Heat began to spread forth from his head then flowed in rivulets down his neck to his back. The world went dark. Sounds muffled as the angelic face before him faded, to be replaced by a nauseating ache, a dreadful ringing, then... nothing.

Coleman, by now uncertain whether to yelp like an animal or let his fists fly, flinched as a steadying hand was placed on his trembling shoulder. Even as he sobbed and quivered amid the assurances, entreaties for calm, and lofty, awkward terms of comfort, he realised slowly what had happened. Opening his reddened eyes just a little, he gradually beheld the familiar shape of a shiny bald head and long ragged beard, and heard, like sweet music, the strangely muted high-pitched squeak.

'Sarn't Friday!' he gasped, incredulously.

'Boy safe. Boy safe, now,' Friday repeated over and over, standing stock still and patting Coleman mechanically like a dog, bulbous eyes fixed, staring madly into nothingness.

'W-what... happened to you, Sarn't?' Coleman stammered forth at last.

'Animal,' Friday cursed, those same eyes now lit up with hatred at the pathetic pile of dark blue serge cloth heaped around the prostrate lieutenant. 'Him an officer... no choice... God's hand struck, Friday his hammer. Not Friday's choice.' The eyes narrowing slightly as he focused, Friday added, 'Should have done him proper,' in a stentorian voice, hitherto unfamiliar to Coleman.

'He isn't... dead, is he Sarn't?' gasped the wide-eyed boy in horror.

Friday sighed gravely and shook his head. 'Ought to be dead,' he muttered angrily. 'Didn't deserve to live like *that*.' The words spat out as he spoke them, venom tainting every syllable.

'Sarn't?'

The meaning was obvious, to Friday at any rate. 'Sodom and Gomorrah. No right, I tell you. Best I came back.'

'What happened to you, Sarn't?' Coleman sniffed a second time.

'Fired a shot off. No one heard,' Friday replied stiffly.

'I heard,' Coleman replied, looking to Friday for approval.

'Good lad,' Friday whispered. 'Always said so, did Friday.'

'Friday knows best, Sarn't,' Coleman murmured, smiling weakly. Then, as he looked at the sergeant, Coleman realised that he was hobbling.

Friday saw his concern and sought to dismiss it. He took off his greatcoat, wrapped it around Coleman's broad shoulders and told him quietly that they had better be off before someone came and found them.

'What do I do? What do *we* do now, Sarn't?' Coleman whimpered. 'That's it for us now: both out the army, both for the rope!'

'Nah, not that. Not that,' Friday repeated monotonically. 'God's will, that's what it was. God's punishment on that sodomite. Disgusting. Worst sin in the scriptures.'

'Mr Albert!' Coleman whispered, eyes suddenly widening in both hope and horror as his officer slowly re-entered his consciousness. 'I thought it was... you see, I weren't turned out right, proper like, Sarn't. That's why... my shirt... What's he goin' to think of me? Of what I done? What I let *him* do!'

Mercifully, Friday was far too distracted to follow the nuance of Colman's self-reproach and thereby his incautious disclosure. Only the officer's name rung in his ear.

'Yes, lad. Go to your officer. Not a word of this, mind,' he added warningly. 'Not a word! Best he don't know. What he don't know, can't hang him.'

Chapter Seven

From the moment that the body of Lieutenant Simonides was discovered by a sentry on his way to roll call at 4:00 a.m. the following day, his death was treated as murder. Not least among the plain and apparent circumstances left pointing to this conclusion was the fact that, in addition to the heavily inflicted blunt trauma to the back of his head, he had been found skewered to the ground with an assegai.

Much of the blood from the head wound had been washed away by the heavy rain, and the nature of the impaling had meant that much of the blood from his stomach and intestines had drained down through the soil, which the body lay directly above.

Consequently, it was not so plain as perhaps one might assume how exactly the officer had lost his life. Despite having no friends, either amid the ranks of the Ninety-First, or indeed the sappers, the death of a British officer in circumstances that were questionable left provision for only one response. A killer had to be found, lest low morale be permitted to elapse into desertion or even mutiny.

The rain had well and truly stopped by the time Coleman had woken up. Looking around and about him, he discovered to his relief that he had passed the night under the protective canvas of Lieutenant Bond's tent. Indeed, Bond lay beside him even as he woke. A freckled, bronzed bicep curled protectively around the young sapper's chest as he dozed, occasionally shifting, or sniffing a little in his sleep. Calmer in his own mind, and yet somehow transfixed with a fear that the worst was still to come, Coleman snuggled up against the warm, comforting body of the nearby officer, and all the horror and dread of his previous imaginings began to evaporate. Yet, as the sensation of waking began to take the place of that semi-consciousness in which we all prostrate ourselves for a time, convinced that the pain, anguish and certainty of the things we fear most are far away, he knew that he was wrong. Did all that really happen, or had he simply imagined it? If not, where was Sergeant Friday? Had he been a dream, an apparition? If he hadn't, what on earth would happen now?

'Of course, though it's wrong to say, I shan't miss him,' Earnest Penfold remarked grimly, as he and Lieutenant Knight stood examining the body, still hideously pinned to the ground outside the supply tent.

The corpse's shoulders were hunched; the fingers splayed out and grasping at the grass and soil around his body, apparently clawing for dear life or hanging on to this world with vigour. The muscles in the officer's scrawny neck were strangely contorted, drawing the muddy, blood-stained face into a leering death mask, twisted and fixed in the form of some hideous old tree.

'That's hardly a reason to kill him, old man,' Knight replied quickly. 'If you ask me, the poor wretched fellow had enough troubles. Talking of which...'

His remarks were designed to herald the arrival of Captain McGonagle who, having been roused from his tent and informed of the murder by Sergeant Stag, could now be seen tramping across the muddy ground in his spectacles, his nightshirt billowing in the morning breeze.

'His flies are undone,' was the sum of the officer's opening gambit.

'Taking comfort, no doubt,' Knight observed. 'Terrible business, Captain. I'm sorry.'

'No need to be sorry, lad, unless you took his life,' quipped back McGonagle, to the sappers' minds a little too lightly to befit the circumstances.

'Who could have done this?' Penfold found himself saying. 'I mean, I know no one really liked the poor chap. I tried to be brotherly, you understand. But why?'

'Why, it's plain as your nose, man,' McGonagle retorted simply. 'One of those wee African boys crept up, hit him with a knobkatacari, and stabbed him in the back to zila.'

'Zila?' Knight repeated incredulously. 'And might you mean a knobkerrie, sir?'

'Aye,' replied the captain stoically, and ignoring the correction. 'Pagan ritual they enact after battling. Slit open the body to eat up the spirit of the warrior within.'

'Surely you mean to free the spirit within, Captain?' Penfold ventured cautiously, since McGonagle was evidently not at all concerned about the death of his subordinate, even less so the particulars of Zulu beliefs. 'Lest they fear the bloated ghost will haunt them. Furthermore, as to the assertion, nay, assumption that it was one of my men who did this, I can only protest in the strongest terms.'

McGonagle shrugged. 'Aye, protest all you will. Prove me a fool, if you've a mind to,' he suggested. 'It's there for you to see, whether you like it or not. One of those damned hirelings bashed in his brains, then stabbed him through the backbone before robbing him clean.'

'Has he been robbed, then?' Penfold retorted quickly. 'What about his money? Is it gone?'

'He had none, of consequence,' McGonagle replied, again a little too lightly for decency.

'Then I shall find out some other way to disprove your theory, sir,' Penfold asserted, adding, 'and will someone please cover him up, now!' as his parting shot.

'I suppose we really ought to have a check parade, roll call and such,' Knight remarked to McGonagle, but the will to do so was certainly not evident in his tone.

'I'll have Sergeant Stag fall ma boys in before breakfast,' McGonagle replied briskly. 'You call your sappers together, and we'll soon see what's what.'

'Captain,' Knight added, as McGonagle turned to go.

'Aye?'

'Well, sir, I just hope to God that it *was* one of Earnest's boys, and not a white soldier. I mean, I know how the poor thing feels about those men of his but, well...'

'I know, laddie,' the Scotsman replied quietly, reflectively, and with almost a rare hint of pathos. 'I've seen this all before, remember? The mutiny.'

Knight nodded and trudged back to his tent through the dew.

Less than five minutes later, the two senior officers were standing once again in conference, this time in McGonagle's tent, when footsteps without and a hasty sound of parted canvas heralded the premature return of Earnest Penfold. Bounding into the tent at such speed that he almost fell over and did for the other arm, it was several moments before the little subaltern had caught his breath sufficiently to be able to address his assembled colleagues.

'You'll never guess what has happened, Gideon. Sorry, Captain McGonagle, but you'll never guess either.'

'Earnest, what on earth is the meaning of this?'

'What on earth's the matter with you, laddie?'

'You'll never guess. Never!' Penfold repeated, and it began to look as if torture was going to be the only way of extracting the information out of him.

'Here, take some of this Lieutenant,' McGonagle interrupted, handing Penfold his hip flask and exhorting him to sip the spirits and recover his composure.

'Thank you, sir,' Penfold returned, as soon as the liquor had taken effect, and his nerves had been returned once again to a state of coherent sensibility.

'Come on then, Earnest,' Knight persisted irritably. 'Don't you think the time's a little bad for riddles and japes just now?'

'I'm sorry, Gideon, it's just that you'll never believe what's happened, but...'

'Oh, don't start that again, for heaven's sake!' cried McGonagle.

'What's this, then?' added Bond, who had just walked in behind Penfold.

'This is just what I've been trying to tell them, Albert!' Penfold replied excitedly. 'Old Friday's come back! If I could only just please finish...'

'You mean they've found him? Alive?' Bond demanded.

'Yes!' cried Penfold, by now exasperated at not being able to finish a sentence.

'Well, thank God someone is,' McGonagle grunted ironically.

'Sir, please!' Knight remonstrated. 'That sort of irreverence is hardly fitting—'

'You talk some rubbish, Lieutenant,' returned McGonagle angrily, and much to the surprise of all three officers. 'I left my sentiments with my wife in a temple overlooking the Ganges, so don't talk to me about respecting the dead!'

The three sappers fell silent.

Bond was stunned. 'I never knew I had an aunt in India,' he found himself mumbling.

'I know!' snapped McGonagle, before storming out to examine his men.

In the end, it was Earnest Penfold who broke the silence. 'I still maintain that it wasn't one of my earners who killed Simonides,' he informed them, before following in the wake of the captain.

'It seems almost strange to me,' Knight remarked to Bond. 'Here we are, in the middle of a war in which we have all seen death and killing—'

'And killed,' interrupted Bond.

'Yes, Albert, I'm sorry,' Knight retorted quickly. 'It's just that I never could have imagined how one more death would be so significant, or how much it might affect us.'

'It certainly has changed everything,' Bond sighed wearily. 'I just wonder who, how, and why, that's all.'

After so long a march and such dreadful conditions, McGonagle's men were not in good shape. All had thick beards; the mud and the dirt ingrained itself in their skin, their clothes, and their hair. Uniforms stank of mud, damp, and gun oil, while spots and boils had broken out all over many of their bodies, and the thick red clay hung from their tartan trousers like cobwebs from a ceiling.

Now, as they stood to attention in three ranks before their NCOs and their surviving officer, they looked as if any one of them might have been moved to murder.

'You all know by now what has happened,' McGonagle was

telling them loudly. 'In the small hours of today, some person or persons saw fit to avail himself of native weaponry and take the life of Lieutenant Simonides. I have now to warn you, ma boys, should we find the man or men responsible, their lives will be forfeit.'

A few yards away, Gideon Knight had been charged with delivering a similar sermon to his own company. 'Men, it is a grim responsibility with which we are burdened here in Her Majesty's colony, but it is a duty that we face as soldiers of the Crown. Early this morning, an officer of the Queen's army was brutally murdered and impaled to the ground with a Zulu spear. I intend to find the man responsible for this act of villainy, and if he were found to be one of you, I should be compelled to deal with him as I might at home. Further, if any man were found to be concealing from his officers any evidence relevant to this crime, I shall personally undertake to serve on him the severest punishment conceivable under the law. Men, you have been warned.'

Despite such warnings, it was clear to all that the blame for such an incident could lie only with one party of men: the African pioneers under Earnest Penfold. The presumption of guilt had been evident from the moment Simonides's body had been discovered. Between the roll call in the morning to the considerably lacklustre burial in the late afternoon, Penfold became increasingly convinced that his men were about to be made into scapegoats.

'It's utterly unspeakable, Gideon!' Penfold complained to Lieutenant Knight. 'You saw them when they arrived yesterday – they couldn't have been better behaved after so long and rotten a trek with that impossible old man McGonagle. They ran up to me as happy as if I had been their father, crowding round me so that I could hardly see. Didn't they, Albert?'

Bond, who was beginning to feel the noose of his association with McGonagle tightening around his throat, simply nodded back in silence.

'I can even tell you why McGonagle's so keen to blame my boys, if you like!' Penfold persisted, until Knight rather peevishly ordered him to drop the subject.

'Now look here, Earnest. Albert knows his sappers; I know mine, and I'm damn sure there isn't a murderer amongst any of the worst of them. Your boys – for all they might work their little hands off – are untrained auxiliaries who don't speak a word of English. How can you take their part before that of your own soldiers?'

'Jacob Christmas speaks perfect English,' Penfold protested, earning himself a warning look from Bond and a simmering glance from an increasingly impatient Gideon Knight. 'That's why McGonagle is so desperate to see them blamed,' the little officer continued bravely. 'I spoke with Sergeant Christmas when they first came in, and he told me that old McGonagle managed to take them round in what amounted from his descriptions to be a forty-five-degree arc, landing up miles out of their way and days off course. He's hardly likely to want that publicised, now is he? Oh, and while we're on the subject,' he continued, 'wasn't it queer, old Friday suddenly turning up out of the blue, just like that?'

'Now look here, Earnest!' Knight finally snapped, seizing hold of Penfold's good arm and propelling him behind a wagon with such force that even Bond was tempted to intervene. Knight was worried. He did not like the fact that a senior officer, with unknown orders, had suddenly wandered into his camp and superseded him. Now his men fell under suspicion of murder. His fury found its vent on Earnest Penfold. 'Captain McGonagle is, aside from being Albert's uncle, a senior ranking officer who has just had his only subaltern murdered. He is well within his rights to want a culprit found before he goes, and is probably quite correct in his assertion that this crime was not perpetrated by a regular soldier. Whoever the culprit, this reflects on him and his command!'

'But he never liked the man!' Penfold protested, but Knight's grip grew even firmer.

'Earnest, either let it go or I'll let your boys go. Imagine if it was Albert or myself who had been bludgeoned to the ground and stabbed. Would you be so focussed on your African allegiances, or the first of our brother officers to fall here among us?'

Penfold scowled and forcibly withdrew his arm from the officer's grip. 'You may be in charge, Gideon,' he whispered menacingly, 'as our senior officer here. You might even be a captain before long, but if you ever presume to lay a hand on me again, I shall have no option but to react—' He broke off in mid-sentence and departed, leaving the other two stunned and silent.

'I have never seen the like, have you?' Knight found breath to gasp at last. 'What the deuce has gotten into him, do you suppose?'

'I seem to remember saying something similar about Warren before we left Natal,' Bond replied. It felt oddly cathartic to be playing arbiter for once. After all, it was usually him getting into trouble rather than the other two, and things were becoming stranger by the minute. 'I've never seen him like that before,' he had to admit to a still silent Knight. 'Still,' Bond found himself admitting, 'I expect I would be just the same if it were Friday or Coleman under suspicion. An officer owes it to his men to take their part, doesn't he?'

'Albert,' Knight resumed at last, breaking the silence with a ghostly, slightly muted murmur, 'I think Earnest Penfold just threatened to kill me.'

Nor were matters improved later that day when, after hours of toiling away on entrenchments and road improvement under Lieutenant Bond, Earnest's unfortunate earners were rounded up, disarmed, and dragged off to parade before Captain McGonagle. Humour was not evident, in McGonagle, his men or the unfortunate pioneers most whom were now struggling considerably.

Many were roughly treated, jostled, and shoved about, while others were subjected to yet more divisive taunts, jibes, and physical abuses to get them into order before the captain. For whatever reason, the Highlanders had lost an officer, and from sapper to sergeant to officer, Earnest Penfold's African pioneers had become the chief suspects.

'Come now, it's no good doing that now, lads!' Gideon Knight remonstrated lightly, as an enraged African solider tried to stab a sapper through the arm for perpetually manhandling him. 'If you push them about they're only going to get more uppity.'

Earnest Penfold was by no means as relaxed about the situation. He ran up and down the line, yelling like a madman and pressing threats upon anyone who harmed his men. He complained that the way in which the Africans were being treated amounted to little more than scapegoating and that he refused to countenance such arbitrary condemnation. For the most part, he was politely ignored by his sappers, and even rebuked by McGonagle's troops, who catcalled and swore at him openly.

If such an undermining display was distasteful to Bond and Knight, it was downright humiliating to Penfold, who ultimately turned and rounded on the man whom he held to be responsible for this injustice and his subsequent loss of authority, who stood calmly observing proceedings some feet away.

'Captain McGonagle!' he railed. 'These men are neither your troops to deal with as you think fit, nor the proven subjects of anything beyond your own groundless suspicions. I demand that you and your men desist at once from this thuggery and restore my men to their arms until someone has presented some evidence of wrongdoing!'

McGonagle seemed utterly unruffled by such rank insubordination from a junior officer. He had clearly been all too used to Simonides's outbursts, and treated Penfold's petition with equally impassive disdain. Utterly dismissing the little raving officer's passionate attack and turning instead to Gideon Knight, McGonagle calmly pointed out that the English-speaking NCO of the irregulars would be afforded adequate opportunity to make representations on behalf of his fellows at a mass court martial.

'Until this time tomorrow, they will be relieved of both their duties and their arms and held under guard by my boys.'

'That's monstrous! You cannot try them collectively.' Penfold was beside himself with indignation. 'You've no right. They're not slaves! Technically, they fall under Commandant Flambard's authority to try, in any case.'

'My officer has been murdered, you silly wee man!' McGonagle exploded back at last. 'I am in command here, and I say they will be detained until tomorrow.'

'Really, sir, I don't think that's a very good idea,' Knight intoned, now thoroughly worried about his own situation as officer commanding. 'If you haul one of those men out and, well, take summary action, we'll face a mutiny!'

There followed a long, painful silence. The Highlanders

went quiet, and the African troops even stopped protesting and complaining as the ether of McGonagle's unspoken rage wafted chillingly around the camp. They all knew that word, if not all its meaning.

'My apologies, sir,' Knight mumbled in embarrassment. 'That was indelicate.'

It was too late however, for the muted contrition of the careless lieutenant was already becoming lost in the elderly officer's boiling rage.

'Don't you dare to talk to me of mutiny, laddie!' McGonagle roared, causing even Bond to shake with fear at the ferocious onslaught. 'I set out one night with my officers, leaving the women and children under the protection of a few guards – my own sepoys. As soon as I had gone and those wretched gates had shut behind me, my sentries were stabbed; officers, surgeon, children, and all. By the time we returned at dusk, not a single woman or child of the garrison lay alive in that accursed keep, and never again shall I underestimate a subjugated colonial's capacity for vengeance upon his occupiers!'

From the relative safety of their entrenching, Coleman and Friday looked on in alarm.

'We done this, Sarn't,' Coleman whimpered despairingly. 'We done it ourselves.'

'Never killed the bastard, though. Never done that.' Friday intoned, still leaning on a long wooden crutch from twisting his ankle.

This was in fact the reason for his prolonged absence without leave. Friday, having been so taken up with the little lost olivette and utterly consumed by wonder, had simply misplaced his footing on his way back to the camp and fallen down a donga, where he had remained until the constant barrage of rain had obliged him to escape. Having clawed his way both tooth and nail from the bed of the donga, the dedicated sergeant had then sought not to alarm the sentries by crawling through the outermost trench and scrambled into the camp underneath one of the newly arrived wagons. Now, as he stood supervising the sappers at their digging, he looked straight at Coleman with all the candour and straightforwardness of his profession, mixed with the stalwart authority and solidity of his position to support him.

'We done nothing,' he told the quaking sapper firmly. 'Done what was right; what was God's will. No one done more. Got that?'

Coleman nodded, smiled weakly, and carried on digging. *But if Friday didn't go back and finish Simonides, then who did?* He could not bear to imagine that it was any of his officers, and yet deep down he knew the one thing he really didn't want to know at all. For the truth was, if Mr Albert had known; if he could have seen what had happened, or disturbed Simonides in the act, Coleman knew his protective officer would most certainly have shot the man on the spot. Then again, if he had waited, that would have meant that he must have seen what was happening and done nothing to help. Coleman told himself that was impossible.

Even so, the doubt was there, and it was a feeling that he loathed. For the last dreadful few hours, he had toyed with telling Mr Albert everything, but he had made a pact with Friday after all, and it was a pact that Friday had rightly demanded for saving him. How could he now go and rat on him, as well as dump such an unbearable burden on a man already beset with problems of his own? *Worse still*, he thought as he lifted yet another spade full of earth with the pulsating muscles in his strong arms and hurled it over the barricade, *what if Mr Albert doesn't want me after such a soiling? Or doesn't believe me at all?*

Chapter Eight

The remainder of the day passed badly enough. Poor Lieutenant Penfold continued to rant backwards and forwards that his men were innocent, blaming everyone else in sight and even suggesting that some external force had been somehow responsible, an opinion that won him short shrift from absolutely everyone, including his friend Lieutenant Bond.

'For goodness's sake, Earnest!' Bond complained, after about an hour or so of prolonged badgering from Penfold. 'I can't seriously see how you expect anyone to believe that one solitary Zulu crept in here, struck a blow to one single drunken officer and then stabbed him to death before retreating into the darkness. It just defies reasonability. I'm sorry.'

'He could have fallen!' Penfold continued to rage. 'You saw the state he was in – we were all in – that night. He could have tripped up, fallen and struck his head.'

'Having enough strength left over to roll onto an assegai, point up, and then stick himself into the ground with it? Do be sensible, Earnest!'

Penfold looked thunderous and stormed off into the gathering twilight, swearing a discovery of proof and retribution for the hundredth time. As he stomped past, the little officer could barely have noticed poor, handsome, and once again utterly wretched Coleman, huddled beneath a covered wagon, and looking simply ghastly. His hair hung lank and without its usual sheen, his eyes were dull and turned tragically down at the corners, and his soft pink lips were pursed in a permanent frown. He looked as if he was about to cry.

As he sat under his own awning, Friday glanced across at Coleman, but the lad was too lost in the blues to notice. What else was he, Friday, supposed to have done, after all? He couldn't possibly have left Coleman to that devil Simonides, nor could he have reported the matter to McGonagle, Knight, or least of all Bond. Such things did not bear speaking of after all, and an allegation like that from a non-commissioned officer against a lieutenant of an infantry regiment would only have resulted in disgrace for the army and the shaming of the boy. And him.

It would also be career ending. The mere hint of such a scandal might have been even more damning than the murder, even if they were believed. It would be viewed as such, and the mud would never unstick.

Meanwhile, back in the mess tent, which young Coleman had so carelessly and happily thrown together for that much maligned reception for McGonagle and Simonides, the elderly captain and an apoplectic Gideon Knight were still slogging it out over command and commandments.

'Captain McGonagle,' Knight found himself repeating, 'you may be the senior officer in terms of rank, but it is I who have been placed in command here by Colonel Roystone himself, and have orders from my major to remain here until the supplies arrive.'

'Which they have,' McGonagle replied curtly, and returned to the notes he was writing.

'Sir, I don't think you quite understand what I am trying to tell you,' Knight persisted, with such monotonical repetition that even he grew tired of hearing it.

'You've done your job, laddie,' McGonagle replied. 'Now let me do mine. An officer has been murdered, and a pioneer detail stood down from active service. I'm too short of men to continue alone, so tomorrow I intend to take an officer from your company, at least one troop of sappers to get me as far as the main column, then you and your fellows can do what the devil you like.'

'What?' Knight demanded, incredulity getting the better of protocol. 'Do you seriously suggest that I simply hand over one of my officers and as many of my men as suits this caprice of yours, notwithstanding any orders save your own?'

'Take care, Lieutenant!' warned McGonagle severely, 'That is the second time you have presumed to call me capricious, and I'm minded saying that I intend to take no more of it!'

'May I remind you, sir, that I am junior to you by only one rank, and that by virtue of my appointment from the column commander I am at liberty to comply with or reject your requests as I see fit, so long as you and your men remain within Fort Penfold.'

'A miss is as good as a mile,' McGonagle quipped back, sipping the whisky from his hip flask, and refusing to be provoked a second time. 'You will comply with my orders, Mr Knight, or I shall be forced to dismiss your authority and see if ma nephew and wee Mr Pendragon out there feel like weighing your rank against mine!'

'You wouldn't dare!' Knight broke forth, utterly abandoning his position as the servile second-in-command. 'Come to that, neither would either of them!'

At this point McGonagle merely glanced up from his papers

for a fraction of a second, belittling the enraged subaltern immediately with one acidic glare. 'You sure about that, Lieutenant? My only subaltern was skewered to the ground last night with a native pigsticker. I don't know who's guilty of it, but I'm damn sure going to see the culprit strung from the highest gibbet I can find before you see the back of me.'

It was at this point that Knight felt he wanted to say something rude regarding that notion, but the politics of self-interest had prevented him. A sudden thought had occurred; a more troublesome and distressing thought than that which had been presented so far. McGonagle was a well-known wordsmith, and often kept things from those around him. What if he had received orders to proceed with the sappers and for some reason, perhaps concerning the murder, had elected to keep it from him? No adjutant with aspirations to senior rank would wish it known as insubordinate, and McGonagle was certainly not a man to keep such things to himself when, or if, they got back to Natal. With a deep sigh and a gesture of frustrated capitulation, Gideon Knight tossed his helmet into the corner and subsided forlornly on a drum. *If only Warren was here*, he thought miserably to himself. Now he would have to be the bigger man and lead from beneath.

Knight's sentiment, could he only have known it, was being expressed in the same manner, if slightly louder, by the highly vocal Earnest Penfold.

'I agree with you entirely, old chap,' Bond replied, as he and Penfold made a slow progressive inspection of the fortification once more. 'This is far too great a responsibility to be placed on a subaltern. Had Gideon only the rank to back it up, he might be able to put his foot down a bit more.'

'I doubt your uncle would listen, even if Gideon was a captain,' Penfold replied peevishly. 'In any case, it is for the precise reason that he is so keen to become one that makes him so reticent to intervene on behalf of his own men.'

'Now look here,' Bond chided severely, 'let us not make bones about this. You and I know perfectly well that it is your African men in question here, not your sapper troop.'

Penfold looked pained. The rain had eased off just a matter of minutes before, and the ground now sang and gurgled once again with the sound of the earth absorbing the moisture of the previously torrential downpour. 'It's just that it all seems so unfair to me, Albert,' Penfold continued miserably. His righteous indignation had quite deserted him now, leaving a worried and seemingly helpless little man to wail and moan in a manner that his companion felt quite displeasing and disturbing.

'Look here, Earnest old chap,' Bond ventured at length, 'don't you think you might be taking the Africans' part just a little bit too far?'

'Well, I suppose I'm doing the wrong thing by poor old Simonides, I do see that,' Penfold replied after giving the matter a little thought. 'Yet the more that I think about it, the more I see that no one else is going to do it for them. Honestly, Albert, if those poor fellows were only given a little respect and dignity, and treated as proper British soldiers, they might just be a little more likely to mimic the regulars' behaviour.'

'That's all very well, Earnest,' Bond returned unmercifully, 'but have you paused to consider exactly how a "proper British soldier" is treated at home? They shun him; they don't want him in the public houses or around and about the local fairs and music halls. They don't really want him anywhere except on the other side of the world so they can remember him on plates and toby jugs. It's fine for a fellow to be holding the line in India or Africa, so long as he's still sending his pay home, but bring him back and stick him in digs at Amherst or Chatham or let him look for drink in town or a table to eat at, it's a different matter entirely. It's blatant hypocrisy, like the late lamented Simonides. Suddenly he's gone and everyone is bent on vengeance out of guilt!'

Penfold nodded gravely. 'I do see that, you know,' he replied forlornly. 'It's just that, well, what with this being my first proper command of men and all and so on, I just want to see the thing done properly, for all my men. You understand?'

'Oh, I do,' replied Bond. 'Indeed I do, Earnest. It's just that I would hate to see our friendship or your friendship with Gideon suffer for your libertarianism.'

'It's just too bad, that's all,' Penfold replied, and the two of them walked on a little further, pausing by a stack of mealie bags, the contents of which had been ruined for being left in the rain, and were thus incorporated in the overall defences.

Bond lit a cigar, offering one to Penfold.

'No thanks, old man,' he replied wearily, waving away the proffered tobacco with a sad smile and a gesture of restraint. 'I don't think I could afford to take that up as well.'

Bond initially said nothing about this enigmatic remark, but his bronze eyebrows did move a little closer together and bemused creases began to furrow the smooth forehead. He took another puff on his cigar, and Penfold plumped down resignedly on a biscuit box, removing his sun helmet with his good hand, and placing it between his knees. Then, with his left arm still slung across his chest, the little officer proceeded to reach inside the leather straps that supported its weight and removed from inside it a small piece of paper. This document he gave to Bond, and the latter could tell from the grave silence that followed that the portent was not one of good fortune.

'Is there anything you want to tell me before I read it?' he asked quietly, as he accepted the paper from the outstretched hand of his troubled friend.

'It came from my father's notary the day before we sailed,' Penfold commenced.

Bond winced. Such subjects were still too close to home to be treated with any level of objectivity, even in such circumstances as those prevalent then and there. 'I never knew your father had died.'

'That's probably because he hasn't,' Penfold replied simply. 'In fact, he's even more alive and alert than I am at this precise moment.'

Once again Bond said nothing. He knew well enough to know that these things were like watching a dam burst: it all began with a trickle, yet he knew that the whole lot might tumble forth eventually, and he was jolly well going to be ready.

'Take your time, old fellow,' he murmured.

A cricket got up a row in the long grass beyond the outermost barricade, and soon a whole army of crickets had joined in with the deafening chorus, until it began to sound as if the whole world had gone a-chirping. Neither officer turned a hair; they were used to it by now.

Penfold covered his face with his hand, took a deep breath and began. 'You see, it all came about when I became engaged to Hen,' he explained in tones of woeful gloom. 'Father didn't care for the match at all, you see. He thought I was marrying below myself. At least,' he added quickly, 'we're not exactly in the top drawer ourselves you understand, but there is a little money, and with it a deal of pretention.'

Bond nodded grimly. The tale was beginning to sound

familiar, this time with his and Clara's roles reversed for the narrative. 'Go on,' he encouraged, feeling oddly liberated by his little friend's disclosure.

'Very well.' Penfold replied. 'I never thought that I would marry, you see. No, Albert, don't feign to protest like that. I know I'm not gifted the way you and Gideon are, and this is all quite hard enough, so please let me finish what I am trying to say, will you?'

Bond nodded and muttered an apology.

Penfold resumed. 'Anyway, Mother and Father quarrelled terribly. She took my part all right, but I could tell from her face that she agreed with his view of things. There is an awful lot of snobbery about those of us who haven't had our fortunes all that long, you know.'

Bond had to suppress a smile. He knew better than most.

'The long and the short of it was, they had the most frightful row with Hen's parents when they met, and Father rounded up by refusing to consent to the marriage.'

'Don't tell me,' Bond interrupted unthinkingly, 'he threatened to cut you off without a penny, and to see you and Hen on the street?'

'By no means, Albert. He's far too proud to permit a scandal of that sort,' Penfold retorted mirthlessly. 'He told Mother and I that we could sort out the cost of the thing between ourselves. Hen's poor father hasn't a bean, you understand, and told me that he'd cut me off in a matter of months. I had been at Royal Military Academy a year by then, and Mother persuaded him to commute the severance to my being commissioned, to save face.'

'Well, here you are,' Bond smiled warmly. 'It looks to me as if you've made it, Earnest.'

'Yes, that's all very well,' Penfold added miserably. 'But you know how things are in the army, what with expenses and all. It costs a chap to turn up for duty most days.'

It was true. Officers when at home or abroad lived on a purely credit basis. Salaries were meagre, and hardly covered domestic mess bills, so a young subaltern, new to the ways and methods of the system, found himself obediently signing chits left, right and centre. In such circumstances, simply doing as one was told often resulted in some considerable financial difficulty later. For a gentleman with significant personal means or separate income, such salutary lessons could be easily learned in short succession, and the results met out of the private purse at the end of the first month of an officer's commission. For officers like Bond and Penfold, social and financial obligations had to be approached with considerable caution and no small measure of prudence, or the debts mounted.

At length, Penfold rose from his seat and the two of them carried on their circuit.

'We did quite well to begin with,' he explained to Bond, as they walked past the little nooks and crannies where the men lay huddled together under hastily improvised awnings, or bunched up alone amid the boxes, bags, and canvas of the supply wagons. They all looked utterly wretched. 'I had the costs of course, but then we were expecting that. We budgeted, you know?'

Bond nodded again. He was growing all too accustomed to that aspect of real life himself.

'Hen took modest lodgings away from the barracks, and we seemed to get by on what I was bringing in. Then the news of the war broke, and I suddenly realised that I was going to need far more than my sword if I was to stand any chance at all. The truth is, Albert, I hocked it to buy the revolver and the field glasses.'

'Oh, Earnest, you didn't?' Bond sighed disapprovingly, and all the time feeling a complete hypocrite.

Penfold nodded gloomily. 'It was then that we had our talk. I explained that there was a good chance of brevet promotion, and that we might end up with a little more money, but only if I did well.'

'What did Hen say?' Bond found himself asking.

'She saw the necessity, and we gave up our little rooms by the barracks for a modest little place above The Bull in Chatham. Hen taught needlework, reading, and piano to young ladies. Modest, appropriate things, you know?'

Bond nodded.

'Anyhow, finally we saved up enough to buy my kit, and pay the bills from Brompton.'

'That's why we saw even less of you in the mess than the others saw of me,' Bond remarked, enlightened. 'I feel a brute, Earnest, for we had you down as a bit of a piker.'

Penfold nodded and smiled weakly. 'I know I've been a bit testy of late,' he added. 'I'm sorry, Albert.'

Bond nodded acknowledgment, but seemed suddenly to be somewhere very far away. Penfold, slightly embarrassed, continued with what he was saying for a while, until the hopelessness and utter exhaustive pressure of the past few days finally caught up with him and he slumped down against a wagon nearest to the tents.

'You know how it is for us, Albert!' he groaned miserably.

Bond turned sharply around and looked properly at his companion. His shoulders hung limp and exhausted beneath the crumpled cloth of his serge jacket, and the heavily laden, baggy eyelids shifted and flickered as if they might just succumb altogether. A deep sigh forced the contortions on the officer's minute frame to pulsate even further, rippling up and down his weary form like a chill wave of death.

Bond looked pained. 'You know that I would help if I could, don't you, Earnest?'

Penfold nodded again, and again he forced a smile. 'I would neither ask it nor want it, old friend,' he replied. 'The situation is quite hopeless, and I really have no idea what to do.'

'Gideon has private means,' Bond suggested tentatively, but to his horror it was a suggestion that provoked the most stinging response.

'Are you trying to lose me my commission, Albert?' Penfold exploded. 'Have you any idea what it would be like if Warren or the colonel found out about this? The way subalterns are treated when they fall behind with their bills is worse than the debtor's prison. I'd lose my independence; they would allocate a field officer, probably Warren, to take over my accounts, and then they'd soon see that I'm too poor to stay in the army and I'd be booted out with nowhere to go. Don't you think that Hen's been through enough without the adjutant getting involved? It might get out of the barracks and about town!'

Bond sighed and fell quite silent for a time. He was all too aware that he too might well have found himself in such a position. Then again, he hadn't a wife to support, and the way he was beginning to feel about Coleman suggested to him that there wasn't really much point in pretending any further. Hard as he tried, he simply could not supplant the image of the young sapper with the visage of his long-deserted intended, Clara. In any case, he was no nearer to those allusive and spurious stories of brevet promotions and gallantry medals than he had been in a chair at his club, so there was so far really very little gained. With a deep sigh of resignation, he bade the forlorn Penfold goodnight, and set off in the direction of the only remaining comfort he knew he could rely on: the adoring young soldier waiting for him in his tent.

Back in the relative protection of his sandbag redoubt, Gideon Knight sat by the flickering oil lamp and gloomily ruminated on his all too brief command. What on earth could he do to prevent McGonagle from simply superseding him?

There was nothing to qualify the officer's right to command. He could offer no evidence of McGonagle's unfitness, and there was no suggestion that a subaltern should do anything other than submit to the authority of a captain.

He couldn't talk to Bond, the man was his uncle after all, and he could hardly talk to Penfold when he, Gideon, had just spent all day playing devil's advocate for McGonagle. Abandoning his principles of stoic isolation, Knight quit the cover of his meditative sanctuary and set off in search of a brain to pick.

He was just about to stroll across to Bond's tent and throw back the flaps, when the appearance of some strange, silhouetted images against the dimly lit canvas disrupted his train of thought for a moment. Gazing numbly at the mesmerising, animated shapes on the stained, parchment awning, the officer was suddenly brought up sharp by the clicking of boot heels and a short, dry cough of introduction.

'Sergeant Friday, good evening,' Knight found himself mumbling distractedly. 'I was going to call on Lieutenant Bond, but now I think about it, I wonder if we might pass a word back at my billet?'

Friday nodded obediently and followed in the wake of his officer. It was a good thing, he reflected, that the darkness had begun to overwhelm the pale red rays of evening sunlight, or else Lieutenant Knight might well have seen the colour of his sergeant's own features, or worse still the beads of sweat as they broke across his brow.

'Look here, Sergeant,' Knight resumed as they stepped inside the redoubt. 'I know Mr Albert is your own troop commander, and I am aware that your loyalty must be to him, but I wonder if you could help me. I'm simply all at sea for knowing what to do. Are you aware...'

Bond, who meanwhile was utterly unaware of how close he had come to being walked in upon, approached his young batman with slow and steady deliberation.

Almost as soon as Bond had entered the tent Coleman, who stood with his back to the officer, suddenly stopped what he was doing and stiffened. The footfall grew heavier and Bond, who was less than a foot away, breathed in the scent of the young soldier's body like some exotic elixir of damp and sweat. Coleman was stripped to the waste, his broad, bronzed shoulders tapering gradually down the smooth golden skin of his back, and descending into his pair of firm buttocks, still keenly emphasised despite the heavy folds of his baggy navy trousers. Gently, tentatively, Bond placed both hands with almost provocative tenderness on Coleman's exposed back, bringing them slowly down the contours of his exposed body and clamping them firmly on his hips. Coleman let out a yelp, spun around and almost knocked the officer across the tent.

Bond, shocked rigid by this sudden change in tempo, almost cried out himself. As he struggled to retain his balance he looked on, wide-eyed and open-mouthed, horrified and confused by the trembling mass of emancipated emotion before him. Accustomed to Jack responding with tenderness to such tactility, Bond found himself a little frightened.

Stunned, open-mouthed and very red indeed, Coleman could only look back at the horrified Bond in a sort of ashamed horror at his own reaction. He had never looked more vulnerable, or more physically and emotionally attractive than at that moment in the tent at Fort Penfold, when the two of them stood surveying each other in stunned silence, only feet apart. Under different circumstances spontaneity might well have been crushed and suppressed by the severity of such a reaction, had not the trembling Coleman suddenly abandoned all pretence of rank or martial discipline and burst helplessly into tears. Leaping instinctively forward like an animal defending its own, Bond bridged the gap and took the young sapper firmly in his arms.

Seeking comfort as never before, Coleman buried his head in the officer's chest and sobbed as hard as he had ever done. Just as an animal in the pouring rain whose instinct tells it to make for the nearest point of cover, so the young sapper's instinct was to roll into the officer's arms like a ball. Mollies and Nancy boys didn't survive the docks, nor the barracks for that matter, and he had always been as tough as any other – tougher, even. His life had seen to that.

Bond, himself almost transfixed with grief, desperate to help, simply let him cling for dear life. Stroking and caressing the long strands of soft blond hair betwixt thumb and fingers, he gently kissed the back of Jack's neck, sensitively murmuring words of comfort and endearment, always with one eye on the door of the tent. Gradually the grief subsided, and Coleman began to respond to this loving and gentle treatment by rubbing his cheek up against Bond's chest and snuggling under his chin. Bond placed a hand on the young sapper's cheek, stroking and smoothing away the tears, reiterating his affections and assuring him all would be well. Coleman sniffed, shifted position a little and then began to kiss him back. Warmly, firmly but slowly at first, and yet with far more passion and animation as the energy took over, he began to unbutton the olivettes on the officer's tunic. Breathing a deep sigh of elation, Bond closed his eyes, his arms providing a haven of sanctuary, determined to scare away anything that might seek to harm or upset him, but equally determined to know what had. Bond could smell every bead of perspiration, sense every move, and feel every sensation as Coleman kissed him, the moment perpetuated and magnified a million times over, until he thought his heart would explode. Never in his life had he loved anything, felt so close and protective of anything, and yet sought so deeply to understand something before.

Withdrawing, eyes still closed, Coleman allowed himself a moment before breathing a deep sigh and looking plaintively up at Bond.

'You don't have to tell me anything,' the officer murmured at length. It seemed like a sensible place to begin, with no pressure applied and no demand being made.

Coleman promptly broke down again, and thrust his head back into the protective enclave of Bond's hard shoulder. He absorbed the ferocity of the boy's misery and frustration as an anvil under a hail of blows from a blacksmith's hammer. Jack sobbed hard, stifling the sound in the officer's body. Bond whispered tenderly that he loved him, and that everything was going to be fine, which seemed only to intensify the boy's grief. Only after considerably warm and tactile encouragement did the officer manage to coerce the grieving sapper into confidence.

'It's all right, go on then,' Bond whispered reassuringly. 'Go as hard as you like, I'll take care of you. Just keep it coming but keep it quiet. The sooner it's out of you the better.'

Coleman sniffed, whimpered, and clung to Bond's back with such primal despair that he felt he must surely be crushed. Gradually however the convulsions subsided, tense limbs and contorted grips slackened, and the two of them were once again lost in a world of each other, tenderly caressing and sliding close together until the strength of one began to infect the other. At length Coleman once again felt strong enough to look up and speak, and this time he managed to hold his composure long enough to recount the horror that had so radically afflicted him before.

Chapter Nine

Bond listened in rigid horror as his batman explained, for some measure, the bizarre and hitherto inconceivable events, and shocks of the past forty-eight hours, of Simonides's attack, and Sergeant Friday's miraculous reappearance and heroic prevention of the evil that the officer had been so close to perpetrating. Moreover, Coleman's principal fear appeared to be that anything should befall his sergeant on his own account.

'W-we never stabbed him though, Mr Albert, honest we didn't,' Coleman stammered as an afterthought.

Bond said nothing for a moment, but slowly removed his revolver. He checked that it was loaded, cocked it, and then laid it down on the drum beside his bed, which he used as a table. 'You see that?' he said at last, gazing glassily at the primed weapon beside the bed.

'Please don't leave me to do this on my own, Mr Albert. Believe me, I never done it!' Coleman whimpered, clamping shut his eyes and pressing his face against the officer's knee.

Bond snapped out of his reverie in seconds. Falling to his knees also, he took Coleman once again in his arms and held him tight a few moments. Once again, his lifted Coleman's chin with his knuckles, looked long and hard into his reddened blue eyes, and then at the gun on the table.

'Now just you listen to me,' he began. 'I would never hurt you in any way, nor let some bastard like Simonides, and I swear by all things both holy and unholy that I shall never, never leave you, or fail to be there for you when you need me again. Listen, if anyone dares to try and harm you ever again, I'll kill them myself. Understand?'

Coleman looked at the officer to the pistol, and then back at the officer. Never had he seen the passion burn so bright, the blue eyes so aflame with indignation, or the sincerity radiate so humanely from the handsome face as it looked down on him.

Comforted at last, he smiled for the first time that evening and gently rested his head on the young lieutenant's shoulder. 'Promise, Mr Albert?'

'Never,' Bond repeated. 'Nothing is ever going to come between us, or try to take you away from me again. I promise you that.'

The blond head nodded up and down against the exposed right arm, gently tickling the tanned skin with its glistening silkiness.

'You'll have nothing to fear, so long as I'm alive, and neither will Sergeant Friday. We can never speak of this, mind you,' he added severely. 'No one must ever know what happened to Lieutenant Simonides.'

'I weren't dressed proper, all wet and... open, like,' Coleman admitted weakly. 'I heard someone come up behind me and I knew how I was... my shirt buttons... I just thought it would be you if anyone came near me. That's why I was loose, easy like. That's how he saw me. Like he was you... coming to me.'

'What?' Bond breathed in amazement. 'And you imagine for a moment that implicates you, do you? Or excuses him in some way? What on earth possesses you to even entertain culpability? You weren't drunk, you didn't invite Simonides to defile you by your posture, dress... by anything! You didn't kill him, either.'

'Nor did the Sarn't!' Coleman exclaimed suddenly. 'Please, Mr Albert, say you believe me. He only hit him to get him off of me in the first place!'

'I know, I know,' Bond repeated, squeezing Coleman tighter and holding him closer to his chest. 'I just know what I'd have done if I had been there, and hitting him wouldn't have been half of it!'

Bond's first move the following morning was to call Sergeant Friday away from the considerable and burdensome responsibility of organising the mobilisation of McGonagle's transport for an immediate conference concerning the revelations.

'Now look here, Sergeant,' Bond commenced. 'We've got to keep this to ourselves, do you understand? On no account is this business to become public knowledge.'

'Sir?'

'Sergeant, I have to confess that I don't know you terribly well,' Bond resumed hastily.

Friday was giving him the monosyllabic treatment, just like their first meeting. In this case it was exactly the reaction that the officer had been expecting.

'Even so, what I do know of you, both from the accounts of my fellow officers and from my own experience, is that you are an excellent troop sergeant, with an impressive period of service and an exemplary record of conduct. You have the medal to prove it.'

Friday remained silent.

Bond was not thrown by his silence and tried a different tack. 'Look, Friday, no one is saying that what you did was wrong... at least, I'm not saying that at any rate. Nobody in our position, that is to say, a position of responsibility, wherein we have a duty to the men under our command, would view what you did as anything other than reasonable, under the circumstances. In short, I believe you acted to protect another, having no alternative presented at the time. I will not see a man of your reputation and aptitude hanged for murder.'

Friday, who had so far stood and listened in officious silence, almost exploded at the mere mention of the word. Yet such was his discipline, conformance to title and faith in the order of things, that he waited until the officer had finished orating before allowing his own voice to be heard.

'Permission to speak? Never stabbed him, sir,' he stated abruptly, before Bond had been afforded the opportunity to nod. 'Done the rest, though. Ain't proud and I ain't ashamed neither. But I never stabbed him.'

Bond sighed deeply and pointedly rubbed his eyes with his fingers. 'Pride and shame have no place in this matter!' he broke forth with a hissing sound so menacing that it almost made *him* feel afraid. 'Let me tell you the truth. You must know by now that I hold Sapper Coleman in some affection. Are you aware of that, Sergeant?'

Here, Friday became somewhat awkward. They both did, albeit for no reason that Friday would have been able to quantify with words, beyond the customary, perfunctory: 'Sir?'

Bond was colouring himself now and was evidently becoming more and more agitated as the possible inference from his admission began to affect his speech. 'When I heard what he tried to do to Coleman I, well, I didn't—' He paused for a moment, and just as Friday was beginning to think that his officer had broken down completely, he returned with acidic alacrity. 'I dare say that, should I have been there, I should have taken out my pistol and shot him dead. As it is, I wish to God that I had, if I had seen what you saw.' Bond's speech faltered.

Friday looked pained and, for a moment, it looked as if he might have to witness the officer weep. This, he attributed to religious sensibility, a notion soon to be debunked.

Coleman, who had so far remained silent, raised his head, and let out a string of contrite noises scarcely commensurate with an articulate sentence.

'Hold your tongue!' Friday sniffed indignantly. 'Spoke out of turn. No business bringing officer into this. Boy gave his word, so Friday thought. Between us, and God.'

'I'm here, Sergeant Friday. God isn't!' Bond barked, looking up sharply.

As he did so, the pencil with which he had been fiddling snapped in half and the rough wooden end plunged into the palm of his hand, ripping the skin. He didn't even notice the blood. The whole interview was beginning to remind him very much of that so far distant morning at Brompton Barracks when Friday had first introduced him to the endearing young sapper, now standing so forlornly and so full of guilt in the corner. *Damn it*, he thought. *Friday shouldn't be talking as though any of this is Coleman's fault.*

'Would you wait outside please, Jack?' Bond asked restrainedly.

'Sir?' Coleman looked pained, and it was a stiff fight for them both to hold on to composure as they exchanged pitiful glances across Bond's campaign desk.

'I said *dis-miss*!'

For the young soldier at least, such a dismissal smacked very soundly of the gloomiest portent. Bond's eyes said, *trust me*, yet still, doubt crowded the young sapper's thoughts, albeit fleetingly. Had they suddenly decided he was guilty? Did he simply wish to get rid of him to patch the mess up with Friday, the sergeant?

Even so, love and loyalty won out. Coleman simply nodded in obedience and quit the tent without a further murmur.

As soon as he fancied the boy to be clear and as soon as the dark silhouette had disappeared off the pale sunlit canvas, Bond's anger spilled forth in tumult. 'How could you do such a thing, Sergeant?' he demanded icily. 'To say such a thing to Coleman after all that he has been through! You ought to be ashamed, man!'

'Boy's tough,' he muttered defensively. 'Thinking of officer. Didn't want no trouble for you, for the corps. For—'

'Yourself?' Bond interjected. Friday looked wounded, but the officer continued. 'What, pray tell, do you fancy to have come about as a result of your silence?'

Still, Friday said nothing.

'Sergeant, I have already told you that I would have acted as you did, were I to have found myself in your position. But to expect him to shoulder all this alone. And to keep this from *me*. Do you not respect me, nor care for that boy at all?'

Friday, who had just about been maintaining his composure so far, boiled over. His face grew very red, and his eyes grew like blisters. 'Care?' he repeated. 'Care for the boy?'

A silence followed, and Bond began to wonder just what exactly so candid an exchange was about to bring forth upon them.

'Friday saved boy. Gave him to you 'cos I knew you'd take care. Mr Albert's good officer, thinks Friday. Mr Albert care for boy.' Friday blushed even harder. 'Ain't had much, has lad out there. When Friday sees that sinful sodomite—' Friday stopped mid-sentence.

Bond bristled, then sighed and rubbed his eyes forlornly. 'What I am saying, Sergeant, is that now *I* know all this too, we are in a better position to act in unison. It is imperative that no one save we three should gain access to this matter. He *must* be protected from the consequences of this, even if it means we two must hang as a result.'

Friday's eyes widened, but the stalwart NCO had allowed himself enough open talk for one lifetime. Snapping smartly to attention, he saluted and then nodded. 'Officer knows best,' he said at last. 'Friday keep his tongue, sir.'

'Thank you,' Bond replied, adding as the sergeant turned to leave, 'Friday?'

'Sir?'

'What do you suppose would have happened, had not Lieut— I mean, had not Mr Simonides died?'

Friday thought for a moment, then replied, 'Gone after the boy.'

Bond nodded gravely. 'Let us but comfort ourselves with the fact that he can't any longer,' he suggested, regaining his composure, and gazing numbly at the papers on the desk before him. 'Remember, no confessions.'

'Sir.'

'Remember also, I'm in this as deep as you are now, so if they hang you, they'll hang Jack, and me besides. Neither Simonides's exposition nor mine will protect the corps.'

'Sir.'

Coleman re-entered the tent almost as soon as Friday had left, and from the look of partial relief on the young sapper's face, what passed between them outside had not been acrimonious.

He looked at Bond in dumb readiness, and the officer could see from the puffs around his red eyes and the lines down his grimy cheeks that he hadn't stopped weeping. In an instant the officer rose, placed his hands on the young sapper's shoulders, and smiled for the first time since that terrible storm had broken over their heads.

'I told you we were in this together,' Bond whispered lovingly. 'I'm here, and believe me, nothing on earth will protect you like I'm going to.'

Coleman smiled, then faltered a little. 'I've had dreams, all right. Nightmares.'

'It's to be expected,' Bond replied, himself a little haltingly. 'Innocent people often suffer in war, Jack. Yet just occasionally, it takes a war to wipe a bad stain off the face of the earth. Even if there was a debt, it isn't yours. Do you understand? This is not your sin, and no sin of yours engendered it. Do you understand my meaning?'

Coleman bowed his head, looked up again and smiled weakly. 'Do I – do *we* – deserve this? Sarn't Friday, what he says about God, the bible 'n' all?'

Bond said nothing. He couldn't even if he wanted to, for his tears choked back speech. Wasn't there enough of a war going on for two people to simply pass by unnoticed in the chaos? Must they really undergo all this and more, just to be together?

'God,' he murmured at length, in accents so deep and dark that Coleman barely recognised his voice. 'Sodom and Gomorrah God punished, or *man* punished what he regarded as immoral, or what other men had told him God regarded as immoral. What god forbids love, Jack?'

A cry from without snapped the moment in two like Bond's pencil, and from the two distinctive voices raised in opposition, Bond knew that his uncle was going hammer and tongs with Gideon Knight.

'Time to intervene,' he told Coleman, touching his cheek gently. 'Best you get off and see to our kit. You will be all right, won't you?'

Coleman smiled and nodded. 'Got you, ain't I?'

'Definitely.'

'Then I'm fine, sir.'

Chapter Ten

Captain AW McGonagle awoke at the crack of dawn by way of custom.

Even as he lay there, listening to the early morning sounds of the veldt, harkened to the insects moving and chattering, the birds calling and the occasional creaking and clanking as a nearby sentry rested his rifle between his boots, he closed his eyes again and smiled peacefully. He had never been entirely happy since his wife had died, and the drink had certainly not helped either that or his own career. Neither had all those years of frustration, inactivity, and staff duties, watching as all those younger men ascended the ranks above and around him while he remained a captain, simply growing older, drinking whisky and resenting. Yet now he was back again, and at last the years of suffering and solitude had begun to drop away from him as he lay there, out in the field, and composed poetry in the privacy of his tent in the early morning light.

Command of this supply column was going to provide that long-awaited and much maligned mounting block that a man of his age and temperament required to resume the saddle of the horse of life. He liked the sentiment and decided to commit it to verse. *If only those prating bookworms under my command had cut their teeth on the Indian mutiny rather than at the academy*, he thought, *perhaps they might be a little more respectful of my long service and infinite experience as a solider.*

The canvas flapped and rustled above; shadows and silhouettes danced across the brilliantly illuminated canopy as the men were roused from their slumber and fell in for breakfast. McGonagle snorted, sniffed, blew his nose, and put on his neat little gold-rimmed spectacles. Then he felt around for his pipe, bade a fond farewell to the last beautiful moments of true and comfortable repose, and clambered out of bed with a groan. This damp was not for arthritics, he decided.

Lieutenant Bond had risen early. Once sleep had left him and the stirring and shifting of the young sapper in his entrancing slumber had rendered the tiny camp bed much too small for two people, the officer had decided to take advantage of the early sunrise. It had taken all his strength and reassurance to get the young soldier off to sleep after the stress of their interview the previous day, and the poor wretch seemed to still be beset by torments concerning his late attacker. He was not unduly bothered about Coleman being left asleep in his tent. By the time anyone got around to striking tents, the young batman would be sitting in his shirtsleeves, alternately gobbling his porridge and cleaning things.

In the back of his mind, was the pressing notion that, should McGonagle decide or be badgered into leaving one sapper officer behind to guard the depot, then it would be Penfold and not *he* who answered to the charge.

"'All things bright and beautiful',' Bond began in a wavy tenor, and thinking all the time of the golden-limbed, blond sapper still cuddling up to the warm blankets in his camp bed.

The decidedly dubious note of his solo choir was suddenly interrupted by yet another, this time more impressive voice from the other side of the laager.

A loud, deep yet perfectly pitched solo voice was just launching into, "'Oh my love is like a red, red rose...'" when

Bond came face-to-face with his uncle, stripped to the waist and very much at his toilet with soap and water behind one of the wagons.

There followed a mutual cough of embarrassment, during which both impromptu renditions ceased abruptly. After some pause, the silence was broken only by the screech of a distant sakabuli bird.

'Good morning, Albert,' McGonagle laughed, a little dryly.

'Good morning, sir,' Bond replied, doing his best to look away from the ample rolls of fat, which had come on considerably since middle age, and seemed to him to be spilling over the waistband of the older officer's tartan trews like an oil of the Victoria Falls.

McGonagle laughed uneasily again. 'No need to call me sir in private, Albert,' he remonstrated gently. 'Tish, if I can't call you ma nephew and you can't call me uncle, what on earth are we coming to?'

Bond shifted uneasily from one foot to the other. 'Forgive me. I didn't wish to presume, well, in front of the other chaps, you know?'

'Aye, very well,' McGonagle replied. 'I spent a lifetime of dealing with men who thought they could advance by the men to whom they were related. I've no time for nepotism, Albert, and I've never done you favours, have I?'

'Never,' Bond replied, rather too robustly and readily, had McGonagle been minded noticing. Checking himself, Bond sought to move matters on. 'Uncle,' Bond began enquiringly. 'Well, I just wondered, have either Earnest or Gideon made, well, representations at all?'

'Why, what on earth do you mean by representations?' McGonagle demanded, snatching an eruption in his skin with a curse and trickle of blood.

'Well, sir,' Bond resumed, conscious of the time passing before them, 'I wanted to know who... well, I mean, *which* of us is to be left behind to guard the drift.'

'Guard the drift?' McGonagle repeated incredulously 'Why, who should I leave in charge here?'

'Earnest,' Bond suggested innocently. He hated himself for doing it, but Penfold had been wounded after all, and that slung arm would hardly lend itself to riding roughshod across the landscape for days.

'What, wee Pendragon, here all about his own business?' McGonagle enquired, equally innocently. 'What on earth should he do if the worst were to occur?'

'He's as trained and experienced as I am,' Bond retorted hotly. 'He's seen just as much action, and that little body is a good deal stronger than it looks.' A chuckle from McGonagle suddenly caused the young officer to halt abruptly, and with a sigh of dismay, he realised he was turning into devil's advocate. 'What about Gideon?' Bond resumed hastily. 'As senior lieutenant, wouldn't he be more suited to an independent command?'

'What about you, ma boy?' McGonagle suggested lightly. 'Don't you fancy an independent command of your own?'

Bond went white. 'I beg your pardon, Uncle?'

McGonagle laughed. 'There's no need to get worked up over nothing, Albert, for I have absolutely no intention of leaving you behind. D'you really think I want to face the colonel and tell him that I told off my own flesh and blood to guard this God forsaken corner of nowhere while taking his fellows on, and deeper into enemy country?'

Bond smiled in relief. 'As long as you don't leave any of my boys behind.'

'Don't leave who behind?' intoned a third voice.

It was Gideon Knight who, having decided against his better judgment for the men to muster and fall in, had subsequently set about locating McGonagle.

'What's the occasion if I may ask, sir?' Knight enquired cordially, upon seeing McGonagle engaged so busily about his toilet.

'I'm taking a bath, laddie,' the officer replied. 'After all, it wouldn't do to roll up at the column looking like an unmade bed now, would it, Albert?'

'Absolutely not,' Bond replied, eager to desert the scene of his earlier brown-nosing before the conversation resumed. 'Shall I fall my troop in yet, Gideon?'

'Sir?' This time it was Knight's turn to brown-nose, as he looked to McGonagle for his approval of the order.

'Aye, best be away with it,' McGonagle replied, wiping the remnants of the soap from his considerable body with the remnants of an old shirt. 'You can fall in that local rabble while you're about it too, Albert,' he called after the departing Bond.

'Shouldn't they have left already, sir?' Knight murmured thoughtfully.

'What?' cried McGonagle in outrage. 'Do you really think that I'm about to take those wee murdering spear pinchers halfway across Africa with me? They were bad enough before they killed one of my officers!'

'Sir, there is still no evidence readily apparent to us that would indicate an African soldier killed Simonides,' Knight remarked quietly. 'In any case, won't it be up to Commandant Flambard to interrogate and, if necessary, serve justice when we rejoin the column?'

McGonagle thought for a moment, then nodded slowly. 'All right, Lieutenant,' he conceded warily. 'You may tell wee Mr Penrose that he can take his Africans with him should he wish, but it is his responsibility, should ought else untoward occur. Do I make myself clear, Mr Gideon?'

'Yes, sir,' Gideon replied grimly. 'Very clear.'

The sapper officers took a leisurely breakfast, while the camp gradually began to disappear around them. Their work had, after all, been in digging the trenches, fortifying the position, and widening the latrines where necessary. They had already drained off the roads sufficiently to take McGonagle's convoy of supply wagons, and besides which they still had a long march ahead of them that day, so a quiet amble into it was hardly to have been begrudged them. The smoke from the morning campfires was grey, scented and strangely comforting, especially to Bond, whom it reminded of long holidays taken at his grandfather's country house in the chilly Yorkshire winters.

Sergeants Friday, Andrews and Stag fell the men in before 8:30 a. m., fresh issues of ammunition were drawn by the sappers as well as their new Highland comrades, and the stragglers from the West Rutlands who were being left to guard the hitherto unmolested position.

A sober, if slightly unsentimental, huddle was quickly organised by Lieutenant Knight so that the late Simonides's possessions might be catalogued, and any non-personal items auctioned off among the officers in the time-honoured custom. On this occasion however, there being no known next of kin to whom such items as his plate watch, silver signet ring and other items of modest value might be returned, the decision was taken to leave such chattels as items of memorial on his grave. Time was pressing after all, and since there was no one at home to whom the money raised from the sales of his revolver, shoulder belt, sword and binoculars might be sent, all were entrusted to McGonagle.

'It's a black day when a man's watch and chain must hang upon his cross for want of someone to pass it on to,' Penfold remarked to Bond, as the latter assisted him in mounting his horse. 'I tell you, Albert, I shall be glad when this arm is right again, and you won't have to do such things for me.'

'So will I,' Bond replied. 'For all you're a little fellow, you're no lightweight either, Earnest, and that's the fact.'

'What did you have?' Penfold enquired of Bond, gesturing with surprising melancholy towards the little pile of stones and small wooden cross that denoted the last resting place of their brother officer.

'Oh, nothing special,' Bond replied coyly.

The fact was that he had already squared it with McGonagle that Simonides's revolver, belt, strap, and spare ammunition would come to him at a moment more private than at the auction. There was no talk of payment. McGonagle forbore to ask, and he to offer. He could have done with the watch as well, however meagre a substitute for his gold one, but hadn't wanted to seem overly acquisitive.

Bond harboured secret intent toward furnishing Coleman with the weapon, should any other life-threatening situation arise, or in case the boy for whatever reason fell outside his protection. *Never again will I see you threatened*, he had promised Jack. *Even if I cannot be right there beside you, I'll be fine if I only know you're safe*.

Spirits were generally quite good among all concerned. Gideon Knight seemed reconciled to his loss of command, although his behaviour did seem to be becoming a little furtive. Penfold was still badgering McGonagle over his African pioneers and begging for them to be allowed to come, while the handful of slightly sick and walking wounded Wolves under their own sergeant seemed to be adapting to their new station as guardians of the drift, due in part, no doubt, to the officers' departure.

The only hint of an upset came about when one of the handfuls of men from the West Rutlands tried in vain to snaffle Coleman's blanket to use as a carpet bag. Fiercely protective of anything given to him by his officer, Coleman saw to it that the soldier was given a black eye for his trouble, and it was all that the sappers could do to prevent "their boy" from being set about by the villain's disgruntled comrades.

In the end, it was McGonagle who defused the situation for them. Having, like most people, taken quite a shine to his nephew's endearing and usually friendly young batman, he declared that the sappers had done wonders for the camp. Threatening that anyone else who was apprehended while interfering with his property would be stripped of his clothes and forced to march along with an assegai in place of his rifle, McGonagle went on to further antagonise all concerned. 'Any man who steals and shirks like a heathen deserves base treatment,' he declared, arousing such hostility from the already incandescent Africans that a bloodbath was only averted by a whisker, and finally defused when Lieutenant Penfold was finally informed of the old man's concession to taking them with him after all.

This gesture was not universally welcomed, however, and the smouldering embers far from dowsed amid ranks.

'Much more of this and the men will run away, sa,' Jacob Christmas informed his officer. 'They are the Queen's soldiers, sa, they deserve to be treated like it.'

'I know,' Penfold replied gloomily. 'But what can I do, Sergeant? It took all my courage to convince him to bring you along at all.'

Sergeant Christmas made a sign with his hand and dawdled back to his men, who were being drilled before Lieutenant Bond by an increasingly impatient Sergeant Friday. Looking from one to the other, Bond could see that the pioneers resembled an even more sullen and aggressive-looking bunch than the individuals under his command from the West Rutlands. Here, an African soldier would scowl, look sulkily up at him as he and Sergeant Friday proceeded down the line, and snort a bit; there, another one would spit out a lump of sugar cane, which would land just beside the officer's boot. Not one seemed to show any signs of the happy, willing, and amenable troop of about whom Penfold had been so lyrical, and absolutely none of them took at all well to a strange officer and NCO looking them up and down and ordering them about.

'Don't look so happy, do they, Sergeant?' Bond remarked to Friday.

'Perhaps because they *have* their own NCO!' Penfold protested, as Sergeant Christmas, who had sought to join Bond and Friday's inspection as befitted his rank, was shoed back into file by Friday.

The dignified African never spoke a word but fell quietly in and to attention on the flank, despite his stripes. Dissent simmered at this affront and, as Bond and Friday passed him, one soldier scowled a little harder and spat a lump of tobacco on the ground. Friday, incensed by such behaviour, motioned to strike the man with his cane. Seconds later, the bald sergeant found himself flat on his back and very much pressed to the earth by the impeding point of an assegai. Looking up with a start, a high-pitched wheezing sound emitting from his throat, Friday looked as if he was going to burst. Two sappers were upon the man in seconds. He was disarmed, restrained, and laid out flat with a single blow from a rifle butt before any of his mates could even break sweat.

McGonagle, who up until then had been talking to Lieutenant Knight only a few feet away, suddenly sprang forward, jabbing manically with his finger. 'Gentlemen, we have our killer!' he cried triumphantly, as the seething soldier was held fast by his outnumbering captors, blood pouring from the open wound in the side of his mouth. 'The culprit reveals himself. Hot-tempered cuss!'

'You all right, Sarn't?' Coleman asked earnestly, as poor Friday struggled back to his feet and tried desperately to regain his ascendancy over proceedings.

The NCO continued to wheeze and gasp with incredulity as the now apprehended man began to writhe and struggle with the sappers who held him, cursing and kicking out with his legs until yet more men were obliged to abandon their preparations and assist in restraining him. For a moment, it looked as though Earnest's earners might mutiny completely, but for one quiet but clear spoken command. At a single order for their own sergeant, Jacob Christmas and the Africans fell in, to a man, as straight and orderly as on parade. For a moment only, Christmas exchanged glances with Friday. The bug-eyed sapper NCO then nodded slightly. Christmas returned the acknowledgement, his face resumed its wonted calm placidity, and he too fell in, this time before the Africans, rather than amongst them. As Christmas reverted to "eyes front", so too did his men.

'I must say, it does look rather bad for the chap,' Bond remarked grimly.

'It's a settled score,' declared McGonagle. 'The man is clearly mad.'

'I do have to admit that it is regrettable,' Knight responded, and even Penfold had to struggle for words of mitigation.

In the end, the detained man was lashed to the back of one of the wagons, relieved of his red headdress and placed under close guard.

At another word from their sergeant, whose primacy was questioned no further, the Africans moved into left file and trailed arms for the march.

Gideon Knight, now deposed from his role as officer commanding, shouldered the burdens of the late Lieutenant Simonides, joining McGonagle at the head of the column.

'We seem to have gained another senior NCO,' Knight observed quietly, as Jacob Christmas saluted the mounted officer party.

'We always had one,' Penfold retorted quickly. 'Christmas has worn the same three stripes since we left headquarters, if anyone had had a mind to notice'.

Bond cast a glance toward Friday, who seemed to have confronted his brush with mortality and the subsequent obliged acknowledgement of his new brother NCO with stoicism. Faced with little alternative, Friday appeared to behave as though this had always been so.

'You won't regret this, Captain,' Penfold beamed, as the Highlanders trooped past him with their officer riding at the head.

'We shall see,' McGonagle replied sagely.

'They will be good, sir. I know how well they can work if they're handled properly.'

McGonagle gave Penfold a dubious look but said nothing in response.

'Thank you for what you did, Albert,' Penfold called across to Bond, who was still waiting at the head of his own sapper troop for an order to march.

McGonagle raised his hand, and Bond manoeuvred his horse accordingly. 'Sergeant Friday, when you're ready.'

'Sir!' Friday replied briskly. 'Comp'ny... forwaard *march*!'

The command was repeated in Zulu, before being taken up by the junior NCOs.

Coleman glanced up at his officer, as if for reassurance, and Bond winked back at him. So, they set off once again, sappers trailing along behind their mounted officers in a squelch of boots and hooves in the mud, groaning and snorting until they vanished into a thick fog of rain, far from the eyes of the remaining garrison.

About halfway through the morning the sun came blazing through the fog, and the pace of the march soon warmed the frozen joints and constricted limbs of the soldiers.

The soft yellow grasses swayed back and forth, and a delicate breeze began gently to caress their cheeks as they struggled up the rough track, bearing gradually north and leaving the river far behind.

A few hours later, however, the heat was beginning to take its toll. The mist, having burnt off the hills completely, had now given way to a shimmering haze. The ground, once muddy and constricting to hoof, boot and wheel now began to boil, bake, and crack under the fierce white sun.

'Come on now, just keep going,' Bond murmured to Coleman, who was putting a brave face on it but looked as if he might well peel off at any minute. 'Take hold of my bridle,' Bond suggested. 'Trail arms and I'll tow you along.'

'Sir,' Coleman groaned, then almost fell flat on his back.

'Watch him!' cried Bond in alarm, as the mechanical stomping of the sappers almost caused them to march right over their flagging comrade.

He reigned in his horse, dismounted, and dashed back to the point by the roadside where Coleman had fallen. He looked wretched up close, the sight of those screwed up blue eyes struggling against the glare almost reduced the officer to tears.

'Come on,' he whispered, gently elevating the young soldier back up into a sitting position. 'We'll soon have you right again.'

'Sergeant Friday, we need water here, now!' cried Earnest Penfold, pausing to offer assistance. 'Will he be all right do you think, Albert?'

'Fine, if only I can get him hydrated again,' Bond replied. 'Really, Earnest, it's about time we stopped for a rest, especially in this punishing sun.'

Penfold looked around him and nodded. The men were tired, moral was at an all-time low, and scuttlebutt had it that more than one of the African troops had deserted, despite headcounts to the contrary. Nevertheless, any desertions would render their compliment dangerously low by nightfall.

The best way in which to compound sweaty clothes, sore hands and feet, sticky pores and blistering skin seemed simply to grit one's teeth and carry on with it, but this strategy could only be maintained so far. Rifles became like anvils, their weight dragging them from the slippery grasp of the exhausted soldiers; valise equipment rubbed and rent the skin beneath the serge jackets, belts, and webbing cut into the flesh as their packs became heavier. Horses stopped and simply refused to move, and several seasoned men even fainted on the road.

Harangued from all sides by the three sapper officers, himself tormented by flies, sunburn, and exhaustion, McGonagle entertained the entreaties in silence for a short time, then conceded with outwardly surprising rapidity that the troops might need a rest. The truth of the matter was of course – not that he would ever be found to admit it – the death of Simonides had taught even the ageing officer one or two things which he did not intend to forget. After all, they could stop for a while, pitch camp, set off at first light the next day and still join the main column within the next couple of days.

'All right, Lieutenant,' McGonagle announced at last to a final burst of nagging by Gideon Knight. 'We'll make camp by that hollow depression on this side of the riverbank before nightfall. We must keep going a while longer, but when we get there, we'll pitch camp down by the water, and see about getting the wagons across in the morning.'

'The men are very tired now, sir,' Knight reported, earning himself a filthy look from the captain, and an order passed straight back to the others to keep the column moving a further mile and a half.

'I'm old, I'm tired, and I'm not up to a running battle with you today, Mr Knight,' McGonagle muttered irritably. 'The truth is, I'm shattered. But we can't allow the column to go without these supplies for too much longer. Colonel Roystone expects a large engagement soon, you know, and these ammunition stocks might well be needed.'

Knight nodded dutifully and rode up ahead of the rest to scout the landscape. The sapper officer did not respond, however. His mind was still on other matters.

'I'm going to have to take the boy on my horse, sir.' Bond called up to McGonagle, as they crested the top of a long grassy slope, which dropped down on either side and ran into a track by the riverbank itself. 'It's all right, Jack,' he whispered in the exhausted sapper's ear, and they struggled into the saddle together. 'You'll be fine soon, I promise.'

Chapter Eleven

It was almost dusk by the time the small column reached the river. They had travelled on and off pretty much all day, the men were exhausted, they had lost several oxen, and the *hors de combat* was growing with alarming rapidity. This was compounded when Sergeant Christmas, with officious dignity, reported the actual desertion of several his beleaguered pioneers.

'It's almost as if they know something we don't,' Lieutenant Penfold remarked with a levity which was not entirely insincere.

He was ignored.

Either way, it was no surprise that the scuttlebutt turned self-fulfilling prophecy. Mistrust and prejudice abounded, and the uneasy respect between the white NCOs and their singular black contemporary became a mere matter of appearance.

Coleman had just about recovered from his uncharacteristic episode of heat exhaustion, and Bond's overworked mind subsequently became free to worry about the considerably altered footing of his relationship with Sergeant Friday, rather than the health of his batman. Since leaving Fort Penfold, neither man had passed a word to each other beyond the most necessary military dialogue, but both could see the whole time that the other was thinking of only one thing: Coleman and how best to protect him.

The bald sergeant seemed to stick to the young sapper like

glue, and whenever they halted for so much as a moment, the sharp-eyed old soldier was buzzing round his charge like a fly. Strangely, Coleman did not seem to object or take exception to such paternal interest, certainly from Friday but especially from Bond. To him, it was all part of that wonderful, constant care and concern for his own wellbeing that the young officer had so long shown him, and Coleman, for his part, could not help feeling the safest he had ever been before, at least since infancy. Never in his life had he felt so well cared for, and the love and gratitude he felt towards Bond was to manifest itself again and again in the form of the most steadfast and unquestioning loyalty.

McGonagle had also been quite an altered figure in the life of Lieutenant Bond. He chatted away, freely, and gaily, as the small convoy picked and scrambled its way across the floor of the valley, surmounted on either side by the most breathtaking scenery of such titanic proportions that the individual traveller could not help but feel dwarfed from a distance of twenty miles.

'I tell you, lad, I've na'er been so happy in years. Do you know that, Albert?'

'Sir?' Bond responded, in some surprise.

'Aye,' McGonagle continued. 'Love made me happy in my youth. Just like you, eh?'

Bond looked at McGonagle for a moment before letting his eyes glance back to Coleman.

McGonagle smiled a knowing smile. 'Not been this happy since I lost your aunt in India. I never thought to hold a proper command again, and yet here we are, all these years on, and with you and these bright young buttons, n'all!'

Bond smiled reflectively. *How come the old man has never talked like this before*, he wondered?

'I'm thinking,' the captain commented, as they began to climb the foot of a long and winding grassy slope down one side of the valley, 'that I might just get myself measured for one of those blue patrol frocks like you young fellows. I've always said red was too conspicuous, you know.'

'I remember,' Bond retorted dryly, and was just about to ask why McGonagle had wasted the greater part of his career, and very nearly his nephew's, by writing so many scathing articles and publishing ruinous pamphlets, when a dreadful row among the Africans distracted all their attention. The reason for the rumpus soon became evident.

About half a mile to the left, and again on the right, two thin bodies of Zulu warriors seemed to be massing in front of them. They were high up, positioned on one of the rocky shelves that hung above the riverbed, and the lower summit of the other respectively. There scarcely seemed enough of them to have made getting up there in the first place worthwhile, but McGonagle was not to be robbed of his first action in so many intervening years. Throwing his men out in two prongs, either side of the wagons, he ordered Knight to do the same with his sappers.

'I want to beat those wee devils at their own game,' he called out above the din of loading rifles and the shuffling of boots on the loose rock as the men took up their positions. 'Spread out wide, and we can keep them well away from the wagons.'

'They're not going to attack us down here though, sir, surely?' Knight retorted. 'They would never get their men back down here for one thing, and there are far too few of them to make an attack a plausibility.'

Bond, however, was by no means as reserved. 'Captain, let me take Earnest's boys up that low shoulder over there. We can run them back down on the other side, and then the infantry would have a clear field of fire to make what they liked of them.'

'Good man, Albert,' McGonagle replied.

'Sir, I must protest this order!' Knight remonstrated. 'It might be a feint to draw us out from the wagons. Albert's men might get slaughtered.'

'If that was the case, they'd have come down the valley,' McGonagle returned. 'Besides, there aren't sufficient men up there to make shooting at us worthwhile, let alone launch a disciplined attack on our wagons.'

'That, sir, is precisely my point!' Knight persisted.

'We should laager, sir,' Penfold interjected. 'Just in case.'

'Snuff!' replied McGonagle. 'Let Albert and your Africans flush them out into the open, then we'll see what a little disciplined musketry can bring, won't we, boys?'

The captain's words were greeted with a rousing cheer from his men, swiftly replaced by looks of horror and disappointment. McGonagle, stunned, took out his field glasses and scanned the horizon in bewilderment.

It was Penfold who finally broke ranks. 'They've cleared off, sir,' he observed.

'All of them?' Knight demanded.

'Well, I'll be—' McGonagle began, but was very soon interrupted by a cry from Bond who, having rode at full pelt as far as the foot of the cliffs, could now neither see his objective, nor the reason for their disappearance.

The Africans stood around their sergeant in a bemused silence. They had not altogether relished the prospect of bating their traditional enemies into action at close quarters in open ground, and stood looking insolently from Bond to McGonagle, each as red and flustered as the other.

Bereft of leadership, they looked to their own induna, Sergeant Christmas. As rigidly disciplined and conformist as

Friday, Christmas looked in turn to the officers. No one moved.

'Ah, they've broken,' Corporal Denham remarked aloud to anyone and no one.

'Don't be so sure, Corp,' Friday muttered, casting an accusing glance at Christmas. 'Sly, them lot. Never like it looks. Always more behind them eyes... lurking.'

'Well, I ain't sorry, Sarn't,' Coleman put in sharply. 'I ain't sorry that Mr Albert won't be climbing up there all by himself, without us to watch his back.'

'You take a lot on yourself, don't yer, boy?' demanded the corporal severely.

'Leave boy alone,' Friday interrupted.

'Cheers, Sarn't,' Coleman added, apparently oblivious to the malicious expression of Denham. Then, to his surprise, Friday smiled at him. 'Blimey!' Coleman gasped aloud.

'Snakes alive!' Denham added in wonder. 'He ain't never done that before, not in the twenty year I've known 'im.'

'I shan't be sorry to see the end of this valley, you know, Gideon,' Penfold remarked to Lieutenant Knight, as a very flustered McGonagle began issuing orders for the company to move off again.

This time however, they kept going until they were well past the overhanging cliff faces and had followed the river back into relatively open ground once more.

Back at the main column, Captain Horace Fenton scratched his face, squinted in the harsh sunlight of the cruel midday sun, and tried to take his mind off the wound.

The sun was utterly blinding, and all he could see for miles was the abundant yellow grass of the seemingly featureless landscape, broken and intermittently detailed by one or two scrawny trees, the odd dongas, and the otherwise regular sight of Colonel Roystone's column encamped on the hillside. A fly buzzed ruthlessly around the officer's head until irritation forced him to swat it with his riding crop. He was fed up with being bitten, his skin was red and sweaty, his palms were clogged with dirt and grime, and the thick brown beard covering half his face seemed to be littered with swellings, bumps, and irritations. Wiping the beads of perspiration from the back of his neck, yet still taking care to avoid the hundred and one blisters and boils which stung every time he touched them, Fenton glanced across the sprawling camp towards the colonel's headquarters tent.

Since about 11:00 that morning, when a handful of mainly elderly Zulus had emerged from the shimmering heat under the protective banner of a large white tablecloth, all three senior field officers and Commandant Flambard had been in endless conference.

'What the deuce do you suppose is going on, Horace?' enquired Snooker Collingwood, who had plodded up the embankment to join his old friend in his observations.

'Well, something's up, and that's a matter of fact,' Fenton replied quickly. 'They've had old Flambard in and out of there like a jack-in-the-box all the last hour, so they must need to translate something badly. Hold up, Snooker, it looks as if there's someone coming out at last.'

Collingwood raised his field glasses to his sharp eyes, then handed them to Fenton to see what he made of the two figures now made visible by their departure from the tent.

'It looks like the colonel, and Colonel Henderson,' Fenton remarked, as the unmistakable blue patrol jackets of the battalion commanders emerged into view, one of whom was still supported by crutches.

'It also looks as if they've been chucked out by Colonel Roystone,' Collingwood remarked to the chagrin of Fenton, who did not appreciate speculations concerning his superior officer. 'What on earth could be happening?'

'It's an absolute disgrace, especially at this point in the proceedings!' Henderson snarled in irritation. His arm was still bound up from his gunshot wound at the pass, and although the swelling had decreased considerably, this did not diminish the officer's bad temper. 'That colonial radical Flambard being allowed to interrogate those Zulu prisoners without so much as a by your leave, and Harry bending over backwards and sending us out like errant schoolboys. It's my prerogative as intelligence officer.'

'Well, perhaps if you were to start by exhibiting some of that intelligence yourself, Harry might start to take account of your opinions,' McEnry retorted sharply. 'Besides,' he added, as Henderson's rage looked fit to boil over into violence, 'I might remind you that those Zulus came in under a white flag and are thereby no more prisoners than we are.'

'They might be spies under a flag of parley,' Henderson returned sullenly.

'True, but they might also be here to capitulate for Matabyana or a member of his family,' McEnry replied. 'If so, that means that they will want reassurance, and it might take a while to get what we want from them.'

'I'd have had it all by now.'

'What with?' McEnry demanded, turning swiftly on his crutches to face his old adversary with the venom of frustration evident in his flashing grey eyes. 'Hot coals and the cat, I suppose. For God's sake, man, use your brain for once.'

'It's still a wretched liberty,' Henderson snarled in disgust. 'And I still don't see why we are to stand out here and wait on Flambard to call us back in. This isn't his courthouse in Oscaarsberg, you know, McEnry.'

'It's not India, either,' muttered the colonel. 'No Rajas' dungeons to repurpose.'

'I demand you repeat that, Colonel!' Henderson exploded.

'I said I imagine that there is a reason,' McEnry sighed wearily. 'And I might remind you which of us is the senior officer, *Colonel*.'

The retort was to prove symbolic. Henderson had stormed off under a cloud, and McEnry knew he had lost his audience.

Flambard meanwhile was utterly oblivious of the derision that his demand for privacy had caused, although he was aware of its potential to ignite the simmering Henderson.

'I couldn't care less, Harry,' he had told a worried Colonel Roystone. 'Bloody little man demonstrated his affinity for diplomacy in India when he executed those sepoys under an amnesty. I'm not having him ruin this opportunity by waving his fists and upsetting things generally.'

The commandant was, if anything, a little daunted by the prospect of brokering so crucial an arrangement, and sought to find Lieutenant Faunce-Whittington, knowing he could deal with the lesser members of the Zulu delegation, thus leaving him free to barter with the chief and his adherents.

Red-coated soldiers jumped left and right as the burley commandant stormed back and forth through the tents of the second battalion and lumbered off in the direction of the irregulars' camp.

Flambard found Lieutenant Faunce-Whittington exactly

where he had been expecting. The officer stood in his tent, shirtsleeves rolled up to his elbows, and delicately balancing a keenly sharpened cutthroat razor betwixt thumb and forefinger as he tentatively attempted to execute a particularly awkward contour of his double chin.

Almost as soon as he entered the tent, the commandant realised the danger in an abrupt salutation. He paused, hovered in the doorway with one foot in mid-air and struggled to retain his balance in silence. Unfortunately for the junior officer, this gesture came too late. Suddenly aware of the presence of another, Faunce whipped round and let out a yelp of pain, followed by a trickle of blood as the blade encountered an eruption in the skin. This was followed in turn by a stinging sensation and a most unsightly red weal where the blood had settled into a clot.

Flambard was beside himself. 'Faunce, my dear fellow, I'm so terribly sorry!' he exclaimed in horror. 'Oh, how dreadfully clumsy of me to burst in on you like this, I simply can't imagine what I was thinking of.'

'Oh, please don't fuss, Colonel, think nothing of it,' Faunce replied, infinitely more excited by the prospect of a drama than a little loss of blood and a slight disruption to a countenance already ravaged by months of campaign life. 'What's happening, anyway?'

Flambard, who was still flapping madly over his impropriety, very quickly returned to earth when the matter of his visit was once again brought home to him. 'Faunce, the matter is this: I need your Zulu tongue as a matter of some urgency over in the colonel's tent. There are over a dozen Zulus come in under a white flag this morning, and they're all up there chattering nineteen to the dozen if you please, and I can't get a word of sense out of any of them!'

'Prisoners? Oh!' cried Faunce, delighted to be in on a major event at last. 'I'll come at once, Colonel.'

'Oh, for goodness's sake, Faunce, finish your shave first, man!' Flambard boomed in embarrassment. 'Really, I can't apologise enough, my dear fellow. I had simply no idea.'

'Oh, not to bother, Colonel,' Faunce replied, hastily snatching up his pistol belt and discarded blue patrol jacket. 'Perhaps we shall discover where that stray impi is hiding. Do you suppose they will tell us anything about the rest of the army?' he persisted doggedly, as he and Flambard proceeded to further disrupt the infantry camp's dining arrangements by dashing between the ordered ranks of long trestle tables, whereon the cooks were vainly trying to prepare the evening meal.

'Well, they must have come for something, that's for sure,' the commandant replied, angrily parting the dishevelled queues of troops as they lined up for their grub. 'So, it's either a surrender, or a trick of some description.'

'Trick?' Faunce repeated in alarm, struggling to keep up with the commandant and fasten the hooks on his patrol jacket at the same time.

'Yes, Faunce, a ruse. Some sort of plot perhaps. Either way, we shall soon find out when you and I have had them properly questioned.' Pausing, the magistrate removed his hat and began mopping the sweat from his ruddy countenance with a handkerchief before resuming his formidable gait.

Before they could go a great deal further however, the two officers once again found their way blocked by thronging crowds of infantry, artillery, irregulars, and civilian contractors.

'Please excuse us, gentlemen!' cried Faunce in his most authoritative tone, as he and Flambard struggled to part the human curtain of disordered humanity.

'What the devil do you suppose is going on here?' Flambard boomed in annoyance. 'Out of our way, all of you!' he demanded, waving his arms around pushing and shoving like a spectator at the foot of the gallows.

'Colonel, what's happening?' Faunce wailed above the din.

Flambard paused, looked around at the melee going on before them, and then back at the flustered lieutenant. 'Faunce!'

'Colonel?'

'Faunce, how many years have we known one another?'

'Ten years, if a single day, Colonel. More in fact,' replied the officer innocently.

'And in all that time, have you ever known me rude, Faunce?'

'Why no, Colonel.'

'Well then, for goodness's sake shut up, man, and help me part this red sea of blessed serge before the world comes to an end around us, there's a good fellow. Oh, and Faunce?'

'Yes, Colonel?'

'Do stop gassing, man. Save your breath for those wretched Zulu prisoners!'

'Yes, Colonel.'

By the time the two irregular officers had finally struggled through the crowds and traversed the grassy camber on which the colonel's tent was pitched, the scene that greeted them was once again that of the utmost devastation and indiscipline. Here, officers of every rank from junior subalterns to majors could be seen pushing and shoving at one another, and squabbling like children. Whispers were going up and down the masses of red and blue-coated officers like wildfire, and everyone seemed to be jostling everyone else, or grabbing and tugging at sleeves to persuade them to share their information.

'What the devil is this, do you suppose?' Flambard demanded loudly. 'Gentlemen, what on earth do you mean by carrying on in this manner? Gentlemen!' he repeated, but even the magnificence of the old soldier's booming oratory was not yet sufficient to drown out the shouts and clamouring of the mob of officers outside the colonel's tent.

Several irregular officers had also joined in the frantic pantomime, and these were soon joined by their NCOs and even the other ranks of the volunteer movement who, following their officers' example, demanded to know what was happening, utterly regardless of their military rank or civil status.

Such unspeakable breaches of propriety were evidently too much for the commandant. In seconds, the tumultuous noise and endless barracking was silenced by the piercing report of a single pistol shot as it ripped through the clear blue sky. A buzz of muted excitement went rippling down the assembled company as each man cast about to discover the source of the discharge, and the reason for its happening.

'That is enough, do you hear?' Commandant Flambard stood upon a wagon, revolver held high above his head a large plume of smoke rising incriminatingly from the mouth of the barrel.

He stared at the ashen faces of the bewildered assembly, glaring even more sternly at those of rank. Just the sight of this huge man standing amid the flotsam and clutter of the abandoned wagon dissolved the ardour of even the most vocal. When he spoke, the effect was cutting.

'Gentlemen of the West Rutlands, gunners and sappers, volunteers! Fellow Africans! I cannot believe what I am hearing! Never in my life had I thought to see such a hubbub among men in the Queen's uniform, and worse, hold a Queen's commission! You should all be ashamed! Be off, lest you lead by example.'

Humbled, pale, and dejected, the various ranks trailed off and returned to their duties.

Faunce, who thought he was well used to the commandant's stirring rhetoric, still stood utterly transfixed as the burley magistrate struggled to compose himself.

Eventually, once the spectacle had well and truly passed, and Flambard's florid complexion had faded back to its usual boiled beef consistency, he stepped forlornly down from his place on the wagon and marched into the headquarters tent.

'Just like a sergeant major!' Faunce simpered delightedly. 'Well done, Colonel.'

Flambard said nothing, though a thoughtful, wry smile was discernible on his face.

Chapter Twelve

Even by comparison to many enlisted soldiers, Colonel Roystone was tough. Yet now the young ensign who had once taken on a Russian hussar with only his commission sword in his hand, hung over the sprawling maps of Zululand, supporting his weight on his great solid arms, and looking mistily into the ether.

Enlisted at the age of seventeen, a varied career had taken Roystone from an eager adolescent in the trenches before Sebastopol to a Victoria Cross for valour, and the eventual brevet colonelcy that was to see him command his regiment in Zululand.

As the two irregular officers entered, they found that the colonel simply looked straight through them.

Hardly aroused from his perpetuated state of vacancy, Roystone grunted acknowledgement of his old friend's arrival, before returning to that matter of apparently absorbing interest, which kept his gaze fixed firmly on the ground before his table.

Faunce opened his mouth to speak but was silenced by a gesture from Flambard.

'Harry,' began the commandant, crossing slowly towards the campaign table at which the colonel stood. 'I want you to tell me what has happened. Will you tell me, Harry?'

'Colonel, look!' Faunce, who had only just stopped

blushing, and was now beginning to look around at the sea of pale grey faces, now lit upon something of real interest.

Flambard, who was just about to round on the young officer and order him to hold his tongue, suddenly stopped dead and sighed. Over in one corner of the tent sat Lieutenant Colonel Henderson, still as a corpse and gazing just as vacantly as Colonel Roystone. In the further corner sat the three senior Zulu emissaries, fixed and frozen, apparently too terrified to either move or speak. Lieutenant Colonel McEnry sat in a collapsible chair next to the bed. His face was perfectly ashen, and the tear-stained redness around his eyes indicated to the observer that the news was of the severest magnitude.

'Gillespie, you were right,' Henderson offered at last, and so alarming was his apparent state of lethargy that Flambard abandoned all previous prejudices and instructed Faunce-Whittington to pour the officer a brandy.

Looking further down the tent, Flambard realised that the presence of the three Zulus had since been augmented by the arrival of another deputation, this time bearing all the hallmarks of a torturous journey across country. The first was an officer, a subaltern, heavily bearded and wearing a severely degraded patrol jacket. The second was a scout, an African dressed in the uniform of one of the armed and irregular mounted units, holding his wide-brimmed cloth hat with the red puggaree portentously on both hands before him. The third was a sergeant of the regular mounted infantry, whose collar tabs and severely threadbare serge proclaimed him to have come from centre column. Words were not necessary. With a deep sigh, Commandant Flambard removed his hat, rubbed his eyes, and subsided in a chair beside the dazed McEnry.

At last, he broke the silence. 'How many?'

'Fifteen hundred, sir, all His Lordship's Number Two

Column. Volunteers, natives and police as well as the infantry,' replied the officer.

Here, the African soldier accompanying them looked fit to sob.

'It happened on the twenty-second of January,' Colonel Roystone finally managed to announce in monotone. 'The invasion is aborted and support unlikely.'

Faunce, who had up to this moment been obediently pouring a brandy for Colonel Henderson, suddenly gave a gasp and swallowed the measure himself.

Flambard rubbed his face. 'The border?' he asked.

'We don't know, sir,' replied the officer who had brought the news. 'The Zulu reserves tried to follow up the massacre by attacking a depot on the Natal side, but they were warned in advance and managed to throw up a barricade.'

'Were many men killed?' Faunce exploded suddenly. 'What about the other forts? What about the depot on Flambard's drift? What about Oscaarsberg?'

'Faunce, enough!' Flambard remonstrated warningly.

Faunce looked pained. His cheeks had begun to swell, and his beady green eyes dashed from one senior officer to the other, then back to the three messengers.

'We are alone, unsupported, and likely to be attacked at any moment,' Roystone rejoined. 'His Lordship is in no position to move until he has regrouped, reordered his forces and redrafted his invasion plans.'

'What about the lines of communication?' Flambard resumed hotly. 'Has anyone told Warren Westgate that his men are fit to be butchered at any moment?'

Colonel Roystone, however, was not entirely listening. 'I am to dig in or withdraw as I see fit,' he repeated wearily. 'What a choice, Gillespie, and all my own.'

'Hardly that, Harry,' put in Flambard. 'I can't surely be expected to drag my volunteers halfway into the country and simply stop in a laager until someone from home government sees fit to pull us out again! What about the supply routes?'

'He's right, Harry, we all know it.' This time the voice was McEnry's.

Everyone looked up as the silver-haired lieutenant colonel rose, albeit with considerable difficulty, and hobbled across to the brandy decanter perched in readiness on a small sideboard.

It looks so damned incongruous, thought Flambard. *What the hell is a sideboard doing in the middle of a tent in South Africa?* Even so, he allowed the observation to pass.

McEnry poured a large glass of spirits, swallowed hard and contemplated. 'Speaking for myself, I really can see no sense whatever in abandoning Major Westgate's sappers in hostile country to guard a supply depot that might, well, never get resupplied. We really do need to think about pulling them out, you know.'

'What if the party sent to relieve them gets attacked as well?' intoned Henderson irritably. 'Do we really need another slaughter on our hands, McEnry?'

'I think we had better hear from Major Westgate,' Flambard suggested, adding, 'Faunce, be a good fellow and go and fetch the major, would you?'

'Colonel?

'I said do it, man!' Flambard bellowed.

The officer was gone in seconds.

'What are we going to do, Colonel?' Faunce wailed in anguished tones for the hundredth time, as he and the magistrate sat mournfully outside the former's tent, sucking on cigars, and gradually taking in the shocking developments of the day's revelations. Flambard said nothing for a moment.

The sun was by now beginning to set, and a weird red glow had begun to envelop the land, bathing all in its fiery light as the pale beige tents of the infantry camp began to disappear among the lengthening shadows. As the great infernal ball descended, the last lingering rays played upon the weathered face of the commandant, his huge white whiskers drooping from his crestfallen countenance like willow fronds in still water.

Glancing at his commanding officer in quiet contemplation, Faunce took in the rows of medal ribbons that ran from one side of his left breast to the olivettes on his patrol jacket. There was the familiar red and white of the Indian campaign, the white with the single, broad red stripe of Lord Napier's Abyssinian expedition, together with the blue trimmed with gold of the commandant's service in Crimea. In addition to these, Faunce was able to discern the claret and yellow of Flambard's ribbon for the Far East, and the blue bisected with red of his first ever campaign in Canada at the tender age of fifteen. Only one ribbon did the knowledgeable young officer fail to identify: a single, plain silk ribbon of a dark red colour, worn in deference to the otherwise chronological order of the commandant's many war medals. Pondering this queer anomaly, Faunce was just about to break the silence and inquire after the strange and simple ribbon when the commandant suddenly spoke.

'I've made up my mind, Faunce,' he announced. 'I know what I have to do – what I am *going* to do.'

'Colonel?'

'I'm not prepared to leave those young men out there with only the spurious possibility of support from an elderly eccentric. To rely on McGonagle for help and the voice of highly questionable reason would be just as good as parting the wagons in the laager and sleeping in their tents without so much as a dog on piquet duty.'

Faunce, who had managed to distinguish the tone in the officer's voice as being the same as that which he had used on the day they crossed the river, suddenly felt an eruption taking place in the pit of his stomach. 'Colonel, I take it that you mean—'

'Yes, Faunce, I do,' the commandant interrupted. 'I cannot and I will not leave those poor fellows out there in the veldt to be slaughtered at the will of the Zulus. Roystone can keep my men, he can keep all the volunteers who are prepared to remain with the column, but I shall take the main body of my own African troops and one company of white militias with me on my mission.'

'You might be killed,' Faunce was heard to murmur, but his response lacked the gusto of his earlier protestations. For the truth was that, much as he might wish to deny it, Lieutenant Faunce-Whittington was no more prepared to leave his friends the sappers to their fate than Flambard.

'Damn it, Faunce! I've been a soldier all my life. I fought for the Queen in Canada when she came to the throne in '37, I've fought in every corner of India, fought the Tzar – everything. I was at Magdala, I was shot at leading the forlorn hope at Pah-Lum-Pah, and I've even fought close quarter in this land and lived! Throughout this campaign no one has done anything, save to underestimate the Zulu, and look where we are for it. Fifteen hundred dead, the whole of the invasion wrecked to ruins and a distinct possibility of even more dead to end the week on. And for what? So that men like Henderson can say "look how savage they are" and demonise and divide still further? I tell you, Faunce, I shall see those sappers safe before the Zulus cut off our supply routes and see each man dead! If I don't, I'll die hard trying!'

'I could refuse to come,' mumbled Faunce.

'You could,' Flambard replied. 'What is more, you would be perfectly within your rights to do so. I fancy you won't though,' he added knowingly.

Faunce shook his head. 'I shan't. I can't.'

Flambard smiled to himself.

'You might be charged,' the subaltern found himself adding. 'Colonel Roystone has already said how much he needs the irregulars, especially since Isandlwana.'

'I've already told you, Faunce, he shall have the irregulars, plus my own men, and the native companies in addition to what's left of the police. All I need are my own mounted squadron and a squadron of good and reliable local troopers.'

'The Lyndhurst men?' Faunce suggested.

Flambard smiled openly this time. 'They'll do nicely!'

Chapter Thirteen

The sappers, it was true to say, felt in dire need of rescue. As it was, since early that afternoon both Gideon Knight and Earnest Penfold had been rowing hammer and tongs about the navigation. Whereupon McGonagle, who hated maps and, he had just remembered, liked sappers about as much, threw up his hands in a temper and relieved the two subalterns of their itinerary. Much squabbling ensued, and to such a degree that Sergeants Andrews, Stag and Friday were hastily obliged to call for hymns to be sung to keep the row from filtering through to the other ranks.

Through it all Bond, perhaps understandably in the circumstances, was keeping his own opinions well and truly to himself. Things had changed a great deal since his graduation from the academy, and if there was going to be an out and out struggle for power between captain potential and captain eternal, he was damned if he wanted to become embroiled in it.

Eventually, McGonagle's unpopular decision to divert brought them, not onto the lowland shortcut that his predictions had surmised, but slap bang into yet another river. This was a major blow indeed, not least for Bond whom, having spent the last few nights battling with his conscience, his loyalties to his friends, and his newfound rapport with his uncle, had begun to believe that McGonagle was right. They paused for a while at the top of a gentle camber, just off the wagon track, to consider their position. It was late, pushing on for dusk, and the men were nearly shattered. Furthermore, the discovery and subsequent rousing of an enraged secretary bird had caused lunch to be delayed and resulted in the men taking their meal on the hoof with whatever small provisions could be most easily consumed in this manner.

'They could do with feeding properly, Captain,' Bond remarked, looking pityingly at poor Coleman, who seemed utterly devoid of life or spirit.

'We could all do with stopping, sir,' Penfold added ruefully, while scratching absent mindedly at a bite beneath the neckline of his faded and tatty serge jacket.

McGonagle looked from one to the other, then he looked at his men. A short silence was followed by a few grunts as the officer fumbled with the case of his field glasses; some further muted grunts and observations as he scoured the landscape for features, and then another short silence while he decided what to do.

'Mr Knight?'

'I say we stop, sir.'

'Hmm,' McGonagle replied thoughtfully. 'You concur with this, Albert and Edmund?'

'Earnest,' Penfold corrected.

'Sure I am,' replied McGonagle. 'Just answer the bloody question, will you?'

The comic error was greeted with a rumble of amusement and served to defuse the situation a little.

McGonagle chuckled, replaced his field glasses, and turned to address his troops. 'Men, we make for the ground on the other side of this embankment. There is a drift about a mile and a half from here that can be widened to take the wagons. We move off at first light tomorrow, but tonight we can rest and sleep and get some food down our necks. What do you say to that, then?'

A lacklustre cheer went up from a few of the Highlanders, but other than that the men were too tired to do anything but wearily obey their orders.

McGonagle nodded sagely. 'We move to this place— What's it called?'

'Stockhouse's Drift, sir,' Knight amended, reading the map over the captain's shoulder. 'Probably the namesake of the trader who established its use.'

'Well, there we have it,' McGonagle concluded. '*Short*house's Drift it is!'

Another rumble of laughter was heard above the noise of the column moving off, and the three sapper officers, for their part, spurred their horses with a heightened sense of relief and satisfaction at the end of so long and tiring a day.

The position itself, when finally they achieved it, lay in a sort of natural bowl, ringed and dotted on all three sides by aloes, cacti, and other assorted rocky and botanical debris. The ground was mercifully dry, and the flat sandy depression of the riverbank appeared to offer a most welcome change from the men's usual groundsheet of mud and anthills. A shoulder of high rocky cliffs jutted an impressive three hundred or so feet into the air about a thousand yards from their position, dominating the skyline and overshadowing the riverbank for the better part of half a mile.

An old, long-deserted lean-to stood rotting in the lee of a clump of trees, and the skeletal remains of an equally antiquated flatbed wagon suggested that this place had been a settlement vacated in some considerable haste in its day. The ground around the grassy knoll on which the gloomy ruins were situated was bisected even further by ditches and dongas.

Ancient aloes rose and loomed above the rocks at the base of the craggy escarpment, and vicious-looking cacti, together with malignant thorns and brambles, choked and scrambled about the caves and crevices below the dominating outcrop.

'We'll move nearer to the river,' McGonagle announced briefly. 'We're too exposed here, with all this cover all about us.'

'Yes, but, sir,' Knight protested, 'if we move away from here, we're further out into the open, and that leaves us even more vulnerable to attack from all three sides.'

'You would rather have us enfiladed from the cliffs, those nullahs and the undergrowth, Lieutenant?' McGonagle retorted coolly.

'Sir, I really think that Lieutenant Knight may have a point, you know,' Lieutenant Penfold added sheepishly. He had seen the way the old man dealt with the late Simonides's petitions and did not want to become the next casualty of scorn. 'Don't you think we could at least use the position as some basis for a defence, should the need arise?'

McGonagle thought for a moment. 'How the hell, may I ask, would we laager the wagons in a topographical nightmare like this, Mr Penrose?'

'Penfold.'

'Um.'

Hasty confabulation ensued, but with Bond's being the casting vote it was eventually decided that, despite its exposed position, the riverbank offered a greater plausibility for defence, providing the wagons were properly run into a defensive formation as soon as the soldiers made camp.

'We'll camp over there, and we'll just jolly well have to keep our wits tonight!' McGonagle concluded, and no more arguments were heard for the ruins.

Thus did the combined companies of engineers and

Highlanders camp for the night by the lonely, desolate and subsequently rechristened Shorthouse's Drift. Some deserted Zulu huts were discovered nearby, and these were pulled down without question. Piquets were placed at strategic positions up and down river, although the piquet that had been tasked to watch over the ghostly and exposed outpost, overlooked from the stretch of road where the decision to halt had been taken, worried the sapper officers terribly.

'I can't stop the old man throwing his beats out as far as he likes,' Gideon Knight complained to a characteristically silent Sergeant Friday. 'But when it's our men and not his own troops that get dumped out there in the dark, one can't help but feel a certain responsibility. Do you see my drift, Sergeant?'

'Sir,' was the extent of the feedback from the circumspect Friday.

By the time Bond had exhaustedly seen to the execution of rudimentary procedures, hastily bagged some food from a nearby cooking pot and plumped down in his tent to eat it, he was almost too tired to notice the absence of his favourite sapper. He had been worried sick about Coleman the entire time they had been settling in. The boy was fit, strong and energetic – Bond's own experiences could testify to that – but that last episode by the roadside had really shaken him. If the truth were told, the young officer was not exactly in the best of conditions himself. Since he had thus far tended to measure his own discomfort by that of his uncomplaining young batman, and since the cracks were apparently now showing in the young lad's previously dauntless constitution, he himself must be in a bad state.

Bond took a puff on his cigar, unfastened the first three hooks and eyes on his patrol jacket, and lifted his aching legs up onto his camp bed. It was true to say that the areas between his thighs and his ankles were raw indeed, constant friction betwixt saddle and cord breeches, his failure to have Coleman sew on leather patches had seen to that. His feet were sore as well, having been jammed into the sweaty and increasingly deteriorating leather riding boots, purchased so long ago from his little place in London.

Lumps and bites were beginning to swell under his beard, while skin eruptions on the back of his neck rubbed against the mohair on his jacket collar with ruthless persistence, and an odour that was perceptible.

The rumble of distant thunder and the deep orange glow of sunset pierced the canvas of his canopy, rousing the young lieutenant. Feeling sorry for oneself, he decided, had never been an acceptable pastime for a Yorkshireman. Snatching up his topi and shoulder belt, the officer bid a remorseful farewell to his bed, wincing at the pain as he stood upon the earth once more. The clouds massing above the towering escarpment clustered together in great daunting plumes of animated grey, shifting, and billowing out across the illuminated red sky and covering half the land in shadows. Another rumble sounded to the west and Bond, with a sigh, tapped out the growing stock of ash from the end of his cigar before trailing off across the camp in search of Coleman.

'What the devil do you mean by "on piquet"?' an incandescent Bond demanded of Sergeant Friday, as the two of them plodded slowly across the still open defences of the camp.

'Captain's orders, sir,' the NCO explained helplessly. 'Friday not to know.'

'How could you allow this to happen, Sergeant?' Bond persisted irritably. 'To let that poor bastard be sent out there in the dark after all he's been through. Do you realise, he hasn't had an hour of—' Here the officer checked himself in mid-sentence. The reference which he had been about to make concerning Coleman's sleeping habits, not to mention the nightmares, would have been unfortunate, not to say incriminating. Instead, Bond chose a different tack entirely. 'How many men did McGonagle send up?'

'Six men, sir. Two sappers, three Scots along sides Corp Denham, they are, sir.'

Bond closed his eyes. His mind was racing and his heart thumping as the realisation of his powerless situation began to overwhelm him. *Should Zulu scouts be active tonight*, he thought, *he would be utterly helpless out there.*

'That's quite enough without Coleman,' Bond stated firmly. 'I have work for him, so I suggest we go and relieve him, and you can go up there on the half hourly round to check that all is well.'

Whatever expression Friday's bulbous green eyes were betraying in the gathering darkness of that sheltered spot, they did not make themselves apparent to the lieutenant as his sergeant snapped to attention and gave a salute in acknowledgment of the instruction.

'And I really do not like these open embrasures,' Bond remarked to the departing Friday. 'Gideon should speak to the captain about those.'

As fortune would have it, Captain AW McGonagle had chosen to pitch his own tent at the top of a gentle slope, upon which the rising ground levelled out into a small grassy area overlooking the river.

At around the same time as his nephew was busily engaged in saddling his already exhausted horse in preparation for a ride back up the wagon track, the elderly officer himself was gradually preparing for bed. Consequently, he was none too pleased by the sudden reappearance of Lieutenant Gideon Knight, still suited and booted, and apparently quite bent on hounding him from beyond the realms of his bedroll.

'Captain, I know you think me an upstart,' Knight began cautiously, 'but I really do feel that I must be frank in these circumstances. We should laager properly, especially in such open country as this. Furthermore, sir, I really do suggest that you do at least re-pitch your own tent within the confines, such as they are, of the circle. I should feel so much happier if I knew for certain that we were all together, and that there wasn't any part of the camp around which I couldn't at least throw out a line of defence, if needs be.'

'Lines of defence are my worry, Lieutenant,' McGonagle replied, wearily removing his boots, and placing them in regimented order beside his camp bed. 'As are,' he added, 'where or why I chose to sleep. I might also remind you that I survived for many years in India, in the middle of the worst bandit country imaginable, and what is more we only had muzzle loaders. You lot have breech-loading carbines.'

'Yes, sir, and speaking of which,' Knight continued doggedly, 'perhaps you might consider having a rifle, or better still a rifleman, join you up here between now and morning. I'd feel a lot happier—'

'No thanks, laddie,' McGonagle interrupted, unusually without a hint of annoyance. 'I'll do all and fine with my old Joe Manton here.' He patted a burnished and, to tell the truth, rather elderly looking shotgun, which the captain took with him everywhere he went, and which now also stood next to his awaiting camp bed.

'I'd still rather you had a carbine, sir,' Knight persisted. He knew it was useless.

McGonagle shook his head and smiled. 'I'll have ma pistol

if the old girl fails me,' he chuckled, adding, 'Besides, can you imagine any Zulu popping his head round here, only to have it blown off by an old Highland grouser?'

Knight smiled and shook his head. 'Good night, sir.'

'Night, Lieutenant.'

'Oh, sir!'

'Yes, Lieutenant?' McGonagle asked patiently, one leg still sticking plaintively out from beneath the sheets and blankets.

'About the piquets, sir. I fear *we* may have placed them too far out to be of use.' If the veil of mutual culpability was designed to elicit less chagrin, it was wasted.

Tired, out of arguments and all set to drop onto his bolster, McGonagle waved away the anxious entreaty with a gnarled right hand and instructed Knight to do what the devil he pleased. Breathing a sigh of relief, the beleaguered young officer replaced his topi on his head and tramped off down the slope in search of his horse and Sergeant Friday.

Yet, as he re-entered the confines of the semi-laager and the low lights of the freshly built campfires, the heady tang of the wood smoke and the rustle of the dry dusty grass beneath his feet began to remind him of his lost command at Fort Penfold. It was not that he was ill disposed towards the old man personally – he seemed amenable enough when he wasn't addled with drink or suffering from the effects of the march and his terrible deafness. This was supposed to have been his chance to shine, yet here was he, Gideon, next up on the army list for promotion and expectant of a captaincy on return to England, poised to turn the pages of his own historical career and discover his future here in Africa. Had he really resigned his adjutancy back in Brompton for this, he wondered? This, which was supposed to be his first big show, destroyed because he had to play butler to a frustrated old failure who never quite made major. Knight snorted to himself in pent up resentment. Why hadn't the old man simply bought a promotion before the practice had finally been phased out?

Another distant rumble suggested yet another change in the fortunes of the weather. Scratching his beard and trying desperately to ignore the equally imposing rumbling noise that was at that moment issuing forth plaintive entreaties from his own stomach, Knight decided that his best course of action would be to call in the piquets. He would then redeploy them according to his own interpretations of the landscape. Even so, he reasoned it was still late, and if he didn't get some food down him soon then he would be liable to drop dead, or at any rate be no good at all to anyone. He was also aware, despite the remonstrations of his mind over his heart, that he hadn't put down so much as a line in that little book, which Flora had given to him prior to embarkation on the *Castle*. With yet another long sigh, he seized a handful of biscuits, took a casual glance round the open embrasures, well-lit by the men's cooking fires, and set off on his quest for Friday.

Chapter Fourteen

Ludo Friday considered himself to be one of a dying breed of non-commissioned officers. He first attested in 1854, at what he would go no further than to describe as the age of "boy". Back then, the British Army principally comprised three types of social grouping: the officers – the gentlemen of fortune, who came and went according to the price of rank and to the length of their purse; the men – drinkers, gamblers, criminals, paupers; and professional soldiers – who, like the colours of the Queen, were presented to their regiments for life. These were the men who, like himself, had risen from boy, then spat, polished, and drilled their way up through the chevrons until they died, retired, or finally attained those prized gold stripes of authority and distinction. As with many of his own school at Chatham, Friday did not agree with men who secured themselves quartermasters' commissions and went about pretending to be officers. That was not as the Duke of Cambridge liked things, and who was he to argue? Mind you, he had the undeniable advantage of a long and distinguished family history of service to Crown and country, and his own father, Sergeant Major Magnus Friday, had been one of the most highly decorated sappers of his time. A history that only aided the less than fortunate, prematurely bald youth, aspiring to achieve better things for himself.

Even so, things had begun to change radically since that

long-forgotten day many years before when the young Ludo had been accepted into the corps as a boy recruit. Stripes had used to be so much harder to get hold of, but these days they were handing the rank of colour sergeant to mere lads of twenty-five. It was a culture that did not sit with the strict, simple, and conservative Friday – respectable chapel man, bachelor, avenging angel to those of inferior rank, and strictly reverential of those set above him in the social order.

Still pondering the demise of gentlemen engineers, the steady old navvies of his father's time and the long whiskered, leathery skinned and middle-aged NCOs of his own, Friday thanked God that he had the good sense to bunk down for the night in a supply wagon. Filling his clay pipe with some of the mountain of tobacco securely stored within his choice of bunk, the sergeant decided to allow himself the unusual indulgence of a little reading before making his tour of the beats. Ordinarily, such flagrant self-gratification as smoking pilfered tobacco would have provoked the most tumultuous backlash from the authoritarian NCO.

Yet, with no Coleman to set on the path to righteousness, no Denham to pull up for profanities, and none other to gainsay him but God, he decided that one little snip wasn't going to lose anyone the war. Lighting the pipe with a deftly struck match, Sergeant Friday puffed away contentedly, until the strange orange glow of the still sunlit canvas awning wafted with the smell of smoke and the blue haze of blended leaves.

This simple sin absolved, he then dug deep into the pocket of his shabby blue worsted trousers and was rewarded some moments later with an equally shabby, evidently well used, dog-eared little bible. With yellowing pages, crumbling black leather, gold worn from the once gilded leaves, this holiest of books spoke simply of his firm belief in the virtue of austere and unbending conformity. Adherence to the rigidly defined protocols of discipline was Friday's creed, and his preference for stories of Israelites and the pages of the *Old Testament* seemed, for him at least, aptly to reflect that link between soldiers and their faith.

Not that it ever occurred to Friday that there might be another way. The pages of the *Old Testament*, with its epic battles, fire and brimstone, appealed to his firmly cherished beliefs. Separating right from wrong seemed inseparable for his adherence to his duty. Hard work, devotion, retribution for sins and strength in the face of temptation were the only rafts to which he could cling in these apparently endless times of change.

Friday reconciled his soldierly duties to his calling. He had shot and, for all he knew, killed, back at the drift. Those men had been pagans, and the decision God's will.

Striking Simonides, an officer, would have been anathema, had it not been the will of the Almighty working through his humble servant... leastways in *his* case, he rationalised. He had not considered what he might do should God, in his wisdom, grant him survival until his retirement. The life of a porter, a ticket inspector or a police constable did not appeal to him. He had been a sergeant too long for any of that. Furthermore, the very idea of leaving the army and retiring to a dingy basement room with spartan brown furniture, grey walls and a coal scuttle neither filled him with hope for the future, nor supplied him with the desire to see it come to pass.

In fact, he was just beginning to think about replacing his bible and taking another nip of tobacco when yet another rumble of thunder echoed a deeper grumble, reminding the sapper that he had not yet taken his evening meal.

By the time Gideon Knight had finally located Sergeant

Friday, the NCO was found to be sitting cross-legged in the back of a supply wagon, busily engaged upon the vilest-looking stew imaginable and, to the officer's mind at least, looking uncharacteristically shifty about something or other. Clouds of steam rose from the sergeant's unappetising dinner, and when the long shadow of his officer fell across his plate, his look was one of martyrdom.

Knight coughed pointedly and Friday, who was bent so low over his repast that the end of his long straggly beard was almost dipping in stew, nearly choked on his food, and sat bolt upright and to attention. Knight was even less impressed when, after Friday had finished coughing and spluttering enough to get a coherent sentence out, it transpired that his petitions and entreaties to McGonagle had clearly been, if not a waste of time, then certainly a superfluity.

Lieutenant Bond, he was informed, had, upon hearing that Coleman, Denham, and the others had been posted so far from the camp, chosen to forgo his dinner and ride directly out there to relieve them.

'Well, that does it!' Knight exclaimed in outrage, exasperated still further by the apparently nonplussed expression being sported by Sergeant Friday. 'If it isn't McGonagle with his idiotic orders, his wretched Indian anecdotes or his *bloody* poems, it's Earnest Penfold crowing about his African men and brothers, or Albert running around behind my back with young Coleman in tow. I tell you, Sergeant, I've just about had enough of all this nonsense!'

Friday looked painfully from his officer to his spoon, and the rapidly cooling stew on his plate. There followed a short yet painful silence and, for a while, it looked to Friday as if the officer he had known for twelve years was almost fit to turn with the weather outside.

Swallowing the officer's profanity, which went down about as easily as the stew, Friday finally permitted his hunger to overcome protocol. 'Permission to, er, return to rations, sir?' Friday inquired shortly, yet with the plaintive appeal evident in his tone of voice.

Knight's momentarily glassy eyes cleared. He looked into the wide green eyes of his patient sergeant and fought to recollect what it was he had come for in the first place. 'Sorry, Sergeant,' he sighed at length. 'Here am I on a full stomach, interrupting your own meal and complaining about matters you can't mend at all. No matter, carry on with your supper. We shall speak again at daybreak.'

Friday nodded compliance and mumbled vague courtesies through his beard full of stewed oxen, while Knight wandered off in a dreamlike state and left him as before.

As soon as he was back in the centre of the laager, watching the long shadows of the day as they danced and flickered with the glow of the firelight and the last clinging amber rays of the setting sun, something somewhere began to trouble him. From somewhere, deep in the chasms of the officer's mind, an alarm bell had begun to ring. Not, as the laws of comparison would have it a peel of bells, nor particularly loud, but from one small, clear, faintly tolling bell from somewhere in the ether of his innermost consciousness, and he knew that something was wrong somewhere. Bond's priorities seemed, somehow, elsewhere. Not ostensibly with his uncle, nor with their situation. Knight mulled over these thoughts as he walked.

All Coleman had done for the last four hours was wander up and down with his rifle slung over his shoulder, alternately cursing his deployment so far from his officer, and lamenting the anxiety of their separation. The last thing he wanted to do was commune, so it was almost a relief when Corporal Denham, who was in command, had told him to take up a watch on the top of the craggy little outcrop overlooking the river. Plumping down on a rock, Coleman loosened off his choking collar and miserably caressed the raw skin left by the fraying yellow worsted that trimmed the neck. His feet were in a wretched state, too.

As soon as he took the pressure off them by sitting, the pain was even greater than when the blisters had been compressed by his body weight. Looking tentatively around for a second, he stooped, removed his helmet, and began to unfasten his boots a little. He knew full well that it was a charge if the NCO caught him, but some things were undeniably worth that risk. *Bastards*, he thought. *I didn't want to stand around with you lot, in any case*. Now, as the day began to draw in all around him, the shadows grew longer, and the air began to cool a little, he started to wonder what might happen to him, all alone out there with only his rifle for protection. Jack had seen the damage that Colonel Roystone's battalions had done to ward off the rampaging Zulu warriors. What could he do with one Martini-Henry and no bayonet?

'Calm down, Jack, mate,' he remarked aloud to himself. 'Ain't no good fretting yourself. They ain't going to come for old me, way up here on me own.'

After all, he reflected, they were not expecting to be attacked. Why, he could still see the blazing campfires and the open embrasures between McGonagle's wagons down there in the camp. Besides which, if Albert's uncle, the old captain, thought everything was shipshape with all his years in the army, who was a lad from Chatham to question?

The local impi had, as far as they all knew, been utterly shattered by the battle with the main column, and anything that might be left of the routed Zulu chieftain's forces were steadily swept aside or driven towards Ulundi, while the colonel's victorious column blazed even further into Zululand.

Something rustled in the tall grass a few yards down the slope, and Coleman found himself bringing up his rifle, checking that the sight was up and fingering the trigger with paranoid anticipation. Nothing happened, however.

The sunset continued to thrill him. The sky grew more colourful, and the imposing black thunderclouds began steadily to advance on the encampment below.

As his worried mind strove to move on to other matters, the throbbing pain in Coleman's feet became almost too hard to bear. It was no good, and there was nothing else for it but to remove the boots all together and try his best to inspect the damage. Ever since his fall on the road he had been suffering from them. At first it was the rubbing of the sores on his heels, the ends of his toes, and the sides of his feet as the constant marching reduced his already dishevelled socks to shreds. The boots were half the problem. The profusion of sweat combined with the immense heat and the stewed leather caused the blisters on his heels and the balls of his feet to sting and chafe until he winced at the agony. The pressure of remaining vertical was still unbearable, and it was with a gasp of pain that he tried pathetically to resume his feet and shift his weight from his tortured heels, and almost fell base over apex as he tried to balance his rifle. Every time he tried to place on foot in front of the other a terrible sting vibrated up his muscular legs and sang in his ears with uncontrollable vibration. His eyes began to water under the strain, and he knew he would just have to sit down again. *Hang the bloody corporal*.

He groaned again. The resumption of an upright position had caused him to arch the muscles in his feet, and his lower tendons were utterly bound and senseless from spending all day so tensed up. Finally, he found the courage to remove the boots completely. The stinging sensation was hell, and the debris in the bottom of his disintegrating boots, combined with the dye in his socks and about six weeks of no proper washing, had left them black and swollen and stinking to high heaven. Coleman winced again then he began to whimper a little. No way was he going to let it show to the others, but his body felt just about ready to pack it in. His toes were murder after being crushed together by his boots; the callused hard skin all around the edges of his feet did nothing to prepare him for the agonisingly bulbous swellings that were his marching blisters. The sensation of removing what was left of his socks and bandages proved to be painful enough, and so long had they been stuck to his feet. Thus, when he finally did succeed in removing them completely, the two great sacks that resembled melted cheddar cheese in his heels and toes had begun to weep and bleed uncontrollably. He gasped in horror. The smell was overpowering.

For the few seconds he teased and prodded the swollen sacks of shifting fluid, he thought that no assegai could ever be as painful. At least he'd get that wound from fighting – this was just taking the mick.

He was just about to lance the biggest swelling with his fingernail, when a cry from a sentry further down the slope alerted the agile young sapper to the emergence of a rider, and the dull thud of a horse's hooves as they fell on the dry dusty ground. Hastily gathering in the ruins of his boots by their laces, Coleman righted himself and, with a small hiss as the sores began to rub again, replaced his topi and hoisted his rifle.

Slipping and stumbling down the grassy slope, completely oblivious to the thunder overhead as the clouds began to move in still further, Coleman brought up his rifle just in time to see the handsome stallion mount the ridge before him. Breathing a sigh of relief that manifested itself in an incredulous smile as the dramatic shape of the mounted officer stood silhouetted against the red and orange panorama before the setting sun, he felt all his pain and anxiety vanish into the shadows.

Bond was off his horse in seconds, both boots landing squarely in the dust with a satisfying thud, a clink of spurs and a rattle of leather accoutrements. He beamed at the sight of Coleman, those steadfast sapper eyes looking back at him as the young soldier broke into a broad smile and the sparkling blue sapphires, lately so dull and heavy, creased up at the corners in their usual endearing fashion.

There he was, Coleman's Mr Albert: broad-shouldered, strong, and steady; brave and mighty enough to turn aside anything, and ready to protect him.

Jack was tired. He had been marching all day in full kit under the cruel sun. His body was covered in webbing sores and insect bites, and his feet were still being blistered and boiled like lobsters. His whole body was running with perspiration, his face and hair were utterly saturated, and every stitch of his dirty uniform was soaking and cold against his wet skin. Yet even so, the second the officer had righted himself and straightened his back from his landing, Coleman was responding with yet another disarming grin.

After glancing warily around for witnesses, the boy's topi was off, and he was stumbling forward. A few poor, pathetic, scuff-booted steps forward and his saturated blond head was laid across the officer's shoulder, his body pressed against the solid chest of the young lieutenant, his hair dripping cobs down the back of Bond's patrol jacket.

Bond held Coleman and smiled. Then he lifted the young soldier's head, stroked back the hair from over his bruised blue eyes and gently nudged the boy's chin with his hand. *Jack's hair has grown one hell of a lot*, he thought, since the last time he'd stopped to take notice. Those sleek, glossy blond strands, neatly parted over to one side that he had first taken such delight in back at Brompton, were now thicker, pushed back off the face in two wings, and rapidly edging over the cropped step at the nape towards his serge collar.

His face had matured, too. Still fresh and handsome to look at, but coloured a darkish brown, with a clear emergence of shaving stubble around the jaw area. The clean, curved forehead was now ridged and pitted with skin eruptions from the helmet band, but still to the officer, he was beautiful.

'I'm so sorry they left you here,' he said at last, once the pressure of Coleman's embrace had worn off slightly, and he felt more able to breathe and speak at the same time. 'I'm sorry they dumped you on your own, and I am truly sorry that I didn't even realise where you were until now.'

Coleman smiled. There was no rebuke or chagrin, just pitiful gratitude that the officer had come for him at last. Bond thought he wanted to weep.

'I'm so glad you're here, sir. I've been hopin' you might come out here and see me all the time. I never thought you wouldn't... I didn't want to, I mean.'

'You shouldn't have been out this far to begin with,' Bond replied sourly. 'I don't know what the old man was thinking of, truly I don't. Come on, then,' he added kindly. 'Let's call in the others and I'll redeploy them nearer to the camp.'

'Me too, sir?' Coleman asked brightly. He was doing his best, but the weepy eyes and the look on his face said it all.

'No chance,' Bond replied quickly. 'You know that I need you with me. The others can go hang, but I'm not leaving you out here on your own again, not for a moment.'

Coleman smiled again, and Bond felt his heart skip a beat.

'Look at your hands,' Bond found himself saying. 'They're too nice, too good for working so hard. Look at those red blisters and that dreadfully hard yellow skin.'

'I am a working man, sir,' Coleman corrected softly.

'Oh, stop being so wise, will you?' Bond retorted. 'When I get us out of this hell you won't be. I'll buy us both out of the army, we'll get away somewhere else, abroad perhaps, and I'll see to it that you're properly looked after and that you don't have to live like this anymore.'

'Leave the army?' Coleman repeated hazily.

'Oh, Jack. I've had such a decent life. I never realised how easy it was until I joined the army, until I met you, until we came out here. Both of us, with the same equal chances to win or to lose, both of us with... what we have together.'

'I feel the same,' Coleman replied tenderly. 'I never knew... well, I never knew what love was until you came to Chatham. Tell me you'll never leave me,' he added imploringly.

'You know I won't, you silly boy.' Bond sighed despairingly. 'Now go on, get your mates and the corporal, and tell them I told you to call them in.'

Only once Coleman had picked his way back up the hillside on his errand did that smile fall from the officer's face. Glancing warily about the surrounding countryside, Bond checked the contents of his revolver, snapped it shut and replaced the weapon in its tarnished brown leather holster.

'Best be quick,' he found himself muttering. 'I don't like this place one bit.'

The sooner they were back inside the laager, he decided,

the better he would like it. Really, he decided as presently the young sapper reappeared with five of his mates and Corporal Denham – all of whom were delighted at being let off so early, there could be nothing so well worth fighting for and no battle more worth winning than for Jack. Bond knew well that it would not be easy. He knew that the odds were stacked heavily against them; that numberless enemies might well be waiting in the wings to strike them down and rip them apart from each other. He knew also that nothing about the future could possibly be relied or counted upon. Nothing could be taken for granted, no certainty was beyond doubt. Their lives had never been exactly easy, had they? Those two kindred spirits at one in an increasingly maddening world. There was still the war to win, too.

Tired, hungry, and resentful of missing dinner, the small detachment of sappers and Scots tramped back into the laager, only to be greeted by an animated and, to tell the truth, rather florid-looking Lieutenant Knight.

More than one man must have remarked to himself how impressive the handsome officer looked, his broad shoulders fitting neatly into the red undress frock, buff cord-clad legs wide apart as he stood with his booted feet firmly planted in the dusty red soil. His face was burned a dark russet brown, and his normally neatly trimmed moustache curled into his dark, pointy beard like some avenging saint as he glared unmercifully at the approaching soldiers. The adjutant was most definitely agitated.

'Albert!'

'Gideon?'

'An explanation if you please, in my tent... at your earliest convenience.' The officer forced a tight smile.

Bond, being conscious of Gideon's position in relation

to his own in the lists, was usually the very model of courtesy and sociable deference towards his high achieving comrade. On this occasion however, with the sun almost set and the rumbling bellies of his men sounding loud and hard above the approaching thunder, he was not best disposed towards humility.

'I'm afraid I am rather busy this evening, Lieutenant,' he replied, pointedly laying emphasis on the official equality of their common rank. 'I have piquets to post, my men haven't eaten yet, and I really should see to the state of my paperwork. It hasn't been touched for days, you know.'

'What's this then, chaps?'

Gideon Knight, who as it was seemed just about fit to explode and now faced with a third participant in the swordplay of military politics, turned to thunder. 'Earnest, whatever it is that you want, may I suggest you go and wait for me in your tent, and I shall see to it presently.'

Penfold, who had merely popped across to make the offer of a hot drink and unwittingly walked into yet another subaltern's war, turned on his brother officer like a cobra. 'Gideon, may I request that you reserve your rudeness for one who better deserves it and, furthermore, do you think that it is entirely appropriate for two officers to be berating one another in the middle of the camp and, more importantly, in front of the men?'

'Earnest,' Knight managed to hiss with simmering menace only thinly veiled in affability for the troops, 'this is really one of those matters which is best left as it is and not made worse by spectators. Further contributions are not pertinent. Do I make myself clear?'

'No, Gideon, I think it is *I* who have not made myself clear on this occasion,' the flush-faced little officer retorted shakily, but more firmly as his anger took over. 'I wish to make it known that I regard your behaviour as unforgivably out of line, and by my commission, I demand that you two desist from rowing in public!'

'That's it!' Knight stormed in absolute fury. 'I'm raising the captain!'

'You already did,' intoned an unmistakably imposing Celtic baritone.

All three men went very red indeed. Coleman and several of the sappers turned away in embarrassed alarm. These were their officers that were rowing after all, and many had noticed the gradual deterioration in the relationship between their top brass since parting company from the main column.

Corporal Denham shivered. All in all, the stage looked set for a grim spectacle. There was no sport in such scenes. If the officers couldn't maintain the respect of the men, how were the NCOs supposed to hold their own?

'Now, gentlemen,' began McGonagle as he advanced on the party like some malignant shade in his billowing nightshirt, but still with his tartan trews and riding boots to complete the picture. 'Would somebody please tell me what by hell in saints is going on out here? What the hell are you doing with all those men, Albert?' the old Scot demanded, peering through his gold-rimmed spectacles.

'They've just come in, sir,' Bond replied hastily. 'I thought, well, that the piquets were too far out from—'

'Very well, very well,' McGonagle interrupted. 'Now look here, Albert, I want you to pick a fresh squad of men, collect your tools and go down river and see about widening those wagon ruts for your Uncle Alec, there's a good fellow. We need to be off early at first light.'

'But, Uncle, it's almost last light now!' Bond protested. 'It's about to pour with rain, and my lads still haven't eaten—'

'I don't care a hat what they haven't done, Albert,' McGonagle shouted back in anger. 'Now don't you *uncle* me. Just get on, laddie, and do as I say. Collect your tools and your sergeant and be off with the digging! Dear God, your mother, my sister, was a wilful one withal. That must be where you get it from!'

That was it. So personal a reference in company, especially one concerning his late parents proved to be too much for the already outraged lieutenant. He was hardly able to appeal an order, not in front of the other men, especially after so demeaning and personal an exchange. With a hiss of suppressed rage and a sharp intake of breath, the young officer turned swiftly on his dusty boot heel and barked at a terrified Coleman to rouse Sergeant Friday.

'At the double!' Bond found himself snarling, for once not just for show.

'What about the other piquet, sir?' Knight demanded, himself far from pacified by Bond's humiliating dressing down.

'Fetch it in, laddie!' the frustrated captain barked back in annoyance. 'Or do you need a royal warrant to do that as well?' He stormed back to his tent, mumbling various obscenities about those 'bloody sappers and miners', leaving Knight cornered and in a position of supreme embarrassment.

He was stuck, caught between the devil and the deep blue sea as far as saving face was concerned. What could he do, he wondered? Not only had he succeeded in managing to row with both his fellows and undo, at a stroke, his hard-won progress with McGonagle, but he was also now in danger of losing his standing with the men. Somehow, he knew, he would have to say his piece.

The world had gone a bit grey by this time. The spectacle

of the romantic sunset had long since vanished, swamped like everything by the malignant advance of the swirling storm clouds. Insects and other airborne pests flew, buzzed, and wafted around the position, further tormenting the soldiers who already wanted to dig a big hole and get in it while the row was taking place. He couldn't call out and risk compromising his already precarious authority by having the old man simply ignore him and carry on. He couldn't very well run after him, tell him to stop or even order him to halt. For a few short seconds he toyed with the notion of supplanting McGonagle and relieving the old man of command. That might just get past senior officers in Africa who knew the old buffer and his ways, but was unlikely to wash with high command, and could potentially be career damaging in the long term. This would be too extreme he decided, even for McGonagle, and since any more tactful approach might well result in a further rebuff, Knight decided in the end to go with his initial instincts and pursue the retiring captain to his tent.

McGonagle seemed amused rather than surprised to find Knight running after him up the slope, and went so far as to suggest that it was a shame so young and studious an officer should forget his orders so quickly and need run to his captain for a reminder. Knight felt he wanted to hit him.

'Captain McGonagle,' he began in a manner that smacked of the late Simonides. 'I feel obliged to say that your conduct throughout this campaign had been little short of unprofessional. You have acted in a manner, which I for one consider to be sloppy and even foolhardy, risking the stability of your command and disregarding any adherence to accepted military practice based on your own, may I say, outdated experiences of an altogether different theatre and... questionable, at best, in this one.'

'Unprofessional? Questionable experience?' McGonagle repeated, rounding on the mutinous young officer with a fury that was almost palpable. His eyes bulged, his neatly oiled hair fell from place above his weathered brown forehead, and his yellow teeth flashed from beneath his beard like those of a rutting stag. 'Unprofessional, is it?' he demanded in outrage. 'Let me tell you a thing or two, laddie. I can remember when soldiering was a duty and the Queen's commission was taken as a vocation, a calling, not some damned trade, or an appointment to be had for sinecure!'

'Sinecure?' This time it was Knight's turn to repeat things. 'Do you know how long I served as adjutant at Brompton? Do you know how long I'd been a lieutenant, ere they sent me to war? Twelve years, Captain. Since I was eighteen years old, I have been waiting for an opportunity to undertake an active command, and I'll have you know that my personal fortunes render my army pay a mere trickle! Good God, sir, I don't think I could pay *my* mess bill on the salary of a lieutenant, let alone fund the amount you drink!'

'So, I drink! In fact, I'm going to have a drink right now if you'd care to join me in one!' McGonagle retorted angrily, snatching up his hip flask and pouring the contents into two tin mugs even as he spoke.

Knight was so furious that he simply snatched up the beaker without as much as a nod, swallowing half the contents in a swift gulp.

'A toast!' snapped McGonagle. 'I know, Lieutenant, we could drink to your being charged with disobeying your orders when we get back to Natal. That would be a shame, wouldn't it? I mean for you to end up having to remain a lieutenant for as long as I have a captain.'

'All right, sir,' Knight snapped back. 'Very well, so I didn't *buy* myself a profession, then *buy* myself a promotion when they didn't think me good enough to give me one on merit. Did you buy your lieutenancy as well as your captaincy? Perhaps,' he added unwisely, 'if you Scots had longer arms and shorter pockets, you might have made major before they abolished promotion by purchase!'

One Simonides too far, McGonagle decided. In seconds, the acid sting of the measured spirits seared through Knight's eyes like hellfire. The initial rawness of the projection was soon superseded by the most hideous pain, so deep and terrible that for a moment he thought he was blind. The burning agony was worse than anything he had encountered in his life before. It ripped and tore through his head, wracking it with intolerable vibrations and hurting so badly that he just had to screw his eyes up even harder and wonder if he would ever see light again. Rigid with anger, yet still a veritable bastion of dignity, Gideon Knight spat the dregs of scotch from his mouth and wiped the running spirits from his face and beard. His eyes were still too sore to open.

McGonagle, could the young officer have only seen it, had gone perfectly ashen beneath his suntan. 'I am truly sorry, Lieutenant,' he said quietly at last. 'I don't know what I was thinking of, and you have my word that it will never happen again.'

Knight said nothing as the old man fumbled about his belongings in search of a handkerchief with which he might dry his face. He didn't even look at him, although admittedly this owed more to the fact that his eyes were still so clouded with a watery haze that he could do little beyond opening them a crack in any case. Feeling for the tin mug in which he had accepted his own libation, Knight lifted the vessel calmly to his lips and, downing what was left in a single gulp, calmly turned, and quit the tent in silence. Only when he was well clear of the canopy's moorings and safe from the prying eyes of the sentries did he plump down beside a wagon and do his best to clear the still stinging teardrops from his brown eyes. This done, he replaced his helmet and, simmering with unquenchable rage, tramped off in search of his horse.

Back in his tent, McGonagle reflected in gloom. For the first time ever, he accepted that he had gone too far. The sad fact was that he quite admired the sharp, academic, and ambitious Knight, and now they would retire him for one moment of unpremeditated madness. For an instant, he glanced at his revolver. Then, as he took up a pen to put to paper for the last time, he thought again. There were still words to be written.

Should I die, he thought, *it's vital I leave behind a legacy of prose.* Taking out his poetry book, he leafed through the pages until he came across something he really liked. Not one of his own tonight, he decided. Perhaps Browning, or Chaucer. After all those years, many of which had been spent in complete loneliness, he felt he was entitled to feel fed up with the incomplete works of Captain AW McGonagle.

'Don't let the bastards have the last word,' he sighed to himself, as the rich scotch whisky in his belly began to out slosh the food already down there, and a nice warm tingly feeling began to creep from his toes to his extremities. 'It's probably time to retire, anyway. After thirty years, they're nae gonna promote you now, ma lad.' To his surprise, McGonagle found himself chuckling. Perhaps he would go back to India or go home and see Willie and the boys, he mused.

The fishing season should be on by the time he got back to Scotland, and the idea of sitting in front of a great fire in one of those old tartan chairs telling war stories to his enthralled nephews and grandnephews really began to appeal to him.

He began a lilting Scottish tune in a wavy tenor, not aided by the drink. As his mind began to wander back amid the pines and the dells and the great sweeping acres of heather overlooking purple rocks and a rushing burn, and the clear cold smell of the Highlands began to filter back from his memory, he knew that it was time to go.

Chapter Fifteen

When the first tiny drops of rain came pattering tentatively on the canvas above them, Earnest Penfold was in the company of his young batman the bugler, meditatively reading through his treasured letters from home while his companion saw to the cleaning of his boots. The letters were contained in a small paper bundle, done up with a piece of ribbon and generally kept in the little officer's brown leather satchel for safety when on the march. Among the three, which Penfold had received since his arrival in South Africa, was one small white envelope bearing his name and instruction that it was not to be opened until the campaign was over, and he was safely back in Cape Colony.

'I really don't suppose I ought to read this until we get back, should I?' the officer enquired of his young servant. 'After all, a promise is a promise, isn't it?'

''Spose, sir,' replied the lad, pausing in his labours to humour his officer by looking up.

Penfold smiled and sighed. Why couldn't he have got a Jack? he wondered gloomily. He was so envious of Bond's bright and endearing sapper who followed Bond everywhere, and generally looked up to him like he was the Duke of Cambridge.

'I have great troubles on my brow just at the moment, Fletcher,' he told the bugler. 'Although I should say from the noises coming from above that we shall be in for even greater ones before the night is through.'

'Aye, sir. I don't much fancy crawling back to the underbelly of a wagon if it's goin' to be a flipping downpour. 'Scuse the language, sir.'

Penfold nodded and smiled sadly. 'It's funny,' he observed, pointing with his good arm at the bowl of water in which Bugler Fletcher was busily engaged upon washing the muck from his boots. 'I always remark on how nice it is to see water when it ripples and reflects off the canvas like this. Do you see, Fletcher?'

The youth feigned interest for a moment before returning to his work.

Not one of nature's romantics, thought Penfold, as the reflected lamplight in the water danced and flickered on the canopy above. 'Oh well, I shan't tell if you don't, Fletcher,' he observed, tearing open the seal on the envelope with his teeth, while holding the paper betwixt the thumb and forefinger that protruded from the sling in which his arm lay cradled.

Having read only a few lines, Penfold dropped the paper. The colour drained from every inch of his face, and he began to breathe much quicker.

Fletcher looked up, wondering if his young officer was about to have heart failure, when the crumpled piece of paper fluttered to the ground before him.

'It can't be helped now, I suppose,' he sighed miserably. 'She was bound to run out sooner or later, so I suppose this is really the best thing all round.'

'Sir?'

'Money, dear Fletcher,' Penfold sighed resignedly. 'You might just as well know, since I'm going to have to tell someone: I've run out of the stuff. Well, that is, Henrietta my wife must have run out of what I left her with back in Chatham and writes me she's gone to live with her married sister.'

'I thought officers always 'ad money,' the bugler sighed wistfully.

'Did you, indeed?' Penfold replied, but his eyes were glassy and vacant, and his melancholy almost palpable to the bewildered young soldier before him. 'Of course, Albert would have helped me if he could, I know that now,' Penfold suddenly began again in a monotone that seemed to his batman to be addressed to another. The little officer snorted and shook his head, as if to emphasize his point. 'I couldn't hear of it of course, not even if he had the money to do it. I mean, can you imagine the ignominy?'

Fletcher could find nothing to say, and wasn't entirely sure he knew of *ignominy* anyway, so he simply knelt there staring.

Penfold nodded frantically then shut his eyes up tight, as if trying to shake some tormenting foreign object from somewhere deep inside his brain. 'I've been thinking as hard as I can,' he continued, 'but the truth is I just don't know what to do. Hen's parents thought we were mad to marry so young, and yet here we are, virtually bankrupt and Hen moving back to Gravesend because she can't keep the rooms in The Bull.'

Fletcher simply opened his mouth and closed it again. If Mr Penfold was heading for an asylum, or penury, another officer would have to pay his wages. Yet what of his arrears?

'Gideon Knight was the best that Bond could come up with,' Penfold resumed, with such blithe countenance and light-heartedness of manner that Fletcher was left no room for doubt that his officer was going mad. 'Of course, he was right. Gideon is by far the best person to know what to do, having been in the job so much longer than all of us. That's no good though, you see, because he's served as adjutant. It's his duty to report this sort of thing, and I don't want to end up being discharged. I should have to enlist again, only this time for a sapper!'

Fletcher, who had by this time become almost as worried about his officer's disclosure as he had about his own back pay, began to consider sending for help.

Penfold had risen from his seat now; the letters were strewn across the floor of the tent, and the little officer was looking decidedly vacant.

'You sure you're awright, sir?' Fletcher managed to ask at last.

'I know I should think better of him,' Penfold continued, pacing mechanically towards the open flaps of the tent. 'I just want to do what's right by Henrietta, my wife, but Gideon's a decent sort, and by far the richest man I know. All pulling together for the corps and all that, we can't have chaps falling off the boat.'

With that, he left, leaving his bewildered batman in a complete state of flux, and calling madly after him to take his shoulder strap, or at least his revolver.

The rain had begun to fall properly by this time. It pattered down hard on the roofs of the tents, hammering harder and harder as the clouds began to open overhead. The hitherto dry and dusty floor of the riverbank began gradually to darken as the little plops of water threw up patches of dust, and a strange smell of wet rock began to cling to the nostrils.

Gideon Knight tugged on his tan leather gloves and was just about to spur his horse and ride out in search of the second piquet when Penfold ambled across the laager, evidently taken up with something. Knight, who was not in the best frame of mind after Earnest's betrayal of earlier on, and still fuming over his row with McGonagle, eyed the approaching officer with an impatience that was painfully apparent. Penfold seemed not to notice however, ambling quite absent-mindedly across to where the mounted officer sat waiting, the rain falling with increasing force on his unprotected head. A flash of white lightening tore across the black and thunderous sky, illuminating the camp and lighting up the approaching Penfold for several seconds after. He looked utterly pathetic, nose covered in spots and swellings, while bites and blackheads littered his oily forehead as the water ran off his thick beige hair and into his squinting eyes. The skinny little body, further depleted by physical exertion and army rations, looked even feebler in the soggy white shirt, while his poor useless arm hung from his neck in a sling, and the raindrops fell from his pale, straggly little beard.

'Gideon.'

The voice was strangely high-pitched, even for Penfold, and the tone was one of almost inaudible pallor.

'Earnest, what on earth are you doing out here in the pouring rain with no proper clothing on and no weapon in case of danger? You ought to be ashamed of yourself.'

'Gideon... I need your help,' Penfold continued, still in a dreamlike trance. 'I thought it would all be all right, but now I see that it can't be.'

'Earnest,' Knight replied sternly, as the rain began to pour off the brim of his helmet and down between his legs. 'Whatever it is will have to wait until I get back. Can't you see I'm busy?' With that, he spurred his horse and thundered off into the stormy night without even pausing to await a reply.

Poor Penfold just stood there forlornly looking after him, the rain beating down on him and his wet, shivering shoulders, his boots becoming gradually more and more caked up with mud and his mind wandering further and further from his body as his last chance rode off into the darkness.

While Penfold had been slowly agonising over his impending financial disgrace, Bond, thus lumbered and faced with the unenviable task of digging out the riverbanks under those strange and threatening cloud formations, had tramped off with Sergeant Friday and an unhappy squad of sappers. They came to a halt about a mile from the Highlanders' camp. Bond dismounted, waited for all his men – who were naturally on foot – to catch up, and in the meantime surveyed the scene before him.

The view of the river was a blurred reflection of black, blue, grey, and brown, resembling something like a pool of oil as the murky waters began to merge in his eye with the dark storm clouds massing overhead, which had now totally engulfed the dwindling colours of sunset. It seemed as if the land were now completely absorbed in a colourless pall of gloom and darkness, while the overhead rumble of thunder reminded the officer that the rain could not be far away. The grassy bank upon which they would have to improve dropped away some twenty feet from the water's edge, declining steeply from top to bottom. The walls of the bank were crowded and cluttered with small trees, brambles, and aloes, inverted and hideously distorted as they struggled to remain vertical against the uprising banks. A low and well-concealed furrow just below a tangle of shrubbery suggested a time-honoured place of passage used by some sort of animal and yet might, with some considerable clearing, serve as a start for their crossing.

'Here,' Bond informed his men, as young Coleman doubled over to where he stood, shovel in one hand and his Martini-Henry in the other.

A sudden flash of lightening lit the dark sky for a moment, followed by the pitter-patter of raindrops upon their helmets. A dry, dusty smell that was strange and alien to the nostrils came at the first fall of rain, and the thick red powder beneath their feet was very soon a sloppy red paste, seeping through their soles.

At first it was just a gentle, tell-tale fall of drops that flecked their faces, hair, the shoulders of their jackets and the toes of their boots; so light in fact that they might hardly have noticed anything at first, had they not been waiting for it. Then, it began to fall harder, and the droplets began to hammer down on and all round them harder and faster still, until the tops of their tunics became soaking wet, and the mud was washed from their helmets and down their backs. Dark patches began to form across their saturated shoulders, and even larger ones started to take shape down the front and back of their trousers, until the smell of wet wool and human sweat became overpowering.

There was a chorus of derision as the downpour grew heavier, and Bond knew well that standing around did little for morale.

'Bloody hell,' Corporal Denham was heard to mutter.

'Language!' hissed Friday. Rain was one thing; profanities were quite another.

'Sergeant, detail to begin by clearing this rough foliage from around the trench,' Bond instructed. 'Then I want that furrow widened out enough to get the gear down there for assembling the pont. You and Corporal Denham see to that with your detail, and Sapper Coleman and I will take the rest of the men downstream to see about improving a crossing for the wagons themselves.'

Despite the rain, Friday assented with customary formality,

and the men were soon downing their rifles and valise equipment in favour of their picks and shovels.

Yet another horrendous flash of purple sheet lightening lit up the wide-open veldt for a few seconds. This was followed in no time at all by a cataclysmic boom of thunder, which shook the ground like an overhead barrage. The rain lashed across their faces by this time, their hair began to flatten, and little clusters of droplets began to form on their eyebrows and run down the ends of their noses. A few seconds and they were soaked completely. A sudden chill followed, and clothes became heavier as the wet cloth of the outer garments clung without mercy to the sodden undergarments, which clung in turn to their wet and shivering bodies.

'Sounds like a war going on,' Coleman sighed, yet somehow with far more maturity, masculinity, and strength of character.

As he turned to look at Jack, Bond began to realise that no more was the boy an innocent, viewing the world with the incredulity of a Chatham lad sent overseas. If he had ever been afforded innocence – fighting to survive by fists, wiles... or by other means entirely. Another stolen glance showed the officer that Coleman was smiling, having noticed his regard.

Another blinding flash tore across the sky. He saw the young man framed against a backdrop of black rocks, pale unearthly yellow pastures and the dark, swelling, brooding storm clouds up above.

'Best we off kit, sir,' Coleman said at last, removing his dripping wet topi and shaking out his lengthening hair in the rain.

He looked so attractive just then, so solid and dependable one moment, and then all at once so open, even vulnerable, as the rain began to stream off his flat blond head and cascaded down his face, dripping off his nose, chin, and eyelashes. Bond fought for breath. It was going to be a rough task to maintain his composure under such circumstances, yet they had a rougher task in hand just at that moment.

'All right, men, take off your jackets, packs and your headgear,' Bond instructed, himself removing the already sopping wet patrol jacket and casting it aside. 'The rain will only weigh your clothes down even more, and the work will seem much easier if you can move around properly.'

'Shirts too, sir?' Coleman whispered tentatively in his officer's ear.

The rain was incredibly heavy by now, beating down on their heads like a hailstorm, hammering them into the growing sea of mud and soaking every inch of their bodies. Bond, who was down to his satin shirt when the real attack came, was drenched in an instant. His hair hung over his eyes until he pushed it back with his hands, so that it now resembled the silky coat of an otter.

He spat out the water from his mouth and tried to wring some of the water out of his shirt. It was useless. Coleman moved a pace closer, pressing his tender lips against Bond's lobe, shouting to be heard above the torrent. Tendrils of wet hair brushed against the bare skin of the officer's shoulder as his own soaking grey flannelette fell away. The rainwater surged in glistening rivulets down the boy's firm body and the gleaming, animated muscles in his chest. Bond gasped aloud this time and was forced to close his eyes and nod to covey the order.

Most of the men had abandoned trying to preserve their clothes in any case, simply chucking their serges and their saturated shirts where they might, snatching up their tools and throwing themselves into their appointed tasks with vigour, though more to generate warmth than from any more noble motivation.

The rain showered down so heavily that it soon became almost impossible to see beyond one's nose. A two-foot spray jumped from the surface of the river as the men waded into it, struggling with their long wooden stakes, and battling for movement as their boots sank into the mud and their baggy trousers began to fill with water.

The lightening, when it occurred, lit the entire landscape for miles around, and the thunder burst directly overhead with a ferocity equal to a thousand artillery salvos, clapping across their ears like nothing they had ever experienced, and deadening other sounds for a considerable time after. They struggled to dig. The mud was soft and ran with the consistency of wet sand, but movement and the action of digging became so difficult that many abandoned their tools and began to scrape out great sloppy sods with their bare hands. The result was that the men and their officer were soon utterly smeared in thick, scented reddish brown mud.

The rain continued to fall unmercifully and splattered relentlessly down upon their heads so hard that most were literally running water from their scalps to the ends of their beards, or the stubble on their chins. Several times they had to struggle up the slippery bank and make sure that the rifles, secreted beneath two or three greatcoats and tucked up in scraped out stretch of bank, were not to be washed away by the rising river.

Slipping, stumbling, and falling over constantly in the merging mud bath of wood, water, and bodies, soaked to the very bones, stung by the rain on their backs and half blinded by the sporadic lightening and rising spray, they battled on.

At one point, Bond snatched hold of something that he took for a piece of wood, only to discover that what he held in his hands was the stiff and decidedly dead remains of a large bird. Gasping in disgust as the maggots welled up and dripped off the body like raindrops, he raised the carcass above his head and flung it as far as he could manage. There came a cry from just beyond the bend in the river, and the unmistakable shriek of Friday arose above the tumult, threatening reprisals and stern recriminations as soon as the perpetrator of the projectile was identified.

Helpless with laughter, Coleman, stripped to the waist, his blond hair flattened and moulded as the water streamed off it, almost dropped his shovel as he struggled to remain upright in the increasingly swelling current.

Bond, his dark russet curtains collapsing over his face no matter how many times he tried to smooth it back, and gallons of icy cold water pouring off over his eyes and down his back and legs, grappled with a huge timber and tried in vain to save it.

The rain clung to the back of Coleman's neck, slipped down around his ears and gushed like a busted drainpipe every time he leaned forward or bent down to dig.

'Oi, Jack, lad!' came a cry from beyond the bend, where they knew Corporal Denham to be assisting Sergeant Friday in assembling a heavy pont. 'I thought the sun was meant to shine out of your arse, boy?'

'Language!' cried Friday but was drowned out by the thunder and his waterlogged beard.

Coleman, unable to see beyond a cascade of saturated blond hair, spat out a quantity of water and cupped his hands to his lips. 'Happen it does, Corp,' he retorted cheekily, emboldened by the proximity of his officer.

'Well, how's about givin' some light down here,' Denham returned unperturbed. 'Cos it ain't half bleedin' dark this end!'

'Language! *Langu-age!*' cried Friday, who was himself

struggling to hold a stake for one of his sappers to hammer into the silt.

Bond, nearly shattered and wracked with the giggles, placed his foot against a rather rotten-looking lump of wood. It snapped and the officer tumbled back into the enveloping waters with a curse, snatching at anything he hoped might afford him purchase. A cry went up from one or two of the nearest men, and Coleman only just managed to slip into the rushing brown foam in time to catch hold of his officer, both men nearly unable to move for hysteria.

'I bloody nearly went there!' Bond wailed, as his head emerged from the water and the freezing rain hammered down even harder upon them, and they struggled to regain the bank together.

Coleman, wrestling frantically with the current, finally succeeded in setting the officer back on his feet. They pitched back against a depression in the bank, gasping.

'Language!' came a cry from Friday, not knowing who had spoken, and apparently yet undaunted by the fearful clash of the elements around them.

Writhing in the mud, Bond's broad freckled back pressed against Coleman's slippery, smooth, and glistening chest, they could only lie there and wallow as the laughter overwhelmed them. Their naked torsos were completely caked in soggy wet mud, their hair slicked back off their faces with more of the same, and their flailing, saturated trouser legs slipping and squirming in the rushing water. Bond's chest hair was matted with the brown pulp, and every inch of fabric cladding their exhausted legs was utterly absorbed in an ocean of mud.

A thick mist hung only inches above the tops of the riverbanks, and somewhere in the distance an even greater barrage of thunder seemed to be tearing the night still further in two, shaking even the very foundations of the mountains themselves. Each man was blinded to anything beyond his own hands and what they contained. In any case, no one was in any position to look up from his work. As it was, the spray and fog were so dense that, even if they had looked, no one would have been able to discern more than the mere shadows of the two men, as they lay helpless and panting in each other's arms, just a few yards down river. Bond, utterly and completely drained and unable to shift the thick, damp smelling mud from any part of his body, rolled onto his front as he lay on Coleman's chest and rested his head against the young sapper's cheek. The boy gasped as the officer's manoeuvre forced the back of his sleek blond head still deeper in the mud and wriggled so hard that he almost succeeded in burying himself. Spluttering, he wrestled with Bond for a few seconds, until the pair of them were completely covered from head to foot and utterly unrecognisable from the undulating contours of the banks themselves. They were in so much of a mess that it simply couldn't matter anymore. In fact, so thick and clingy was the mud that it was almost a blessed relief from the harsh, cutting rain and the lashing current. Their hands ran all over one another, shoulders, arms, and chests, exploring, teasing, tormenting; Bond stroking Jack's face and Jack stroking Bond's wet, silky hair, both men lost in each other. Lost in love.

Exhausted, they lay there and watched as the steam rose from all around their begrimed bodies. The smell was vile, and they were in desperate need of a drink. For a while that must have been only a few moments they just lay there gazing at one another, utterly devoid of all barriers concerning rank and hierarchy by their semi nudity, proximity and by the hopeless state of their soaking wet, mud-splattered skin.

Another crack of thunder followed a flash of lightening,

and the ground shook beneath them once again. The rain was utterly blinding as it fell in sheets, washing the mud from their faces and, but for the occasional bolt as it tore across the night sky, obliterating everything from view.

'Listen to that thunder, sir,' Coleman shouted in Bond's ear. 'It's so heavy, it sounds like the artillery opening up, or the butts at the Hythe rifle ranges.'

'Either that, or the wind ripping through the trees. It's blowing a gale!' Bond retorted.

Even in the dark, and camouflaged as they were by the mud, he could sense Coleman looking at him in bewilderment. The silence spoke volumes.

'What trees?' he added, seemingly to answer his own mind as well as Jack's. 'To quote Uncle Alec there *are* none... in this drift, at any rate!'

'In Africa there *are* no trees!' they chorused.

As the joyous atmosphere died down and the rumbling cacophony of the storm surrounded them, a feeling of unease permeated through both sappers. Bond found that Coleman had instinctively curled a bulging right bicep around his shoulder. *So,* you're *protecting* me *now, are you*? he thought in wonder.

Chapter Sixteen

In the instant it took Lieutenant Bond to struggle free of the protective swamp in which he and Coleman had been wallowing, another sheet of lightening illuminated the world. In the one clear moment, in which he was able to see as far as the hallowed encampment wherein his uncle, Earnest and the Highland troops were reposed, Bond struggled with the impositions of his mind and the vague, dancing shapes of half imagined motions between the embrasures. Cursing the thunder as it clapped across his ears, even harder than the report of rifle fire of which his inner consciousness had clearly told him from the camp, he struggled against the driving rain and the howling gale to gather the fragments of his operation.

In the space of something like an hour, the alarmingly swollen river, together with her ally the relentless rain, had soaked, broken and physically exhausted thirty typically strong, fit men. More importantly, she had also lost them much of the wood needed to build the ponts and wearied the spirits with her constant barrage of sounds and sensations, reducing the sappers to sap and all hope of a successful undertaking to a futility of drills and gestures.

Coleman, shattered and just about ready to be washed away by the fearsome current, stumbled up the embankment, rifle in hand. Almost unconsciously, he placed his hand on Bond's shoulder.

'What did you see, sir?' he asked as gently as he could above the din.

'See?' Bond repeated. 'I couldn't see a damned thing, that's the trouble.'

'Hear then, sir,' Coleman retorted, now thoroughly alarmed.

'Neither,' said Bond. 'It's all up here,' he added, placing a finger to his temple as the water streamed down his face and down the slick hair as he smoothed it back once more.

They were soon joined at the top of the slope by Sergeant Friday and Corporal Denham who, having struggled free of the mud and snatched up their weapons at the first distant sounds, were now both surprised to find their officer and sapper also standing-to.

'Thought we'd imagined it, sir,' Denham managed to bawl above the torrent. 'Sarn't fancied the thunder like to a battle goin' on overhead, or nearby here.'

Bond said nothing for a moment. Then he sighed. 'Get the men out, fetch the rifles and get their kit back on. I don't care if it's wet or dry.'

'Yes, sir,' replied Friday.

'D'you think there's something wrong, sir?' Coleman enquired, now once more at liberty to embrace his officer in the absence of the two NCOs.

Bond looked grave and shook his head. 'I just don't know,' he replied.

Bond and his sappers were not the only ones to be disturbed that evening. The thunder cracked overhead, and the thick fog of rain swept down upon the canvas awnings of the soldiers'

tents, rendering sleep impossible and nightmarish imaginings highly probable.

McGonagle, who had well been used to the monsoon season back in India, lay awake and pondered his impending retirement with the aid of a hundred-gun salute from the rampaging elements outside. He knew that his purse would go further in India. Then again, all his mistakes were in India which, along with his late wife, had been the main reasons for his leaving to begin with. After all, it was over twenty years since last he set foot on Scottish soil, and even though people had long memories, it was hardly London or Oscaarsberg. There was little society north of Edinburgh, and none in the Highlands. Besides which, he reasoned, with a Zulu war medal to accompany his Indian one, he might call himself major for all anyone would know, or care. Then again, no. A captain was a captain and so, he reflected, was he. The soldiering uncle from afar should hold mystique enough.

'Captain Alec Wilbur McGonagle,' he chuckled away to himself. 'Eightieth Indian Regiment, and Ninety-First Highlanders... retired.' Already, the scribe in him was marching in quick time. 'The modern Martini-Henry is quite different from the old muskets they used when I was first commissioned,' he heard himself telling an enthralled audience, gathered around the fire in the great hall of the family seat. 'Hard pounding in squares... Solid lines kept out cavalry, infantry, and Zulus alike. File firing, front and rear rank with every man husbanding ammunition and placing shots to kill. Raised markers, that's your answer.' And pause for applause. 'In India... there are no... *teas*?' he enquired of himself. Though the rhyme was there, it seemed to offer no natural return but "ganges", which was geographically tenuous, at best.

Hang poetry for good and all, he decided, AW McGonagle

must live for the present and enrapture others with tales of the past. Living for yesterday was unhealthy, and perhaps all those wasted years of poetry and verse had blinded him to the real talent, the real vocation and calling in his need for critical recognition. He would plan, draft, and write his autobiography: *The life and times of the British soldier*, or perhaps *The memoirs of a Scottish soldier*.

Suddenly the pressing call of an altogether more immediate vocation began to grip him. With a curse, he remembered his chamber pot was still in a wagon. *Of all the damn stupid things!* It was no good, he would just have to get out of bed and find a place to go. There was no way he was going to scrabble around in the rainy darkness in search of the latrine – and risk falling in it, more to the point – when there was a perfectly good tussock just outside his own accommodation.

'It's no good, ma boy,' he murmured over to himself, setting down his pen with finality. 'You'll just have to cut down upon the drink, and that's the fact.'

Almost falling out of bed, McGonagle almost thought that he could hear an even harder pattering, sounding above the dogged driving rain. *Better be sure*, he thought. Then, as if to satisfy himself, he tucked his sprawling nightshirt into his enveloping tartan trews, tugged his red undress coatee on over the top, and replaced his rather comical nightcap with the Topi helmet he so rarely wore, his preference generally being for a straw hat.

The rain continued to fall in sheets on the miserable, sodden camp and its equally miserable inhabitants. Those left out on sentry – their fires long since reduced to a pathetic smoking splutter – huddled up with their rifles under their long grey overcoats and tried their best to close the gaps between the peaks of their helmets and tops of their collars.

Everything looked rotten outside, and the instant he set foot in it, McGonagle's boots sank into the thick soggy mud.

At least I had the sense to camp on the ridge, he thought. The rain was soaking merrily down the gentle embankment by this time, and the poor fellows in their tents inside the laager were bound to be passing a most disagreeable night. It was worse than anything he seemed able to remember, and the storm seemed to him to be almost more menacing than those that occurred during the monsoon. He must write all this down for the book, he reflected.

Yet another stinging spray of iced water hit him fairly in the face. Cursing, the elderly officer removed his neat little gold-rimmed spectacles and was just in the process of wiping them as near as he could get to clean when a sudden flash tore through the darkened embrasures on every side of the camp. Momentarily raising his gaze from his glasses, McGonagle suddenly realised to his horror that the flash and bang still echoing off the mountains, which he had taken for lightening, had suddenly been joined by the groans and screams of his sentries. For that brief few seconds an icy chill ran through the old captain's bones as the wretched soldiers died at their posts or called out piteously for reinforcements amid the continuing bombardment of rain, sleet, and this more sinister infiltration.

From somewhere up on the mountain as both he and his men picked their way back down towards the river, Gideon Knight watched the flashes with a growing sense of helplessness.

Earnest Penfold, himself aroused from bed to answer a call of the utmost necessity, suddenly spotted what he thought was one of his earners dashing across the inside of the muddy laager. This time however, the little officer had also taken care to bring his revolver and, as the figure made its way across the camp towards him, he pointed the weapon at the source of his irritation and ordered him to stop.

By this time many of the Highlanders were up and about, running to and fro with their rifles and hopelessly attempting to strap on their valises over shirts and, in some cases, the bare flesh of their semi-naked bodies. Furious with his own men for their apparent apathy in allowing one of their number to desert with impunity, Lieutenant Penfold cried out to the Highlanders that one of his men was running away and instructed them to restrain him. It was only at this moment that the terrible truth of their predicament finally dawned upon him, with the awful realisation that it was not one of his men, and that the camp was under attack.

He froze. A cold thrill of anticipation wracked his whole body and before he knew it, the little officer found that his need for the latrine was rapidly catching up on him. Before he knew what to do, the warrior whom he had taken for a deserter had stopped, drawn back his arm and, emitting a howl of chilling finality, flung his assegai at him.

There was a deafening ripple of gunfire, the very air of the encampment illuminated by a kaleidoscope of orange flashes as the shooting started. A long, low chilling whoop sounded in the darkness, apparently from all sides, as the Zulus closed in on the laager. Then, as the dense cloud of obliterating smoke began slowly to clear, the sudden shape and form of semi-clad Zulu warriors began to emerge before the very eyes of the terrified Highlanders.

'The gaps! The gaps!' cried Lieutenant Penfold, revolver in one hand and gesturing frantically to the dazed, confused men about him, exhorting them to pull themselves together and help him pull the wagons in on one another. It was too late, however.

A dense, dark, and seemingly endless swarm brandishing spears and shields of a piebald animal skin emerged from the inky blackness and through the open embrasures, emitting a baritone hum as they ran towards the spitting muzzles of the soldiers' carbines. A few of the Highlanders had managed to squeeze together under the deadly close-range fire from the darkness outside and, under the steady and commanding voice of their sergeant, Linus Stag, succeeded in firing a well-directed volley into the oncoming ranks of the enemy. They fired again, but this time the relentless hoard of angry Zulus would not be stopped, pressing onwards between the wagons, left open so accommodatingly by the officers responsible for their dispositions.

Screaming hoarsely for those who had them to fix bayonets, Earnest Penfold could only fall back and watch in horror as the Zulus outside the camp came on, a mere few occasionally dropping as the great mass surged forward, seemingly oblivious of the feeble spatter of bullets from the disorganised soldiers.

Only those who had been snatched by their NCOs and organised into firing parties managed to put down any serious fire on the Zulus. Several of the men, who had rushed forward to take up a better position for firing, were now engaged in a feeble attempt to wage a fighting retreat, their disciplined rank divisions reduced to a maddening dash as they abandoned resistance in favour of survival. Some managed to fall successfully back on the wagons, many mounting the beds to return fire, slicing down several warriors in their tracks and bayoneting any others who managed to get near them.

Yet still the Zulus came on, rushing past their wounded adversaries before many had even hit the ground, stampeding through the British position, and slipping easily past the hopeless stands of the bewildered Highlanders and sappers. Once within the laager, there seemed to be nothing that the soldiers could do to stop them – shooting, stabbing, and thrusting wildly with their assegais, half blinded by the rain and ferocious in their relentless assault.

Still standing, watching with growing numbness and incredulity as his fighting force was gradually cut down into mere fragments, McGonagle was suddenly aware of a party of warriors advancing on him at speed up the slope. In the seconds it took to bat an eyelid, the old soldier had ducked back under the canvas of his canopy, snatched up his shotgun and now stood facing his attackers as they swarmed towards him, lit up by a flash of purple lightening.

'So, you want me, do you?' he called out in defiance, raising his weapon to his shoulder. 'Will I give you some of this?' he cried, firing wildly with both barrels, and blowing four warriors off their feet in a billow of gun smoke.

None the worse for wear, the other pair scrambled up the slope, quite regardless of their colleagues' bodies, as they lay scattered around the captain in a sea of blood and damage. Realising he was out, McGonagle quickly tugged open the leather flap of his brown revolver holster. His pistol spat out five rounds, hitting both Zulus as they came on, lead slugs punching holes through their hopelessly inadequate shields and killing them stone dead before him.

'Attack ma camp, will you!' he exclaimed, as another Zulu struggled up the slope, only to receive the full force of the officer's shotgun as the butt hit him squarely in the face, and he sank back down with a dribble of blood and teeth.

Animated, his heart thumping harder and harder, McGonagle looked about for another suitable candidate for the remaining round in his revolver. Sure enough, a seasoned warrior of about thirty summers mounted the slope in the wake of his comrade, waving his assegai and screaming a war cry. His blood up, his glasses utterly obliterated by his own breath and the pouring rain, McGonagle could only cock his revolver, fire, and curse as the bullet missed its mark by the strength of a mile. Backing steadily, fear for the first time ever beginning to grow in his straining heart, the elderly officer realised that he was within inches of his life. He *must* get hold of his sword. Staggering across the grass, slipping in the mud, and struggling not to become caught up in the sprawling ropes of his solitary tent, McGonagle made a concerted dive and succeeded in plunging between the flaps. The darkness made it almost impossible to see any further, but a vague glow of silver plate and the barely discernible anagram of Her Majesty glimmered away in the corner of the tent and caught his attention. As he stumbled forward, his fingers within reach of the hilt, McGonagle suddenly felt a sharp blow in the small of his back, as the breath was struck from his body. This was followed in turn by yet another, this time keenly defined pain as something cut through the cloth of his tunic and cut deep into his flesh. A sharp, agonising sensation rippled through his entire body as the blade plunged into his shoulder and he felt himself fading with every second. He fell to earth with a low moan, snatching at the side of his camp table as he went down, holding on for only a moment, then crashing to the ground amid a sea of ink and disordered papers.

The Zulus were swarming all over the position by now and, but for depleted clumps of resistance, had otherwise gained control of the camp. Many were in amongst the tents themselves, adding to the noise and the chaos of the gunfire as the sickening sound of rifle butts hammered down on shields, and the gruesome rip and tear as metal pierced and cut through serge and flesh. To every man left alive it seemed as if the Zulus just kept replenishing themselves in endless numbers, rising from the mist and smoke like some terrible realisation of a mortal nightmare, dashing in amongst their colleagues and stabbing them mercilessly to death.

Firing his rifle, seized with the manic zeal of self-preservation, Sergeant Stag made a last desperate attempt to save the defence. Almost as soon as they had spilled out of their tents to fight, the men had been reliant on the ammunition stored about their person, or secreted in their expense pouches at the back of their kit. Now, as Stag and his boys poured their fire into the enemy, their supplies began to dwindle and the intensity of their volleys to decrease. Ignoring the call of warning from his corporal, Stag broke from his cover behind the wheel of the wagon they had been defending to dash across the muddy laager and secure fresh supplies. Before he had made it a few yards, a shot rang out and he collapsed across the ropes of an abandoned bell tent. Wheezing a final plea for his lads to "keep going", the sergeant suddenly felt the blade of an assegai plunge between his shoulder blades, striking the curse from his lips as he died.

Lieutenant Penfold meanwhile was still holding out, dodging, and dashing towards the farther side of the laager, deafened by the crackle of the gunfire and his eyes unspeakably sore from the smoke. He had endured fear, fatigue, countless nights of flies, fleas, cold and sickness; his arm was probably septic, and now this unforeseen attack, pulling the company apart with their spears and slaughtering his sappers as they ran to assist their brother soldiers. Frantically, he glanced both this way and that. *There must be some means of salvaging the defence.* Manic, with all the fire and frustration of his miserable life and the reality that there was no way out finally welling up inside him, Penfold opened fire. Pain and horror fused together to fan the flames of aggression, and he ran from his position, firing his revolver at the innumerable enemy and shooting into their midst for all his one-armed little body was worth. The results of such frenzied and indiscriminate pistol shots were soon apparent however, and his work soon expended the five bullets left in the chambers. With a click of resignation, the smoking revolver subsided into silence and, declaring itself finally to be empty, slipped from his trembling grasp and landed in the mud with a slap. All his life he had been backed into corners by bigger, stronger people, and now, as Penfold gradually retreated into a space wherein two wagons had been run together and stacked high with sandbags to form a windbreak, he realised that the game was up. Ever since school he had allowed it to happen, merely curling up while the others poked fun at him, scrappy, meek little Earnest with his bony little elbows and kneecaps, who didn't like rugby and couldn't pull an oar for his house. This time, he thought, as the warriors pressed home their attack, he would not simply let go. It was then that he spotted young Fletcher about a hundred yards off, helplessly wounded and crawling under the canvas of a bell tent for some desperate measure of protection. If there had ever been one thing that the little officer had in his favour it was his height. Barely five-foot five, Penfold had always just scraped by in rugby by his being able to duck and weave in and out of his opponents' clutches. Now, as the big, well-built Zulu warriors fell towards him, the lieutenant suddenly took a dive. Dodging beneath the arm of one, he narrowly missed being assegai attacked by another and succeeded in slipping between the shields of a third man in his desperate strike for freedom. He knew it was only a momentary advantage, but he had to keep it going.

Fletcher's feet were still to be seen sticking out from beneath the saturated awning, indicating that the young bugler's injuries had left him with very little time at all. In a last concerted effort, Penfold slipped out from under a wagon and ran the last few steps towards his goal: the flapping doorway of the tent. Then a look of disbelief mixed with shock and abject agony rippled across his contorted face. This was followed by a gasp. A feeling of breathlessness and a scream of fear welled up and burst forth from his mouth as the point of an assegai struck him in the chest. For a moment he wrestled with the broad blade seeking to pull it free, but the point had gone right through him, pinning his arm to his chest and fixing into his body. His strength was soaking away and the life ebbing from his small body as he clawed his way inside the tent.

Young Fletcher was still alive when the officer succeeded in hauling himself the last valiant few inches inside. His short fair hair was soaked and transparent, his spotty chin smeared with mud and blood, and his lips spitting more blood as his big brown eyes searchingly gazed back at his officer. For a moment or two they exchanged glances; their hands struggled out to meet one another and their fingers entwined as the wretched world of pain, fear and horror gradually left them behind. They died within a heartbeat of each other.

Lance Sergeant Jacob Christmas was the last man to fall. Having managed to collect a few stragglers, many of whom for the first time placed his white stripes above his black skin, waged a fighting retreat as far as an outlying donga, with the intention of securing the old, abandoned outpost.

Gradually, as his men were picked off by fire from the camp or overwhelmed as the rampaging warriors came streaming down the dongas and killed them, the valiant stand was whittled down to the one man. Out of ammunition, backed up against the wall of a donga and faced with two impending Zulus, Christmas hissed, and cursed as they held back their assegais and thrust forth their shields as bait for his bayonet. The bayonet has not been issued to him, rather recovered from the body of a fallen white soldier who had been permitted to carry one in life, like the rounds he had fired in defence of his camp. Already wounded and bleeding heavily from the left arm, he turned aside the shield with the point of his bayonet, before emitting a fearful cry and plunging it between the warrior's ribs. The second man backed away slightly as Christmas relinquished the rifle and took up the weapon of his ancestry, an assegai, and fought on. Fate found the brave; steadfast Christmas just moments later; a moment's gasp and a fight for life as the bullet entered his body before he too lay dead amid the chaos.

In truth, the whole disastrous spectacle must have been over in less than twenty minutes, the troops taken completely by surprise amid the awful maelstrom of the nightmarish fight for Shorthouse's Drift. Yet those brave souls in the camp were far from being the only ones engaged in a bitter struggle for supremacy as the darkness swept across the veldt.

Chapter Seventeen

Almost as soon as the firing had begun, Gideon Knight and his nine-man piquet had scrambled into positions of cover among the rocks and boulders along the cliff and opened fire on the Zulus investing the camp. Due to their lack of numbers – not including Knight since the officer did not possess a rifle, the action did not represent a catastrophic hindrance from the Zulu perspective. Even so, the sight of more red soldiers moving about on high motivated many of the warriors to abandon their work in the camp and launch a rather forlorn assault against the insurmountable cliff face. All those who tried were shot down in their tracks, the most successful getting only about nine yards from the boulders at the base of the cliff. Several within the camp attempted to return fire but their muskets, combined with the poor conditions and the even poorer quality of Zulu marksmanship, resulted in a few balls idly plopping home around the bodies of those killed at the base. At one point, it appeared as though the Zulus might mount the gentle shoulder of the mountain on the far side, but these soon broke off and streamed down the donga in pursuit of Sergeant Andrews' rear guard.

Knight, by this time weak and exhausted by the relentless rain, the hopeless state of things below, and the deafening fire from the rifles of his own men, could only watch in dismay as the last clumps of his boys fell amid the slaughter, while the mouths of their carbines spat a few pathetic rounds in an effort that looked to be more of a gesture than anything more offensive. From his position on a knoll of rock, his revolver hopelessly puffing away at the shadows below and a sob gathering in his heart, Gideon Knight murmured a prayer of supplication to whoever was listening.

'Please, God,' he begged, 'just don't let my friends be counted among our dead...'

Dazed and exhausted, with aching brows and heavy eyelids to accompany the severe weight of the mud around their legs, boots and equipment, Lieutenant Bond and his troop stopped again to recoup their strength and take an impromptu roll call.

Since the rain had eased off, all they had been able to see of the camp was a circle of dim shadows resembling wagons, ominously surrounded by a cloud of what appeared to be rifle smoke and a heavy mist resulting from the torrential downpour.

Muddy, bloodied, and bruise from their exertions and the odd stray lump of driftwood washed downstream by the current, they subsided in a miserable pile in the relative cover of a donga and awaited their officer's instructions.

Bond glanced around in the murky darkness. His men looked utterly broken; many of them were wearing their valises over their shirts, forlornly carrying their saturated serge jackets along with their muddy tools and carbines. They were wet, freezing cold and utterly drained of all hope.

In the end, it was Coleman who broke the hellish drama of silent communication between the animated faces of his officer and his two NCOs. 'It's the camp, it's under attack, ain't it?'

he asked imploringly, his blue eyes open so wide that Bond almost felt moved to tears by his sapper's courage in speaking the truth he could not.

Corporal Denham opened his mouth and raised his right hand to chastise Coleman, but an icy warning grip on the arm from a coldly passive Sergeant Friday quickly dissuaded him.

'We'll just have to see, and do the best we can,' Bond announced at last. He knew it wasn't very original, but what else could he say in the circumstances? 'If the camp is in fact being attacked, the chances are that they outnumber our men by a ratio of ten to one.'

There was a curse and a groan of despair from somewhere in the darkness, which was soon quashed by a swift cuff across the ears. Bond could neither see, nor did he care, who it was. If the truth were told, he felt the same, but it was supposed to be him who encouraged the men in the face of danger, not simply join in with the lamentations.

'We must assume the worst, however,' he continued, raising his exhausted body to a crouching position in an assumption of authority belied by his physical condition. 'It will be hard, but we must assume that all is lost to our men in the camp and act according to our wits. The Zulus do not know we are here, neither do they know how many of us there are and, if we are careful and prudent, they needn't think that there's any fewer of us than there ought to be to relieve the camp.'

Despite his noble discourse, the officer's mind was racing as he modestly acknowledged the whispered assent of the men nearest to him as he drew his revolver, carefully checking its contents and cocking the weapon by snapping back the hammer. The motion was almost painful against the blistered skin of his thumb, and the sharp click as the drum rotated sounded as loud and clear as a pistol shot to the men presently cowering in fear of their lives. They were less than two thousand yards from the camp by now, and about as near to the river as it was reasonably safe to be.

Bond looked at Coleman, who looked searchingly back at Bond, who promptly turned to the despairing faces of Denham and Friday, waiting on their lieutenant to issue them with instructions. What on earth was he to do? They were all shivering from the cold by this time. Their uniforms were utterly soaked through; their toes in their boots frozen solid and bitten by cold from their being so full up with mud and river water during their punishing sojourn. So, what *was* there to be done? To simply launch a mindless counterattack on an indefinite number of warriors in open country would be utterly foolish. Every infantry-based scenario he had undertaken at the academy had involved attacking something or defending it, usually based on a well-documented historical action. There had been nothing, to his recollection, covering forlorn, outnumbered counterattacks in near pitch darkness, with the enemy strength unknown. If the Zulus had, by whatever means or devilry, managed to gain control of the camp, then thirty worn out sappers with only their personal ammunition rations and a sorry absence of cold steel would be of little to no use at all. To break out in the open meant clearly to be butchered.

There was no way in which Bond could ascertain the Highlanders' situation without compromising his own position by cutting out into the open, but then again hiding out in a donga while your company is massacred was hardly the ethos of any solider, let alone an officer. He had thought he heard firing coming from further away but that, he reasoned, was probably just the sound echoing off the mountains, and besides there was no sense in imagining his position to be stronger than was the case. He must think a bit harder. Time was clearly running out, and a decision would have to be made. In desperation, he turned to his sergeant.

Friday, for one, looked completely and utterly helpless, almost as lost as his officer. His breath came and went in long, thin little wisps, and his mouth, when at last he opened it, would emit little more than a high-pitched sound like the boiling of a kettle. Despairingly, he turned to his second NCO.

'Corporal Denham?' Bond demanded, whipping round irritably, and staring at the corporal as if the whole thing was entirely his fault.

Denham was a long-serving sapper of some twenty years with the corps, nine of which he had spent as corporal. Now, his brow darkened with the prospect of having to pronounce upon a situation that his friend and superior seemed unable to judge.

He scratched his black beard and sorrowfully shook his head. 'Ain't my place to say, sir,' Denham responded at last. 'Even if it were, I can't say I should rightly know what to do then, neither.'

Bond, not sure whether to curse his sappers for their apathy or simply fill his own eyes with the tears streaming down Coleman's muddy cheeks, nodded gravely. His clothes stank; the smell of mud and wet was beginning to mingle with the smell of rifle smoke as it drifted across from the camp and causing him the most appalling nauseous sensation. If this was his show, he decided, then it must fall on him to quite literally call the shots if necessary. Something had to be done... there and then.

Chapter Eighteen

Commandant Flambard, despite being known to take physical conditions and the worst of unpredictable situations in his considerable stride, did not enjoy being rained upon. If questioned on the topic, he might well have admitted that the dislike harkened back to his days as a young soldier, when gunpowder and shot were the order of the day and when the former was apt to be ruined by a dangerous amount of water.

Well used to the outdoor life, Flambard was by no means naïve when concerned with the perils of the elements. Almost as soon as the first flash of lightening proceeded the first rumble of thunder, and the first spots of rain had begun to patter on the brim of his slouch hat, the pragmatic commandant had abandoned their trek in favour of a suitable hideout.

Since leaving the main column in the company of thirty men of the Lyndhurst Mounted Rifles, and a further squadron of his own men, Flambard had ridden the land in search of the elusive supply column. By no means a fool, he had ascertained quite early from the various Zulu civilians in the area that at no time had red soldiers passed their homesteads since the main body had defeated the impi at the river. He knew full well that the sappers would still be well entrenched in the earthwork at Fort Penfold, and that the notorious Captain McGonagle would quite likely have taken some alternative route to the one prescribed. With all of this in mind, the practical magistrate had promptly set about scouring the riverbanks for signs of the Highland company, knowing that any officer with an ounce of experience would, failing maps, use them for the basis of his navigation.

By late afternoon however, matters had taken an altogether more sinister course. Riding well ahead of the main body of troops, two scouts of Flambard's Horse had spotted a large body of Zulus moving very rapidly towards the slopes of the mountains overlooking the river. Wondering what on earth an apparently disembodied impi was doing buzzing around the countryside when the main British column was considerably further north, Flambard concluded the warriors must have been looking to cross the river with the intention of attacking Fort Penfold or pushing on as far as Natal.

'Oscaarberg!' he cried. 'They're going to attack my magistracy! We *must* cut them off.'

'Not today, Colonel, surely?' Faunce-Whittington had protested. 'Look at the way the weather's turning. We can't be out in the middle of all this! Why, we might even get struck by lightning if we're not careful!'

Annoyed as he was to retire, Flambard had to concede that the lieutenant was right. They would alter their course for the range of mountains, camp for the night in some caves that the commandant knew existed, and then be able to move off and intercept the Zulus nearer to the crossing at Stockhouse's Drift. By late afternoon they were in sight of the river, and by suppertime, Flambard's Horse and the Lyndhurst men were safely ensconced in the caves below the mountain, trying to enjoy their mealie porridge, tea, and biscuits with the threat of a counter-invasion hanging over their homes.

'We have to stop those men,' Flambard repeated, as he had on countless occasions since he and Faunce-Whittington had bagged the cave with the smallest mouth.

'Try to eat your supper and not worry so, Colonel,' Faunce suggested sympathetically. 'It really doesn't do, you know. Clouds the judgement.'

'Judgement,' Flambard repeated hoarsely. 'It seems the judgement of everyone with more than a crown on his collar has been clouded by this miserable war, from the high commissioner to that bloody old captain we still can't seem able to track down.'

Faunce poured his tea in silence. He did not enjoy Flambard showing fear and chastised himself for being selfish in his expectations: of gruff commands, booming oratory and the steadfast comebacks to his own neurotic doubts and misgivings. What was worse, not once since the news of Isandlwana had Flambard told him he was being foolish about anything, nor rebutted a single suggestion. Suddenly, it all felt very real, and it was not a notion that Faunce felt he enjoyed.

'I expect we shall just have to leave McGonagle and old Socrates, or whatever his name is, to fend for themselves while we stop the Zulus,' Flambard sighed at last. 'I suppose it was to be expected. After all, the man's bent on self-destruction.'

'He's from a very aristocratic clan, you know,' Faunce-Whittington remarked critically, something of the old society gossip popping up from its place of long repression in the officer's brain. 'They're a bit bottom drawer now, but I think there was money... once.'

'Very worst kind, Faunce,' Flambard replied sullenly. 'All they know how to do is fish for some of the year, shoot for another, and drink whisky for the rest.'

'Oh, Colonel, I do hope you're not a radical!' Faunce retorted in alarm.

'Radical? Good God no, bless you Faunce!' Flambard

replied. His great red face lit up with laughter as it rumbled from his belly and shook the water from the roof of the cave. 'I've served Queen and country all my life,' he chuckled. 'I am a simple soldier and a moderate Gladstonian with it. However,' he added severely, 'it is true what I said about McGonagle, nonetheless. The absolute aristocracy and the underclass have one major factor in common, did you know that, Faunce?'

Faunce-Whittington, himself the socially exiled son of a powerful family title of over five hundred years, simply shook his head and remained silent.

'What binds the old gin hag on the steps of a public house to some feckless heir awaiting his inheritance?' Flambard asked rhetorically. 'I shall tell you: neither one knows of any difference, neither understands consequences nor fears them, and neither one knows how to change. Let me explain. The working man is an honest soul. He earns his living, has no time for the moans and grumbles of his brother man, and holds no love for those who shirk. In the same way as the gentry, the small, landed titles and gentlemen of England have been endowed over centuries with a notion, not only of right, Faunce, but responsibility to their people as well. So, the truly upper classes with nothing to do, no betters to judge them and nothing for which to apologise, carry on as if they had nothing at all. With no one to censor them, why should they not?'

'I don't understand, Colonel,' Faunce replied truthfully.

'It is like this, Faunce,' the magistrate resumed patiently. 'The truly genteel are far more radical than many of their lower peers or the rising middle classes. They do more weird and wonderful things themselves, so they are more likely to accept eccentricities in others. It's the same with the underclass, and varies at all stages in between. The lowly pickpocket is endowed with the same inability to be shocked as one who has spent his or her whole life being waited on hand and foot and getting up to *exactly* what they like.'

'I still don't see what that has to do with McGonagle, though,' Faunce returned, sipping his tea with prim disapproval for the commandant's subject matter.

'Poor man has run mad, Faunce,' Flambard replied, himself taking a swig of his tea and gazing meditatively out of the cave mouth and into the rainy darkness. 'He's been an outrage to many for so long, most have simply stopped noticing his own antics or considering his actions. He's spent so long being told he's got it wrong, the poor fellow has become convinced he's the only one who has it right. He's probably doing it as we speak, camped up somewhere, sipping his malt and reciting his awful poems, ranting.'

'Even so, Colonel, all that duty and ancestry must be better than all this new money?' Faunce protested.

'Indeed, Faunce?' Flambard challenged. 'Industrial money is engrained in the palms of hands. Those same hands have spent years working for what they have and understand the value of their labour and what they have spent so much of their lives creating for themselves. It is a creed with which they endow their children. They know their trade, they know what they must do to make a business work well, and by God, Faunce, they've made the nation great in the last hundred years or so.'

As soon as he had eaten and retired however, Faunce-Whittington was back on their earlier topic. 'We *are* a great nation though, aren't we, Colonel?'

'The greatest,' Flambard replied heartily. 'What is more, we are blessed to live in a great age, Faunce, an age of expansion, of discovery and of prowess. Yet a greater time has yet to come, and that is when we shall need the Empire. Imagine the coming together of all these counties – Africa, India, and Asia – all for the common good. Such a commonwealth of riches might stand against any empire on the earth: Russia... Prussia, even. That is why we must incorporate the Zulus and Boers and develop Africa together. Should we unite in peace and common purpose, we might just outlast old England!'

'I thought you admired the Zulus, Colonel?'

'Oh, I do, Faunce, don't ever mistake me,' Flambard replied, setting his empty cup down on a rock beside his improvised camp bed and wagging his finger. 'Yet every empire has its bloodstains, Faunce.'

'Colonel?'

'The crushing, Faunce. The killing time, when King Shaka consolidated the tribes of his people into one nation, one common power, and one common good. In the same way as the Empire has drawn in India, Canada, Asia and now the Africas, Shaka brought all his warriors, their wealth, and their houses together, gave them an identity and turned them into the most terrific force to stand against the whole of the outside world. It was bloody, cruel – there is no room for doubt – but the result far outweighed the evil. Look at them, Faunce. The greatest African nation in history, and the force with which *we* now must reckon. This war has been started, right or wrong. Now one side or the other must end it!'

'We fight for our homes, at least. Civilised life...' Faunce quipped back at him.

'Don't be so hasty, Faunce,' Flambard replied. 'Their nation's morals may not be our nation's morals, I'm not to deny that. Yet they have forged an unimaginably agile army, who presently seem capable of not only defeating modern military technology but have also the ability to threaten our very borders. Borders, I might add, which we crossed to invade *their* home, and borders we now leave poorly guarded against counterattack!'

Faunce went quiet, and Flambard fell to preparing his bed for occupation. There always seemed to come a point in their little standoffs when it was better to simply shut up and simmer down before cordial conversation was fit to be resumed.

'Colonel,' Faunce probed tentatively, when the cold had become so awful that there seemed to be no danger of Flambard leaving the confines of his blankets to get up and hit him, 'won't the Africans, white or black, have something to say about all this confederation, occupation and such?'

'You can't expect them to overturn centuries, perhaps thousands of years, of their way of life and accept the developments of a mere fifty or so,' the commandant replied. 'So yes, I should expect that they will have something to say, Faunce.'

'Are we wrong, then?' Faunce persisted, as the hammering of the rain outside grew even heavier, and the relentless drip of water on the floor of the cave looked set to drive them mad, was silence permitted to prevail.

'As I told you, Faunce, the bigger picture,' Flambard concluded. 'King Shaka sold the port of Natal to the British settlers many, many years before Cetshwayo ever came to be. We must share our advances with all African peoples, but in the meantime, we must trade with those who will accept our ways, and fight with those who can't. It's the same as if the Anglo Saxons, suddenly decided that they no longer wanted those of Roman, Norman, even Celtic blood among their nation, and suddenly arose to throw them out. Centuries of coexistence would be overturned; all those whose forefathers made up Britain would suddenly be treated as foreign. Even the Queen!'

Faunce nodded. 'The irony being, I suppose, that Saxons are Prussians?'

'Broadly, I suppose,' Flambard replied. 'Point is, Faunce, that it all goes beyond simple invasion. We have been settling all over Africa for the last century or more. Children have been born here to families from Europe, who regard themselves as much as Africans as the Xhosa and Zulu. The Zulus are an empire, like the Russians, the Prussians, or us, doubtless smaller, yet forged in blood. Now our two empires conflict.'

Here Faunce-Whittington looked at the commandant. He looked at him long and hard. 'Do you like it then, Colonel?' he asked.

'No, I don't like it,' Flambard replied. 'But then it isn't up to me, is it?'

The lieutenant thought for a moment, then he smiled. After all those years of knowing the man, it was only now, looking at him across a darkened cave in a rainstorm, that he realised what set the man apart from his fellow men. Usually, the commandant he knew was the same man that everyone else did: the big, brave, ostensibly fearless old soldier and irrepressible leader of men of all creeds.

It was his eyes that made the difference; those bruised, slightly turned down and watery grey-blue windows on an old soul who thought more than he said, saw more than he let on, and cared more than he would allow anyone to begin to imagine. The ruddy, scarred, weathered face held within its leathery countenance those wonderful old eyes that spoke to Faunce of a man who had been both a father to the many men who had served under him all those years and all those who did so at the present time. They spoke as well of a man who had been a loving husband to his late, much-lamented wife, a friend and brother to his fellow officers, and a beloved leader to each man below him in rank, quite regardless of the colour of their skin. During his many campaigns, Flambard had commanded troops of all complexions and creeds, many different castes, and many more religious sensibilities. All these facets the man had taken on board, and all over the world there must have been men to look up from their work and say how proud they were to have served with him.

No wonder, he thought, *that Flambard is so loved by his men, so trusted by those close to him, so revered by men who know him, and so envied by those who do not.* How many times, he reflected, had the commandant told him of the young soldier whose baby he and his wife had helped to deliver on the frontier, or how that great man had wept over the body of a drummer boy in the breech at Lucknow?

Brushing away a tear himself as he recollected the sad story, Faunce looked again in wonder at the fearless giant who had for the past twelve years been his friend and father figure, his loaded revolver lying just beside his pillow as he slept.

With such a man as that, he thought, *how on earth can we lose?*

The storm continued to rage. The captain and officers of the Lyndhurst Company came and went. Their soggy grey uniforms and the black velvet of their cuffs and collars seemed to grow darker and wetter with every hour that passed. At one point, a flash of lightening tore through the sky, lighting up the entire cave and rousing both Faunce and the commandant from their sleep. Flambard, when awake, needed to be active. He looked at Faunce, looked out of the cave mouth into the blustery night, and began to empty, clean and reload his revolver. Faunce watched as the bushy eyebrows closed in on one another; those watery blue eyes struggling to cope with the darkness as the commandant squinted over his work.

'I expect you need a monocle,' he suggested.

Flambard never looked up but continued to insert the brass-cased rounds into the chambers of his pistol. 'I have one,' he replied at length, 'but I don't wear it on campaign. I could hardly have it in to ride a horse. The wretched article would simply drop out.'

Faunce went silent for a while, then he changed the subject. 'Colonel?'

'Faunce?'

'Colonel, would you mind if I ask you a question?'

'Not a bit,' Flambard replied, still apparently disinclined to look up.

'Well, I can't seem to fathom what exactly your rank was… in the regular army, I mean,' Faunce began awkwardly. 'I mean, you're a colonel now, but were you a lieutenant colonel or were you a brevet rank? If I may ask?'

For the first time, Flambard looked up from his weapon and laughed. 'God bless you, Faunce. I was nothing so spectacular.'

'You weren't?'

'No, Faunce, I was just a major.'

Faunce, however, was not inclined to let the matter drop until his curiosity had been properly satisfied. 'I'm sorry to keep on, Colonel, but I shan't sleep otherwise.'

'Of course not,' Flambard replied, still giving nothing away.

'Only,' Faunce resumed uneasily, 'I can't understand why, after all your years in the army, they didn't promote you further. Besides, you've always been called *Colonel*.'

'Only since this war, and only by your misnomer, I might add,' Flambard chuckled.

'Well, it's just that Colonel Roystone, Arthur McEnry and even that fellow Henderson succeeded to their colonelcies, and you were better than all of them.'

Flambard said nothing to begin with, but from the way he snapped shut his loaded revolver it soon became painfully apparent that he had wearied of the subject. 'When I was in the regular army it was a different world, and I was a different man,' Flambard explained, breathing a deep sigh, and closing his eyes as if on the brink of some terrible confession. 'Officers bought commissions and promotions like horses. I began my military career at the Royal Hibernian Military School.'

'In Dublin?' Faunce exclaimed incredulously. 'Are you Irish, Commandant?'

'No, Faunce, I'm from Gloucester, but my father was serving with a garrison there at the time. We were very poor, you know.'

'Colonel, I never knew!' Faunce sighed. 'How ever did you afford a commission?'

Flambard opened his mouth to speak, but his intended statement was suddenly interrupted by the clear, unmistakable crackle of rifle fire, apparently no more than a mile away. 'What the devil was that, here at this hour?' he demanded. All thoughts of childhood reminiscences were soon cast down for the present as the huge magistrate sprang from his bedclothes and snatched up his revolver.

'Thunder?' Faunce suggested, all other obvious alternatives being far too distasteful for the young officer to consider volunteering.

'Spitting like that?' Flambard demanded sternly. 'No, Faunce, it's shooting.'

'You mean we're under attack?' wailed Faunce. 'I must get my Swinburne!'

'No, blast you, it's not *us* they're attacking at all!' The commandant was now fully out of bed, his boots tugged on over his cord riding breeches and his shoulder strap slung across the mighty dark blue shoulders as he strode out of the cave.

Horrified, a thrill of hopeless excitement and adrenaline pumping around his large body, Lieutenant Faunce-Whittington grabbed his hat and carbine, before charging off after Flambard and almost smacking his head on the low vault of their improvised bedchamber.

After a brief conference with his officers and the hastily recalled piquets, Flambard was able to ascertain that reports of rifle fire had been heard on and off since late evening, but nobody had been entirely sure of the direction from which the sounds originated. The rain was still lashing across the rocks as Flambard, Faunce-Whittington, and the officers of the Lyndhurst Mounted Rifles scrambled up towards the summit of the escarpment and peered tentatively out across the windswept veldt. Flambard said nothing as they climbed the rocky shoulder, and no one else was brave enough to break the endless sound of the rain and the increasingly ominous sound of distant gunfire by talking. A moment's sweep of the landscape gave the magistrate his answer.

With a deep sigh, which soon developed into a long moan of despair, Flambard turned back to his officers and pointed. 'Look,' he said grimly, as the direction of his finger gradually dictated the direction of the men's view. 'We've been right on top of it the whole time and never known a thing until now.'

'Oh, Lord,' Faunce gasped, genuinely horrified by what he had seen.

Just the other side of the mountain, and the caves beneath wherein they had so long been resting, was a river. About a mile or so from the nek of the mountain was a sandy drift, and about five hundred yards from the water's edge stood a circle of wagons containing several tents. The entire spectacle was lit with the grim flames of a blazing firefight and, from the summit itself, could be heard above the storm the sounds of men engaged in mortal conflict.

'We've found them, Faunce,' Flambard murmured menacingly, as a chill of horrified anticipation rippled through his body like the icy blood in his veins. 'McGonagle and the others. They've been here all the time. Trouble is, now the Zulus have found them as well!'

Chapter Nineteen

Commandant Flambard's troops moved in two sections. The first, commanded by the magistrate himself, consisted of the main body of Flambard's Horse, together with the Lyndhurst men and a small number of mounted Africans. Their objective was to pick their way down the far side of the mountain and, once down, quickly take possession of the deserted outpost and give fire from the cover of the surrounding dongas. The remaining smaller group of Flambard's men, under the command of Lieutenant Faunce-Whittington, took up positions on the flat top of the mountain to provide cover fire.

The section under Faunce-Whittington made good progress and managed to creep down among the boulders of the mountainside.

From their vantage point on the opposite slope, Gideon Knight's men mistook the dark blue uniforms and black irregulars for a fresh wave of Zulus.

Already stretched beyond the limits of his nerves, with the wind howling in his ears and the rain lashing against his red flecked cheeks, Lieutenant Knight instructed his men to turn their attention towards this new threat, presently creeping up on them from the other side of the valley.

Fortunately, poor conditions, combined with the shattered nerves of his sappers and the quick thinking of Faunce, who shouted at his men to duck the instant he espied the redcoats, the potential for further tragedy was averted.

The Zulus in the camp meanwhile, who, by rights at this time should have been looting and enacting their spiritual rites upon the dead, were suddenly being popped at from all sides. As it was, the fire previously directed towards them by Gideon Knight's secure yet essentially marooned piquet had represented little more than an annoyance. The surviving soldiers had become a thorn in the fleshy pride of the now victorious warriors, and several of the younger groups set off in the direction of the mountain, seeking to climb up the slope and put an end to the irritating persistence of the outnumbered men. In the event however, the feeble spattering of bullets from the dwindling stocks of the sappers on high were suddenly augmented by a deafening roar of musketry from apparently every donga for several miles around. Several warriors fell in the first wave, and the sound of horses' hooves, doubtless magnified sevenfold by the surrounding slopes, sealed the bargain entirely.

The warriors threw down their muskets, turned and dashed back to the relative safety of their newly acquired territory, the laager, to take cover from the firing and doubtless complain loudly to their indunas that somebody somewhere wasn't quite playing fair. After sweeping to victory over an entire company of the enemy, the warriors were naturally inclined towards ill humour. The party of men on the mountain had been little more than an embarrassing irritation, but now that they were being enfiladed from apparently the same quarters as that from which the warriors had directed their own assault, plundering the camp no longer seemed so important.

From somewhere deep in the bottom of his boots, Lieutenant Bond found his quaking heart at last. Next, he found his tongue as well as his heart, and set about dictating his plan of campaign to his highly relieved troop of sappers, who crowded attentively around him, quite prepared to obey any order that did not involve squatting in the mud and thinking.

'Take the men down the dongas, Sergeant Friday,' Bond instructed. He had to be clear, authoritative, and at least to appear as though he had a plan. 'I want at least one point of concentrated fire, interspersed by pockets of intermittent fire up and down the line. You will direct, and as each pair of men fire, the next pair will follow and so on, reverberating up and down. Is that clear, Sergeant?'

Friday simply nodded.

Coleman, who had been gazing awestruck at his officer for several moments, as Bond turned to look at him, lit up with a smile that simply glowed with admiration and love.

'Let 'em think there's more of us than there is, sir,' put in Corporal Denham.

'Precisely,' Bond replied, swiftly precipitating Sergeant Friday's inevitable admonishment of the NCO for addressing his officer unsolicited. They hadn't time for those games. 'Which is why, Corporal,' he added quickly, 'I want you upon my command – which incidentally you shall recognise when it comes – to advance.'

Here, the corporal's previously elated expression turned to one of dismay. He was not amused. 'We'll be cut to bits, sir,' the NCO retorted, horrified.

'Solider!' Friday hissed in remonstration.

'Which is also why, Corporal, you will not go until you have my signal,' Bond replied with growing impatience. 'When you receive my command, you will move forward, taking advantage of cover and firing as we practiced on field days. When you get to the donga, I want you to stop, give covering fire for the same advance by Sergeant Friday, by which time we should have driven the attackers out. No more than five hundred yards in, and keep well to your cover as you go.'

'What if we ain't, sir?' Coleman asked quietly.

'Then we shall be in for a stiff time of it,' Bond replied lightly, his offhand response designed to offset his own terror at the potential peril of the situation in which he and his men now discovered themselves. 'Remember, men,' Bond resumed, 'organised file fire up and down the line. No man must be out of time with his comrades, and if any of you do especially well, I'll be happy to recommend you for marksmanship when we get back to Chatham.'

There was a moment's cold pause. Just the mention of Chatham must have conjured up preciously suppressed thoughts of wives, children, and dependents.

That was stupid thought Bond. *I shan't do that again.*

Here, Coleman tugged at the officer's sleeve. Sensing that there was more to come, the brave young sapper once again placed his soft pink lips against Bond's earlobe.

'What about us, sir?' he asked quietly.

Bond looked at him directly, his blue eyes wide open and the revolver cocked and levelling in his hand. 'Jack, you have every right to say no to what I am about to ask. I know you'll tell me you're a soldier, and that I'm an officer and you'll do your duty. I know that already. Rather, I had much preferred that you refuse. It's what I want you to do.'

Coleman shook his head. Bond remained silent for a moment, then he nodded.

'Sergeant, you're in charge. Sapper Coleman and I will follow this donga around as far as we can, then meet up with the river and see if we can get into the camp unspotted. We have our,' he paused, correcting himself, '*I* have *my* pistol, so if you hear me fire it, you know to advance Corporal Denham.'

Bond's words were greeted with a round of nods and grunts of "sir", indicating to their officer that his men knew their tasks. Now it was his turn, this time to lead by example.

They moved through the donga, pausing to listen, ducking as a stray shot ricocheted off a rock or the mound of an anthill. They crept at a stoop, with Lieutenant Bond in front on account of his pistol and the midnight blue colour of his uniform. At one point they paused, and Coleman placed a hand on the officer's shoulder. Bond nearly fainted.

'Sir, there's something I have to ask you.'

Bond said nothing, merely nodding his approval.

'Sir... are you... scared?' Coleman found strength to venture at last.

Bond thought for a moment, then he nodded again. 'Yes,' he replied, 'I'm terrified. But if we don't do something now, there won't be a man amongst us left alive come the morning.'

Coleman managed a weak smile, pushed a brass-cased lead slug into the breach of his rifle, and snapped the breech block shut, cocking it. Then he lodged the butt in the crook of his elbow, tight against his thick right bicep, and moved on.

They were a good deal nearer to the fighting by this time. The rain, so heavy and torrential while they were working, had begun to ease off considerably, and a thick fog hung over everything for miles around. This, when coupled with the ominous pall of white gun smoke, served to aid the two sappers' concealment and mask their advance, for the time being at least.

The sounds of battle seemed to them to be all around now, although something of the fury seemed to have moved yet further away from them. The crackle of gunfire still seemed to hammer their already tortured eardrums with a force more potent than any thunder or lightening, while the mud around their ankles and the sickening sensation that there was nowhere else to go left both men with a fearful feeling of reluctant anticipation.

'I wish we could see them, or at least know where they are,' Coleman whispered bravely. 'I ain't scared no more.' He paused. 'Are you?'

In answer, Bond raised his revolver and crawled forward a few paces.

The air was thick with the sharp, acrid smell of shooting. A peppery scent and something like a struck match seared their nostrils with sulfuric potency.

All around them flashes, bangs and bellows of this foul smoke rippled, cracked, and clung to the air; nauseating, sometimes shocking, sometimes almost consoling by way of its deafening constancy. Suddenly, and before either one of them knew what was happening, Bond and Coleman became suddenly aware of a loud splash, followed by a frantic scrabbling and a mutual gasp of surprise as two Zulus dropped into the donga on the other side. For seconds, their eyes just met and held there.

It was debatable which were the more unnerved. One of the warriors was apparently badly wounded, shot through the knee and almost fit to pass out. He was not, however, too far gone to cry out a warning to his colleague, who sprang into the donga in the wake of his charge and drew back his assegai to strike.

Coleman raised his rifle to fire, but no sooner had he done so the officer had turned aside his muzzle, himself firing off several shots from his revolver, felling them both. An acrid tang of gunpowder clung to their nostrils and stung their eyes. As the smoke cleared, and the painful screeching sound began to evaporate from their eardrums, they knew that their assailants were dead. Neither one made the slightest sound. For some moments Bond watched, mud caked in his fingernails, and the sickening, sensual smell of sweat, mud, water, and this new stench of blood as it welled up from the bodies of his victims seeping into the water around his and Coleman's boots. It seemed as if some terrible claw was drawing its talons across his already expanding chest. The dreadful certainty that he was going to be sick welled up from his stomach, throttling his words in a strangled gulp of fear. A terrible pain laid claim to his head, shutting the lids of his eyes, and bursting in his ears like the sound of a thousand explosions. Briefly, as he thought he heard Coleman say something, his eyes rolled as the officer felt his breath leave his body.

Shocked, terrified and himself hopelessly overwhelmed by the immediacy of the killing, Coleman felt the dead weight of his officer as he fell against his chest in a faint. Casting aside his helmet, sweat droplets of moisture streaming off his glistening blond hair, Coleman gathered up the officer in his arms and struggled back down the donga in search of help.

From his position in the widest part of the donga, his horses clustered together and his dismounted troopers pouring fire through the inky blackness, Commandant Flambard knew that the Zulus would not allow themselves to die in a holding action. With a cry of command, and a single pistol shot as a signal to Faunce-Whittington, Flambard and his men and advanced. If the ripples of gunfire and the dismay at taking casualties so soon after claiming their objective had been upsetting to the exhausted indunas, the ground shaking thunder of hooves signalled the very last straw. The defence was abandoned, and every warrior who did not have to carry some dead or wounded comrade threw down what he was doing and filtered off into the enveloping darkness.

Zulu casualties had been less on taking the camp than abandoning it, and angrily, sullenly, they seemed to melt away, fading into the fog as it crept in around the bodies of the dead.

Upon hearing pistol shots, Sergeant Friday ordered his men to fire. They were spread, as their officer had instructed, out along the dongas in separate pockets of two or three men. When they commenced their reverberating volleys, the ripple of gunfire crackled up and down the line, spitting out smoke and flames and creating the desired effect of a considerably larger liberating force.

Tense, his fingers trembling and his heart in his mouth, Corporal Denham was just about to give the order for his own little party to advance as ordered, when young Coleman came staggering back into view, struggling under the combined burdens of his rifle, ammunition, and Bond. He was clearly in some difficulty, the young officer's body weight and slight height advantage providing a serious obstacle for the sapper's progress through the muddy donga.

'Officer's down, Corp!' cried Coleman, regardless of their situation in the dark. 'Can you help me? He's out!'

'Out?' repeated the corporal, terror mounting with every syllable. 'You mean—?'

'He's hit!' Coleman sobbed, breathing a sigh of relief as the burden of his rifle was passed to another soldier. No one was touching the officer though, that was his job.

'Hit?' Denham found himself repeating monotonically. 'Like, he's been... shot?'

'No, hit!' Coleman retorted with growing indignity, gently resting his officer against the grassy side of the donga. 'Knocked down, got with something, I think. It was all over so quickly, Sarn't,' he pleaded, turning to a swiftly advancing Friday for help. 'Mr Albert killed them both. He was so brave.'

'Hush, boy!' Friday hissed in panic. 'Don't gabble at your corporal.'

'Sorry, Sarn't, sorry, Corp,' Coleman replied, still clinging relentlessly to the unconscious officer in his arms.

'We have to get him back,' muttered the corporal to his sergeant. 'The boy's going to be fit to be tied at this rate, and we can't stay out here for ever.'

Friday simply hummed in response. His large green eyes lit up, and he began to scan the gathering darkness in search of an answer.

Little could either man have known, but just at that moment Lieutenant Faunce-Whittington was making the same feelings known to his senior officer.

Flambard, on the other hand, held no such inhibitions. Drawing his revolver and instructing his men to fix bayonets on their Swinburne carbines, the magistrate drew himself up to his full height and, at the top of his voice, ordered a further, final advance. Trembling with fear and anticipation, Faunce obediently produced and cocked his revolver. *At least I've come this far*, he thought, *so I might just as well go the whole nine yards*.

'I heard fire from the opposite side, sir,' Faunce's sergeant piped up several seconds later. 'From across the water it was, or at any rate somewhere nearby.'

'Oh, really!' the officer muttered impatiently. 'It was probably just the echoes of our own fire off the rock faces. Make yourself useful and go fetch those redcoats down from off the cliffs, there's a good fellow.' His orders were instantly countermanded, however, as the flapping officer found himself looking into the watery blue eyes of a seriously irritated commandant.

'No, Faunce!' he boomed, heedless of their situation in the darkness. 'If Sergeant Behr thought he heard shooting, it might well be worth taking into account.'

Faunce looked pained.

'Well, it's hardly likely to be the Zulus, Faunce!' Flambard barked in annoyance. 'Listen carefully... there!' he exclaimed. 'Can't you hear it too, Faunce?'

'Oh yes, Colonel, I can!' replied the officer, straining his ears as the steady clap of the Martini-Henry sounded over the thumping of his own heart.

'That's organised fire, Faunce. Some of them must have survived!'

'Oh, Colonel, is it true?' Faunce cried in delight. 'Come on then, we must get them in!'

'Down, man!' bellowed the commandant, seizing the lieutenant's shoulder belt and dragging him back down to earth as the bullets ripped through the canvas only a few hundred yards away. 'They don't know we're here yet, so they might just as likely start shooting us for Zulus.'

Flambard thought quickly. Then, gradually, he rose to a crouching position in the donga. Whatever Faunce had been expecting the resourceful commandant to do next, nothing could have prepared him for the stentorian boom that shook the ground from under him and seemed to bounce back and forth the very mountains around their position.

Lieutenant Bond was just beginning to come round when the deep, clear, unmistakably British male baritone roared like the wind across the open veldt.

'Ceeeeease fiaaaar!'

'What the hell was that, Sarn't?' Corporal Denham gasped in surprise. Even Friday couldn't shout like that on a good day.

'Language!' hissed Friday. 'We must revive the officer. Call the men in, Corp,' he added, before projecting his own, considerably higher pitched order for the sappers to end their volleys.

Taking advantage of the distraction, Coleman stooped over his officer in the mist and, gently removing his helmet so as not to hurt him, leaned over Bond and kissed him on the forehead, whispering, 'Please wake up, sir,' in plaintive tones.

Bond, who had been alternately swimming in and out of consciousness since the sound of Flambard's resonating command, suddenly felt the warm sensation of the young sapper's lips on him like a miraculous touch, lifting the chill from his body and causing him to open his eyes.

Coleman groaned aloud from relief. 'Were you hit, sir?' he

asked in concern.

Bond, still unable to speak, simply shook his head and continued to gawp at Coleman in delight, horror, and amazement.

'Sarn't, Corp, come quickly!' Coleman called out triumphantly. 'Mr Albert's alive, and he's waked up!'

'Jesus!' cried Denham in surprise. 'Hallo, sir, we thought we'd lost you.'

Such was the incredulity of Friday, coupled with relief that he would no longer have to remain in command, that he completely ignored his subordinate's worst blasphemy to date on account of his officer's miraculous recovery.

If Bond's mind was a whirlpool, his legs were even less substantial as he struggled to retrieve their use. 'What... happened? Jack, Jack!'

'I'm fine, sir.' Coleman beamed. 'We heard voices. They're alive!'

'Boy saved Mr Albert,' Friday assured him. 'All's well, camp's not taken after all. Someone called out just now.'

'Well, thank heaven for that,' Bond breathed, closing his eyes in sweet relief.

The reality, however, was to prove far more disturbing than anything they could possibly have imagined.

Chapter Twenty

As soon as the shooting had stopped, and the reports of gunfire had died away like the call of a distant bugle, the sombre commandant rose to his feet and listened intently for a minute. Then, slowly and with deliberate action, he raised his revolver above his head and stepped up onto the grassy side of the donga wherein his men were sheltering.

'Now listen carefully,' he said quietly to those nearest him. 'I am quite sure we are not in any danger. However, I want you all to watch me the whole time. Watch my movements and, should you see me lower my hand for any reason or at any time, you are to take cover and await my orders. Is that understood?'

There was a ripple of excitement as the order was conveyed down the line in the form of whispers. Everyone closed in a pace and, as the world grew so still that all one could hear was the creaking of the leather boots, or the rustle serge as the commandant's arm went up above his head, that great man stood up above the mist. Taking large, slow paces forward, Flambard mounted the side of the donga and began slowly to advance on the smoky silhouettes of the gutted campsite.

Faunce-Whittington was the first to follow, creeping along behind his steadfast leader at a wary pace, his revolver aimed searchingly into the darkness.

Then, as the paces went from five, to six to seven and eight, the remaining men rose from their positions and began to advance in their awesome numbers across the lonely ground.

At the same time as the bold commandant was advancing into the unknown territory of their lost encampment, Lieutenant Albert Bond and his sappers were steadily taking the same course, albeit from a different direction. They moved as one, with Bond at the head, armed as he was with his revolver, followed closely by Friday and the inseparable Coleman. As they closed in on the silent camp, the scene around them began to take the form of one of the fashionable horror novels so popular at home.

They were cold, damp, and afraid as all around them thin little veils of mist clung to the earth, creeping around their boots, and obscuring all vision much below their knocking knees. It hung in ghostly white mantles over the deep, glistening pools of rainwater that filled the wagon ruts, so recently cut and thereby so chilling a reminder of all that had so lately happened. Valiantly they pressed on, every footstep hissing and sinking into the unforgiving mud, oozing through the cracks in their boots and weighting down their tired bones with the consistency of lead.

At one point Bond raised his hand as if to indicate a halt, advancing but a few paces by himself before signalling for his men to come on behind him. Gradually, as they advanced, with their fingers inching nervously towards their triggers, the images of horrific truth began slowly to emerge around them. The pall of smoke and fog began to drift, almost as if the spirits of the dead were already at liberty and, thus disturbed, had sought to move away from them at speed, wafting through the remnants of the camp and filtering away in the night. Vague suggestions of the shapes and horrors of battle gradually dredged up to greet them as the fog cleared. Coils of smoke still rose and trailed away from the dormant rifles, while the departing pall lapped against the canvas of the nearby wagon tents, waves in a sea of gloom against some lonely harbour wall. Even as he took yet another pace forward, Bond suddenly felt his foot touch something solid. Scarcely daring to look, yet unable to avert his gaze, the officer brought his men to a halt where he stood, before gradually sinking to his knees amid the sodden grasses. Feeling the ground in front of him like some poor blind old woman in search of a needle, Bond moved his hand around until the very tips of his outstretched fingers met something firm, smooth, and deathly cold.

Hardly daring to breathe now, let alone look, he groped a little further until his touch met with the rounded contours of that which he knew could only be one thing: a human face. His fingers moved a little further still, sensing first the tender, parted lips, then the wide, flat nose and unmistakable African features. He almost wretched as fingers fell upon the open eyes, soft, still wet, and horribly squashy to the touch. With a shudder, he moved his hands across the brow until his fingers located a small, deep, round hole in the middle of the corpse's forehead. The wound told of a direct hit from a modern rifle and, to his horror, Bond realised that he was kneeling in a pool of this dead man's disembodied brain matter. He was nearly sick on the spot. Instinctively, Coleman moved forward a pace.

'What is it, sir?' he asked innocently.

Bond could find no stomach to answer. The death grimace glinted in the dark before him and, with an effort, the officer managed to rise and gesture for his men to advance in close order. The scene was taking on the heady tinge of an induced nightmare. All they could see within the periphery of their limited vision were the bodies of men, animals, and the mutilated remains of people they had known by association. Shot, stabbed, bloodied, with tangled limbs of men cut down in their tracks and left to cool amid the human debris of their friends and enemies, utterly regardless of age, rank, or colour.

At one point, Coleman saw what his hideously overworked imagination fancied a ghoul. Dressed in red serge and tartan trews, his orange beard in startling contrast to the luminous pallor of his lifeless skin, hung an old sweat of McGonagle's Highland Company. He was placed in a crouched position, with his back against a wagon and his arms stretched out on either side of him in a gesture that looked horribly like an invitation to embrace. As they drew closer, the sappers could see that his glassy eyes were frozen wide open, and that the yellow teeth were clamped shut across his red tongue, which was lolling from one side of his mouth. Coleman gave a yelp, then dropped his rifle and took an involuntary step backwards. Before he knew where he was, yet another limb concealed from him by the fog had caught him off guard. He stumbled backwards and, with nothing to save him from falling, flung out his arms on either side of him and cried out for help. In seconds, a pair of strong arms had been thrust under his, and to his relief, Jack felt his blond head fall against something firm.

Bond, having sprung forward to catch the boy as he fell, now clung onto him for dear life, holding the young sapper close to his chest and whispering tender words of comfort and assurance.

Reinforced by the embrace, Coleman looked up in terrified wonderment. 'Is he— Oh, Christ, sir... that *man*!'

'It's all right,' Bond retorted gently, raising his revolver arm to point. 'Look.'

With another gasp and a sob, Coleman realised that the poor dead soldier had been speared to the wagon, and that the shaft was now protruding from him.

'You knew him,' Bond whispered reassuringly. 'That was one of Uncle Alec's men.'

Coleman composed himself a little and nodded.

'Come on, steady now.' Bond managed to sound almost bright as he reassured the young sapper. 'Sergeant Friday—' He paused.

A sound had begun that filled all of them with a helpless terror. They all listened, rigid with horror as that which purported to be a single, clearly toned bell sounded its doleful peel with steady repetition throughout the silenced camp. Each man went cold, hairs stuck up on the backs of necks and even Sergeant Friday was heard to whisper a prayer as it echoed through the mist, off the sides of the wagons and deep into the very inner chasms of their fear. There seemed to be no earthly explanation, and no one wanted to offer one.

Coleman shut his eyes and hugged his rifle. Bond, similarly more disposed towards the corporeal rather than the moral for comfort and protection, cocked his revolver and aimed the muzzle into the darkness, listening intently to every mournful chime.

'That ain't Zulus,' murmured a cowering Friday, convinced that the hand of God himself had been moved to strike a funereal rhythm for the dead of this terrific battle.

Several of the Irish sappers crossed themselves more than once and some were even heard to whimper openly, albeit out of sight.

At last, it was Denham who solved the mystery. With a strangled gulp that was clearly somewhere between a sigh of relief and a muted sob, he tapped the officer on the shoulder and pointed about twenty yards in the direction of one of the wagons. Bond closed his eyes and cursed himself for his own superstition. For there, suspended from a spit, hung a row of cooking pots and pans, apparently washed, and left in readiness for the following morning's breakfasts, left swinging like lifeless limbs in the breeze.

They were almost in the centre of the laager now, and by the aid of a lately emerged and chillingly clear moon, were able to see something of the unhappy fate of their camp. All around them lay the bodies of sappers and Highlanders, together with a pitifully small number of the enemy. Nothing stirred, apart from the odd wisp of smoke or the resigned thud as a rifle dropped from lifeless hands to the earth.

To Coleman, eyes wide and fixed with horror, it seemed as if they had all paused in some terrible game, as if the smoking guns and the swinging limbs might suddenly return to life and resume their furious fight, just as soon as the moonlight had passed over them. It was almost as if they had grown shy, and that the reality of their carnage could somehow be lost in this childish pretence at sleeping where they lay. Coleman hated the silence, and longed to break it by firing his rifle, or kicking one of the nearby corpses that littered the field, stirring them into action and ridding the place of that dreadful stillness. There was little but a dim sense of reality about the whole sorry spectacle, but nobody minded. Reality, as they had once known it, was an illustrated newspaper at home, *this* was the stuff of nightmares. In silence, the remaining sappers came on.

The moonlight lit the way by this time and, as well as the grotesque spectacles already discovered, the lifeless forms of the surprised sentries could be seen slumped about the charred and blackened remains of what had been their campfires. It was only a matter of time before they came upon one of their own.

Sapper Whelan, moving steadily forward amid the ruins of

his tent, inadvertently dislodged the body of a comrade. He was dressed in a long greatcoat and had evidently been told to relieve one of his mates on sentry duty. This poor sapper had clearly died as he was stooping to fasten his boots, because the stab wound was placed right in the centre of his back. This was not the worst part. As Whelan reached out and cautiously turned over the boy, he was suddenly heard to let out a shout.

Bond turned from examining the wreckage of a supply wagon, only to witness possibly the most horrific sight ever known to a solider unfamiliar with their adversaries' post-combat rituals. The young sapper had been stabbed, that much was clear enough. Yet when the voluminous shroud of the bloody greatcoat fell away, it soon became clear that the soldier's stomach had been deliberately sliced open, leaving the intestines and internal organs open to view and, as it seemed, fit to tumble out at any moment. Whelan cried out again, but his vent was lost amid the terrible moans, sobs and guttural wrenching noises made as the rest of the men succeeded, by degrees, in discovering the enormity of the garrison's crushing defeat by the overwhelming Zulus. Not a soul failed to wince.

'All of them, Jack,' Bond sighed in disbelief. 'Sappers, Highlanders, Africans. All of them cut like this.'

He halted over the words as he stabbed with his finger, pointing in mystified curiosity at the horrible gash wounds inflicted to the stomachs of the overpowered troops. All had been stabbed several times, and many had clearly been subject to what appeared to be a bizarre and superfluous butchery.

Also apparent as the fog lifted was the feeble nature of many of the last stands put up by the doomed defenders. Pathetic little groups of two or three men, sometimes with no more than one rifle between them, were in evidence, either slumped across the beds of wagons, driven into corners amid bags and boxes, or laying in an orderly row across the bloody ground. Some were even strung out in small rows, as if the rank-and-file fire of so small a number could somehow offset the ferocity of so terrible an onslaught. Not for a moment did it occur to Bond that anyone of *his* could be among the dead.

The smell was utterly unspeakable, and the ground gurgled hellishly as the rain soaked in amid the blood and gore. Ammunition boxes lay broken open, men and animals lay slaughtered within feet of one another, and one or two of the vanquished campfires still hissed and spluttered pitifully as the last dying embers fizzled out amid the damp, death, and misery.

'What are we going to do, Sarn't?' Denham muttered to Friday, as the two of them stood gazing vacantly at the bodies of two of their own comrades in the doorway of a bell tent.

Friday simply shook his head. It seemed to him as if the ground were seeking to swallow up the very essence of her murdered sons, and the thought made him start up a-wheezing all over again.

'Shan't be any sleep in this place again,' he said ominously. 'Be many a soul set to wander abroad tonight, there will.'

'Do you mind, Sergeant?' Bond chided irritably, mindful of the shuddering Coleman.

'They won't be at peace?' Denham asked of Friday.

'Ain't for us to say or not,' Friday retorted, grimly looking over the carnage and resting his rifle on a pile of ruined mealie bags. 'Many here died godless. One thing I do know, Corp, they ain't going to let them get away with this.'

'So oughtn't they, an' all!' Denham cursed. 'I tell you something, Sarn't, I ain't going to rest until we've seen them given this back for seven times what they've done to us.'

Friday nodded portentously and gave amen.

'That will do, thank you, both,' Bond snapped angrily. 'Enough campfire talk.'

Fear takes different people in different ways. For some it creeps up, the culmination of a protracted period of thought or worry, finally merging into that dreadful realisation that something is truly going to happen to you. For others it is almost instantaneous, jumping out and seizing the unhappy sufferer by the very throat, leaving no pause for breath or consideration. When fear caught up with Lieutenant Bond, in that already dreadful pale moonlight, littered with the corpses of friends and subordinates, it came in a form of a muffled cry from somewhere across the other side of the camp. Involuntarily, just as Coleman had done several moments before, Bond took a step back. This time, his unwilling passage landed him, not in the arms of his brave young sapper, but firmly in the middle of a gutted private. His foot sank to ankle depth amid the slippery mass of the poor soldier's intestines, with an audible squelching sound that might otherwise have been comical, were it not for the horrendous circumstances of its conception. He gave a cry as a fountain of blood squirted into the air and showered his patrol jacket. Just as he was beginning to feel his own insides as they eased the contents of his stomach into his mouth, the reason for this sudden alarm call became apparent and Bond found himself frozen in the motion of vomiting. For there, through the darkness and just outside the piercing rays of moonlight they all could clearly see figures emerging from the dark shadows and mists, which still clung to the dongas around the laager.

Bond, his heart hammering faster and faster, could find nothing to do but simply remain where he was and cock his revolver again in readiness for whatever was to come.

Frozen to the spot, the sappers were compelled to follow

their officer's example and keep perfectly still. As they looked, they beheld the wide, horn-like brim of the hat, the great claw held aloft above his head, apparently jabbing at the moon with his finger. Only when the figure stepped out of the shadow and into the direct pool of moonlight did the combined sighs and even shouts of joyous recognition resound in that hitherto quiet and desolate place.

Coleman looked across at Bond, the image of abject terror plain and apparent on his face as the approaching apparition lumbered towards himself and his officer.

'It's all right, Jack,' Bond cried out in relief. 'Can't you *see* who it is?'

All around the faces of the sappers were simply lighting up. Pictures of relief were painted across every single one and, after the stress and horror of the previous few hours, many gave in completely and found themselves reduced to tears of relief, and even dry, mirthless laughter. Each sapper watched as Bond moved slowly to the centre of the laager, while the unmistakable form of Commandant Flambard, his revolver arm stretched aloft and followed by Lieutenant Faunce-Whittington, warily advanced from outside the perimeter. With a ceremonial slowness like a parade drill, the men themselves hung back while their officers approached each other, both groups carefully picking their way across the laager so as not to further defile the already mutilated dead of a battle in which they had taken no part.

Coleman on the other hand was by no means so bashful. He was always sticking close to his officer from now on, and no one was getting around him so easily.

From the farther end of the camp, Gideon Knight and his ragbag piquet of nine men could be seen cautiously approaching the scene of the gathering, the look of abject shock evident on their weathered faces as they moved towards the camp.

Faunce-Whittington gasped. All around them now the images began to form, and the thinly veiled horrors broke forth from the soft mantle of fog to reveal the true carnage that the last few hours had witnessed in that lonely place.

Tears ran down the large lieutenant's face as he heard the commandant murmur a prayer for the dead and saw the still curling wisps of wood smoke from the guttered campfires, and the tops of the once hospitable bell tents, which now rose from the enveloping darkness like gravestones.

Bond and Flambard met in the middle. For a few moments, the young sapper officer did not know what to make of it all. Then the commandant stretched out his hand, and Bond found himself seizing it and grasping it with all the conviction and genuine gratitude of a man who less than half an hour before had imagined himself to be completely alone.

'Hello, Colonel.'

'Lieutenant Bond! Thank God you and your men are still alive. How on earth did this happen, do you know?'

Bond shook his head forlornly, and suddenly all the exhaustion, terror and physical demands of the previous twenty-four hours seemed to catch up with him. With a moan, he stumbled forward and almost fell into the arms of the burley commandant. Coleman was on him in seconds.

'I'm so sorry, sir,' he whimpered. 'Mr Albert was wounded you see. We met some of the Zulus coming down our donga and—'

'All right, all right. Compose yourself,' Faunce-Whittington told the young sapper gently.

He had not forgotten those blue eyes from Oscaarsberg, nor had he forgotten the enigmatic, beautiful young soldier who loyally assisted his officer with the initial crossing under fire, way back in those safe, optimistic days holed up in Fort Flambard.

'Bond, listen carefully, man,' Flambard instructed. 'How many men have you left? I know it's hard, but we must think quickly if we're to stand a chance out here tonight.'

'Just over thirty, myself included,' Bond replied groggily, as Faunce attempted to pour a half bottle of brandy down his parched throat.

Flambard was categorical. 'Forget about including yourself,' he said firmly. 'You and your batman get some rest. You're exhausted and may both have grave work ahead. Oh for goodness's sake, man, don't give him the brandy!' he cried in alarm, causing Faunce-Whittington to yelp in fright and almost drop the bottle. 'Poor fellow needs water!'

At the mere mention of water, poor Coleman could hardly contain a wistful squeaking noise as it came into his throat, and his plaintive blue eyes searchingly gazed up at the irregular officer, seeming to him an appeal for charity. Coleman, who had long since learned that switching from tough street talk among his peers to the supplicant, "deserving poor" look that had occasionally filled his belly when dealing with clergy and other worthies, did so this time involuntarily. That was it. One look at the exhausted little-boy-lost, and Faunce was on the case. Pretty soon, both Bond and his devoted batman were wrapped in blankets, and sipping hot coffee hastily boiled up by the waiting troopers, while the dismounted irregular troops began to rummage around for the necessities of a meal.

'Embrasures wide open as harbour mouths,' Sergeant Behr of Faunce-Whittington's troop remarked to the captain of the Lyndhurst Mounted Rifles. 'What with that and them fires, the Zulus must have seen them a mile off and strolled in!

Professionals? Huh!'

The officer said nothing, but merely nodded in agreement. This show had turned into a shameful bloodbath for the regulars, and he for one was glad to have been kept out of it.

'Does anyone have any clear idea of what happened yet?' Flambard asked of the exhausted sapper officers.

Neither one managed a response.

Bond was utterly defeated. His hair and clothes were covered in mud and blood, he was unrecognisable from the bodies that littered the laager, and the horrific truth of what had happened in his absence was refusing to sink into his exhausted brain. He merely closed his eyes and shook his head.

Knight sighed heavily. If the truth be told, the officer was utterly stricken by the course that events had taken in his absence. Not only had the outcome of the battle shocked and horrified him as much as any man present, but he also resented the hand that fate seemed once again to have dealt him. After all, he reflected bitterly, what had he done wrong? Gone up a mountain to call in a piquet on the orders of McGonagle, whence he had promptly been trapped and, with less than twenty rounds per man, forced to lay up and watch as his friends and comrades had been ignominiously defeated.

'They just came out of the ether,' he told Flambard hopelessly. 'One minute all was well, then there were reports of musketry from every side down below, and the next thing I knew there were shields and spearheads dancing around inside the camp.'

The two officers watched as the commandant scratched his head and considered their imposed predicament. Despite his rank, Flambard still habitually wore the silver stars of majority on his dark blue jacket collar, and there was something undeniably comforting in the old soldier's experience and bearing. Retired or not, there was no man anyone there would rather have had in command, including, at that moment, Gideon Knight.

'I think I see what must be done,' Flambard announced at length. 'Since you might just as well know now as tomorrow, I believe the impi that attacked your camp was well on its way to crossing the border into Oscaarsberg. Your action here, whatever its outcome, has undoubtedly had the effect of forestalling them. Whatever else they may believe, they've received a sting tonight, and many of their number won't be waking tomorrow to follow up the kill with another. For that we have undoubtedly to be grateful, and it does serve to help our position a little.'

Knight looked pained. 'What do you suggest, Commandant Flambard?' he asked in tones which, had the burley old magistrate had a mind to notice, did little to defer to his seniority, or the miraculous way in which his forces had arrived to save the day.

'What I recommend, Lieutenant, is to hold,' Flambard resumed, pointedly ignoring the interruption, as well as the implied snub. 'We have the cover of darkness, true enough, but so do they and, I might add, to a much greater extent. They know where we are, and this ground. We know no such of them and must therefore use deception to create a diversion. Faunce and his men will run those wagons in, as they should have been before,' he added pointedly. 'Next, we shall relight the campfires within the laager confines. We shall then retire to a man, taking what shelter we can among the caves and rocks of the mountain, at least until daybreak when we might be in a better position to decide what to do.'

Bond was too weak to answer, and Knight, for all his lack of enthusiasm, found himself unable to see any alternative but compliance. Both officers wearily nodded their assent, and Bond was spirited off by a waiting trooper to have his wound examined and subsequently re-billet with Coleman in the caves overlooking the drift.

Under such circumstances, no one gave a thought to who slept where or, more to the point, with whom.

'Faunce, be a good fellow and see poor Bond has all that he needs, will you?' Flambard requested of his charge.

Faunce nodded willingly and, turning to go, paused to ask whether the Zulus would attack again.

Flambard shook his head. 'I cannot say,' he replied gloomily. 'I fancy not. They will have their own wounded and their post-combat rituals to observe, which are of grave importance to them. However, if we leave the fires out as decoys and post sentries to watch over the caves all night, we should be all right. It's going to be grim, Faunce, make no mistake, but with a bit of luck we *may* live to see sunrise!'

The large lieutenant raised a watery smile and toddled off about his business.

Flambard paused for a while and shook his head sadly. He had seen some sights before, but if this was the way this war was going to end up, he was damned sure he didn't want to see another one. Some minutes later, he called together the officers in charge of the Lyndhurst men, together with Faunce-Whittington and his own colonial officers, who had subtly been probing the campsite in search of clues to the disaster.

'Any idea, Austin?' he asked of the captain.

'Looks rather bad, sir, for the regulars, I mean,' he replied.

Captain Austin Tyler had lived in the colony all his life, had fought in the last African war and was also the secretary of the settler's association. A former schoolmaster, he looked at Flambard with the same loyal eyes of so many men, but even the awe in which he held the formidable magistrate could not conceal his utter disgust at the turn of events.

'All the Scots are dead, Colonel,' Faunce interjected. 'We found one or two of the poor devils as far out as our donga, who must have been caught in the crossfire when we opened up on the camp.'

'Officers?' Flambard enquired, although he already seemed to know the answer.

'Two, sir,' came the halting reply from one of the lieutenants under the command of Captain Tyler, seeming somehow unsure of how he should proceed with his report.

Flambard nodded gravely. After all those years he was just as well qualified to ascertain what he was not being told, as well as to digest what he was. 'It's a hard morning those poor boys have ahead of them tomorrow,' he announced to the assembled officers. 'I just hope that some of their friends managed to get away in the chaos. Have we organised a search party, Faunce?'

The lieutenant shook his head. 'The Africans won't do it, Colonel,' he replied simply. 'Not with corpses still turning up here, there and everywhere. We're sickened enough,' he added wisely, 'so they must be fairly terrified, both of unquiet spirits and of further attacks by the Zulus.'

Again, the old commandant simply nodded and sighed. 'Ah well,' he said at length. 'Poor boys that they are, identifying sappers is still their own officer's grim responsibility. Now we must attend to ours. Captain,' he added, turning to the Lyndhurst officer. 'I want piquets left on the mountains overnight, and some mounted men as far out as safety will permit. Have some more men on the opposite side of the river as well, just to be sure.'

The officer nodded and duly departed to do his bidding.

'Faunce.'

'Colonel?'

'I want you to take care of the survivors for me, do you understand?' Flambard told the officer severely. 'This has been their first close quarter action; they've all lost friends, and many have suffered through this terrible business. Bond,' he added, 'has probably suffered the most, little he may know it. His ordeal is far from over.'

'Doesn't he know yet?' Faunce enquired sincerely, both understanding it was Captain McGonagle to whom they referred.

Flambard sighed. 'There seems to be little room for doubt that the man himself was one of the officers. It's just that I can't bear to think about it. One of the dead was certainly an officer from the colour of his shirt, and Lieutenant De Tourney thought they found another in amongst the tents. Either way, we must take care of them until the morning, when we shall all have some hard decisions to make.'

'About Oscaarsberg, Colonel?'

'About everything,' replied the commandant briefly. 'Now come on, Faunce, we have a lot to do before we can retire. Where is Bond, by the way?'

'Retired,' Faunce replied. 'He's in the driest cave we could find, although most of his things were ruined when the camp was overturned, so he's with his batman who presumably has their blankets, kit and such.'

'Good for him,' Flambard replied distractedly. 'It's going to be one hell of a night.'

'You called, Commandant?'

Flambard turned in surprise. Knight must have mistaken the use of his name as a cue for a summons. It was a confusion the sapper officer had sought to create, being somewhat ill disposed towards waiting for someone to include him in their council. Even so, the wise commandant was well used to ambitious young officers, their stratagems and pretentions. The knowledge that Lieutenant Knight did not hold with being superseded married all too veraciously with the implied condescension.

'*Mr* Knight,' Flambard commenced patiently. 'This is the second occasion you have chosen to address me as though my rank were some quaint honoraria. I feel for your pain, and the doubt you must now be feeling over things done and... *not* done. You may be a regular officer, but may I remind you that I once was as well and, furthermore, that I rose to field rank upon retirement. If you find the title of commandant unpalatable, then I suggest you call me major. Do we understand one another, Lieutenant?'

Knight went the colour of his undress frock, but no one could see in the dark. 'M-my apologies,' he stammered at length, highly relieved that there were no other spectators.

Public humiliation was not the commandant's norm, but having already been coaxed down cowering from a mountainside by Faunce-Whittington, Knight was not prepared to risk further ignominy by further arousing the magistrate's ire. Besides, he needed advice. The disaster was down to McGonagle – no military court in the empire could possibly find otherwise – but in the aftermath, Knight was bankrupt for ideas. There were no medals to be had for surviving a massacre, especially not for officers. Quite the reverse, in fact.

Flambard seemed to sense this apprehension and softened a little. 'No one can blame you, Lieutenant,' he told him kindly. 'Sad day as it is, we know full well that this must lay squarely at the feet of the officer in charge. It's a difficult position, second-in-command. Believe me, I know,' he added. 'So, try not to be too hard on yourself.'

Knight managed a tight smile and nodded. At least this old man knew the ground and wasn't likely to become a liability like the last one. 'Sir,' he piped up. 'Thank you.'

'No trouble,' Flambard replied. 'Just don't be too quick to judge the dead, that's all. I know what you must be thinking right now, but whatever else happened here tonight, those who stayed answered for their mistakes with their lives, as did many more who bore no blame. No one could ask more, and no man living is fit to sit in judgement.'

Knight went very quiet and walked away in search of a cave. If no one wanted to hear what he thought right now, he would just have to save it for the inquiry. Assuming he could bring himself to defame the dead further, in avoidance of his own shame.

Chapter Twenty-One

The sky was very nearly pitch-black when the lantern, swung by a helpful Faunce-Whittington, lit the steps to the cave in which Sapper Coleman and the blankets awaited.

Bond turned at the foot of the short climb and thanked the volunteer officer for his help.

'Terrible night,' Faunce replied, clearly slightly embarrassed and trying hard not to look at the blood and mud on the sapper's face and clothes.

Bond nodded and turned away.

The cave itself was a curious structure, of none too comfortable dimensions and very little cover, the roof being a mere three-foot or so from the most extreme stalactite to the smooth, hard surface of the rocky floor. Sheered, apparently by the elements from the face of the mighty cliff, to lay in it felt like being sandwiched between two very large slabs, down which the rainwater trickled relentlessly. Consequently, it was only after considerable wriggling that the two sappers were able to lay their heads on their improvised pillows, namely their numb forearms, and stretch out their legs without too much pain or discomfort. It was too dark and therefore dangerous to try and find one another, so they just held hands.

The rain continued unmercifully throughout that night, and now and then icy sheets would lash across the mouth of the cave and saturate them further, gushing down amid the rocks around them and causing the most chilly and unpleasant sensations as they tried to sleep. Thunder continued to crack overhead, and at one point the ferocious lightening lit up the cave with such alarming brilliance that both men sat bolt upright.

The flash also illuminated Coleman's face, albeit for an instant; that anguished, pitiful, rain-soaked and chilled face, which reminded Bond so painfully of a terrified animal taking shelter from the raging storm.

Reaching out instinctively, Bond had, however neglected to allow for the terrible dreams besetting the poor young soldier since his assault by Simonides. Consequently, when the officer stretched out to him, and Coleman recoiled like whip, the shock caused both to overbalance, and both promptly tumbled backwards into the darkness amid cries of surprise and horror. Coleman landed on his back with yet another yelp, and Bond, to his conflicting emotions, found himself landing almost on top of him, the boy struggling and wailing as the two of them subsided somewhere dry, grainy, and soft. Bond breathed yet another sigh of relief. Whatever they had landed on was more comfortable than those agonising rocks, and whatever it was, it seemed an improvement on nothing. Reaching out an arm, he managed to locate the trembling Coleman. Their uniforms, already soaked and dried to their bodies, were now wet through again, and the two men found themselves shivering violently as they pressed into each other's arms.

'Will we ever get out again?' Coleman whimpered through chattering teeth.

The shock of the sudden flash and subsequent darkness had shaken him out of whatever wits he had left, leaving the poor boy with the terrifying thought that he had gone blind. He could feel the grit in his hair, and it moved.

'Right now, I don't care,' Bond replied, squeezing him even tighter. 'I don't care where we are, and I don't care if this soft stuff is wormcast, just so long as we can keep warm and get some sleep here.'

Coleman, too frightened to reply and too lost in love to want anything different, simply pressed his body to Bond's and did his best to absorb his warmth.

Smells of wet wool, serge, sweat, mud, blood and damp clung to the air. The chill and stink assaulted their nostrils, as they shook and trembled in unison, clinging to each other with every part of their cold contorted bodies.

'When I was a nipper, at times like this I wanted my ma,' Coleman whimpered softly. 'Now, I just want you, but more. Ain't that queer, Mr Albert?'

Bond shook his head in the darkness. 'There have been times when I thought I wanted mine,' he replied. 'I still mourn, yet I know I'm lucky to have what I've got here, now, even amid all this.'

Coleman's brow puckered. 'You do mean *me*, right, sir?'

'Well, I didn't mean the sand,' Bond chuckled, squeezing his brave bundle even tighter than ever. 'Now you hang on to my dripping wet coat, and I'll hang on to yours, and between us we might just keep warm until the sunrise.'

There followed a short silence, and to his joy, Bond realised that Coleman had dropped off to sleep in his arms.

Chapter Twenty-Two

The following morning saw the sun rise ominously over Shorthouse's Drift.

Gradually, as the piercing rays of amber sunlight came filtering within the soggy debris of their last night's resting place, at least two of the drift's former garrison were well pleased to feel its gentle caresses against their skin.

Bond was the first to open his eyes; breathing in the damp morning mist, he thanked providence for their deliverance. For the dawn had found them together once more, huddled in each other's arms under the protective outcrop of rock which had proved so unlikely a place of comfort and shelter during the horrific events of the previous night.

Jack, his sleek blond head laying against Bond's broad chest, wriggled into a more comfortable position, and gazed adoringly up at his officer through bleary eyes and a damp, silky fringe. Only when the relief of seeing him smile again had brought the lieutenant fully to his senses did the rather more sickening smells of damp cloth, stale sweat, and the inevitable urine surge into his lungs like some poisonous, stifling stink.

With a wretch and a gasp as the horrors of the previous night began slowly to come back to him, Bond slithered out of his saturated shirt and jacket like a whelk being prized from its oily shell. Not so much as a bit put off by the overpowering stench of body odour, or the wet matted hair running from the officer's pectorals to his flat stomach, Jack obediently laid his head on Bond's chest once more and kissed his bare skin.

'Albert,' he ventured at last. 'Ma *would* get my pay arrears, right? I mean if—'

'You shouldn't think like that,' Bond retorted lightly, reluctantly running his finger through his matted hair to stop the dreadful itching.

Coleman looked pained.

'I told you I was going to look after you,' Bond replied, this time a little more tenderly as he realised the impact of his words on the crestfallen young sapper. 'I meant what I said, you know,' he added. 'In fact—' He fumbled about in his bundle of salvaged possessions, wincing as the cold rent his stiff and aching limbs.

Jack saw him struggle and moved to help. 'Ouch!' he hissed. 'I can't move my arm, neither.'

'It's cramp,' Bond began.

'I know that right enough,' Coleman huffed. 'Spent enough nights using mine for a pillow on doss house flags.'

Bond smiled a sad smile at his batman before triumphantly disinterring his prize from the dishevelled heap of odds and ends, recovered from his tent by Faunce-Whittington the previous night. Jack gasped as the grimy leather holster and the long, buckled shoulder belt was drawn away, and the dull, burnished black metal of the revolver was slowly withdrawn for him to view. With encouragement from Bond, Coleman placed his fingers gently on the barrel, ran them along the smooth and bumpy contours of the rotating chamber, and carefully fingered the trigger, guarded by its familiar wide guard, and the handle.

'Careful, it's loaded,' Bond murmured deeply, as the young sapper took the pistol from his grasp and, cocking it, held the muzzle up to the light emitting from the cave mouth and stared down the sight in awe.

'I ain't an officer. Can I even carry one of these?' Jack asked, overwhelmed.

'No one can stop you if no one knows.'

Bond paused over his carefully considered words. He had been working himself up the whole of the previous day for presenting Jack with the revolver. Yet even in the face of so sombre a practicality as a personal firearm, the boy managed to look at him as if it was somehow an object of sentiment.

Only after some faltering was he able to make his words fit the occasion. 'Jack, I'm giving you this in case we ever get separated,' he told him. 'No, don't say we won't, last night must have taught you that you can never tell what might happen in war. What I mean to say is, will you please accept this so that, whatever the circumstances, I shall know you have protection.'

Coleman looked lost. He knew exactly what he wanted to say, but under the circumstances "I got you, ain't I?" seemed like a hollow retort. With a sad smile, he nodded acceptance.

'I can't conceive what you've had to live through, night after night not knowing how you might eat, when you might work again, where you might sleep. A boy with the cares of a man, and the strength of one. I've known nothing of the kind, however hard done by I've felt... now all I feel is shame.'

'All I feel is love,' Coleman replied, his eyes searching Bond's face for response, before returning to the pistol in his hand.

'Here, let me take that for you,' Bond added quickly, as he placed his hand over the chamber of the revolver and carefully removed the cocked weapon, slowly releasing the sprung hammer with a loud click. 'There,' he added more easily. 'Just don't go cocking the thing unless you must use it. Those wretched pistols can go off so easily, you know.'

'Thanks, Mr Albert,' Coleman smiled, warmly receiving the bundle of leather, ammunition and gunmetal, as though it were some deeply treasured memento.

This time it was Bond's turn to frown. 'Funny,' he said loftily, turning up his nose with a sly smile. 'I thought we had dispensed with "Mr" lately.'

'Did I?' Coleman replied aghast. 'Oh, I'm sorry.'

'Yes, you did,' murmured the officer.

Reaching out, he took the sapper firmly by the fraying worsted shoulder cords on his serge and kissed him slowly and tenderly on the lips. They continued the exchange for some moments, until the sound of something like a rhinoceros descending the cliff at speed caused them both to recoil in alarm and wonder what on earth was going on.

'It's an avalanche,' Bond muttered aghast, as the loud noise was accompanied by a tumult of falling earth and debris.

The source of interruption was soon revealed, however when, with his feet dangling over the cave mouth like the dead legs of some animal carcass, the hefty shape of Lieutenant Faunce-Whittington was seen, clumsily attempting to execute a descent. Trying desperately not to laugh, the two of them could only watch as the large lieutenant's ample posterior came slowly into view, followed at length by his braces, and an unfortunate view of the officer's middle as his shirt and patrol jacket became hopelessly enmeshed in some overhanging foliage.

Virtually incapacitated with mirth, tears streaming down his face, Bond managed to compose himself sufficiently to call out to the officer, innocently inquiring if he wanted any help. When the answer was returned, or rather helplessly wailed in the affirmative, both Bond and Coleman were left with no alternative but to rouse themselves from the floor of their cave and restrain the suspended officer's flailing legs. This done, and with poor Coleman clinging on whilst battling with the forces of hysteria, Bond tried in his very best authoritative tones to talk Faunce-Whittington into letting go of the rocks above him. When at last they managed to get him down, it was without his hat – which was still suspended from a protruding bower some twelve feet up, and with much of the black mohair tape and olivettes torn, or missing all together, from the front of his patrol jacket.

Red as a peony flower, and acutely aware that both men had lately been treated to a considerable view of his lower middle, Faunce tried to redress the balance by informing them politely that food was on the go, should they want any.

'Thank you, Faunce,' Bond replied, adding swiftly, 'Is there any news?'

Faunce-Whittington, who had of course been dreading such a question, merely shook his head sadly and looked searchingly at his boots. 'Lieutenant Knight is down there now,' he mumbled sheepishly. 'I think he would value your help.'

'I suppose we had better show ourselves,' Bond remarked to Coleman, who was still shivering fitfully with giggles, as Faunce lumbered down towards the laager, gathering alarming speed as he descended.

The gentle, cool sensation of early morning sunlight flowed across their exposed limbs. As it was, young Coleman could think of nothing he would rather have seen than the half-naked torso of the strong lieutenant, while the faint hum of the slowly awakening world rustled and shimmered into life around him.

Bond tugged on his top clothes as an afterthought and,

once Coleman had handed him his revolver, strap, and helmet, the two of them set off down the slope.

Jack left his belt kit in the cave, but took care to sling his rifle over his shoulder. Yawning and stretching out his arms with a ghastly facial expression in an effort to screw the sleep from his eyes and the heavy sensation of waking from his mouth and the back of his neck, the young sapper tried his best to attune to their surroundings. Indeed, these images were no more cheerful than those nightmarish horrors of the lately departed darkness. In fact, they were worse. Somehow, he thought timidly, the darkness lent itself to such appalling carnage, its grim inky blackness almost masking the true horrors of the death, destruction and, more disturbingly, mutilation of their fellow soldiers.

The air was still, but gradually came to life as insects, birds and other native habitation began to stir amid the long swaying grasses, the cool swelling river, and the dominating rocks of the nearby mountain. They shivered simultaneously. Their feet were still wet through from the night before, and their squelching boots and saturated socks left their toes frozen like ice and seemed to be almost detached from their bodies with the numbness of the cold.

At the same time as he and the officer were making their steady, funereal progress down the gentle camber of the foot of the cliff, others were beginning to emerge from the various nooks, crevices and hiding places afforded by the friendly cover. Each bore the same naïve, childishly expectant expression. From officers and NCOs to sappers, irregular troopers and auxiliaries, every face and every look said the same thing: *it can't be true. Please tell me it isn't so.*

They came to a halt at the foot of the slope, both removing their helmets and trying their best to look pathetically normal amid the altogether abnormal appearance of the ransacked camp. Bodies littered the ground, sprawled over wagon limbers or protruding miserably from beneath the cover of the flattened bell tents. The scarlet cloth of the soldiers' uniforms did at least serve to divert a little from the bloody mess and seemingly endless sea of gore. Anything light in colour looked positively sickening. Virtually everything seemed to have a spear stuck in it. A nearby clump of aloes, still dripping with moisture running from the glossy buds right down to the foot-high yellow grass, rose above the clearing mist with serenity belied by its surroundings. It was just like that golden morning, now so lost and far away, when Bond and Coleman had wandered up the hill and lain in the grass together, and the young sapper felt himself almost moved to tears. So much blood had flowed since that time; so much had been done that could not be undone, and now it seemed there was no way back in any sense. Bond seemed to sense his melancholy but could do little to comfort the young sapper as all around them men emerged from their hiding places, gazing vacantly around them for signs of friends and clues as to their fate. Somehow, there didn't seem to be much that was to be left to the imagination concerning the fate of the Highlanders and many of their own men.

A raucous din was kicked up from the other side of the camp. One of the irregulars had discovered to his horror that a scorpion had been sharing his bedroll and gave vent to his emotions in the customary manner and a flurry of blows from a rifle butt. Something unsought and unseen dropped noisily from its home in a nearby shrub, landing in the long grass and scuttling off somewhere.

Bond shuddered. A bird cried out, almost as if it had only just discovered the horrific images of murder and chaos that rested on its doorstep, and very soon its call was taken up by more and more, until the air seemed to be almost alive with squawks and cackles. As well as the constant plagues of midges and flies that had begun to smother the scene of the massacre, several howls had been reported during the night, and by the time the men were roused, the gruesome sight of carnivorous mutilation had met their already blighted eyes.

Unable to stand the silence which, despite the noise of the veldt, seemed still to pervade the campsite, Bond called out for his troop to fall in immediately.

He was joined at length by a very disturbed Sergeant Friday who, fearing the dead would get up and walk, had spent the whole night reciting psalms and consequently robbed himself of some much-needed sleep. As it transpired, he had not been the only one. Several of Flambard's trusted and reliable African troops had broken cover and deserted during the night, and any surviving pioneers assumed to have deserted. Alas, this development had perhaps served to reinforce the long-held and latent prejudices among men so lately converted to a respect and even comradeship with their black brothers under the leadership of Sergeant Christmas.

In sad truth, those pioneers assumed to have survived, now defamed as deserters, likely lay dead beside their white comrades, their identities and sacrifice overlooked in the carnage and mistaken altogether for Zulus.

All of Lieutenant Penfold's troop, most of Knight's and several of Bond's had been killed, either as part of the gallant last stands made by McGonagle's Highlanders or, more sadly, skewered to their bedrolls as they slept.

'Barely conceivable,' Knight remarked to a silent African trooper, tasked to guide the grim sapper in undertaking a rudimentary role of engineer casualties.

The African, as sickened and shocked as the officer, yet without the means to express such feelings to his immediate company, simply looked on in silence.

Knight moved from one displacement of bodies to the other, respectfully lifting heads, examining faces and, where possible, making identification.

Many of his men had died during various stages of preparation for bed and, consequently, many were not wearing the customary blue trimmed red serge of the Royal Engineers by which the officer had hoped he might identify them.

'Don't you recognise none of 'em, sir?' Corporal Denham asked gingerly.

Lieutenant Knight, his face an ashen mask beneath the dirt, sweat and his increasingly lengthening beard, merely shook his head in silence.

A grave Commandant Flambard and a decidedly sombre Faunce-Whittington joined the remorseful party at length, and it was only when the burly magistrate placed his hand manfully on Knight's shrunken shoulder that the officer knew there was worse to come.

'What is it, sir?' he asked feebly, forgetting to address his query to Flambard and causing Faunce momentarily to imagine he had been promoted.

'I suggest you take a look for yourself, lad,' Flambard replied gravely. 'I'm afraid it's grim news, but you might find the answer you're looking for in that tent over there. You can't miss it, it's one of only five still standing.' Flambard kicked aside a length of severed guy rope which, together with a thousand more pegs, ropes, boxes, and toggles, littered the floor of the decimated laager.

Knight looked at Flambard, then at Faunce-Whittington, and then back at his African shepherd. Not one of the three sympathetic expressions seemed either to betray the truth of what he was going to find.

'Wouldn't have hurt you to put names to faces either,' Flambard muttered inaudibly after the departing sapper officer.

Gideon Knight found Earnest Penfold inside the tent, whence he had been rapidly hauled to prevent the flies from getting to him.

Beside the little officer lay the equally mutilated company bugler, his batman, who had apparently died within feet of him. Stooping, Knight carefully examined the bloody mess where poor Penfold had tried in vain to pull free the assegai that fixed his body. The fingers were still outstretched and, although the blood had now run cold in the veins, it was still possible to see the way in which the poor lieutenant had taken the hand of his batman at the crucial moment, despite the horrific nature of his injuries.

'Oh, Earnest,' Knight muttered sadly. 'How could we have let this happen to you, my poor little fellow?'

A sharp click of the heels brought to his attention the presence of Sergeant Friday who, despite the tears coursing down his own rugged countenance, remained in steadfast support of his officer.

'Men are restless,' he muttered. 'Best let the fit ones dig burial pits, sir. Don't do to let 'em... dwell.'

Knight closed his eyes and nodded his permission. 'Oh, Sergeant?' he called back as an afterthought. 'Can you find Albert for me, and tell him what's happened, would you?'

Friday coughed pointedly and studied his mud-caked boots for a moment.

Knight closed his eyes again and cursed. 'McGonagle?' he asked.

Friday nodded grimly. 'Up in his tent, sir.'

'Very well,' Knight replied. 'Just tell him to come as soon as you can.'

Yet again, Friday simply nodded, and left.

Once the men had taken a cold and unappetising breakfast, Bond and Coleman retired once more to the protection of their cave, wherein they received a call from an unsmiling Commandant Flambard. As soon as the whiskered officer's formidable form appeared in the cave mouth, Coleman was on his feet and stood to attention. Bond also rose to his feet, yet less with the customary ease and civility observed between officers, and more from the sheer exhaustion of the previous night's depravations.

Flambard's reaction was discomforting to say the least. Gravely, without even acknowledging the presence of the sheepish young sapper, Flambard cleared his throat and motioned for the lieutenant to sit back down.

'I'm frightfully sorry to disturb you, Bond, but I really thought that you ought to know as soon as possible,' he began sadly.

As it was, Bond's reply spoke both for himself, and for Coleman, who was sitting open-mouthed and alarmed by the unmistakable implications of the visit.

Flambard sighed and scratched his whiskers. 'I think we both know what I have to say, don't we?'

Bond nodded gloomily.

'My men have discovered the bodies of two men, both of whom they believe to be officers by their dress, their weapons, and the locations in which they... fell. I truly am sorry, Lieutenant, but there doesn't appear to be any room left for doubt that they are your uncle, and your brother officer from the Corps of Royal Engineers.'

Bond, who could find no words with which to answer, simply sat there blinking. 'Thank you, Colonel,' he sighed, eyebrows raised and a misty look beginning to drift across his expressionless face.

Flambard, saddened as it seemed by some private grief himself, grunted a word of condolence, before rising awkwardly and darkening the cave mouth as his huge body squeezed out and into the sunlight.

'Albert,' Coleman whispered tentatively, but Bond was too preoccupied to notice.

'What are we to do?' Bond called out to Flambard, as the magistrate's hat began to disappear below the rocky lip of the cave mouth.

The hat halted, and Flambard paused to consider a response. At length, he turned back and peered once more into the gloomy cave.

'A tough fight, to my own mind, is better than the wretched dance which we have been led, and that which has undoubtedly led to this appalling tragedy. We need to take this elusive enemy head-on somewhere, where we will be in a position to dictate the course of any fighting, which we can't do in this high country and on this terrain. We need to push on for the open ground, laager and meet them on our terms. For this reason, I have suggested to Lieutenant Knight that you, the sick and wounded, should remain here another day while we irregular troops scout ahead in search of the safest place to run in.'

'What does Gideon say?' Bond enquired gingerly. Yet to his surprise, the magistrate's retort was positive.

'Seems to agree,' he replied evasively, adding, 'I truly am sorry about McGonagle.'

'Begging your pardon, your honour,' Coleman piped up suddenly, as much to his own surprise as Bond's. 'What about our lads? I mean, well—'

'Don't you worry, soldier,' Flambard replied. 'You take care of your officer; we'll see to it that your mates are properly buried.'

Coleman smiled weakly and shuddered. He had never spoken to a magistrate before, and he didn't want to make it a habit in the future.

'I'll see you, Bond,' Flambard muttered. 'Please remember, I would have given anything for this to have worked out differently, believe me.'

With that he left, leaving Bond and the attentive Coleman to ponder on the strange implications of the commandant's visit, and the sad and tragic revelations of the passing of their two comrades.

Flambard went directly in search of Faunce-Whittington, whom he discovered helping an increasingly bereft Gideon Knight with an inventory of Earnest Penfold's possessions.

'No need to have a sale,' he was saying to the irregular officer. 'I'll send money home myself. After all, a few shillings or a couple of pounds aren't going to make any difference to him now, and his effects should be sent home.'

'Was he married?' Faunce enquired sadly. He had only known the quiet little officer slightly and yet, as a large man with an overtly demonstrative but inward shyness, he found kinship with quiet, small men like the late sapper officer.

Knight nodded gloomily. 'Sweet little woman,' he replied sadly. 'Not really an army wife, poor girl. Still, it can't matter now, I suppose.'

'She'll be lonely, I think.'

Knight nodded again and breathed a deep, regretful sigh. 'Are you married yourself, Faunce?' he enquired.

Faunce-Whittington sniffed, grunted slightly, and was

just wondering where to put himself, when a dry cough from Flambard interrupted proceedings.

'Sorry to barge in, gentlemen, only I seem to be making something of a morning out of doing so.' Looking sadly down at the few scattered chattels of the lately departed officer, Flambard realised that, even though he had seen this done so many times, for him the tragedy never seemed to abate in the slightest.

Faunce-Whittington looked pained. 'Has Albert been told? About his uncle, I mean,' he asked gingerly.

Flambard nodded and smiled slightly. Whatever else he was, or whatever else his drawbacks, Faunce certainly had the knack of evaluation. 'I need you, Faunce,' he explained. 'It's difficult, but I simply can't help myself. I must see the old devil one last time, but I must confess that I cannot bring myself to go alone. Will you accompany me?'

'Oh, of course!' the officer replied heartily. 'We must go right away. Whyever didn't you say something sooner, Commandant?'

Knight groaned inwardly. At least the magistrate had seemed more together than old McGonagle, and now it seemed as if the pair had been old friends. 'You go, Faunce,' he muttered with a weak smile. 'I shall finish up here.'

Faunce-Whittington nodded and the two subalterns shook hands, while Flambard drifted off outside the dilapidated awning.

This really is going to be the worst of days, he thought solemnly.

Chapter Twenty-Three

They discovered the body of Captain AW McGonagle almost resting exactly as he had fallen, amid a sea of disordered papers, consisting chiefly of poems, tracts, and articles, together with preliminary notes for his book, all intended for publication upon the elderly officer's return to his homeland.

His empty revolver lay just outside the lank flaps of his bloodstained bell tent, while the old Scottish sword by his side was spattered with yet more blood.

They stood and regarded in silence for a moment. A sort of grave horror mixed with respect for the circumstances of the death and the state of the dead compelled thoughts to remain unspoken and condolences to pass unsaid.

'What happened to you, Alec?' Flambard muttered, to the combined shock and surprise of Faunce-Whittington. 'How did you come to this end? All that time, the town, the fort, for this.'

Mournfully, the magistrate removed his wide-brimmed hat and, kneeling almost in the middle of the blood and matter, bent down and gently closed the elderly captain's eyes.

'There we are, you can sleep now,' he whispered, slowly taking in the devastation, scattered material, and unnerving smell of the mutilated body. 'May you attain *moksha*.'

For all his faults, it appeared that the captain had died sword in hand, while taking on more than one of the now mythical, almost supernatural, enemy. Indeed, there was some comfort to be drawn from the fact that McGonagle had been found face up, and a pile of bullet-riddled bodies outside served as testament to the fact that the old man had not died quietly.

Even so, Faunce was unable to remain silent. 'I'm sorry, Colonel,' he said at last, tentatively fingering the empty silver hip flask that the Zulus had not been given a chance to loot from the officer's belongings. 'Do you think he had been drinking?'

'I think I should be troubled if he hadn't,' Flambard replied, rising awkwardly to his feet, and groaning as his knees cracked and his back straightened.

'Colonel?'

'It's simple,' Flambard answered gravely. 'In all the time I have known this good man, I have never once subscribed to these commonly held misconceptions about him. He was a once good officer whom time, grief and disappointment made into an eccentric. Yet he always *did* take a drink.'

'I am sorry though, Colonel,' Faunce muttered, thoughtfully removing the bottle from the commandant's trembling grasp and gently replacing it on the improvised camp table. 'I know how much you wanted to help him.'

Flambard chuckled mirthlessly. 'Dear Faunce,' he said. 'I know you mean well, but I am very much afraid that you do not know nor understand at all. My history with Captain McGonagle began long before this foolish war, and many years ago on a beautiful continent miles away from here.'

Faunce swallowed hard, and to his horror found himself subsiding heavily on the bed amid the late captain's sheets, the coarse linen spotted with his blood.

'Many years ago—' Flambard began, when suddenly he was interrupted by a dry cough emitting from a little way outside the tent. The magistrate righted himself and muttered heavily about removing the body to a place of burial.

'Let Coleman do it, Colonel. I think Bond would appreciate that.'

Flambard nodded. 'I'm sure he would, Faunce,' he replied, patting the officer on the back as the two of them left the body to the care of the waiting sappers. 'We really should be getting along now,' added the magistrate, pausing momentarily to salvage a single, solitary sheet of paper that was nestling amid the endless reams, ignominiously spread across the floor of the tent, of which countless pages were smudged unrecognisably, and others stained with blood.

Once outside, Flambard and Faunce-Whittington stood and regarded the black and blustery landscape, while the wind tossed and disturbed the lifeless canopies and mournfully swayed the grasses to and fro.

'What a queer continent this is, Faunce,' the magistrate remarked wearily. 'Four seasons in one day, and not one of them in the correct time or place.'

The officer in turn grunted painfully but failed to offer a reply.

While the commandant had been busily engaged upon paying his last respects to the fallen, young Sapper Coleman had been comforting and consoling in the only way he knew how. Having collected some odd bits of wood, which he found at the back of the cave, the resourceful young lad had not only built a small fire but had also succeeded in drying both his and his officer's saturated greatcoats, giving them both something dry to lay on.

'We badly need a bath, don't we?' Bond muttered, scratching furiously at the dry, crusty mud that stuck to his hair, beard, face, and clothes.

'Take your jacket off again,' Coleman whispered, tenderly laying his head against the officer's cheek so that Bond could stroke his hair, as Jack knew he loved to do.

Bond, feeble, miserable, and emotionally exhausted, simply did as he was bidden and slipped out of his upper garments, laying back against the young sapper and resting his head against the boy's firm chest.

Coleman, simply overwhelmed by pity as Bond looked helplessly back at him, slipped down beside him, and closed his eyes. 'I'll do anything,' he said at last. 'Just tell me how to help, sir.' He looked at Bond, their blue eyes meeting.

Still the officer could find no words with which to answer, but tears had begun to well up, and ran down the officer's begrimed face as he surrendered composure to grief. Kissing him warmly on the cheek, then on the mouth and then ever so tenderly again and again, the young sapper tried his best to soothe the agony of Bond's loss. One thing Coleman had learned was the time in which it took to remove his red serge jacket, and the rough grey-blue shirt underneath. The incredulous lad had always known, yet never quite understood, why people always wanted to be close to him, from pretty Kentish maids to the twisted Simonides. He had learned quickly to apply his physical attributes to hard work and fair reward, but could never reconcile the times when necessity had obliged him to use his beauty to purchase advantage. To do so would have been to accept prostitution, as he had known his mother do, out of necessity, when singing didn't pay.

Yet one thing he knew perfectly well was how much the officer liked to touch him and, right at that moment, he knew he would do anything at all to make him happy again.

Bond, eyes still streaming with tears of remorse, loss, and gratitude towards him, laid his head on the smooth broad shoulder and, trying his best to ignore the dry, flaky mud that covered both their bodies, began to rub away at the knotted muscles. Coleman shut his eyes once more and gasped. He delighted at Bond's touch, and was only too happy to have his supple, toned limbs manipulated by the officer's warm hands, made so, he knew, by his own efforts in collecting and building the flickering fire. Wrapping themselves in the two dry greatcoats, regardless of the darkening skies without their little dwelling, they subsided on the sandy floor and slithered into each other's arms. Slowly, Bond's hands began to work their magic on the smooth contours of Coleman's body. With a gasp of pleasure and a murmur of contented adoration, he closed his eyes and wriggled up against the officer's chest. Stroking back the thick, matted brown hair, he looked into the young subaltern's eyes and kissed him gently on the lips.

'I'm so sorry,' he whispered. 'I know you loved him, even though you quarrelled before, and I ain't going to let you be alone until you've said goodbye to him.'

Bond said nothing at first, laying his head on Jack's shoulder and breathing in the smell of his body. 'I love *you* too,' he whispered. 'Thank you for being so good to me.'

'You're good to me,' Coleman protested, nudging the officer's chin with his nose. 'Is it alright to say I love you too, to an officer? I mean, I ain't out of line by sayin' it, am I...?'

Bond wasn't sure whether to laugh or cry at the absurdity of it. One man professing love for another, wondering whether to prefix, or to close with an honorific.

'I really meant what I said, you know,' Bond muttered into Coleman's hair.

'What's that?' the young sapper retorted blissfully.

'We really *do* need a bath!'

Coleman chuckled, then he kissed him shyly, peeping through his oily curtain of hair and, smiling coyly at the handsome Bond, began to lick his finger and wipe away the grime from the officer's matted moustache. 'We got to bury the captain,' he muttered soothingly.

'I know,' Bond replied. 'I just can't bear to go out like this.'

Coleman smiled, shifted himself up on his elbows and studied the officer's smooth, muscular chest, freckled shoulders and the dark, rusty colour thrown about by the flickering firelight. 'If we need a bath,' he ventured, 'I reckon I got an idea...'

'Someone can fill you up a pan of hot water!' Faunce-Whittington called after Bond, albeit at a respectable distance as the expressionless sapper thundered past him in the direction of the river with Coleman in tow.

Bond, refusing to look round or stop for even an instant, called back blithely, 'I shan't need it, thank you, Faunce. We'll use the public baths,' he added, as a tantalising prelude to his intended actions.

Coleman, who had stowed his pack, rifle, and his sun helmet, struggled to keep up with the officer's determined gait, all the time following in a trail of discarded accoutrements as the other sappers in his troop gradually cottoned on to what their lieutenant was up to.

'What on earth?' Lieutenant Knight was heard to demand of Sergeant Friday, as Bond was seen to pause, unfasten his shoulder strap and plump down on a rock to remove his muddy boots.

'Sapper!' Faunce-Whittington called out after the departing Coleman. 'You know him, your officer, surely?'

'Oh yes, sir,' Coleman replied proudly.

'Well, what on earth does he think he's doing?' demanded the officer curtly.

He was presently joined by an equally dumbstruck Knight and Friday who, having watched the exodus for a matter of seconds, tramped across to the nearest visible source of information and stood there open-mouthed.

'Excuse me please, sir,' said Coleman politely, chiefly addressing Faunce-Whittington. 'If you please, I think I'm needed by my officer.'

'What with?' Friday demanded, but so breathless and high-pitched was the actual utterance that the young sapper could have been forgiven for not hearing at all.

Whether he heard or not, Coleman was off.

The fact was that the appearance of both Bond and his men had changed quite considerably for their labours at the river. This, when followed by a restless night of mud and rain in the dubious cover provided by the caves and scrapes, and the heartbreaking – not to mention backbreaking – work of digging burial pits for their brother soldiers, had left their uniforms in a terrible state. A thick crust of mud clung to every inch of their exposed bodies, trousers, boots, and kit. Only those who had thrown off their upper garments under relative cover still retained the customary scarlet of the British Army, while everyone else including and especially their officer looked to have been baked in a pantry and left to cool by a window. His normally silky bronze hair was shocked back and dried into a starchy brown; his unrecognisable cord riding trousers stuck to the hair on his legs in an atrophied armour of flaking scales, which cracked and crumbled with every footstep. His beard bore more of the same, while streaks of yet more mud covered his moustache, cheeks, and eyebrows.

Friday too had a thick mat of clay for a beard, stretching from his chin to the third, mud-caked button on his stiff and starchy serge. The top of his bald pate was covered in a layer of dry brown scales, while his thick protruding eyebrows stuck out from his face as if touched by the frost of a hard winter morning. He stood and watched, bulbous-eyed and horrified as his men trooped off behind their officer, casting aside bits of their kit and seemingly stripping off as the hot sun burned once more through the heavy canopy of fog that covered the river valley.

Knight caught up with Bond by the outermost wagon of the laager. 'Albert,' he began in frustration, having been made to run all the way from the foot of the cliffs to almost the banks of the river itself. 'What on earth do you think you are doing?'

'Taking a bath,' Bond replied coldly. 'We can't bury McGonagle looking like this. I simply won't have it, Gideon.'

'Bath!' Knight repeated, incredulity rising with his temperature and that of the world around him. 'How?'

'I'll show you,' Bond replied defiantly.

Quite a little audience had begun to accumulate now, and even Commandant Flambard stopped mid-sentence and turned to look.

Coleman, who was almost completely unrecognisable after two consecutive nights of mud and rain, stripped off his serge jacket and grinned approvingly at his beloved officer. His hair was caked, each thick clump of blond dried into a pointed strand, identical to the colour of his mud-splattered face and giving him the look of some pathetic homemade corn doll. Only his soft pink lips and his bright, twinkling blue eyes shone through the mask. As he tore off the matted shirt from the skin on his back, Bond could only smile and nod his approval.

From their rock at the base of the cliff, Flambard and the three irregular officers had tramped down to join Friday and Lieutenant Faunce-Whittington, who had just turned very red in observation of the sappers' ritual, as they trooped together towards the bank. There they paused, turned, and awaited the arrival of their officer. Then, as if the whole thing had been engineered with the intention of annoying Lieutenant Knight, Bond tore off his own shirt, and flung it down in the damp grass. Next, he removed his riding breeches, the dry, crackling mud ripping and clinging to the thick dark hairs on his legs as he peeled them away from his skin. These he also cast aside, and Coleman, who had been right behind his officer the entire time, slowly began to remove his own apparel and dumped it down in the grass as he denuded his limbs of each filthy article.

Faunce-Whittington, who had previously been reduced to watching open-mouthed, now could only gasp as the handsome officer and his equally endowed batman wriggled free of the last threads of clothing and proceeded utterly stark naked to the riverbank.

Coleman, terrified but hopelessly exhilarated by the shock of events, blushed as his horrified comrades tried their best not to stare at his firm white buttocks and the trefoil of blond hair from which his genitals swung unashamedly, and followed his officer the last few steps to the water.

The sun was beginning to warm things up nicely by this time as, to the cheers and applause of the far less repressed African troops, the naked sappers took a last, tentative look at one another and plunged into the rippling water.

'Good God!' cried Knight.

'Fancy,' gasped Faunce-Whittington.

'Brave men indeed,' chuckled the commandant.

Sergeant Friday on the other hand could only be heard to simmer and squeak like a boiling kettle. Such sights were above and beyond him all together, and in more ways than one, he reflected in outrage.

'Well done, Bond, for ingenuity,' added the magistrate to Faunce who, if he had been blushing before, was by now a rather less than fetching shade of beetroot, trying his best not to stare too hard as Bond and Coleman ducked and plunged in the icy water and began to wash themselves free of the mud and scales.

'Colonel,' Knight burst forth, staggering up the grassy slope and rejoining the officers and a panting Sergeant Friday. 'I really cannot apologise enough.'

Flambard, who considered himself too old and experienced, decided not to suffer such affectations patiently. 'I shouldn't worry, my dear chap,' he remarked blithely. 'Until you mentioned it, I assumed that smell came from elsewhere. Faunce,' he added, turning to the smirking officer, 'I suggest you direct Mr Knight to a cave and offer him a cake of soap, since he seems to be too shy to bathe in company.'

This last blow was too much for the fiercely conservative Friday, who turned, saluted, and marched slowly off in the direction of anywhere he could go. Someone would have to pay for this reckless display of indiscipline, he decided. Familiarity between the ranks, his officers rebuked and mocked by colonial veterans.

At length, he happened upon his old stalwart Corporal Denham, who was standing in the lee of a wagon, himself utterly stark naked, washing his hopelessly dishevelled uniform in a pale of muddy water.

Friday paused, closed his eyes, and groaned heavily. 'Not

you as well, Corp?' he squealed in horror.

Denham, his black hair pushed back off his face and his black beard dripping into the pail of washing, calmly scratched his testicles and grinned at the incandescent Friday. 'Good Lord, what a pair, Sarn't,' he chuckled lightly. 'I never seen the likes of that before, what with him an officer an' all. The pair of them 'n' all. My word if I weren't wrong about that one. Seems that boy does have summit to brag of after all, eh, Sarn't?'

Friday, who had turned to an alarming shade beneath his muddy coating, clamped his eyes shut and made a guttural noise a bit like the crank of a mangle. 'Never seen nothin' like it,' he hissed. 'Never want to see the like again. Never!'

'Oh, I shouldn't worry, Sarn't,' replied the corporal, to Friday's mind a little too blithely. 'You'll not see the like of that again, and not for long if the water's cold!'

There was a monetary pause, then Friday's eyes suddenly burst open again. 'Where are you goin', Corp?' he demanded sternly, as Denham dredged up the contents of his improvised copper and rang the bulk of the water from his saturated clothes.

'Bath, Sarn't,' he replied calmly. 'I ain't been in yet.'

With that, he left Friday to his noises, dashing off across the encampment to more cries and chants from the delighted Africans, who had never seen such behaviour by their colonial comrades, and were never likely to do so again.

'This must appear rather a demeaning display to a volunteer,' Knight muttered half-heartedly to Faunce-Whittington.

'Oh, on the contrary, I was rather impressed,' the officer replied.

Knight looked bewildered, interpreting the reply, but the lieutenant was unrepentant.

'No offence, Gideon, but if you pass so much as a criticism

of Bond either before or during the funeral, I'm afraid I shall be obliged to shoot you. Now, if you'll excuse me, I think I have remembered something that might come in useful,' he concluded sweetly, offering a sarcastic wink and abandoning Knight as Denham had Sergeant Friday.

Coleman, who let out a ferocious shriek as his body met with the water, jumped, and splashed about to keep warm. 'It's bloody cold, this is!' he yelped.

Bond managed to smile, for the first time that day. For a few, brief, blissful moments they had been alone in the water together. Bond looked lovingly at Coleman, his glossy wet hair hanging down over his face, his tanned shoulders just visible as his neck rose from the dark river water.

'Stop whining and get washing,' he laughed, incautiously taking hold of Coleman and plunging him beneath the rippling surface.

Coleman obligingly remained under for several seconds, jumping and lurching as the icy chill rippled through his body before rising to the surface gasping and spluttering afresh. All around them sappers charged naked into the swell, thrashing, and splashing each other as they struggled to keep their body temperatures up. Bond, his solid constitution already fully acclimatised to the cold, stretched out his arms just below the surface of the water, and out of sight of all but Coleman, beckoning for the boy to come and get him. Grinning, his blue eyes creasing in the corners and his white teeth flashing against his tanned skin, he plunged forward and soon found himself spluttering again as he and Bond disappeared under once more. They emerged a few moments later, sleek glossy heads restored to their original colours and the features of their faces now free of the clinging mud and dust.

'Here!' cried a voice from the ether, 'catch!'

Bond laughed again, reaching out with cupped hands as Faunce-Whittington hurled a precious bar of soap from the safety of his horse on the now saturated riverbank.

'Not coming in, Faunce?' he called across to the beleaguered lieutenant, who looked as if he had only come down to escape the palpable disapproval of Knight and Friday. 'Where the devil did you come by this commodity anyway, Faunce?' he added as the large officer shyly turned his horse and retreated to a point from which his men stood.

It was true to say that the colonials observed proceedings with a bemused reserve in marked contrast to their gleeful African comrades, who whooped, cheered, and laughed openly, quite unaccustomed to witnessing white soldiers exhibiting themselves unabashed, and without multiple layers of clothing.

With a wince and a grimace, Faunce pointed to his own lengthening beard and waved away the bombardments of thanks and shouts of approbation as he tossed a further two cakes of the precious soap into the water.

'Marvellous,' Commandant Flambard remarked to Gideon Knight. 'Not for the first time, the man is a hero. Just shows you the good in a long purse when one chooses to do such.'

Again, Knight looked pained, but failed to offer a reply. Notwithstanding the agonising self-recriminations over Penfold's penury, he had always been a sportsman, a leader, a mate; one of the chaps. *How and when did my rank make me into a prig?* he wondered dismally.

Several sappers, including their corporal, dived at once for the sinking bounty, and such was the chaos, splashing and general carry on, no one noticed Bond and Coleman recoil quietly against the protective shroud of the overhanging embankment.

Here, their arms knotted around their waists below the surface of the water, cold wet skin pressed against cold wet skin, the two men huddled together, still shivering, and gasping but happy with their concealment. Coleman looked imploringly at Bond, then wistfully at the soap, which the officer was lathering in his hands. With a warm smile, he reached out and began to massage the cleansing oil into the young sapper's hair, gently ladling the water over the top and taking care not to get it in Jack's eyes.

Then, sinking back into the water with a sigh of satisfaction, Bond closed his eyes and handed the soap to a delighted Coleman. 'Just like a bath,' he whispered. 'And yes, it *is* better than goin' under a standpipe.'

Coleman, with a huff of mock indignation, rubbed the soap between both hands and began rubbing his fingers in the officer's hair, scooping up handfuls of water and rinsing out the lather as Bond had done for him. He rubbed hard, scratching the scalp to relieve the frightful irritation and countless insect bites of several weeks with neither proper sanitation, nor protection from the elements. Bond moaned with pleasure and smiled delightedly as he felt the thick, matted strands of hair become de-clogged, and the sapper's gentle hands soothe away the lumps, bumps, privations, and hardships of the past few horrendous days. Then, just as the unsuspecting Bond was relaxing almost as far as one can in chilly a river, Jack forgot himself entirely, clapped both hands on the officer's broad shoulders, and dunked *him* underwater. The world went momentarily dark, and Bond felt himself sinking as the sound of countless gallons bubbled and rumbled in his dulled ears. There was a pervading sense of complete protection and concealment as the water enveloped him for a moment, then a loud rush, a blinding light, and a struggle for breath as two big, strong forearms hauled him once again to the surface. Snorting, spluttering, spitting out water by the mouthful, Bond could only gasp and rub his eyes as the water streamed from his nostrils, and off his thick dark hair into his stinging eyes once more. Coleman delightedly lifted back the glistening strands of thick wet hair off the officer's face and smoothed it back over his ears, laughing as he continued to spit and shake off the water like a dog.

Pressing into the officer's freckled, muscular arms and leaning against his chest, Jack whispered fondly, 'Go on then, sir. It's my turn now.'

Bond, still spluttering, could not help but laugh as his sore eyes focussed again on the soft, youthful face of his young sapper, his sparkling blue eyes now lit up with fun, mirth and mischief, his firm lower body pressed against that of his officer. There was a sense of light-heartedness, despite the tragedy that had framed their time at the river and their reason for being there and, deep down, Bond knew that no circumstance had hitherto contrived to place them in such a unique situation as this. He also knew it was transitory, so he cupped his hands and washed with the soap behind Coleman's ears, the cropped stubble at the nape of his neck and the thick, silky hair above. Gasping with surprise, and renewed shock every time the cold water was splashed over him, Coleman played obediently along, raising an arm, or leaning into Bond so that the officer could reach the extremities of his back. They moved closer together as Bond, relinquishing the soap, closed his eyes and stooped forward for Jack to do what he had just been shown, repeating the process like some bath-time game, or field drill. They both giggled helplessly as Bond bowed his head for Jack to wash, and the eager young sapper ladled water over his officer's thick, glossy locks to rinse out the sobering smell of the toilet soap. As it was, he could hardly resist teasing Bond by pushing him deeper and deeper into the water, and Bond for his part was only too willing to let him get away with it.

'Come on, you,' he murmured into Coleman's ear, which was pressed against his lips as the young sapper nuzzled lovingly into his neck. 'Let's get out and see if we can explain ourselves to Commandant Flambard.'

Coleman withdrew. For a second, he looked pained and blushed, hard. 'I can't,' he muttered, looking shamefacedly down below the surface of the lapping water. 'At least,' he added sheepishly, 'not for a bit, anyway.'

Then, as if to fly in the face of everything he had ever done, as if somehow in apology for the military system that placed a gulf between the two of them for so long, Bond took a deep breath and, to Jack's surprise, plunged back under the water. Coleman breathed sharply, closed his eyes, and groaned. The officer rose a few seconds later, slicking back his thick dark hair with one deft sweep of his hand. Spitting and spluttering yet again, he grinned at the abashed sapper.

'More than a bit from what I can see,' he replied cheekily. 'In fact, quite a lot, solider!'

Chapter Twenty-Four

Despite the obvious pressure on him to have things moving again, Flambard was by no means too taken up with the preoccupations of military pragmatism to realise the effect that recent events would have had on the inexperienced officers. Forty years' military service had taught the officer that, were he to scream, shout or even order the men to move out immediately, none would be prepared to do so until the accepted rites had been enacted over the remains of their fallen comrades. Aside from anything else, Flambard was himself an old soldier, and the sentiments of duty to the dead were ones with which the magistrate identified entirely. He had come a long, arduous way since his service in New Zealand, when he and his comrades had contributed pay to fund a memorial to the Māori warriors they had fought, and even if that hadn't taught him the merits of respecting one's opponent as well as one's friend, then the loss of McGonagle most certainly had. *Damn convention*, he decided, as he watched the sappers emerge from the enveloping waters and stumble up the muddy bank in search of clothes.

Captain AW McGonagle would be buried properly, and something suitable would just have to be said in his memory. Flambard was nothing if not efficient. Accordingly, when the grave had been dug a respectable six feet deep by a dedicated, determined Coleman, and six sappers had been drafted in as pallbearers, and the remaining compliment of officers, NCOs, commissioned and non-commissioned irregulars had been assembled, the service was ready to begin.

'Thank you so much,' Bond murmured into Coleman's ear, as he physically hauled the young sapper out of the mud and silt of the cavernous burial pit. 'Look at you,' he groaned in dismay, as he took in young Jack's begrimed face, damp, sweaty fringe, and the thick coating of mud around the ankles of his boots and trouser cuffs. 'All that sweet work and you're as muddy as hell again.'

Coleman grinned, like some urchin who, ignorant of his mother's warnings, returned muddy and dishevelled after a morning's rough and tumble. 'I don't mind, sir,' he mumbled, adding even lower, 'You can always bathe me again.'

Bond smiled, handed Coleman his serge and belt kit, and boldly touched his cheek. 'Go on,' he whispered lovingly. 'You be off back to Sergeant Friday, and I'll catch up with you when you've packed up our kit.'

Coleman smiled, nodded obediently, and saluted respectfully for the benefit of the nearby colonials. 'See you.' He paused, adding sincerely, 'I hope it don't hurt too bad.'

Bond nodded sadly and smiled, returning the salute, and dismissing him.

Back in his cave, however, Commandant Flambard was by no means as composed as McGonagle's bereaved nephew. 'What on earth shall I say about him, Faunce?' he groaned pathetically, as Lieutenant Faunce-Whittington struggled to prepare his commanding officer for his pivotal role as minister to the funeral parade.

'He wasn't religious, Colonel?'

'Not a bit,' replied the commandant. 'Railed against evangelism, hated missionaries. More so after his wife was killed. So, I can't even hide behind scriptures. What I wouldn't give to read from the bible, or even a psalm.'

'I think Albert has a passage to recite,' Faunce suggested helpfully.

'That's different,' Flambard snapped back. 'That's for his own peace and for the men, and McGonagle's hardly apt to complain.'

Faunce said nothing, carefully assisting the burly magistrate to don his immaculately polished black leather shoulder strap, pouches, and holster.

'I can't recount friendship, not after... not now, at least. And I can hardly mention his poems!'

'Why not?'

'Well, because they were, well—'

'Awful?'

Flambard ground his teeth and nodded. 'Quite,' he added, as they finally abandoned prevarication and began the ominous lumber in the direction of the funeral party.

They paused at the cave mouth, then began at a slow pace across the muddy ground of the laager.

'You said you knew him before, Colonel,' Faunce ventured cautiously. 'In India?'

Again, Flambard nodded.

'Well,' the officer resumed tentatively, 'what I mean to say is, have you nothing from his Indian career that you could draw on for a eulogy?'

'Only its length,' replied the magistrate briskly. 'I mean, he lasted a great many years. But, dear fellow, we can't base a memorial on his longevity. After all, the man has just died in battle, not simply retired!'

They continued a few yards further, then the magistrate stopped.

'Twenty years,' he began sadly. 'More than twenty long and eventful years since I last saw Alec McGonagle. During those years I climbed three ranks, and believe me it was a hard climb, Faunce, with me fighting for every step. I achieved the rank of major without purchase while McGonagle went back and forth between staff posts like a dispatcher's saddlebag, hating the country and people he once not only loved, but advocated for. Since we parted company, it seems the only fighting he's done has been with himself.'

Faunce-Whittington grunted and fiddled awkwardly with the clasp on his holster.

They were within a few yards of the graveside by this time, and inspiration seemed to desert them as readily as it had the late McGonagle.

The assembled officers had observed their presence and were clearly eager to commence with the burial.

Faunce-Whittington scratched his beard. 'Didn't he see any other action, Colonel?'

'Civil disputes, the odd local rising and a stint on the North-West Frontier,' Flambard replied. 'But overall, I think he sat it out behind desks. One thing to his credit I suppose: McGonagle seems to have presided over some of the most peaceful stretches of bandit country in India during his superintendencies!' Flambard shrugged again and shuddered. He really was in a corner now. 'The truth is, Faunce,' he began composedly, 'I really don't know that much about him after the rebellion. He wasn't with us during the Abyssinian expedition, and he only arrived in Africa after the Xhosa and other tribal wars were done with. Other than that, I really have nothing to say for the man.'

'Did you like him?'

Again, Flambard shrugged. 'I did,' he replied. 'We got along in the '50s, and our approaches were very different, but then so were we. I blame myself still.'

'Over what, Colonel?' Faunce retorted, quick as ever to pick up on the rare occurrence of Flambard's revealing something.

'I beg your pardon?' Flambard responded, snapping out of his reverie, and looking blankly at the accompanying officer.

Faunce-Whittington wracked his brains. He had tried his best to think something up for the commandant to say, even allowing his mind to wander back as far as his society days in London, trying desperately to remember the diplomatic nothings he used to say to people whom he disliked at parties.

At last, he gave up the fight with a groan. 'Don't you have anything at all, Colonel?' he asked again.

Flambard closed his eyes and rubbed them with his hands, pulling back the skin on his weathered old face in frustration, and addressing the officer through splayed fingers. 'Oh, Faunce!' he groaned yet again, 'I must say something – anything! We simply can't bury the man without so much as a word, a line, a *verse*.' He paused momentarily, but that was all it needed.

Faunce-Whittington, clearing his throat several times and shuffling uneasily from one foot to the other, seemed to know exactly what he had to volunteer. The answer was plain, yet neither man wanted to be the one to answer for its conception.

'Perhaps, one of the captain's works?' the large lieutenant ventured gingerly.

Wearily, the old magistrate sighed, rolled his eyes, and nodded. 'I know, Faunce,' he replied morosely. 'In fact, I have one here as it happens. I was just hoping against hope that it wouldn't really have to come to this.' It appeared his fate was sealed, and he would just have to read one of McGonagle's wretched poems to the waiting mourners. Even in death, the old man was a pain. 'Very well,' he said at last. 'Come on, Faunce, we shall just have to get this thing over and done with.'

Sergeant Friday brought the parade to attention with a sharp, two-tone command, and handed Coleman a small black bible, which he in turn pressed into Lieutenant Bond's hand.

'Sarn't said to give you this,' he murmured quietly, as Bond, Knight and the others moved past him in the file.

Bond nodded acknowledgement to Friday, who remained at eyes front, but appeared to twitch one eye in reply.

'Well done on your kit, boy,' Corporal Denham muttered in Coleman's ear, as he, being one of the pallbearers, trooped past his assembled comrades.

'Kit, Corp?' Coleman repeated incredulously, then blushed scarlet as the significance of the NCO's words became apparent to him. In embarrassment, he turned to look at the corporal, and realised that he was smirking.

'Had me doubts about you, I have, boy,' Denham whispered out of the corner of his mouth. 'But after today, I sees you're more of a man than I am.'

Coleman, though dutiful and modest, could not subdue a laddish smirk. *At last*, he thought, *the bastard is treating me like a man*. Had he only known his cock would do the trick, he'd have been less coy about his ablutions back at Brompton Barracks.

'Watch out for Friday,' muttered the man behind him, noticing the young sapper's hasty exchange with his corporal.

'He weren't best pleased with them larks today, and you know well as I, he ain't quick to forgive. Sarn't can't touch his nibs,' he added, casting a quick glance after the departing Bond, 'so it'll be you, lad. Watch yer back.'

Coleman's face fell. Then, with practiced caution, doubtless the result of having to look sideways every time he and Bond were alone together, he glanced at Sergeant Friday. His expression was set in a mask of solid stone, the tumbling, starchy beard and the mud-encrusted eyebrows seeming somehow to transform him from the young soldier's mentor into the marble of the unsmiling founder of an alms house, displayed above the door of a paupers' hospital in Rochester's high street. With a ripple of fear running through his tense, agitated body, Coleman straightened his back and returned to eyes front.

Standing forward, a pace from the other officers, Bond gratefully accepted the burley presence of Commandant Flambard and Lieutenant Faunce-Whittington as he read aloud from a lonely passage of the bible. The choice was not a romantic, nor a particularly cheering one, yet seemed somehow fittingly to reflect the state of their worsening circumstances in Zululand, especially since the departure of Major Westgate and their ill-fated, autonomous command.

'"*Man that is born of woman is of few days, and full of trouble*",' he began shakily, as the significance of the words and the knowledge of their meaning flooded home to the sapper officer like the deaths of his parents, and the heavy certainty that he would never see either Penfold or his uncle alive again. '"*He fleeth also as a shadow, and continueth not. And dost thou open thine eyes upon such an one, and bringest me into judgement with thee*"?' he continued bravely, trying his best to ignore the increasing volume of Faunce-Whittington's sniffs, and the increasing advance of his own thinly veiled grief.

That McGonagle might have known of the love he held for Jack and perhaps understood or, by dint of enlightenment, even condoned it, was now too painful to conceive. This and a million unspoken hurts and sorrows cried anguish in his heart and choked the words in his throat.

Suddenly, the sky began to darken again, and a large expanse of cloud once more moved over to envelop the campsite, shrouding the world in a mystical tinge, preparing for the onset of rain. Commandant Flambard cleared his throat, and motioned to step forward, but Bond shook his head and continued, albeit in a broken tone:

'"*Thou hast appointed his bounds*",' he resumed, raising the level of his volume, but wavering with every syllable, '"*that he cannot pass. Turn from him, that he may rest, till he shall accomplish, as an hireling, his day*".'

That was it. The sob burst forth and his voice broke.

With yet another dry cough and a heavy hand laid firmly on the young lieutenant's shoulder, Flambard drew Bond back among his fellow officers and himself stepped forward into the breech. Yet even as he did so, a large black cloud, which had been massing above their position, suddenly moved among the thronging, billowing darkness in the sky. A single ray of light pierced the canopy of gloom to light up their little circle and shone directly down on the grave.

Most of the sappers looked amazed, and Sergeant Friday even went so far as to bow his head and murmur a prayer at attention. Coleman however was determined to be worldly for, as soon as the single ray of golden light had fallen upon the grave of McGonagle, the young sapper, heart in mouth and with blind bravado, suddenly broke ranks, marched up and took his place beside his lieutenant.

Coughing so hard and pointedly that he almost bent double, Gideon Knight found he had to check himself as the sensation of something alien and strangely threatening loomed up on him from behind. With a look of warning, and still more ominous fingering of his revolver holster, Faunce-Whittington shook his head in slow and obvious deterrent, placing himself between Bond, Coleman, and the disbelieving, incredulous Knight.

Oblivious to the insurrection taking place behind his broad back, the commandant took a deep breath and reluctantly commenced his address. 'Gentlemen, volunteers, soldiers of the Queen,' Flambard began, albeit haltingly as a metallic click momentarily distracted his attention. 'We are here to mark the passing of a man who gave his entire life to his profession, the army, and the service of the Crown. From boy, he rose to hold the rank of captain, a position in which he remained faithfully for many years, long after lesser men would have lost heart and retired. His dignity, longevity and loyalty are lessons each.'

Gideon Knight, on any other occasion might have reflected uncharitably on such reverence over the career of a man whom he had regarded as a dangerous failure. Instead, he stood silent and alarmingly pale as the muzzle of Faunce-Whittington's revolver probed his ribs. Whatever else happened, both men knew neither one nor the other was likely to report or recount the incident... to anyone. Ever.

'No man living,' Flambard resumed uneasily, mildly aware from the periphery of his vision that something was not quite right among the officer corps behind him. 'N-no man living,' he reprised, 'has the right to confer blame upon the dead. There can be no higher decoration for any of our profession than that which he now bears in Heaven. He departed this world as any good commander of men, with them to the very last, and I for one salute his courage, his pride and integrity. At the last battle, on the last day, we shall see each other again. He knew his duty, and we that are left salute the heroism of his final act on earth and do honour to his sacred memory.'

There was another rumble, and Flambard knew he must move matters on.

'Above all, it is in our duty to him that we remember McGonagle for that which he was: a loyal and devoted soldier, an uncle to Bond and, above all, a courageous comrade who paid the dearest price for his immortal fame. In his life he was a lover of many things, but perhaps foremost among these have been his' – here it came – 'fondness for the English language, and his...' He paused. '... *aspirations* to write poetry in time of war.'

For a moment, the commandant halted, but a dry warning cough at his elbow from a hovering Faunce-Whittington served to remind him that delay was no salvation. *Damn it*, he thought. *I escaped being dismembered by Afghans, eaten by Maoris and scalped by indigenous Canadians, for this?*

Awkwardly, the magistrate resumed his speech. 'His *endeavours*,' he growled, increasing discomfort made readily apparent by the profusion of sweat as it trickled down his weathered forehead. The sun would be unbearable soon, and the hatless mourners burned to a cinder. Or was it just his brain overheating? It was no good, he had to continue. 'His endeavours are the means by which we shall remember him. I have here a work. A work,' he repeated, aware he was mumbling, and stalling. No one was likely to honour *his* sacrifice, he brooded. 'I have here one of his last, most recent works, and it is this that I shall now read to you. Entitled merely *Africa*, I have a feeling that it is this which, were he to be here among us now, McGonagle would have chosen in celebration of his fame. So, *Africa*.' Flambard cleared his throat. '"*In Africa there are no trees*,' he began, painfully aware that there was a small group only a few feet outside the laager.

He paused again, grunted harder and wondered why on earth he had not had the foresight to read the thing through first. *Spare me*, he thought, before clearing his throat again and soldiering on with the terrible contents of the nonsensical arrangement of whimsy.

'"*In Africa there are no trees*",' he repeated. '"*No snow, no ice, ye see few seas. In Africa they do have bees, hornets, scorpions, and fleas, but no ice, few seas*".'

Silence greeted the first verse. Still, no one had thrown anything, and at least it was better than heckling. This was supposed to be a war poem, or so he had thought.

'"*In Africa there are no trees, and so search I for the green of me*".' He stumbled again, but a helpful nudge from Faunce-Whittington reminded Flambard that he was on the home straight. He feared his reputation would never recover. '"*For in the heat and the dust and the rain*",' he continued, trailing off in places and desperately glancing ahead, just in case the awful text got better, '"*A giraffe, by any other name, would be...*"' *Last ounce of courage and bull*, he resolved, closing his eyes, and gritting his teeth. 'Yes, well...' he muttered, trailing off as the text dissolved into gibberish about walking canes that he simply could not read aloud. More nursery rhyme than war poem, at least to the discerning infant. 'I fear he had not the time to complete—' He paused again, turned a little red and continued to mutter about "works in progress" before rolling his eyes, screwing up the paper and suggesting a pause for prayer and reflection.

A snort of muffled hysteria went up from someone, answered by a silencing thwack from another. The commandant shut his eyes and simmered resentfully.

The hiss of expelled mirth was soon replaced by a choking cough, and everyone studied their boots as hard as they could in order to suppress further hilarity.

Coleman winced with pain. *This was supposed to be the captain's funeral*! he cried to himself. Moreover, some soldiers were now looking at him, rather than Flambard, despite the laughably nonsensical recitation.

The funeral party was swiftly dismissed, leaving the two sappers duly detailed to fill in the whole and erect the small wooden cross, tenderly made by Coleman, shakily inscribed with the captain's initials, and surmounted by his glengarry. Despite the poem, the commandant's oratory had visibly moved all ranks.

Bond, who had been breathing and swallowing hard right the way through, gave way to the inevitable, silent tears. Coleman moved instinctively to place a hand on Bond's arm but paused as he noticed the increasing number of disapproving looks at the young sapper who had displaced himself from his own file and marched up bold as brass to stand beside his officer.

Gideon Knight, who seemed to have fallen into a trance since Faunce-Whittington had pulled a gun on him, stood and stared out across the open veldt and tried his best to reconcile his irrevocable and humiliating predicament.

Friday meanwhile had remained silent and utterly dignified despite his horror at the alarming turn of events with Coleman, clamping shut his eyes and broiling like a cauldron. Never would he be able to forgive the breach in discipline that his poor old eyes had seen that day, nor the impropriety, and with icy rage in his heart, vowed to be avenged. The one his own rank permitted him to punish, at any rate.

Flambard retired from the graveside with the irregular officers. A couple of ashen-faced sappers began to shovel clods of earth into the hole in which McGonagle had been laid to rest. They did not know what was going to happen between their surviving officers, their errant, wilful brother sapper, or their demonically outraged sergeant.

'We have to be ready,' Flambard told the officers. 'Once salvageable tents and equipment have been packed up and Lieutenant Knight's remaining men have availed themselves of any necessities from the infantry's stocks, we must resume our search for the main column. I have examined my conscience, and I now believe that the major question lies, not with the border, but the steady supply of forces already active in the field. There is ammunition in these wagons, which the Zulus thankfully failed to get hold of, and is destined for the men of the West Rutlands. I for one believe that McGonagle would want us to see through his mission as well as our own, so for this reason, I will assume command until we are reunited with the main body of Colonel Roystone's invading force. Do I have any objections or suggestions, gentlemen?'

There was a muted hum from the assembled irregulars, and a shaking of heads by the disheartened sappers. No one was going to argue.

Coleman and Faunce-Whittington had begun to look decidedly sheepish in their respective situations, and the commandant's words were proceeded with yet another click as Faunce released the hammer and un-cocked his revolver.

Muttering dangerously quietly about completing his inventory of Penfold's effects, Knight blanked Faunce-Whittington and abruptly ordered Bond to see to the funeral arrangements of their brother officer. Bond, still shaking and numb with shock, grunted at the two sappers to finish burying his uncle, and then collect Lieutenant Penfold's body from the tent in which it had been laid.

A suitable site was selected for the little officer's interment and Coleman, his tanned muscles flexing still harder, dug a shallow pit in the stony earth of the depression and cleared away the undergrowth with his bare hands. Pale and worried sick at the prospect of Friday's incalculable wrath for his flagrant disobedience, he edged a little closer to his officer and said nothing at all.

Penfold's funeral proved to be yet a sombre, mercifully less farcical affair, with the scene growing darker by the minute as the black clouds rolled in overhead and only two officers in attendance. Bond and Faunce removed their helmet and hat respectively, while four sappers carried the late lieutenant's small body in an old oilskin and set him down in the shallow grave.

The weather, so bright and promising when first they awoke that day, had quickly deteriorated into a grim and blustery spectacle, as black and threatening as the storm which had engulfed poor Earnest and left his wife a widow. The wind blew and jostled, choking back speech, and preventing more than a few murmured prayers from being heard for the dead, and eventually the service was abandoned all together, with rocks being placed over the oilskin by Bond and, as ever, the loyal and devoted Coleman.

Chapter Twenty-Five

'We might be spared rain for one day!' Faunce-Whittington bellowed over the torrent, as he and the still fuming Flambard dived for cover under one of the tented wagons and sat watching the falling rain with a shiver as the droplets cascaded off the canopy.

'Faunce,' Flambard began dryly, 'you do realise that we need to move today, whether this terrible storminess eases up or not?'

Faunce-Whittington, who was about to offer a reply, was suddenly distracted by the arrival of Lieutenant Bond. Having only just got over the young sapper's appearance in an entirely unexpected undress regulation, Faunce coloured deeply and grimaced.

'Colonel,' Bond began, addressing Flambard's chest instead of his face. 'I feel that I must not attempt to explain, nor excuse my actions today. I think you know of my conflicts in respect of my late uncle, and I think you also may be aware of—'

'Not now, my dear fellow,' Flambard interrupted quietly, taking Bond's arm, and drawing the officer towards the mouth of a dry and secluded cave, nestling in the lee of the cliff face.

They stepped inside and, although the rain still dripped persistently down the walls and hammered remorselessly down on all without, their improvised shelter retained both light and an air of confidentiality.

Flambard sat down, removed his hat, and gestured for Bond to do the same. This, the officer did obediently and, placing his helmet beside the rock on which he sat, removed the last of his cigars and offered one to the commandant. Flambard refused but coughed pointedly and scratched his whiskers in readiness for a barrage of questions. Yet none were forthcoming, and the reticence of both men was painfully apparent.

'Lieutenant,' he began. 'What I have to tell you I do so not because I am ashamed, nor that I feel I have any need to justify myself, my career or my place, but because I feel it will help you in understanding the circumstances of your late uncle's—' he paused.

'Disposition?' Bond volunteered.

Flambard nodded readily. 'Thank you,' he replied. 'I was always favoured with some degree of eloquence which, considering what I have to tell you, you might think more remarkable than my present status, and the means by which I came to acquire it.'

Bond said nothing. His interest was not in Flambard, but McGonagle.

'I should tell you,' Flambard told him haltingly, 'that I knew your uncle long before either he or I ever came to South Africa, long before I retired, and a lifetime before the advent of this present war. I was a young man, with few prospects beyond that of my father, and an ambition to follow, not just in his footsteps, but to better both my own circumstances and his modest aspirations for me. Is that understandable to you?'

Again, Bond duly nodded. Familial expectations were entirely relatable, although the following revelation was to strike him, and the others, resolutely.

'I joined the army,' Flambard resumed, 'as a private soldier.'

Bond started, as did Faunce-Whittington, the latter having

been eavesdropping a little way outside the cave mouth.

Flambard was only too aware of the officer's presence. 'Come in, Faunce, since you might as well know the rest,' he sighed.

At this point, Faunce coughed uncomfortably, muttering through his embarrassment something about there being another individual outside, desirous of admission.

This time, it was Bond who nodded. 'Please admit Sapper Coleman also,' he instructed, assuming the most authoritative tone he might under the increasingly bizarre circumstances of their interview.

Cowed, quiet and slightly alarmed by the irregularity of events, Coleman sheepishly followed Faunce into the cave and, dispensing with protocol, sat beside his officer.

'Colonel,' Bond resumed, 'I understand this is to be both a private and personal revelation for you, but I still don't understand what this has to do with McGonagle.'

'Do let me finish, please, gentlemen!' Flambard grunted.

Coleman looked questioningly, but Flambard showed no sign of correcting himself. Only officers were ever referred to as "gentlemen", at least in his army.

'Gentlemen *all*,' Flambard reiterated, gently touching Coleman's sleeve as the boy rose once more to make up a fire and hang the kettle. 'For I make no distinction, nor apology for saying such.'

Silence followed until the commandant, breathing deeply, resting his temples against his gnarled hands resumed his disclosure.

'I attested in 1837, the same year our young Queen was crowned. I had been to the Royal Hibernian Institute in Dublin, where my father had sent me to learn his craft. It was a brutal life, and the curriculum harsh, yet I knew I wanted to do well, so I stuck it out. Old boys of the school often went on to be NCOs, quartermasters or even paymasters, and my standard of literacy and numeracy was good for my age and station. Thence was I accepted into the second battalion of the West Rutlands at the age of fifteen, just in time to take ship for the insurrection in Canada.'

Another short silence interceded with all eyes fixed on the commandant, who sat before them as if in long awaited judgement of some notorious felon.

'I first met AW McGonagle as an officer in India,' Flambard explained hesitantly. 'I had already been in the army for twenty years before, you understand, and through various wars. I had also been fortunate. My education at the institute had afforded me promotion at a most satisfactory rate, achieving sergeant on my twenty-third birthday and sergeant major by the time I was thirty.'

Coleman, who thus far had remained silent, suddenly lifted his head, and murmured aloud at such a prosperous ascension. Could there be such hope for him, he wondered?

'How on earth did you manage to progress so, Colonel?' Faunce enquired gingerly, adding, 'You were really an officer, weren't you?' as a distinctly questionable afterthought.

Flambard sighed, smiled wearily, and nodded.

Bond cursed inwardly. This sort of prevarication was largely irrelevant to his interests. Even so, he listened with courtesy and rehearsed patience as, by degrees, the old soldier took the other two enthralled listeners through his long and varied career, until he was utterly lost in the recital of his story, and Bond was as gripped as the others. Spellbound, they listened as, from a teenaged boy aboard a troopship to Canada, the magistrate brought them up to date through the decades and deployments to their present day, and his command of the

African volunteers.

'Times were hard after the European wars,' Flambard began. 'My own father had enlisted to fight the French, and succeeded to the rank of sergeant, where he remained for a further ten years after Waterloo. Yet times were harder still at home, with so many men discharged sick, wounded, and maimed. Between my childhood in the late twenties and Crimea some quarter century past, passages to Canada rose beyond the capabilities of its small colonial government to administer. Some settlers looked to America and sought autonomy through force, with the indigenous peoples caught in between, loyal to whomsoever expediency dictated for the safety of their families and economies. I was then stationed in Quebec and, when the news of the insurrection reached us, old Sir John Colborne threw up a fort and had the wisdom to commission sleighs and snowshoes for us troops. The conditions were terrible, snow as deep as your waist in parts. I went with my corporal, sergeant, our officer, and the captain under the command of Colonel Gore to St Denis, and there we fought tooth and nail for five hours, until the terrible climate forced the colonel to look to his own men and retire. Until that day, I had never so much as struck a fellow man outside a boxing ring, yet by the time we seized Saint-Eustache in the late November, I had killed – some French, some indigenous. I also lost the top of my little finger to frostbite, and gained my first whiskers, while the powder burns on my face left pockmarks, which you see to this day.' Here, the commandant paused.

The rain grew heavier, and Bond told Jack to go and light the bundle of kindling, which some previous occupant had stacked in a corner. 'Here,' he added, removing the last of his cigars and offering one around.

Flambard refused again, but Faunce, whose tobacco had

long since run out, was only too pleased to accept.

'I should pop it into auction,' he quipped. 'One might raise a guinea!'

'From whom?' Bond shrugged, defiantly handing over the cigar, and lighting his own with careless ease of purpose. 'I expect one might fetch such a price for a cake of soap.'

The fire stoked, Coleman sat back down beside his officer and Flambard, by now weary of interruptions, warmed his big old hands, and gladly resumed his story.

'By June of 1840, I was a lad of eighteen, just like this handsome chap.'

Coleman smiled shyly and blushed while Flambard continued.

'By that time the opium wars had begun, sordid and degrading as they were,' he told them. 'My battalion was sent to fight the Chinese, who still used horn bows and wore skirts, yet they laughed at us in our tailcoats, shakos and collar stocks.'

Here again, Coleman could not help smiling at the thought of a modern army fighting little Chinamen in silk dresses within living and serving memory, but the commandant was indulgent of his incredulity.

'This time we served under Sir Hugh Gough, another good old fellow, and a veteran of Talavera, who recognised the courage, strength, yet also the ruthless efficiency of our foemen. They were also very cunning, with great ornate guns, old and antiquated, and some of them dating as far back as three hundred years! We went as far as Ningpo without the slightest difficulty, and when thousands of Tartar troops dug in their artillery around Canton, General Gough outflanked them, and took their forts in a matter of an hour. On the day of the Tiger, we took Shanghai, Chinkiang and, in the summer of '42, to my shame as I reflect upon it, we destroyed the ancient Celestial Empire for ever, ending two long years of war over opium. I was wounded twice in that campaign, and subsequently came to learn that any solider has the potential to be your equal, however strange his clothes or alien his customs. If naught else, you men must know this from the Zulus. We were shipped to India and took Sindh in '43. I was one and twenty, and a corporal by the time I served under Napier.'

'Lord Robert?' Faunce interjected.

'No,' Flambard replied patiently, 'General Sir Charles, a colourful little gentleman, and a great leader, to my mind the best and greatest Napier of the lot. We braved shot, shell and the most fearful Baluchi tribesmen with butt and bayonet, until we routed the enemy with over six thousand killed, may God forgive us. At Dubba, the old general led the final charge himself, though well over sixty, securing Sindh and restoring peace for our allies. Two summers later I was in the Punjab, back under Gough, and a sergeant for all my service. I was captured and wounded, yet for seven years more I remained in India, even fighting on the North-West Frontier. The Afghans are a ferocious, determined foe and to this day unconquered. Ever will it remain so in my view.'

He was interrupted by a cough from Bond, who rose, left, and returned a few minutes later, windblown, muddy, and soaking wet, laden with his late uncle's cape, cigar box and, lastly, a burnished silver hip flask. This last item the officers eyed with interest, and Bond proffered without distinction. Even Jack took a swig; the warm, rich, tingling quality promoted by the whisky and the crackling twigs of the little fire drying out his still damp clothes and leaving him feeling better than he had felt in a very, very long time. He was even growing more comfortable with the three officers and, as time would reveal, they were growing more affectionate towards him, and relaxed in his company.

Flambard, who had been shifting position to alleviate the numbness in his backside from sitting on a stone, accepted the flask with alacrity and resumed his tale.

'Now, let me see. Where was I? Ah yes, the Afghans. An indomitable foe, some of whom had blond hair and blue eyes, reputed to descend from Alexander the Great!'

Faunce took another slug of whisky and caught himself gazing at Coleman. Flambard quickly followed his gaze and sought to divert it away from the boy.

'They were also excellent marksmen, with a gift for skirmishing and a brutal habit of dismemberment upon any misfortunate enough to fall alive, or wounded, in that harsh, hellish country. Never did they yield, nor sue for peace, nor relent. Nor shall they.'

Bond stirred up the fire with the toe of his boot. Faunce unfastened two olivettes on his patrol jacket, while Flambard took another swig from McGonagle's flask.

'The Crimean War began in '54,' he explained. 'I was, by this time, over thirty myself and a veteran of some seventeen years, promoted to the rank of sergeant major.'

'Ah yes!' Faunce exclaimed triumphantly. 'I always said you had the voice for one!'

'Do let me go on, Faunce!' Flambard grumbled. 'I'm coming to a point!'

Faunce went quiet. Bond leaned forward on his elbow, and Coleman, eyes wide and bright, largely on account of the whisky, fixed upon the old soldier with admiration.

The flickering light of the fire jumped back and forth, from the ceiling of the cave to the weathered lines of the magistrate's face, and the deep, vicious scars, mellowed by time. The light was fading without, and through the rain the three men were dimly aware that the packing up of the camp was fully underway, albeit despite their notable absences. At this stage, none of them cared overmuch.

'For two long years we fought the Russians. Lord Raglan, another old aristocrat of sixty-seven, was also a stale old martinet and a general of the Iron Duke's getting. He would confuse the Russians with the French, to their chagrin, as they were by then our allies!' chuckled Flambard. 'Veterans of Canada might have preferred to bunk with the Russians too, for feelings still ran deep among some old hands, I dare say!'

'France fought beside Britain in Crimea,' Bond explained to Coleman, who didn't care a farthing anyway so long as Flambard continued with his story.

'We were fine to begin with,' Flambard resumed. 'We were well fed, the enemy were in retreat from Bulgaria, and even the French were not proving to be the intolerable bedfellows we had feared. The colour of the towns and the rich, varied ways and customs of its peoples were something quite remarkable, and a real education to me, a poor boy from Gloucester. Then cholera struck us, and terrible numbers died. Ships were lost, supplies ran low, and lines of communication failed. We lost more of my battalion to disease than to the Russians, and as for the lack of medical support...'

'What happened, Colonel?' Bond enquired, for his own part equally keen to know when matters would move on to the more relevant topics of India... and McGonagle.

'Lord Raglan and old General Canrobert received orders to attack Sebastopol. We landed at Calamita Bay in September of '54 and spent the night in the rain. The French troops, it seemed, were much better organised and had looting and thievery down to a fine art, while we stopped out in the cold, with no food to eat and our matchlocks under our greatcoats to keep the powder from spoiling.'

'Much like last night, then,' Faunce suggested lightly.

'Worse,' replied Flambard. 'Now please, let me get on and stop interrupting! Finally, on the twentieth of September, we marched on the enemy at Alma. It was there that I met a young ensign called Harry Roystone.'

'The colonel?' whispered Coleman.

Bond nodded and pressed his finger to his lips.

The commandant continued undaunted. 'Not yet seventeen, Harry Roystone took on a Russian hussar with just the sword in his hand, and then went on to lead us through a hail of shell, bullets and carnage, through the vineyards and onto the heights, to our victory, and his Victoria Cross for bravery.'

Everyone listened in silence from then on; the story was just heating up.

'Our captain had been killed during the first Russian salvo,' Flambard recollected. 'Both lieutenants fell among the vines, and only two boy ensigns remained standing. Harry Roystone, shot and wounded – as was I – continued to lead us over the heights and on to the crest of Alma, where we carried the day amid the Russian emplacements and sent them from the field in a worse state of disarray than was ever to be seen at Agincourt.'

'They should have taken Sebastopol at once,' Bond remarked gloomily. 'I studied the work of the Russian engineers at the academy. They encircled the port, chain linked the batteries, and caused the allies terrible losses from their barrages.'

'Quite so,' Flambard concurred. 'From then on, we endured sickness, disease, cholera, and death. They talk of Florence Nightingale, but Mother Mary Seacole must be remembered with saintly affection for her great work in that terrible desert of mud and snow! I for one will always remember that redoubtable woman as fondly as any man jack of the army!'

A silence fell, the fire leapt, and a fly buzzed lazily around the roof of the cave, as each man allowed his mind to wander in private thought. Mrs Seacole, a formidable black Jamaican widow, had saved many a young British life during that hellish campaign, securing the love of both officers and men by her fearless courage, her kindness to the troops, and her generosity, which finally sent her bankrupt. With her in mind, each man in his own way, fell to wondering whether all Zulus really were so terrible as the ones who had slaughtered their comrades, sacked their camp and mutilated McGonagle. Or maybe just soldiers, fighting as they were trained to do for their homes, farms, and families.

The rain had begun to ease off outside the cave, and everywhere troopers and sappers could be seen scurrying back and forth, packing up the tents, collecting supplies and loading them onto the wagons.

'Go on, please, your honour,' Coleman ventured, as the look of frustration on the face of Bond betrayed the questions he was too proud to ask.

Flambard, numb and aching like the rest of them, shifted his formidable frame once more and began his account of more recent events. 'In the year of '57,' he began.

'The "mutiny",' put in Bond, relieved.

Flambard said nothing, and a painful silence pervaded.

Bond apologised.

'I was well into my thirties at the time of the rebellion,' Flambard continued. 'I had served in the army for a total of twenty years by this time and was a sergeant major with a row of medals upon my breast. I had fought in no less than five campaigns and could go no further in my career as an enlisted man. Harry Roystone, himself a decorated lieutenant, petitioned the colonel to have me commissioned. He too was a fine old fellow and although a traditionalist, persuaded me to accept, but also to remain within the same battalion.'

'Why did you hesitate?' asked Faunce, earning himself a pointed look from Bond, anticipating an end to Flambard's tale, and progression to the topic of McGonagle.

Flambard shrugged. 'I knew what to expect,' he replied. 'Our own battalion was kind enough, yet I knew it was frowned upon by officers *and* men alike.'

Coleman wiped his nose on his sleeve, took another swig from the hip flask and sniffed. The fly continued to buzz. Still, no one else spoke a word.

'Some things do not change with time,' the magistrate continued, this time settling a little as the resignation of his disclosure became tempered by the telling of his greatest story. 'India was one of the few places where a self-made man might maintain a decent lifestyle befitting an officer. Few outside my own battalion cared for my promotion. I had no money, as such, and could not afford to drink in the mess with the others. Only two men were willing to associate with me besides Harry Roystone, and they were Captain Alec McGonagle, and a young Rutland officer called Arthur McEnry.'

'*Colonel* McEnry?' Coleman mouthed to Bond.

He nodded in turn and gestured for the young sapper to listen.

'What happened, Colonel?' Faunce ventured warily.

'The rebellion,' Flambard replied. 'The most significant single event of my entire military career, and one that, while it has haunted me, downright blighted him.'

Bond's eyes brightened, as did those of Faunce. Now they would know the truth, albeit subjective and tempered with hindsight.

'I had just transitioned from the most senior, enlisted ranks in the battalion,' Flambard told them slowly, 'to the most junior station of the officer class, moving among young, educated men and the privileged. I was poor, and I was living in a world of gentlemen, fewer in years and service yet senior to me. My colonel,' he added significantly, 'for all I revered the man, was himself a lieutenant when first I attested. I knew then that if I lived, gained the respect of my peers and the trust of my men, most of whom respected me but opposed my commission, I could no more remain a subaltern than go back to the ranks as a sergeant. I knew then that, above all else, I needed advancement, to see myself satisfied as well as secure. When McGonagle confided that he was to be assigned a non-company officer to assist his administration of his garrison, he suggested I apply and petitioned my colonel to recommend my candidacy.'

Another short silence interceded, and Flambard took a moment to examine the inscription on the old captain's silver hip flask, and the rows of silk decorating his own burley breast.

'Strange,' he said at last, 'to think that this was the very flask that he offered to me the first time we rode out together under the hot Hindustani sun, and that same flask that we drank from in the basement of the surgeon's house.'

Everyone looked puzzled, but by now knew better than to interrupt.

'McGonagle's command was of the fort, the walled garrison town, its people, and the hundred and fifty sepoy soldiers and non-commissioned officers who guarded and maintained order. The nearest British garrison was somewhere between Lucknow and Calcutta, and nearest potential help a matter of several days away. When the first rumours of mutiny began to filter through, albeit in the form of stifled reports and exaggerated, lurid rumours, the Indian troops under my command became unsettled. At first there was nothing much to notice. They became circumspect, spoke only among themselves, and eschewed their regimental mess and temple. Each time I or one of the other officers went about his routine, he felt he was being scrutinised in the queerest sort of way; as if the fellows would clap eyes on you everywhere you went, and I for one became suspicious, if not to say downright windy.'

'How many were you, Colonel?' Bond asked.

'Five,' Flambard replied, 'plus a havildar. Beg pardon, that is a sergeant, who was loyal, and a couple of servants who had been with McGonagle for years. We conducted ourselves as normal, yet, as time went on, we felt ourselves trapped within the town, and later, even the fort. One would give an order, and the fellows would obey, but all the time you felt as if they were waiting for you to act, as you were for them. It was a very strange feeling, and eventually the suspicion and suspense on both sides became unbearable.'

'What did you do?' asked Faunce-Whittington.

'We took to organising meetings, just we five,' Flambard explained. 'We would meet at a certain time and at a safe location, each time staggering the hour by the day. For instance, Monday might be at the chapel at seven, while Tuesday would be in one of the offices at eight and so on. This was so that we could take a special note of any strange activity, or any signs we took for furtive behaviour on the part of our men, who so far had exhibited no outward manifestations of mutiny. We went on like this for a week, with all sorts of strange stories, most of which we attributed to our own sensitivities. Yet we knew something had to come, and on Tuesday of the second week, it came.'

Bond stiffened. This was what he had needed to know –

the answers to questions from way back when – and finally, an explanation for the man he had come to know as McGonagle.

'We met in the basement of the surgeon's house,' the magistrate began. 'It was long after dark, and we knew the dispositions of our watchmen and sentries well enough, for we had made them ourselves according to our plans. McGonagle and I had been the last officers about, so we returned to his office, disguised ourselves in long black robes, and slipped through the darkened streets under our guards' very noses. It was pitch-dark as we stole down the cellar steps and into the basement. If the night was dark outside, it was utterly impenetrable down there, and we five could only see one another when huddled around a single oil lamp on an old table in the centre of the floor. It was then that we discovered both Surgeon James and Lieutenant Saddler were missing. Lieutenant Carver and I wanted to cut out, arm ourselves beyond our personal weapons and search for them, but McGonagle insisted we wait. After all, he said, what can we do? And he was right.'

Bond and Faunce looked especially surprised; Coleman looked downright lost.

Flambard saw the doubt in their eyes and instantly took it for censure. 'Don't ever mistake me,' he said to Bond. 'McGonagle as you may have known him was one man, but the McGonagle I knew was quite different. He was in the prime of life and a fine, stout, black-haired man with every confidence in himself and a mind as sure as stone. When he took a drink, he was merry, but never did it cloud his judgement. That came about much later,' he added grimly. 'So too with his alienation, his eccentricity.'

'What did they do?' Faunce asked again, albeit in a cautious manner. In the ten years he had known Flambard, they had never spoken of the rebellion. Now he began to know why.

'Nothing,' Flambard replied. 'At least, not for the time being. Why, they had done quite enough as it was. After all, there were we, three officers with three knives and our revolvers between us, too scared to leave our basement for fear of ambush and too worried for the fate of our comrades to consider what might already have happened.'

'Colonel,' Bond began, as a pause in Flambard's passage offered him the chance to ask a question. 'McGonagle was married, at least I know that.'

Flambard nodded.

'What happened to her?' added Faunce-Whittington.

The magistrate, however, was determined to tell the story his way. 'There we were,' he told them, 'trapped in a cellar, just the three of us. Even with Surgeon James and Lieutenant Saddler there wouldn't have been enough of us to put up a fight, and besides, the wives and families of our remaining officers were still in the fort, guarded by our sepoys. If we tried to extract them openly, we would surely have been spotted and killed, as would they.'

'What did you do, sir?' interrupted Coleman.

'I was coming to that, youngster,' Flambard replied. 'Our situation was this: there were two or three good men whom we knew we could count on – we knew that much from the first. Where they were, those men, or whether they were even still alive were matters we would not be able to settle from the confines of our basement prison. We knew we had to cut out, yet we had to be able to do so without arousing the suspicions of our soldiers. If they had known that something was up, they would have abandoned their pretence and the game would be over for us. We had to find a way back to the fort without being spotted, and the only thing for it were the sewers.'

Faunce, who had been listening with developing agitation,

now winced. Coleman grimaced, and even Bond closed his eyes and shuddered in distaste.

'The sewers were all that was left!' protested Flambard. 'We had only just made it as it was; we didn't know what had happened to our brother officer and Surgeon James, not to mention what might be happening back at the fort. A moment's pause, or the slightest of margins and we knew they would be in there before we had a chance to stop them. They were guarding the officers' quarters, and it was within those very walls that the wives and children of our company slept unsuspecting. We had to get there somehow, and what did a smell matter against the protection of our defenceless ones?'

Everyone fell to contemplating. What would they do in that situation, they wondered grimly? Bond looked at Coleman, and not for the first time, he knew that should the need ever arise, he would kill, or die, to protect him.

'Did you go?' he asked the commandant.

Flambard nodded. 'McGonagle was undecided,' he explained. 'For the first time since I met him, he seemed to falter. He was so totally unsure. Always bearing in mind that it was his and Saddler's wives with whose lives we were gambling, I knew it was my time to speak. I was a former sergeant major with twenty years' experience, remember. From whom else should McGonagle have the right to demand advice, if not from me?'

No one answered, so the magistrate continued.

'I was spared the evil decision of knowing that it was not my wife or child in there. McGonagle knew that, and so he called upon me to decide matters. "You aren't blinded by love, Gillespie", he told me. "You must decide for us all".'

'What did you do?' asked Faunce.

'We went,' replied Flambard. 'I could see no other way of

gaining access to the fort without first arousing the sepoys' suspicions. The sewers were miserable wading affairs and stank to high heaven. I went first, being the largest, and although the only light was the odd flame above a drain hole, we managed to find our way to the spot where roughly we estimated the officers' quarters to be. That was the trouble, you see,' Flambard lamented. 'The maps and plans drawn up by the surveyors were wrong. We had nothing but a general sense of direction, which at night is always hampered, anyway. We gained our drain, and McGonagle went first, he, being the one in command.' The magistrate stiffened as he spoke. 'It was here that we came unstuck. Almost as soon as he had the grate up and scrambled out on to the cold stone of the floor, he knew something was up from the smell. We had just been used to some dreadful stink, I can tell you, but the scent of the sepoy dorms was unmistakable. Two or three of them there were, all siting around a fire in the middle of the room with their muskets propped against the walls. They were surprised to see us as well when we popped up out of that manhole and into their little coven. From then on there was little choice about it. We had come up in the wrong place, a small bastion just outside the fort, and we knew our plans were ruined. McGonagle was up first, firing away and killing two of them, the third taking flight up the spiral staircase at the far end of the little room. But McGonagle went after him, struggling up the staircase and firing until he brought the fellow down. The shots had soon been heard the length and breadth of the garrison, and very soon we knew we should be swamped. Lieutenant Carver seized one of the muskets – they were still using the old forty-two pattern, since they wouldn't have the Enfield because of the damned pig fat cartridges. Arrogant idiocy that issued them! Insulting their faith and inciting their ire! We rushed the staircase together,

McGonagle picking himself up as he went. I took the first with my long Hindu dagger, while Carver jumped to the windows and fired his musket, killing the sentry placed in the courtyard below. The other was soon off over the walls, but McGonagle had gained his feet by this time, and ran to the window with his revolver. There was soon another dead rebel on the cold stones of that lonely little fortress, I can tell you. Anyway, the problem was that we were stuck fast, once again. There was no way out, so we slammed shut the iron gate on the courtyard, snatched up what we could for weapons and spent the night exchanging answering shots with the mutineers who manned the walls. Throughout that night we heard shooting coming, we thought, from the chapel windows. It later transpired that Saddler and Surgeon James had managed to steal themselves away inside armoury, no doubt having been forced to ground while rushing to attend our earlier meeting. By good fortune, they had seized two brand new and hitherto unused Enfields, which the sepoys had spurned. They made a pretty good fight of it, and certainly kept the bulk of the garrison off our backs during the night, although several times they tried to get in, and we had to fend them off with swords and daggers through that gate.'

Nobody, it seemed, dared to ask the next question, so in the event, no one did.

'We kept it up all night,' Flambard resumed. 'Firing away until our shot was gone and the rebels straining at the gate, the shutters and even a few on the roof pulling tiles to get at us. Poor Carver thought he had the answer: he would make a rush for the wall, scramble over the top and fly to raise the alarm. He was shot dead the instant he left the cover of the doorway, and a merciful blessing it was for him to be so.'

'Why?' Bond asked hollowly. 'What happened, Colonel?'

Flambard sighed. He had waited twenty years to tell this story, why couldn't these youngsters wait more than twenty seconds to hear him tell it? 'We had to do something,' he replied. 'We had fought for four hours, run out of everything and it was only a matter of time, we knew, before our own men broke through the shutters and put us both to the sword. So, we took to the drains again, and this time we knew where we were going. We made straight for the central bastion of the fort, scrambled up yet another stinking drain hole, only to find it had been covered over with a stone, or some such heavy object. By now, we knew, they had guessed that we were beneath the streets themselves. Mobs with torches, swords and axes took to the drains as well, and soon the two of us were crawling through the brackish water, literally in fear of our own lives. We found a shallow cave, probably a flooded cellar.' Flambard sighed ashamedly. 'And there we stayed until the mob had gone, the noises died away, and the smell of effluent had been augmented by the smell of anarchy. They had sacked the town, burnt the bungalows and we knew, left not a single European or Eurasian alive. McGonagle cursed the sappers who had surveyed the tunnels, presumably by estimation rather than exploration, and I blamed myself for my decision. These twenty years, I have feared that McGonagle must as rightly do so as well.'

'Did you speak of it, Colonel, when you met again, here in Africa?' Bond asked.

Flambard shook his head and cast his eyes to the floor. 'No. To my shame, I said nothing. He did not recognise me and I, in my guilt, forbore to stir the embers of such painful memories. In this affair, I fear, I have been a coward.'

'I remember discussion of medals, Colonel, and of India,' Faunce murmured at length. 'I must confess I thought it strange that he should speak of it, and you remain so quiet, though I know of your career and your service there.'

'What should I have said to him, Faunce?' Flambard retorted gloomily. 'What could I possibly have asked, or said, or recollected, that would bring the man anything but pain? Here was I, a retired major of the regular army with silks enough to speak of my life and campaigns while he, a captain, still... with one sullied ribbon, a permanent reminder of his loss? Rebuked, derided, bereaved, and dishonoured, all for want of *my* good council so many years before.'

Chapter Twenty-Six

For a while, no one spoke. Cries from the troopers and sappers outside were taken up by the snort and stamp of the horses, and the jungle and clatter as the oxen were yoked to the wagon limbers. The dribble of rain began to ease down the wall of the cave.

'McGonagle's wife, Colonel,' Bond began tactfully. 'My aunt.'

Flambard nodded wearily and resumed his tale for the last, agonising stretch. 'She was Indian, you know,' he began, chiefly addressing Faunce and Jack, for he assumed that Bond would know the rest. He was mistaken however, and the officer closed his eyes sharply as the slap of his own unknown family history hit him across the face. These were things he didn't even know, being told to him by a man who six months earlier had been a stranger.

'Was she young, your honour?' asked Coleman timidly.

Again, Flambard nodded. 'She was, and the most beautiful girl. The years made no difference to her. She was utterly in love with the man, and he just as utterly in love with her. They were devoted to one another, and that night in the drains, as we listened powerless to the mob sack the garrison, I looked in his eyes and I believe to this day that I saw his heart break.'

'She was... killed?' Faunce enquired.

'McGonagle's wife, together with the wives of my fellow

officers, and Indian servants, women, and children, all butchered as they slept. We returned to the fort the following morning, when the mutineers had gone, and the town lay in ruins. It was a foolish move as there might well have been more of them, but McGonagle would have nothing different, and the least I could do was see him safe after the calamity I had brought upon him.'

'Why do you say that, Colonel?' Bond asked in alarmed surprise. 'You couldn't have predicted what would happen, surely?'

Flambard shrugged. 'It was me he asked for advice,' he replied. 'I had twenty years' experience, and it was me he relied upon for a dispassionate viewpoint.'

Faunce-Whittington shook his head and tutted. 'How can you imagine it, Colonel?' he asked sadly. 'You would have risked your life to accompany him back to the fort. Neither of you could have gained anything by rushing in and both getting killed that night, any more than did that poor lieutenant, when he chanced the snipers outside the bastion.'

'Dear Faunce,' Flambard replied, patting him on the knee. 'How often thereafter I wished that I had been killed with the others, when I thought of McGonagle, his poor dead wife and the sights we saw that day; the faithful ones and those poor, innocent souls.'

Again, he paused, but no one was about to rush him, or interrupt at such a crucial stage.

'We returned that day to a bloodbath,' the commandant told them sorrowfully. 'Corpses littered the streets, bodies lay shot, or stabbed and bleeding on the ramparts, up the stairs and along the passages. Children of the servants lay alongside the children of my fellow officers just as they had played together, their white linen shirts and pyjamas soaked with their blood.

McGonagle's wife we found in their bedchamber, stripped, debased, and cut several times with a sword. Try as we might, we never did get the colour of blood from our hands, our clothes, or the stones she lay on, and McGonagle never trusted his judgement again, nor mine, I should judge. That lovely soft skin, *cut* like that...'

For a moment, the magistrate allowed his mind to wander back to that terrible place, but a sharp, stifled cough from Bond caused Flambard to break his reverie and look up. Sincerely, with the same sorrowful passion as that with which he had told of it, he apologised to Bond for the way he had had to find out.

'I'm sorrier,' he said forlornly, 'because twenty years on I have failed to save even him.'

Bond, expressionless and with a face like stone, rose and looked out of the cave. 'I shan't add to your guilt, sir,' he replied, not unselfishly. 'Though I wish I had known of this long ago or come to some understanding of it before my uncle died.' With that, he left the cave and wandered out into the rain.

Coleman, still stuck fast by the bizarre turn of events that had led to such disclosures and affected so heavily the relationships of those whom he revered, scrambled up and dashed after his officer.

Faunce remained quiet for a time, his face turned from its usual red to a greyish colour, and even his normally beady green eyes seemed to roll in on themselves as he looked both this way and that for something to say to Flambard.

At last, it seemed all he could manage was the inevitable. 'It wasn't your fault, Colonel,' he muttered into his beard. 'Whatever else you were, had done or had been before, McGonagle was the officer in command. It was for him to decide and unfair to impose upon you. You blame yourself, yet

I feel sure he did not.'

'Thank you, Faunce,' the commandant replied mirthlessly. 'I told them the truth back then, but they were bent on blaming McGonagle.'

'Why him, though?' Faunce demanded. 'I mean, he was only something like thirty then, why, you even said so yourself. So why should they be so keen to destroy him?'

Flambard closed his eyes and shook his head. 'The mistake of Alec McGonagle was not in marrying an Indian, not at that time, but in choosing one of a diplomatically irrelevant caste and clan. His choice of bride was a snub to some potentates whom the British had been trying desperately to court. He could have married strategically and cemented both their interests and his career, but he did not. The establishment of India and the army never quite forgave him, nor he them.'

'What happened to him after that?' asked Faunce-Whittington, aghast. 'And why did neither one of you say anything to the other after sharing so much?'

'Oh, questions, questions! One at a time, Faunce!' snapped back the commandant, quickly calming his temper so as not to neglect important detail. 'After we found them, we rode as fast as we could to Ambala, where the British forces under Sir George Anson were preparing to relieve Delhi. We said goodbye to each other as we rode into headquarters camp, McGonagle to have his wounds dressed and I to report to my own colonel before reporting to the surgeon for treatment myself. I never saw him again after that day, not even at Delhi, although I am told he was there, and never more between that time and my being shipped to New Zealand to fight the Maori in '61. When I returned to India in the middle of '65, I was a captain myself.'

'What of the board of enquiry?' Faunce protested. 'Surely your evidence should have been heard?'

'I was never called to testify,' Flambard replied. 'I met Mrs Flambard when I came home in '59. We were married twenty years, as you know, and I miss her to this day.'

Faunce-Whittington nodded and smiled sadly. He too had known the patience, love, and tenderness of that warm, gentle woman, who had been as much a mother to him when he arrived in the Cape as all the nannies he had ever had at home. There had been a special love between her and old Flambard, one that lasted, unquestioning, throughout his long years of overseas campaigning, and even when he took the decision to emigrate and farm in South Africa, she had remained resolutely beside him.

'What happened to McGonagle? Do you know?' he asked.

'I continued to follow his advance, or lack thereof, through the army lists. Yet each gazette, year on year, list upon list, there he was, unchanged and passed over. That was the end of that. Another two years on the North-West Frontier, I accompanied Napier to Abyssinia in '68, they awarded me a majority in '69, and I retired from service that same year to begin a new life with my dear wife, satisfied with my career and position.'

'It's all quite romantic,' Faunce concluded placidly. 'Though terrible, it really is the most wonderful story, Colonel. Albert's aunt an Indian princess too, ah!'

'Not for McGonagle it wasn't,' Flambard retorted sharply. 'He gave his wife a Hindu burial rather than a Christian one, and his career along with it. And now,' he added, 'I have had the added burden of raking up all this pain for poor Bond to come to terms with, as if he didn't have quite enough already.'

As they spoke, the young sapper officer stood outside the cave, rain streaming off his sun helmet as he stared blindly out into the driving gale. Coleman, who had followed him quietly as ever, simply stood beside him and tucked his hand in Bond's.

Touched, saddened, and emotionally drained, Bond collapsed his head into Jack's arms and the two of them remained there sobbing, sheltered from view by the rocks, yet rained on mercilessly from above.

For Flambard and Faunce, their morning of revelations was sharply broken in upon by Lieutenant Knight who, having marched up and saluted, remained outside the cave, and informed the commandant stiffly that the tents had been struck in anticipation of his orders.

Flambard, who was too dispirited to argue or take issue, grunted a few words of thanks, donned his wide-brimmed hat, and set off once more into the rain.

Faunce, dolefully replaced his own hat, dowsed the spluttering fire, and followed in his wake.

Matters moved swiftly on from that point. The rain stopped at about 9:00 a.m., and the commandant issued orders for his men to mount up.

It is proving to be a late start, Flambard pondered grimly, but there was little to be done about it. The wagons were dragged somehow into line, and once again the picks and shovels of Lieutenant Knight's sappers were out in force, digging, widening, and levering wheels out of the sodden mire. A new and unexpected period of daylight emerged about halfway through the morning, and the dark, threatening expanse of cloud seemed to drift off into the distance. With it went the final fleeting glimpses of the last fighting place of their friends and brother soldiers. Everything shone with a peculiar colour after such a downpour, and the stink of wet herbage was heightened further by a damp, sickly smell every time the boots of the soldiers or the wheels, or hooves of the wagon animals and their trains sank into the deep red mud. The ground sang all around them, and slurps and squelches provided the only interruption to the rhythmical dripping from anything that had spent the night outside the caves.

Just before they had mounted up to leave, Bond and Coleman had sloped off up the hillside together. There, they had paused, and the two young sappers took a last long look at the flat grass whereupon the wagons had lately stood; the flotsam and debris left behind on the camp site and, lastly, at the sad, sombre plots of freshly turned earth wherein the dead lay buried. Almost as if he were oblivious to the officer's admiring scrutiny, young Jack removed his helmet and smoothed his blond hair back off his forehead. Bond smiled and looked away again, saying nothing as the two of them walked back down to the waiting column.

'Who would have thought it?' the officer mused sadly, as Sapper Whelan lead his horse up to the point where the waiting officer stood prepared to mount. 'All that time ago in Chatham when you made me read those letters and I didn't want to read. Who would have thought that, less than a year later, we might be here with my uncle dead and all that had happened behind us?'

Coleman, unable to find the words with which to answer, discretely fed his hand into Bond's. With practiced caution, he wiped his nose on the sleeve of his serge, distanced himself from his officer, saluted, and scrambled up on to the wagon.

Not once since the funerals had Sergeant Friday so much as looked at him, and somehow he knew well that things would never be the same between the three of them again.

The poem Flambard could not bring himself to finish reciting.

Africa
By Captain AW McGonagle, 91st Regt.

In Africa there are no trees,
No snow no ice, ye see few seas.
In Africa they do have bees, hornets, scorpions, and fleas,
But no ice, few seas.
In Africa there are no trees,
And so, search I for the green of me,
For in the heat and the dust and the rain,
A giraffe by any other name, would be,
A walking cane.
*But what of rain?
That soothe upon the troubled brain,
That fall upon one now and again,
To sate the pate and cool the air,
To numb the pain of heat.
For them wi' nae hair.
As the bard do say,
"No profit grow wherein no pleasure ta'en,"
As I look across the plane, braw but plain,
And see,
No trees.
But those of me I see.
So green, of heart, must strive te be.

*The content of the eleventh line onwards were discovered by an archivist among some 91st and 93rd regimental records, Edinburgh Castle, 1971. The poem has not been included in the canons of war poetry from the last two centuries. Students of other McGonagle bards will acknowledge its standing alongside the Tay Bridge Disaster and works of that era and of a similar ilk. In part or in full, Africa remains the captain's legacy.

Glossary of Military Ranks

Below are most of the ranks referenced in this story in ascending order, starting with the most junior (not exhaustive).

Enlisted or "other" ranks

ordinary soldiers, usually (but not always) from less advantaged social backgrounds.

Private: an ordinary enlisted soldier of any colour, usually infantry

Trooper: as above, though usually part of a mounted unit

Piper/Drummer: an army musician of enlisted rank

Gunner: an enlisted man in the Royal Artillery, a specialist

Sapper: an enlisted man in the Royal Engineers, from a labourer to a specialist such as a blacksmith, carpenter, wheelwright, and many other trades and professions besides

Non-Commissioned Officers (NCOs)

ordinary soldiers who had served longer and attained supervisory rank through experience, vocational training, and education.

Lance Corporal/Second Corporal/Lance Bombardier: the most junior enlisted Non-Comissioned Officer or NCO, denoted by one white stripe or chevron on the upper arm

Corporal/Bombardier: a more senior enlisted, junior NCO denoted by two stripes

Lance Sergeant: an enlisted, more senior NCO denoted by three white stripes

Sergeant: A senior enlisted NCO denoted by three yellow or gold stripes

Quartermaster Sergeant/Sergeant-Major: a senior enlisted man above NCO but below commissioned officer rank. Usually long serving and highly respected. A warrant officer, with rank denoted either by four gold chevrons worn on the lower forearm or by the wearing of an officer's undress uniform

Officers

awarded a "Queen's Commission" based on education, examination and often social status, these men have entered the army young and automatically hold seniority over even the long serving enlisted men of the other ranks. Many officers serving before the 1870s purchased their commissions and even their subsequent promotions before the practice was abolished. In this story the younger, more junior officers are educated, qualified men. However, some of the older, more senior officers above them would have obtained their ranks under the old purchase system.

Second-Lieutenant: a junior commissioned officer, a subaltern, also known as an ensign (infantry) or cornet (cavalry) at different times during the same era. Denoted by one pip on dress uniform collar only

Lieutenant: a junior commissioned officer, also a subaltern, commanding a platoon, troop and in some cases even a company, subject to seniority, establishment, or assignment. Sapper officers were commissioned directly to a first or full lieutenancy due to their extended military studies. Denoted by a crown on dress uniform collar only

Captain: a commissioned officer senior to a subaltern, often commanding a company. Denoted by a crown and star on dress uniform only

Major: a commissioned officer of seniority often commanding a company/above. Field officers wear their rank on both dress and undress uniforms, in this case a silver or gold pip on the collar.

Lieutenant-Colonel: a senior field officer commanding a battalion or equivalent. Denoted by a crown on both dress and undress uniforms, also worn on the collar.

Colonel/Commandant: a senior field officer commanding a regiment or a unit such as an invading column, as in this story. A colonel was denoted by a crown and pip on the collar, whereas a commandant may have worn different insignia, subject to substantive rank.

About the Author

Having spent many years in uniform, both military and civil, DJG Palmer now divides his time between writing and the heritage and charitable sectors, working in governance and supporting both homelessness and LGBTQ+ veterans' causes. His pronouns are "he/him".

Acknowledgements

As in book one, *A Rougher Task*, I must pay my 1999-2001 tributes to the same pantheon of experts: David Bryant, the Assistant Curator of the Royal Engineers Museum, and his present-day successor, Danielle Sellers, for her help and enthusiasm since Richard Oram's amazing photoshoot. The late Colonel H.B.H. 'Blick' Waring, OBE, of the Queens' Own Royal West Kent Regiment Museum; the former Buffs Museum/Beany Institute staff of 2000; M.I. Moad and the Guildhall Museum, 2000.

To Daren Kearl for adding *A Rougher Task* to Kent libraries wherein I used to research, thank you, I cannot tell you how much that means, and to Gavin Wright for making it happen, and for giving voice to McGonagle's infamous poem! Thanks again to Anne Man-Cheung for work behind the lines 99-01.

In reprise of my previous bibliography, secondary source and literary acknowledgements 1999-2001 include (not exhaustively, nor chronologically): *The Defence of Duffer's Drift* by Major-General Sir Earnest Swinton K.B.E C.B., D.S.O. (1948 ed); *Weapons and Equipment of the Victorian Solider* by Donald Featherstone (1978); *Red Earth, The Royal Engineers and the Zulu War 1879* courtesy of the RE Museum (1995); *Diaries of William Howard Russell* (1995 edition); *Heroes for Victoria* by John Walton and John Duncan (1991);

Brave Men's Blood (1990) and *Zulu* (1994) by the revered authority Ian Knight FRGSS.; *A Widow Making War, The Life and Death of a British Officer in Zululand, the diaries of Captain W.R.C. Wynne RE*, edited by Howard Whitehouse (1995); *Victorian Imperialism* by C.C. Eldridge (1978); *The Victorian Town Child* by Pamela Horn (1997); the journals and periodicals of the Anglo-Zulu War Historical Society, and the writings of Surgeon Blair Brown FRCS, curated by Lt. Col. A. Spicer RAMC, 2000.

In 2024, I have been honoured to receive the support of War & Police Living History Group, who have championed my book at reenactments and become my friends. My thanks also go to The Victorian Society, who act as interpreters of the Anglo-Zulu War on location and as supporting actors and military advisors for film and TV, and The Mid-Victorian Society, who recreate the age of the Rifle Volunteers, for their support of my books and the LGBTQ+ message.

In this volume, as in the last, I have drawn from real life contacts such as Captain Moriarty's defeat by the Zulus at Ntombe River. I would assert that any credible fiction cannot help but parody fact, however fanciful the plot. For the experts among my readers, I offer confession, but not apology, for the occasions where storytelling has corrupted science in respect of weaponry, tactics vs terrain, and natural phenomena. On occasions, I have mixed Zulu military age groups for descriptive value and truncated British unit structure to keep my character pool navigable for my readers. McGonagle's Highlanders being in the invasion vanguard is a deliberate liberty, not an oversight. In 1999, the great captain was destined for The East Kent Regiment. Being besieged in Eshowe meant marooning my sappers in a way that did not suit my fictional, contraflow advance on the Babanango mountains, while romanticism forfended assigning my beloved Scot to a sassenach regiment bereft o' his trews (as well as trees!). Thus, we find him commanding a company of the 91st, earlier in the war than his factual forbears. Those and other deliberate, informed liberties, I acknowledge. Some will recognise and hopefully excuse my informed prioritisation of creativity over history in order to enjoy the story.

Isandlwana, Rorke's Drift, and the cinematic jingoism of the film *ZULU*, I have circumvented quite deliberately, both in parody and in testament. In my now established characters, I aim to offer up plausible Victorian soldiers able to evoke the empathy of a modern readership. My deliberate distillation of "mutiny" vs "rebellion" in reference to India a case in point. To any who find this too WOKE, along with my diversity characters, I can tell you from experience that gays in uniform always *have*, and *will* always, serve, only *now* we are recognised for doing so. If this is a problem, please return this book for a refund. Then please stay indoors and offline, ideally forever.

Thanks go again my darling aunt Irene, who believes in the book as she always did and remembers it, and us, despite the advancing ravages of Alzheimer's Disease, and to my darling husband, who is my everything, thank you.

To my dear departed Captain Alan Florence, BA. The last time we met, only your shadow lingered, as your brilliant mind had swum upstream, like the salmon of your highland dreams. I would not be the man I am today without you, and I will always love you as another father.

To my gorgeous "once and future" colleagues at Dover Castle who have supported me amazingly, and again to all at Cranthorpe Milner, especially my dear friend and fellow

Coleman groupie Jenna, thank you for the love you've shown my heroic sapper boy, my characters and my story.

Lastly, to those same blue eyes, of yesteryear, and the person to whom they belonged. Thank you.

DJG Palmer, 'Englewood', 2024